Shattered

Darnita Collins

Book design by Darnita Collins

Darnita Collins Books are available for order through Ingram Press Catalogues

Visit my website at www.darnitacollins.com

Printed in the United States of America
First Printing: March 2016
Published by Sojourn Publishing, LLC

ISBN: 978-1-62747-200-5
Ebook ISBN: 978-1-62747-201-2

Chapter 1

BOLTS OF LIGHTENING streaked across the evening sky one after another as if they were calling forth the demon that occupied the dark corners of her mind. With every brilliant flash the lightning began to expose the hideous monster that had refused to accept its own death. She wrestled with her demon, trying to take back what was lost and broken and make things right.

The things she had said and done now appeared wrong and hurtful and her mistakes crowded around her like swarms of angry bees. Deanna Guthrie was beautiful, clever, and rich. She was forty-six years old and a partner at a successful law firm. However, her life had been filled with misfortunes and missteps.

She stood by the storm-darkened window, staring at the reflection of a woman who had hidden her fears and pain behind a stone smile. Hair the color of ginger hung in soft curls down her back and her flawless skin had the look of cream. Her gaze was intense and yet like deep pools of still water, her blue eyes were mesmeric that lured everyone she had ever known. Her physical beauty often drew people to her but Deanna had never thought of herself as attractive. She often felt ugly and some days could hardly look in the mirror.

Suddenly, rain spattered the window like a shotgun blast and a sharp crack of thunder caused her to shudder and back away. The methodical rhythm of the machine behind her drew her attention back to the cramped room. The July storm had unleashed its fury on the Tennessee

Valley, but the loudest of thunder could not drown out the sound of the ventilator as it forced air into Eleanor's lungs. The clock that hung above the hospital bed cast an unsettling mood around the room as the scraping hands counted down the minutes before the machine would give Eleanor a final breath. The sound echoed in Deanna's head, twisting, and turning, inflicting its brutal punishment.

She looked at the clock and watched as the hands juddered to seven o'clock. Then her eyes fell to the motionless figure lying beneath the white sheets. They had shared terrible secrets. Everyone else heard echoes of Deanna's demon, but Eleanor was there when it was born and Deanna had blamed her for the sickness of her soul.

She had hurt Eleanor deeply and now she was starting to taste the bitterness of reality. She walked slowly toward the bed. *I never stopped to think what I was doing, I hurt and hurt and never stopped once to think what I was doing to them. Especially to Eleanor.* "I've done everything wrong. I don't know how I could have made so many mistakes." She knew her stepmother could not hear her but she spoke aloud anyway.

Through her tears she stared at the machines and tubes attached to the empty shell. That was all that was left of her stepmother. The vacant stare in her half-opened eyes showed no signs of life. Deanna sat down beside the hospital bed and took the swollen hand in hers; it was ice cold.

Filled with a mix of anger and sadness, she felt sick then the smoldering anger burned fiercely again. "Damn you Eleanor!" she screamed. She lay her head near Eleanor's shoulder and wept aloud like a child. Then she said nothing more. The path of resentment was easier to travel than the road to forgiveness.

Deanna had not always been filled with such anger. Once, before her whole world shattered and before the purity of a young girl had become stricken with shame, she had been a free spirit, pure and uncorrupted by evil. But a vein of ugliness had run through the Tennessee Valley. It ran deep, as deep as the dark secrets between them.

Tears streamed down her face as she listened to the sounds in the room. The clock continued to count down it seemed even louder. She closed her eyes; she was drifting now and remembering. She listened to the clock as the hands jerked from one minute to the next. The room grew quiet as she drifted further, her mind flashing back. Images began to float through her mind and she slid into a sleep so profound her dreams were muddled fragments of memories and fears.

Her mother passed through her dreams and the sweet smell of honey suckles lingered. Her hair was a flowing golden river that covered her shoulders and fell gracefully down her blue gown. A wave of love flowed across her face. She smiled at Deanna but never spoke. Then Deanna heard voices, women's voices soft and slurring. She knew those voices. It was her mother's voice, her grandmother's voice, then they became whispers, and she could not understand what they were saying.

Her dreams jumped from memory to memory like a stone skipping across water. To follow them was like following a voice that speaks too fast. Her mind was plummeting back to her past where reality was the enemy. . .

ten years, twenty, thirty, forty, forty-three. . . .Suddenly they stopped. The disjointed images became clearer.

She saw the big white house with lavender wisteria that entwined the white pillars and shaded the porch with its vines. She saw her tiny hand print on the front porch step. She felt her mother's hand brush her cheek soft as velvet. . . she smelled her mother's perfume, the scent of honey suckles. . . she heard the ticking of the old clock, and then, she could taste salt and the sickening taste of whiskey on his hot breath. . . .

*****

MAY 1962 - in the small town of White Oak Flats nestled in the foothills of East Tennessee. Shadowed by the Great Smoky Mountains where pastures that led up to green clusters of trees which hinted at the presence of a large house. Deanna was three years old, sitting on the front porch of the two-story home. Her father, James, held her mother in his arms and they moved to the rhythm of the music coming from the radio. He touched her mother's swollen belly and then twirled her around. They were all laughing. Deanna jumped up and down clapping her hands and whooping with delight. "Dance with me Daddy, dance with me."

The new baby was due to arrive in June and Deanna was excited to be a big sister. All fall and winter, she had forced bottles toward the mouth of her baby doll and scrubbed its rubber skin in warm water in the bathroom sink. She was eager for the baby's arrival and her mother, Abigale was loving, gentle, and patient with her.

Abigale went into labor three weeks early. That night Deanna fell to sleep watching the golden flicker of fireflies as they weaved in and out of the grass she had put in the Mason jar. The jar sat on the table beside her bed and when her father woke her, she reached for the jar and shook it lightly until she saw three of the fireflies began to crawl up the side of the clear glass. She was still holding the jar when James told her it was time for him and her mother to go get the baby.

"Now go back to sleep, my little princess," James said, kissing her cheek.

Her Grandma Pearl her mother's mother-appeared in the doorway. She kissed her and took the jar from Deanna's hand, then sat it on the bedside table before turning out the light. After Deanna fell to sleep, Pearl made her bed in the room down the hall.

The next day Deanna waited by the window watching for her father's car. She sat rocking the doll. Time went by slowly as she looked down the long driveway. Her grandfather, Charlie, took her for a long walk trying to pass the time.

In the afternoon, she and her grandmother sat side by side on the living room couch. Deanna held a shoebox filled with pieces of cloth; she chose the colors she liked for the quilt and gave them to Pearl. She did not like the shows Pearl liked, she wanted to watch cartoons, but her grandmother said they only came on Saturdays.

As they watched TV, Pearl's favorite, "As the World Turns," she frowned at the woman kissing the man. "Look at her, the home wrecker," Pearl said, her eyes narrowing as she took a sip of sweet iced tea. Pearl sewed the tiny pieces of flowered cloth together, frowning alternately with what was on TV and what was on her lap.

That night, in her favorite pair of pink cotton pajamas, Deanna slid between the cool sheets and laid the doll she called Jenny beside her. "Grandma Pearl, when will daddy get home?"

"When you wake up in the mornin', he'll be here. Now go to sleep, little one." Pearl kissed her granddaughter and tucked the crisp sheet around her.

Deanna felt the breeze as it flowed through the open window. Outside, crickets were chirping. The full moon shone over the Smoky Mountains; it lit her room with a soft glow as long shadows crossed the wall. She lay in the stillness of her room listening to the rhythmic sound of the clock. The ringing of the phone interrupted its chime. Then she heard her grandmother begin to scream. "Oh No, No. Dear God, No!" After a while, strange voices spoke quietly outside her door. Deanna could hear the deep sobs coming from her grandmother.

Deanna clutched her doll in one arm and tiptoed toward the stairs, she leaned over the railing to get a better look; her grandmother was slumped and shrunken on the sofa, rubbing her arms up and down, up and down. She began to cough and choke on her sobs. Deanna felt something bad had happened' she wasn't scared, but she didn't want to know what had made her grandmother cry. She ran back to her bed and pulled Jenny near to her.

She blocked all the voices and listened only to the old clock. For a split second, the fragrance of honeysuckle filled her room; it was her mother's favorite perfume. Like a brush of wind, she felt the touch of her mother's soft hand on her face. “Sleep tight my precious little girl. Mommy loves you.” “I love you too, mommy.” Deanna snuggled into her pillow and fought the heaviness of her eyelids. The sound of the clock faded, and in a few minutes, she was asleep.

The next morning, people filled the house, most of whom she knew, but some were strangers. She walked through the crowded rooms searching for her father. Her Aunt Rebecca, her mother’s sister, was sitting on the living room couch. James was sitting at the kitchen table with Pearl and Charlie. He was slumped over, holding his head in his hands. His body trembled and his face was ghastly pale. Her grandmother’s eyes were red and swollen and when they gazed upon Deanna, they filled with tears. Deanna looked around the room filled with people.

Everyone stopped talking and looked at her. Their sad eyes followed her tiny body as she crossed the floor. The dead silence in the room was followed by a brief moment of sobs, then the sound of Rebecca struggling to catch her breath. The clock striking eight o’clock drowned out the moans coming from a nearby room. The clock stopped its chiming and was silent once more.

James had not looked in her direction once. She held her doll Jenny close to her and walked quickly to where he was sitting and all she could see were his sad eyes. “Daddy.” He turned quickly to her. “Why are you cryin’, daddy?” She touched the tear running down his cheek. He picked her up and sat her on his lap. “Where’s mommy?”

He took a deep breath and as he talked tears dripped down his cheeks like candle wax. “Mommy and your little brother have gone to heaven to live with Jesus," he said softly as he choked on the words.

Deanna's world shattered; she let the doll drop to the floor and jumped from his lap. "Why can't I go too? Tell Jesus I'll be a good girl," she said, sobbing.

She ran to her bedroom and pulled the door shut. She sat rocking her doll and dressing it with the clothes her mother had sown. She could still feel her mother's presence in the room; the delicate scent of honeysuckles lingered. She was confused. *Why did her mother go live with Jesus? Why did she let her brother go with her? Why didn't she take me,* Deanna thought. She wanted her mother; she did not want to live in this world without her.

The house was filled with people dropping in to offer comfort and to leave food. Their muffled conversations swept through the house like autumn leaves blowing across a lawn. Deanna did not want to listen; they talked as if her mother were never coming back. She lay in her bed, listening for her mother's voice outside the door. *She'll come home*, she thought, *she will, just you wait and see*.

"Drink this, honey." The soft voice said as the woman put her hand to Deanna's face and wiped away the tears seeping from the corner of her eyes. For a moment, she thought it was her mother's voice; it was so close.

Deanna opened her eyes and the woman bending over her smiled. Her smile was like her mother's, beautiful and loving. For a fleeting moment, she was happy; it was her mother, she had come back. The woman touched her cheek and brushed back the ginger locks that hung like twisting vines down Deanna's face. "Deanna, it's Aunt Rebecca, sweetheart." Deanna looked at her aunt and her heart hurt. It was not her mother.

She sat up in bed with the covers wrapped around her; her haunting blue eyes dominated her pale face. She took the glass of milk and drank it. "That's a good girl. I brought you a sandwich; you need to eat something, sweetheart." Rebecca sat down on the bed and Deanna could see that her eyes, the same color as her mother's, were sad.

Deanna forced herself to eat, but the food was a lump in her throat. "I want my mommy," she cried. Her soft whimpering was like a puppy crying for its mother. She lay back down. Rebecca tucked the quilt around her and stroked her hair until she fell to sleep.

The next day was the funeral, and two teenage girls from church bathed Deanna. The washcloth made her skin red as it wiped away the tiny soap bubbles. The girls talked about boys and occasionally smiled down at her. One of the girls dried Deanna's hair and wrapped the towel, in the fashion of a cape, around her tiny body. Then she followed the girls down the hall to her bedroom. She raised one arm to her nose, as she held the towel with the other. She smelled like Ivory soap.

The girls continued to chat about boys as they pulled a yellow dress over her head, it was her Easter dress, and then they tied a bow in the back. They pulled on her white anklets, the ones with the pretty lace around the top and buckled her shiny white shoes. After they left her room, she spit on a piece of toilet tissue and rubbed one of the shoes, trying to take the black mark off the side. She was still trying to remove the mark when her grandfather took her hand and told her it was time to go to the funeral.

"What's a funeral, grandpa?" she asked. He could not answer her, his eyes filled with tears.

THE FUNERAL was at a small white church that sat on a hill overlooking a cemetery. The church pews were filled with family and friends. The wood floor of the old church creaked as six pallbearers carried the coffin to the front of the church and then placed it on a stand. Deanna watched a man with thick white hair open the coffin. She could see her mother laying there, her long blond curls swept over the delicate blue burial gown she was dressed in. Church bells began to ring and two men carried a small coffin to the front and placed it beside her mother's coffin but it was not opened. Two women sang Amazing Grace, Deanna knew the song by heart. She sang it with her mother every Sunday morning as they sat in the church choir.

After the preacher recited a verse from the bible, he disappeared behind the Pulpit. Deanna watched everyone walk in single file to the front of the church to get a final look at her mother. When everyone returned to the pews, Deanna followed her father to the front of the church and her grandfather, grandmother and Aunt Rebecca followed her. James crumbled over the opened coffin. "Oh Abigale, Abigale!" he moaned.

Her grandfather Charlie, who was standing beside Deanna, picked her up then carried her to the front pew and gently let her down. He turned and slowly walked back to the coffin and stood between James and Pearl. He placed his arms around his grieving son-in-law and wife. After a long moment and grieving as well, led them back to the front pew, where Deanna was watching and waiting as she tried to make sense of what was happening... The church bells rang again and the man with the thick white hair closed the coffin. The pallbearers carried the two coffins outside and through the cemetery.

James and Deanna walked behind them. . . . Her Aunt Rebecca, grandmother, and grandfather followed leaning on each other weeping. When they reached the open graves, she watched as a bee buzzed from daisy to daisy. The flight of the bee pulled her eyes to all the gray stones; there were so many of them.

She watched the tiny bee until something the preacher said caught her attention. "Ashes to ashes, dust to dust." *What does that mean* she thought? She stood lost and afraid as she tried to listen to what he was saying. He may as well been speaking another language, as she did not understand any of the words swirling around her. All she knew was that her mother was in that box and she wanted her back. Pearl had told her she would see her mother again in heaven. *But how could she get out of that box and get to heaven?*

She held her father's hand while she watched the white and pink coffin as it slowly disappeared into the ground. Then she looked at the heap of red clay dirt beside the hollowed-out ground. Her mother was the center of her world. *Who will take care of me now? Who will read to me and take me for walks to pick flowers?* The questions swirled in her mind like water disappearing down a bathtub drain.

James turned, tugged at her hand, and they walked slowly across the cemetery lawn. Rebecca, Pearl, and Charlie held to one another and fell in line behind them.

Pearl's soft sobs hovered in the air as she wept for her daughter. Then suddenly a dull sound echoed through the cemetery. The awful thud of red clay hitting the top of the vault made Deanna jerk her head. She clapped her hands over her ears to shut out the terrible sound of the dirt closing over her mother. She broke free of her father's hand and ran back to the grave. He tried to run after her but his legs were like rubber, folding beneath him. She reached the edge of the grave. Startled by Deanna, the men covering the vault came to an abrupt halt, throwing their shovels aside and pulling her away from danger.

Deanna struggled, trying to free herself of their grip. "Deanna don't!" Her father's voice was stern as he yelled at her to stop.

"Turn me loose!" She screamed to the men as she fought even harder. "I need to pick mommy some flowers to take to heaven."

James regained his footing and reached the grave fell to his knees again. "Okay, princess," he said through his grief; he could barely speak.

"Mommy likes pink ones and yellow ones," Deanna said, walking to the mound of flowers. She chose a handful of flowers from each spray. After she gathered the bouquet, she walked to the edge of the grave and dropped them one by one onto the concrete vault.

As Deanna and her father turned to walk away, she pictured a vision of her mother holding her little brother. Her mother was smiling. "Mommy has to go away, but someday we will see each other again. I will always love you, Deanna. Be strong." Then she disappeared.

"Bye, mommy." Deanna raised her little hand and waved. She turned around and walked with her father through the cemetery and back to the waiting car.

JAMES FLUNG the baby bed onto the unused mattress and got into the truck, breathing hard. He drove fast over the rutty road to the dump. No one could have known his wife or the baby had been at risk. She had carried the baby for eight months without problems. Abigale told him her back was hurting more than usual that morning, and then a pain ripped through her. James had rushed her to the hospital; an hour later her water broke and it was red. Then with every contraction, there was more blood gushing from her. She moaned in pain when the doctor examined her abdomen. The doctor worked frantically to stop the bleeding but it only got worse. The baby was obstructed in the birth canal and it was too late for a caesarean birth. The doctor did all he could do to save her and the baby, but the bleeding was too severe. Abigale's blood pressure plunged; then her heart stopped. When they removed the baby from the birth canal, he was not breathing. He had turned a dark shade of purple and blue; the doctor tried to revive him, but it was too late.

James had tears streaming down his face as he sped down the road, hitting every pothole. That image haunted him. He drove faster, the tires kicking up dust that hung in the hot air behind them. Deanna bounced against the seat and door of the truck. She held to the door handle, trying not to fall to the floor. The truck came to a sudden stop and James got out and threw the unused stuff on the pile of garbage. He got back into the truck without looking at

Deanna. She turned her head and stared at the crib and mattress receding quickly from them. She did not understand why her father left them there.

That night she woke up screaming from a dream in which her mother was trying to get out of the box. James was the first in her room, wild hair and stumbling, wearing only his underwear and tee shirt right in front of her grandma, who was the second one in. James kissed her forehead and told her it was only a dream, but Pearl held her and rocked her. “Shh…it’s okay now, little one,” she kept saying over and over.

On Saturday, Deanna sat in front of the TV eating a bowl of corn flakes and watching cartoons. Pearl brought her a glass of Tang and gave her a box wrapped in pretty paper. Inside was a book, a thick cardboard woman that stood one foot tall, and a little cardboard girl with red curly hair. Deanna laughed, because they only had on underwear. Pearl sat the dolls on the stands and showed her how to cut the clothing out of the book. Deanna spent the rest of the day with a pair of scissors cutting out the prettiest outfits.

In the weeks and months after the funeral James become more depressed; his grief hung over him like a thick vapor. He tried to fight the bouts of depression and sadness but he was past caring.

MARCH 1963, nearly a year had passed since the death of his wife. It had been a long dark winter for James. Deanna brightened his world somewhat, but like a small flame, the light existed only briefly. It was that spring as Eleanor Barclay traveled through the sleepy East Tennessee town of White Oak Flats; she pulled her car off the road and went inside Guthrie's General Store. She had driven passed the store many times as she made the drive from Birmingham Alabama, but on this day she decided to stop for a cold beverage before continuing the forty miles to Knoxville.

James stared at the raven-haired beauty as she walked into his general store. She took off her sunglasses and turned her green eyes on him. Her long black lashes fluttered from beneath her bangs. He felt as if he were standing near something bright; when she smiled at him he saw a light in his sea of darkness. He looked away but in another instant, he looked at her again. At that moment, she too was stealing a glance.

Eleanor found herself staring, he was tall, an inch, maybe two, over six feet, with broad shoulders, sandy blond hair, and blue eyes. He was strikingly handsome. But there was something sad about those blue eyes. They looked as if the life had been drained from them.

She went to the soft-drink chest and pulled out a cold bottle of Coca-Cola, and then poured a small bag of salted peanuts into the frosty bottle. After she paid for the items, she walked outside and sat in a rocker by the window. James could not keep his eyes off her. Suddenly, like a ship lost at sea, he was being drawn to a lighthouse. He walked to the window and stood where he was out of her sight.

His heart leapt when she walked back inside. She looked him in the eye, her frank gaze lingering for a moment. He nearly melted. Her eyes, the color of bright emeralds, mesmerized him. She strolled to the large chest, and took another bottle out and bought another bag of peanuts.

"This is for later. My mother gets angry every time she sees me pour peanuts into my cola, and heaven forbid I drink from a bottle, not a crystal glass." She smiled at James and reached in her purse for her wallet. "By the way, my name is Eleanor Barclay."

"Hello Eleanor, my name is James Guthrie. You have beautiful eyes," he said finally, fascinated by them. They were so clear and so alive.

"Thank You," she replied with a shy smile.

It did not take James long to strike up a conversation with her. She was easy to talk to. There was something in her quiet voice, something that compelled James to listen to her. She was twenty-two years old and only two months from graduating from the University of Alabama. She had been educated in private schools in Knoxville Tennessee before heading to the Deep South to attend college.

She told him about the work she did with desegregation and about the freedom buses and that she was planning to join a march on Washington in August. The civil-rights movement had taken center stage and Eleanor got in the thick of it, even using her own money to post bail for protesters and civil-rights supporters. Her world was the complete opposite of his.

"You look too young to be graduating college," James said paying close attention to her face. Besides her intelligence and poise, she was beautiful. "So do you live in Birmingham?" he asked, still looking into her eyes

"Yes, but only while I attend college, I'm from Knoxville and plan to move back after my graduation in May. My mother and stepfather still live there." She looked at her watch; the time had passed quickly. Her mother and stepfather were hosting a party that evening to honor the mayor of Knoxville for his efforts to unite downtown storeowners and the black community. Because Eleanor was a member of the Student Nonviolent Coordinating Committee and it was a command request from her mother, she was given little choice but to be there.

"Oh dear, it's four thirty, Mother is going to be furious with me. She was expecting me home a hour ago."

"I'm sorry, it's my fault," he said staring at her. She was calm and intelligent, and he was interested in what she had to say, but mostly he loved just looking at her. He was captivated. He was not sure if it was her voice or the way she looked at him when she spoke.

"No, it was me," she said. "I just enjoy talking about my passion, I'm glad you wanted to listen. But I really should be going. It was nice to meet you, James Guthrie," she said in a quiet voice.

"It was nice meetin' you, too." But this time he could hardly speak as his voice cracked.

"Next time I'll let you do the talking and you have to tell me about you." Her smile was gentle as she gazed into his eyes.

"Okay, but I warn you, I'm pretty borin'."

"Oh, I doubt that's true." She smile again and walked out the door.

From the window, he watched her drive out of sight. After he could no longer see her car, he turned and was surprised to see his father in law and Deanna. As he walked back to the counter, Charlie touched his shoulder and smiled. "Pretty girl," he said to James.

"Oh, was she? I didn't notice." James returned the smile.

"What was her name, Daddy?" Deanna asked, holding a bouquet of flowers she had picked for her mother's grave.

"Why don't we find a vase for those flowers," he said, slightly embarrassed.

Chapter 2

ELEANOR TURNED HER CAR NORTH and continued driving forty miles through the foothills of East Tennessee. An hour and fifteen minutes later, she was in Knoxville. She pulled off the main highway and drove down the wide streets lined with tall oak trees. She drove pass enormous houses that sat back from the street and surrounded by magnolia trees and exquisite gardens.

The tall iron gate opened as she drove onto her family's estate then shut behind her with a clank. The day was warm, she had the top down on her 1963 Corvette. The fragrance of magnolia blossoms floated through the clean spring air. Maneuvering the car up the winding driveway, she noticed Josiah working in one of the gardens on the estate. She waved and stopped to chat with him.

"Welcome home, Miz Eleanor. We sure have missed your pretty smile around here" he said as he removed his hat and ran his hand over his short gray hair, scratching his head. "Don't get many from Miz Cathleen. That is one sour woman." Josiah shook his head. "Yes'm she is all right, that momma of yours has one sour face, and that sour face is lookin' for you," he said as he shook his head again and rubbed his hand along the gray stubble of his unshaven face.

"Is she mad?" Eleanor said with a sly grin.

"Yes ma'am, she's real mad. She told me to tell you to get on up to the house. Don't be out here talkin'." The old black man bent over and picked some daffodils from the garden. "Now go on, get up to the house before she catches us talkin' and has herself a big ole hissy fit," he said with a broad toothless smile. Eleanor reached out and took the flowers from his old weathered hand. He leaned on the shovel and raised his other hand to his brow, wiping the beads of sweat with the sleeve of his white cotton shirt.

"Oh, by the way, your roses are going to be the prettiest in Knoxville." Eleanor raised the white and yellow flowers to her nose and waved to him as she drove away. He nodded and when he could no longer hear the tires of her Corvette bouncing along the old brick, he took a half-pint of whisky out of his back pocket. He removed the lid and closed his eyes as he waved the bottle beneath his nose, enjoying the aroma. He put the bottle to his lips. The aged whiskey burned his gullet as it went down and he made a gentle wheezing noise as he exhaled and shook his head.

Magnolia trees with glossy green leaves and huge white blossoms formed canopies along the manicured lawn. Light flickered in Eleanor's eyes, shining through the dappled shade of the oak trees leading to the fountain. Sparkling water lifted and fell like showering diamonds. The sunlight made rainbows in the dancing waters that vanished and reappeared as she drove closer to the tiered fountain. She braked hard just in time, to avoid hitting the brown-and-white collie that ran in front of the car. Her purse went flying and everything spilled to the floor. She opened the car door and the big dog jumped into the seat beside her. "That was close, silly," she said taking a slow breath of relief. He licked her face. "I missed you too, big boy."

Eleanor looked at the enormous house, her eyes following the pattern of the hand-molded brick as it stair-stepped up to the blue-green gutters that ran along the slate roof. Her grandfather, Henry Butler, had built the stately home in the early 1900's. It stood in North Knoxville, home to elite professionals: doctors, politicians, and business executives.

She was five years old when her grandfather succumbed to a stroke, and her grandmother died a few years later. Eleanor's mother, Cathleen was an only child and inherited the estate, along with a large fortune when they died. Cathleen moved her family onto the estate and became the mistress of the house that she ran with a stern and unforgiving hand.

Eleanor drove her car into the garage and parked beside her mother's Lincoln. Her stepfather's Mercedes was not in its parking space. Eleanor's father, William Barclay, had died of heart disease when she was twelve years old and her mother remarried soon after. "Good he's not home yet," she whispered to the dog. Her stepfather was the only thing that frightened her. She opened the door leading into the kitchen and the large collie bolted through the door ahead of her.

"Hi, Momma Rose," Eleanor, said to the aging woman sitting at the kitchen table.

Rose was a stout woman with warm brown skin the color of chocolate. She was a five-foot warrior and was as round as she was tall. She had on a white uniform and black apron and her coarse gray hair was pulled back in a tight bun. She was shouting orders to the help, as she polished silver. Rose had been the Butler's family cook, housekeeper, and nursemaid to Cathleen and Eleanor. She had raised her own family, and two generations of her white employers.

"Momma Rose, I hear you are as mean as ever," Eleanor said as she took a canapé from one of the trays sitting on the counter. She turned around and walked over to where Rose sat.

"Chile' get that dog out of my kitchen," she said, not taking her eyes off the silver. "You better get yourself on upstairs and get ready."

"Well, I missed you too," Eleanor teased.

"Now go on. I don't have time for chit-chattin'. Got too much work to be doin'." Rose shook her head and laughed. "Lord, that chile!" Eleanor was like her father, William Barclay; she was kind and had always been a sweet child but Cathleen was spiteful and hateful like her father, Henry Butler the colonel, as he called himself. He was never a colonel and was never in a war but his grandfather was a colonel in the Civil War who stayed loyal to the Union, as did most of upper East Tennessee. They did not own slaves but always had domestic help to do the household cleaning, laundry and were nursemaids to their children. Rose's family had worked for the Butlers since the Civil War. And when Rose turned fourteen she started working for them as well.

The dog lolled on the floor beside Rose. "Now you best be stayin' out of sight if you know what's good for you," she said to the dog. She placed both hands on the table and lifted herself up out of the chair. A little unsteady on her feet she walked the short distance to the counter to where the ten-pound ham sat. She pulled the aluminum foil back and sliced a small piece of meat from the end, then replaced the foil. "Here's a piece of ham. Now go on, git." She tossed the ham out the back door and clapped her hands together to encourage the dog to run after it.

Eleanor ran up the back stairs with her sandals in her hand. She was not looking forward to seeing the woman who had birthed her, failed to nurture her, and often forgot her. She hurried down the hall to her bedroom and locked the door. After a quick shower, she powdered her face, and added mascara to her long lashes. She arranged her dark mass of curls and when she had them just right she placed a diamond clip on one side of her head.

Forty-five minutes later, she descended the marble staircase to the large foyer. The pearl necklace and diamond earrings she wore had belonged to her mother and her grandmother. Her sleeveless dress had a kind of quiet sophistication. It fit tight in the middle, showing off her tiny waist; layers of pastel chiffon flowed delicately to her knees. Her pointed heels showed off her legs, making them appear longer although she was only five-foot three. At twenty-two, she was simply elegant.

An enormous crystal chandelier hung from the tall ceiling and cast shimmering reflections on the pink Tennessee marble floor. On one wall of the foyer, a scenic painting of an old plantation covered the entire wall. In one-half of the painting, Union soldiers, mounted on horses, carried an American flag, and on the other half Confederate soldiers walked with a Confederate flag. On the opposite wall was a pair of gilt and crystal sconces and a tall gilt-framed mirror that reflected the light from the chandelier.

She walked past her mother, who was receiving the stream of guests as if she were a dignitary. Because of her family name and wealth, she was a matriarch in her social circle and greatly influenced decision-making among the wealthy and the professional politicians. She did not smile, only shot Eleanor a look when she glided past her.

A pretty girl with skin the color of mocha served drinks. She stopped in front of Eleanor and smiled. She returned the smile, as it was impossible not to. She took a glass of wine. The girl looked Eleanor straight in the eye, and she could see that beneath the timid smile she was a strong black young woman. "Thank you, I'm going to need this," Eleanor said.

"I'll be sure and find you in a few minute ma'am, you may need another."

"Thank you." Eleanor winked at the girl and stepped across the sill that separated the marble from the hardwood.

She could hear the low music and the hum of voices. The large living room had tall night-blacked windows that acted as mirrors. She could see reflections of the guests. Distinguished people, the mayor, council members, and their wives filled the enormous room. Members of the Municipal League and community leaders as well as some black leaders had been invited.

"So there you are Eleanor, Cathleen told me you were driving back to Knoxville this weekend."

"Good evening, Mr. Mayor. I would not miss a chance to see you," Eleanor smiled.

"You're as charming as you are beautiful." he said as he placed his arms around her in a fatherly fashion.

"By the way, congratulations on the award," she said, still holding to his arm. "However, I'm afraid the black community will see the honor as an insult." Her mood turned serious.

"Why do you think that, Eleanor?" The space between his eyebrows wrinkled and he took a half step back. "We've worked very well with the black leaders as well as downtown store owners, trying to unite the city."

"I know but the negotiations have dragged on too long."

The mayor had tried to unite the black community and storeowners. He and black leaders worked together along with ministers from the white and black churches to hold down violence. Although Negroes were allowed to sit were they wished on city buses, they still were not allowed in hospital emergency rooms, hotels, restaurants, theaters, and department stores. Knoxville had a long way to go but it was able to avoid the violence of some other cities. The flames of fury did not burn with as much intensity there as they did in the deeper south.

Eleanor and the mayor were still talking when a lovely older woman interrupted the conversation. The woman had shining white hair crowning her face. The scent of Channel number 5 surrounded her, floating gently from her as she moved. She had on a long chiffon dress and two long strands of pearls around her neck. "What a lovely party, dear." She spoke in a soft voice enhanced with a slight southern drawl.

"Thank you. I am delighted you could join us, Mrs. Lee," she smiled graciously to the tall elegant women. Mrs. Lee was from old Southern money and protected the Southern traditions. She was true to her class. Knoxville was a city divided during the Civil War and her family fought to protect the South. She still ran her home like Scarlett did in "Gone With the Wind."

"Cathleen tells me you will be graduating in May and have plans to go to law school," she said holding Eleanor's hand. "You remember my grandson Richard? He is attending law school at Georgetown University."

"Yes, I do remember Richard. How is he? I haven't seen him since high school."

"Oh he is a fine young man and more handsome than ever. I expect him to be our senator in the future," she said, beaming.

"Please tell him that Eleanor, said hello."

"He is visiting now dear. Perhaps you could join us for lunch tomorrow. I am sure he would love seeing you again."

"Thank you, but I would not dream of intruding on your time with him."

"Oh that is nonsense dear; you would not be intruding at all. I will expect you at twelve o'clock." Before Eleanor could decline the invitation, Mrs. Lee waved to another guest and glided across the room almost as if she were floating.

Eleanor mingled with the guests, remaining completely composed. It was something one noticed immediately about her. She could speak to anyone and go anywhere and was perfectly at ease talking to either women or men.

As she walked around the room, her stepfather, Warren Stone watched her like a hawk watches its prey. Within minutes, he was at her side. He was only inches from her and she could smell the alcohol on his breath.

"You are ravishing, Eleanor," he said in a half-drunken whisper.

"And you're drunk," she said. She held her temper, but her eyes were full of contempt for her stepfather.

"You don't look very happy to see me."

"How did you guess?" She said in a voice loud enough only he could hear. She wanted to run away from him but instead smiled and pretended they were the perfect family. Her mother always saw to that.

Warren had been a drifter and had a reputation of dating older women, especially older women with money. He was irresistibly charming, and in addition to his charm, he was a looker and he knew it. Slim but nicely toned, about six-feet-two, he had black hair and a smile that could dazzle anyone he chose to use it on, man or woman. He was like a cock who thought the sun couldn't rise until he crowed.

He touched her arm and leaned in as though he was going to kiss her on the cheek, but instead whispered to her, "I'm glad you're home, Kitten. I've missed you." Eleanor quickly pulled away, her whole body feeling soiled. She turned her head away from him. She recovered enough to feign a friendly smile to a small group who had gathered in one corner of the room and then slipped out while no one was looking. Once away from the view of the guests, she stopped in the foyer, placed both hands palms down on the large round table and took a couple of deep breaths.

WARREN STONE had a dark side. It started when he was just a kid, eleven or twelve. He touched an eight-year-old girl, in a sexual way, which lived in the same building as he and his family. When his father found out, he beat him with a belt so badly it brought blood. He wanted to send Warren away, but his mother would not let him.

At the age of eighteen, he hung out with the older college crowd. He looked much older than he was and could fit in with them. One night he waited outside the student building; he had been watching a pretty girl for a week. When she came out with a group of at least ten students and he overheard their conversation, he knew right away they were headed to a local bar.

Warren ran on ahead, used a false ID to get inside, and was sitting at the bar when she arrived with the group. He watched her for a little while and then moved to a stool beside her. She was laughing and flirting with one of the college guys when Warren leaned in close to her and struck up a conversation. After thirty minutes or so he took her hand and lightly kissed it, then pulled her away from the barstool. He led her to the back of the bar and down a dark hallway and kissed her passionately, he didn't even try to touch her, and after the kiss, it was not hard to convince the girl to go outside with him.

He shoved her in the ally and raped her. When he finished, he told her he knew where she lived and promised to come back if she told anyone. And he would not be as gentle. After that, he stole a car, and drifted from city to city.

He did not finish high school but he read a lot, and stayed current with newsworthy events, new movies, and best-selling books. It was easy for him to strike up a conversation; he could talk about just about anything. That was when he discovered it was easy to separate women from their money. It was not hard for him to win their trust and when he did, they practically begged him to take their money.

He was twenty-seven when he landed in Knoxville. He was working at the country club sizing up his next target when he set his sights on Cathleen Barclay, recently widowed with plenty of money. She was almost forty, thirteen years his senior, but still a very good-looking woman. It did not take long for him to win her affection and six months later, they were married. Eleanor was twelve years old at the time.

Warren had not had a bad childhood. He was the oldest of three boys. His father worked at the steel mill in Chicago and his mother was a homemaker. There had been nothing in his childhood to cause him to be the way he was. He just liked it. He was an insidious evil; showing no remorse for anything he did.

ELEANOR STILL LEANED on the table. It took her a few minutes to regain her composure. The encounter with Warren had unnerved her, as it usually did. However, by the time she found Rose sitting at the kitchen table she had managed to put a smile back on her face.

Rose was wielding a thick square cardboard fan. "Hi, Baby, come here and sit beside your old Rose. What's bothering you, Sugar." Rose always knew when Eleanor was upset no matter how she tried to hide it. "It's hot for this time of year. Summers a comin' early," Rose said. Droplets of sweat ran down her face and the nape of her neck was wet.

"Momma Rose, you're still here? There are plenty of help to take care of all this. You need to go home, it's late."

"I'm waitin' on Curtis. He had that community meetin', but he should be here soon."

"You know how long those meetings can last. I'll take you home."

"Oh no baby, you can't do that. Miss Cathleen will skin us both alive." She moved the fan more vigorously in front of her face.

"Okay, if you won't let me take you home will you at least go to the maid's apartment and lay down? Curtis can find you when he gets here."

"Sugar, you didn't tell me what's botherin' you. Is it Mr. Warren?"

"No, Rosie, I'm fine."

"Alright baby, Old Momma Rose thinks she will lie down for a while. These old knees ain't what they used to be." Rose looked at her with old, old eyes. "Thank you, baby."

"Good night Momma Rose." Eleanor watched as she hobbled away. It made her sad, then tears came to her eyes. Her own mother was neither loving, nor patient. She was overbearing and most of the time unavailable. Rose had been the one who took care of her scraped knees, and held her and wiped her tears away when the first boy broke her heart. Rose was nurturing and it was Rose who taught Eleanor kindness, generosity, and compassion.

Eleanor loved Momma Rose more than she did her own mother. She had developed a meaningful relationship with her and had told her secrets she would never and could never tell anyone else. It infuriated Cathleen because she knew Rose knew the secrets the old home kept hidden behind its walls.

"When her grandson Curtis gets here tell him Rose is lying down in the maid's apartment," Eleanor said to one of the women as they scurried about placing the food on large silver trays.

"Yes ma'am."

On the opposite side of the house and away from the kitchen, Cathleen stood in the middle of a group of business owners. She was impeccably dressed and her blonde shoulder-length hair was pulled up and away from her face. The diamond earrings that once belonged to her mother sparkled under the light of the chandelier. She always stood out in a crowd, in a movie-star sort of way.

She was a tall slender women and very attractive. She had velvety skin, and her bright green eyes were free of pouches and had very few crows' feet. The only lines she had were very thin lines from her delicate nose to her month.

As she moved around the room, she chatted and laughed comfortably with her guest. She held a cigarette in her right hand; her elbow bent upward showing her slender fingers and perfectly manicured painted nails. A diamond bracelet embraced her wrist: it had been a wedding gift to Eleanor's grandmother from her grandfather Henry Butler. As Cathleen chatted, she glanced at the clock that sat on a table on the far side of the room.

"Please excuse me," she said touching the forearm of one of the men. She placed her cigarette in the nearest ashtray, left the room, and dashed to the kitchen. A black woman dressed in a white uniform quietly put out the smoldering cigarette and emptied the ashtray.

"Why is the food not out yet? Can you not understand instructions? I said to have the buffet set at eight. Where is Rose?" she demanded. "Never mind, just get the food out there," Cathleen barked at the women.

"Yes ma'am." The girl with the mocha skin curtsied. Cathleen glared at her, turned, and walked away. When Cathleen was out of sight, the girl turned and laughed.

"Ray!" one of the older women said. "You goin' to get fired if you keep on actin' like the foolish girl you is."

"It's not disturbin' my sleep," she said, with amusement. Ray's white teeth flashed against her flawless mocha skin.

The women went unnoticed as they carried trays burdened with food to the buffet and quietly disappeared. A low hum filtered through the house as the men discussed politics and women the latest fashions from New York and Paris. It was worlds apart from the colored help who were treated as if they were invisible.

Before dinner, the mayor addressed the guests. Knoxville had been named by the National Municipal League and Look magazine as one of the top ten cities in the US. In April he would accept the award on behave of the city.

It was eleven o'clock when the last guest left. Eleanor was in the kitchen when Cathleen strode through with a lit cigarette between two fingers. "Eleanor, have you seen Warren?" she asked, not bothering to acknowledge the other women.

"No, mother, I haven't seen him since dinner. Could he be upstairs?"

"No, he's not up there either. If you see him, tell him to come to bed."

"Yes, mother."

Quietly, the girl with the mocha skin muttered. "She could try lookin' in the guest house. Last time I saw him he had a bottle in his hand. And that little skinny white girl was with him."

"Be quiet, Ray," said one of the older women. "You ought not be talkin' about things such as that. That's white folks' business." The help avoided Warren like a bad smell since the young black girl claimed he had raped her. After that she moved up north to Michigan. Rumors were that Cathleen had paid her and her family a large sum of cash to keep quiet.

"What skinny white girl?," Eleanor asked.

"Oh that girl has been comin' around hear about a year now."

"Ray, I told you, be quiet," the woman said again.

"It's okay. Tell me about the white girl in the guest house." Now Eleanor was curious.

"Well, the first time I saw her was last summer, she would come here while Miz Cathleen was at parties. . . ." Ray began.

It was one o'clock in the morning when the last of the dishes were stacked in the butler's pantry. And by the time the women finished mopping the floors you could have eaten your dinner off them. After the women left, Eleanor turned out the lights; as she walked through the kitchen, she saw a faint light in the guesthouse. She hurried to her room and locked the door. She secured the chain and before turning out the light, she pushed a chair in front of the door.

During the night she was awakened by a rattle of the door handle. From her bed, she could see a shadow in the small space between the bottom of the door and the floor. It remained there for a short moment then moved away. She sat up in her bed, unable to fall back to sleep until she was sure he was not coming back.

THE DRONE OF THE LAWN MOWER outside her window awakened Eleanor. She stretched, feeling tired after a fitful sleep. Through the open window, the fragrance of freshly mowed grass hung in the air. The hands on the silver clock by her bedside showed ten o'clock. She lay there a few moments longer before getting out of bed. She crossed the room to the window and pulled the curtains back. Josiah was working in the rose garden as he did every day except on Sunday. He reserved the Lord's day for church and rest.

Watching, she knew that by eleven o'clock, Josiah would be finished with the garden and sitting on a bench under the big oak tree. The tin lunch bucket would be open on his lap, he would bow his head and say a prayer before eating leftovers from last night's supper. She closed the window, went into the bathroom, and locked the door behind her.

The hot water ran down her back and the hint of her lavender soap fused intimately with the steam. After the shower, she wiped the mirror. As her hand moved across the glass, she jumped and swiveled quickly, but took a deep breath, relieved there was no one there. Thank God, it had only been her imagination.

Before leaving the bathroom, she wiped the steam from the window, which gave her a view of the back yard. She could see the magnolia tree she and Josiah had planted ten years before in memory of her father. A smile crossed her face when she saw the white blossom. It had taken ten years for the tree to produce its first bloom.

She sat at the dressing table and applied her make-up then stepped into her large walk-in closet, which was hanging full of expensive dresses and racks of shoes. She tried on three dresses before choosing a sky-blue sleeveless cotton dress. The full skirt was a solid blue and the bodice that fit tight had white and blue vertical stripes. Row by row, her eyes moved from floor to ceiling, finally settling on a pair of flats from the dozens of shoes.

She took the shoes from the rack and a white clutch purse from its place on the shelf beside the row of sweaters. She took a pair of white gloves and a white lace handkerchief out of the dresser drawer, and placed them in her purse. The handkerchief smelled like lavender. Rose always made sure she had fresh hankies. Then she rubbed just a small amount of perfume across her wrist and throat, just enough for a whiff. Before leaving her room and going to the kitchen, she looked at herself one last time and adjusted the blue ribbon in her hair.

Cathleen entered the kitchen wearing a pink flowing robe and nightgown. The robe had pink downy feathers around the three-quarter sleeves, and they moved gently as the air stirred through them. Her shoulder-*length* blonde hair was neatly combed and flipped on the ends. She wore no makeup and at fifty, her velvety skin was flawless.

Eleanor leaned against the counter and flipped through the sales ads in the morning newspaper. When she saw Cathleen, she neatly folded the pages and slid the paper across the counter to her mother. The electric coffee pot sat on the counter beside Eleanor, and the aroma of freshly brewed coffee hung in the air.

Cathleen tucked the paper under her arm and took a cup from the cabinet. She poured the black coffee into the cup, lit a cigarette, and inhaled deeply, letting the nicotine saturate her lungs. She exhaled, blowing the smoke over her right shoulder and away from Eleanor.

"Where is Rose?" she asked as she sat at the table and unfolded the newspaper and began to read.

"She wasn't feeling well, so I gave her the day off," Eleanor said as she poured her first cup of coffee. When the toast popped up, she took two pieces of the lightly browned bread and sat the plate of toast and blackberry jam in front of Cathleen.

Eleanor tried to avoid the silent battle between them. She knew her mother never really loved her the way a mother is supposed to love a daughter. When she was just a small child, Eleanor always greeted her warmly because she longed for her mother to look lovingly at her. Then Cathleen would make some kind of comment that seemed unfriendly. Momma Rose, knowing how sad she felt, would take her hand and, leading her away from the table, never failed to say, "Don't worry baby, your momma has just got a lot of worry on her." Eleanor would go to school every morning feeling sad.

"Where are you going?" Cathleen asked, looking over the newspaper but still annoyed with Eleanor's decision to give Rose the day off.

"I accepted a lunch invitation from Mrs. Lee. Her grandson Richard is visiting from Washington and she thought it would be nice if we were reacquainted."

"Richard? Now there is an ambitious young man. You would do well to marry him. I understand he has his mind set on politics. He might even be our senator someday. You could be Mrs. Richard Lee."

"Mother, I would not go buy the wedding announcements. It's just lunch."

Moments later, before Eleanor had her first sip of coffee, Warren entered the room. "Good morning my lovely ladies," he said cheerfully. He walked to Cathleen and kissed her cheek. She did not raise her eyes to look at him, but kept them on the paper. Eleanor could see that Cathleen was angry with him.

Eleanor checked her watch it was only eleven fifteen, but she did not want to spend one minute with Warren. "Bye, mother, I'll be back late," she called as she walked out of the house.

IT SEEMED THE DOGWOOD TREES came into bloom overnight. Clouds of blossoms hung above the green grass of the lawns. *What a lovely sight,* thought Eleanor. The morning light shining through the tender petals making them almost pink. *By noon they'll be white as swan's breast.* She drew in a deep breath smelling the spring green in the air.

Mrs. Lee's home was only a couple of streets over. When she and Rose's grandson Curtis were little, they rode their bikes past the mansion, to the end of the street where they would wait for the ice-cream truck. Thinking about that she smiled. She could remember how the vanilla ran down his dark chin, how she loved his laugh, and above all, how he so often looked so mischievous and naughty.

When Eleanor turned her car off the street the large mansion came into sight. The shining white columns soared twenty feet to support the overhanging roof above the deep porches of the tall imposing brick house. She rang the doorbell and waited for someone to answer. After a few moments, she rang it again and this time a young black woman came to the door. "Hello I'm Eleanor Barclay. Mrs. Lee is expecting me for lunch."

"This way Miz Barclay." She followed the young woman through the foyer and into the formal sitting room. Richard rose from the rigid horsehair chair and walked to meet her. Eleanor offered her right cheek "How have you been, Eleanor?" He said as he waved for her to be seated.

"I have been well but very busy and you?"

"The same."

"I realize I'm a bit early, I hope it does not inconvenient Mrs. Lee."

"Of course not. Grandmother will be down shortly to join us."

After a short while an impeccably dressed Mrs. Lee entered the room wearing a light pink suit and high heels. Large pearl earrings covered her earlobes and a strand of pearls hung delicately around her slender neck. She was impeccable in dress and in manner. Mrs. Pauline Lee was a true Southern lady, trained at birth to be decorative, to manage the intricate and demanding responsibilities of a huge house, the grounds and welcome guest and to be a sympathetic and fascinated listener.

"How lovely you look Eleanor," Mrs. Lee said entering the room. Richard rose from his chair. Pauline strolled across the room and took her seat beside him. "It was a lovely party and the mayor gave an exquisite speech. But I do wonder how our city will prosper with all those negroes going in and out of our stores."

"I think we'll be just fine," Eleanor said trying not to lose her temper. She knew that deep down Mrs. Lee was not mean spirited, but this was the only life she had known. She was seventy-five years old and had lived in the old south her entire life. She could not change her thinking overnight and Eleanor knew that if she had been born in another time, she would understand how the new south had to work.

"Lunch is served, ma'am," the young black woman said from the doorway.

"Thank You Shelby." Pauline rose to her feet. Richard offered his grandmother his arm. "I hope you brought your appetite dear. Shelby has prepared a wonderful lunch for us," said Pauline as she turned to look at Eleanor. She patted Eleanor's hand kindly as Shelby waited at the doorway for them to pass.

Eleanor followed them to the formal dining room. Richard seated her next to his grandmother and after he was seated she unfolded the starched linen napkin over her lap. Shelby sat the silver tureen on the table and lifted the lid.

Steam poured out, clouding the silver and spreading the delicious aroma of lobster bisque throughout the room.

The young black woman took a soup plate from the sideboard and held it next to the tureen. She lifted the silver ladle and silently filled the bowl and deposited it in front of Mrs. Lee. The ceremony continued for Richard then for Eleanor. Mrs. Lee tasted the soup then smiled in eloquent satisfaction and signaled for them to eat.

Pauline Lee took command of the conversation the minute Shelby left the room. Eleanor enjoyed her stories. She was well-read and spoke the romance languages in a quiet accent. "Grandmother you shock me," Richard laughed as he listened to her stories. She was a gifted teller of stories with a repertoire that ranged from accounts of amusing incidents.

After they finished the soup, she kept silent while Shelby removed the soup plates and set down the lunch plates. Once Pauline was sure the young black woman had left the room she began again. "Your grandfather was an incredibly dashing man Richard. Dozens of women were in love with him." She leaned toward Eleanor. "But out of all the beautiful girls he chose me. He sifted through them all and selected the most worthwhile," Pauline Lee said in a mock whisper and began to reminisce. Her large diamond ring caught the light and glistened while the gold bracelets jingled when she moved her hand as she spoke.

Eleanor glanced at Richard often, he was enjoying his grandmother's stories. Pauline's voice was gentle, Richard's laughter a quiet chuckle. Love made an airy unbreakable web between grandmother and grandson. Eleanor had a sudden consuming yearning to know her own grandmother. She'd heard only bits and pieces of stories about her grandmother told to her by Momma Rose.

"Mrs. Lee did you know my grandmother Ellen Butler?"

"Yes I remember your grandmother very well," said Pauline. "I remember how thoughtful she always was, such beautiful manners. Ellen Butler was probably the most fascinating woman in all of East Tennessee. She had a quality of absolute stillness sometimes. She had hair as black as a raven and when she turned her green eyes on you, suddenly you would find yourself drawn to her. Children swarmed to her and men were smitten in her presence. You remind me of her dear." Eleanor lowered her eyes and she could feel her checks begin to redden. "Your grandfather was accustomed to command and could be a mean ole rascal. But your grandmother had only to smile at him and he became her slave. Did you know he was engaged before he met Ellen?" Pauline asked.

"I didn't know that," Eleanor answered.

"Oh my dear you must know this story? Surely someone had told you."

"No, I don't know anything about my grandparents. I was so young when they died."

"Your grandfather was in his thirties when he married your grandmother." Pauline began. "I had a cousin that never got over it. They had been engaged for ten years and she was mad about your grandfather Henry. But then Ellen decided to notice him, my poor cousin Beatrice didn't have a chance. It became quite the scandal the whole city was in an up roar over it."

"Tell me Mrs. Lee what happened?"

"Beatrice sued Henry for breach of promise. My grandfather was so humiliated about the whole ordeal because now the entire city would know that his granddaughter had been having relations with Henry. He would not stand for a public trial so he had her committed to a mental hospital rather than have his good family name tarnished by this scandal."

"What happened to her?"

"Eventually she was released and married her lawyer. Grandfather died leaving her out of his will completely." Pauline lifted her napkin to the corners of her mouth, touched them gently, then continued the story. "By then Henry was married to Ellen and had a child on the way. When your mother, Cathleen was born Ellen had a horrible time with the delivery, she almost died. Henry swore he would never put her through that again. And so it was, Cathleen was his only child and heir to his fortune. He spoiled that girl so, anything she wanted, he moved mountains to give it to her."

After lunch Eleanor and Richard spent the rest of the Saturday afternoon in down town Knoxville. The sun warmed Eleanor's back as they walked along Gay Street and through Market Square. They shopped in a series of department stores, where all the clerks knew her and called her Miss Barclay. Richard waited while she tried on dresses and a few times she invited him to consult at the dressing-room door.

Later they stopped at a small café just off Market Square and enjoyed a delicious apple pie. They drank coffee and talked about old friends and new ones and afterwards, Richard drove her back to his grandmother's house.

"Thank you for a lovely afternoon. I had a wonderful time," she said looking at her watch. "I should be getting back; would you tell Mrs. Lee how thoughtful it was of her to invite me for lunch?"

"Of course." Richard got out of the car, walked to her side, and opened the door.

"It was very nice seeing you again, Richard."

"May I call you the next time I'm in town?"

"Yes," she answered but she was not interested in seeing him again.

It was still afternoon, Eleanor decided not to go home right away. The sun was setting as she parked her car on Gay Street. Shimmering rays of light reflected off the large marquee that hung outside the Tennessee Theater. The title of the movie, "To Kill a Mockingbird" caught her eye. She stepped in line for a ticket and while she waited, a large crowd of black students gathered at the ticket office. The sales clerks refused to sell the students movie tickets and the ushers tried to hold the angry crowd back. Police officers arrived and carried the students away from the theater and down the street.

"Ray!" Eleanor called to the girl with the mocha skin. She ran to catch up with the officer. "Where are you taking her?"

"To jail," he said without slowing his stride.

"If you take them, take us too." Curtis chanted as he and the large crowd that gathered followed the police down the street.

"Curtis, I'll meet you at the police station," she yelled as the officers placed him in the paddy wagon. She could see his face looking back at her through the square glass and watched as his image became smaller and finally the vehicle turned the corner.

Eleanor hurried home to get the cash she kept in her room for emergencies. And because her corvette had only two seats, she drove to Rose's house to exchange cars. It was an old Cadillac and Rose had placed a pillow in the seat to see over the steering wheel. The humongous car swallowed Eleanor's petit body and even with the pillow, she could barely see the black hood of the car.

"Don't you hurt my baby," Rose called out, speaking of the car, and waved a handkerchief in the air. "Be careful with her now." After she could no longer see the taillights, she shook her head and mumbled to herself as she walked back inside the house. It was 10 p.m. by the time Eleanor bailed Curtis and Ray out of jail.

"Are you two all right?," she asked as they walked out of the police station.

"Yes, just hungry," Curtis answered.

"Momma Rose is keeping your dinner warm."

"We can't all three fit in your Corvette," Curtis said.

"That's why I drove Rose's car," Eleanor laughed. They got in the front seat of the old Cadillac and Curtis drove Eleanor back to her house first. Curtis was quiet on the drive to her house but Ray talked enough for all of them about the arrest and the movement.

"Curtis, I'm driving back to Birmingham tomorrow. I don't think I'll see you again until graduation?" Eleanor said when she finally got a word in between Ray's constant chattering. He did not respond as he drove up the driveway. When he stopped the car in front of the fountain, he got out and walked around to open the door for her.

"I'll get your car back to you in the morning." Curtis's cool demeanor puzzled Eleanor and her smile slipped away from her lips as soon as it had arrived.

"Good bye, Ray." Eleanor waved and walked to the front door. She was quite small, still in kindergarten, when she became attached to Curtis. His mother and father had gone north to find jobs and he stayed behind with his grandmother, Momma Rose. He was a slender good-looking dark boy about two years older than Eleanor. They were together a lot when they were kids and when they were, they were inseparable.

The trickling sound as water cascaded down the fountain drowned out the purr of the old Cadillac as it glided down the driveway. The dog startled Eleanor when he touched his cold nose to her hand. "Hey you." She patted the top of his head. "Momma Rose sent this especially for you." She pulled the fried chicken out of the paper bag and gave it to him. The big dog eagerly took the chicken from her hand and disappeared into the shadows.

She did not see the red glow of the cigarette as Warren stood in the shadow of the oak tree. He flicked the cigarette to the ground and gave it a twist with the bottom of his shoe. Emerging from the darkness, he stepped in front of Eleanor. She gasped and stepped backward away from him. She looked over her shoulder but Curtis and Ray had already disappeared down the dark driveway.

"Warren, let me pass," she said in a firm voice, not looking at him.

"Now Kitten, we have not had our special time together," he grabbed her by the arm.

"Turn me loose or I'll scream!"

He put his hand over her mouth and pulled her into an obscure corner of the house. He pushed her against the brick wall. She struggled trying to free herself of his grip but with his hand over her month, no matter how hard she tried, she could not scream.

The fountain seemed to get louder, enclosing her with the sound of falling water. She felt him raise her dress and pull her panties to the side. She clawed at his face with her nails, and felt his blood and sweat on her fingertips. He slapped her across the face with the palm of his hand, not hard, just enough to get her attention. "I don't want to hurt you," he said into her ear. She struggled beneath his weight, which seemed to arouse him even more.

She was exhausted and her body fell limp against the brick. Warren was unzipping his pants when a hand appeared from out of the dark and pulled him around so violently he could not react to the fist coming at his face. The punch came with such force it knocked him off his feet.

Eleanor turned her head and squeezed her eyes shut. She heard a solid thud like someone hitting a piece of raw meet. When she opened her eyes, Warren was lying on his back, Curtis on top of him, throwing punch after punch.

"I told you I would kill you the next time you hurt her," Curtis said as he drew his hand in a tight fist and swung at him again.

"Curtis stop, he's not worth it," Eleanor said as she held him back. Warren lay on the ground, blood covering the front of his shirt. He had a gash above his right eye, and blood running from his nose and mouth. Warren pulled himself off the ground and stumbled to a bench.

"You broke my nose, you bastard. You'll pay for this, boy." As he said it he touched his lip and looked at the blood on his hand. He took a handkerchief from his back pocket and held it to the wound on his head.

Eleanor stared at the bright red blood on the white handkerchief until she felt she would throw up. When she could finally speak, she looked into his eyes, full of hatred. "All I saw was a drunken man trip and fall and hit his face on the concrete bench," she spat. Curtis put his arm around her and felt her trembling. He took his jacket off and placed it on her shoulders as they walked back to the car.

"Curtis, I thought you had driven away."

"You left your purse in the car," he said as he opened the door for her.

"What happen to you?" Ray said, looking at his bloody hands.

"Warren fell and hit his head, Curtis helped him up," Eleanor responded before he had a chance to answer Ray's question.

They drove Ray home; she did not ask any questions, although she suspected what had happened. There had always been whispers among the help about Warren and the abuse to Eleanor. And how overly protective Curtis was of her.

After they dropped Ray at her house they drove back to the outskirts of town to the little white house. Rose had left the front porch light burning and they had to fight their way through a sea of moths. They waved their arms around the light to scatter the winged creatures and ran inside, letting the screen door close quietly behind them.

"Curtis, Sugar, is that you?" Rose called from her bedroom.

"Yes, grandmamma."

"Fried chicken and turnip greens are warm on the stove." Rose yelled to him. "Is that Eleanor I hear?"

"Yes Momma Rose," Eleanor replied. "I'm sorry I woke you." She went to Rose's bedroom; tears began to stream down her cheeks. "Oh Momma Rose." She ran to the bedside and fell to her knees. She laid her head on the bed and Rose reached out and touched her hair. Then she heard Roses tender voice full of affection. "Don't cry chile'. Ain't nothin' so bad it can't be fixed." Rose soothed Eleanor with her words and for a moment, erased her fears.

THE NEXT MORNING Curtis drove Eleanor home and waited in the foyer while she gathered a few of her things. She took only the pieces of jewelry her grandmother had left her and gifts Rose had given her through the years. She looked around the soon-to-be forsaken room, a witness to years of family secrets. She closed the door and hurried down the marble stairs. She left a note by the coffee pot for Cathleen, and walked through the thick solid maple door for what she hoped was the last time. Curtis followed her, looking as though he was relieved she was leaving – and yet there was something sad in his expression.

"Thank you, Curtis," Eleanor said, looking at his face. He simply nodded to her before he turned around and walked away. She stood on the porch of the large brick house and watched him walk down the sidewalk.

"Curtis," she yelled to him. She ran, trying to catch up. "Curtis please stop, wait for me." He stopped and turned slowly to look at her. She looked at him with admiration. He had wonderful brown eyes. He had grown into a very good-looking man; tall, handsome, and slim with an earnest, calm, and intelligent face.

"I'll be home in May, after graduation. I'm going to ask Momma Rose about staying with her until I can find a place of my own. Then we can be together whenever we want."

"Bye, Eleanor." He walked away from her that day with a hole in his heart. He had to set her free. He was a black man and she a white woman: he loved her too much to stay with her.

The big collie was lying beside her car and when she opened the door, he jumped in beside her. "Okay you don't have to stay here any longer," she said.

She drove to Gay Street and parked her car in front of the bank that had once belonged to her grandfather. After Cathleen married Warren, the board of directors felt it was in the best interest of the shareholders to sell it. Eleanor's inheritance from her grandfather and father had been placed in a trust until she was twenty-one. Until now, she had not needed any of that great fortune.

The family attorney maintained an office on the third floor. She walked through the lobby and her footsteps echoed as she crossed the marble floor. On one wall of the lobby, beside the names of the board of directors, hung an oil painting of her grandfather. She studied his face, he had the same stern look as her mother Cathleen.

"You are looking well, Eleanor." Edward Lawson rose from his leather chair and walked around the mahogany desk to greet her.

"Thank you," she said with a smile of a grown woman, not a child.

"Now what can I do for you?" he asked as he motioned for her to sit in one of the matching leather chairs. He sat in the opposite chair and lit a cigar.

"I'm here about my trust fund. I want money put into my bank account each month. And I would like Rose and Josiah to be given twenty-five thousand dollars each and a letter informing them of their well-deserved retirement. After that, see to it that they get two-hundred dollars every month until their death. And there is one more thing: I want twenty-five thousand dollars set up in an education fund for Curtis. Tell him he has no excuse not to get that law degree he has been wanting. If there is any money left after he graduates give it to him in a lump sum."

"That's very generous of you Eleanor. Are you sure, you want to be that generous?" He shifted in the chair and looked at the end of the cigar as he spoke. He was a heavy-set man with bushy eyebrows, a residing hairline, and a thick black mustache.

"Yes Mr. Lawson I'm sure. What am I going to do with all that money?"

"Okay I'll have the checks available for them by the end of the week."

Chapter 3

ELEANOR HAD SPENT THE PAST FOUR YEARS getting her degree in political science and the past week seemed to be one of the hardest. She was tired when she finally walked into her apartment that she shared with two other roommates.

"Eleanor, you have to hurry – we have to be at the sorority house in fifteen minutes," one of the girls called from the bathroom.

"Oh, darn, I forgot all about that," she said throwing her books on the bed. She hurriedly changed clothes and reapplied her make-up.

"Eleanor, phone for you," the other roommate yelled to Eleanor from the kitchen.

"Okay, tell them I'll be right there."

"Eleanor said she'll be here in a minute. Say I haven't heard from you lately. Why are you not calling anymore?" The girl asked flirting with Curtis. "It's the cool cat from Knoxville," she said as Eleanor took the phone from her hand and rolled her eyes.

"Sorry about that Curtis, someone can't mind their own business." The girl puckered her lips and blew a kiss toward the phone. Eleanor closed her eyes and shook her head then motion for the girl to give her some privacy. "I'm so glad you called, I'm feeling a bit overwhelmed with classes and final examines." She loved hearing his voice. "Every time I've talked to Momma Rose you've been out. I've missed you." There was silence. "Curtis is everything all right?"

"Eleanor, I need a favor."

"Of course, what is it?"

"We protested at the Mayor's award ceremony today. We were at the civic coliseum and downtown at the mayor's office. About half way through the ceremony, the cops showed up at the coliseum and arrested some of the protesters. Ray was one of them and I don't have the bail money to get her out."

"Oh." Eleanor felt disappointment and a moment of sadness in her heart. "I'll have Mr. Lawson post her bail. Other than the arrest, how did it go?"

"The store owners have agreed to open the stores and restaurants to us by August first."

"That's great! I have to go, I'll talk to you soon," she said, hurt by his coolness towards her.

"Come on Eleanor," one of the girls said from the hallway.

"I'm coming," she yelled, grabbing her purse and locking the door as she smoothed her hair. "I'm riding shotgun." She slid into the passenger seat, pulled the sun visor down and applied lipstick, then fluffed her bangs. She looked at herself one last time before she flipped the visor up.

ONE MONTH LATER Eleanor walked across the stage and received her college diploma. There were no congratulations, no smiling proud faces in the audience. No one had come to celebrate with her. She went back to her apartment and packed a few things, as much as she could fit in her Corvette. The telephone rang as she was packing her toiletries.

"Congratulations, Sugar," a familiar voice came through the phone.

"Momma Rose. It's good to hear your voice," she said.

"I wish I could be there but I'm just too tired, baby, don't think I could make it all the way down there to Birmingham," she said in a faint whisper.

"Momma Rose, are you alright?"

"Yes, baby, just these old bones are tired. Don't be worryin' about your old Momma Rose. Okay now, you be careful drivin' home."

"Where is Curtis?" Eleanor asked.

"He's with Ray. He said to tell you he's proud of you."

"Tell him hello for me," Eleanor said as tears trickled down her cheeks. She was hurt and sad because she knew that Curtis's thoughts were not with her anymore. She stood there for a moment. *Where is home*?

"Eleanor, have lunch with my family and me," one of her roommates said. "My parents would be happy for you to join us."

"No, this is your special day." She embraced her roommate. They held each other for a long moment, then she gathered a few clothes and the dog. It was twelve o'clock when she headed north. As she drove farther into the foothills of East Tennessee, she found herself being drawn to the little store again. The closer she got to White Oak Flats the more anxious she became to see James.

At 6:30 p.m. she turned her car off the highway. She pulled in front of the general store and stopped. She instructed the dog to stay in the car while she went in. He did what he was told. James was helping a customer and did not see her right away. She wandered over to the metal Coke chest and took out a cold bottle and then picked up a bag of peanuts. She walked to the counter where James stood. When he looked up and saw her, his heart skipped a beat.

"Hi again," he said.

"Hello. Do you think the motel up the road would allow my traveling companion to stay with me?" James looked over her shoulder and out the window, laughing when he saw the big dog sitting in the seat.

"The owner is a friend of mine. I'll call if you like and make the arrangements."

"I would like that." Eleanor wandered through the store, picking up items and setting them down again.

"You're all set. They'll have their best room for you and your companion."

"Thank you," she smiled at him. "Oh, I forgot to pay for my things."

"It's on the house. And by the way, the diner closes at seven so I made you a sandwich; I thought you might get hungry later."

She smiled at him and took the paper lunch bag. "Thank you, that was very thoughtful."

"I put an extra one in there for your companion." James walked to the window and watched her pull away.

A half mile north of the store, she turned off the road and checked into the motel. After she showered, she curled up in bed and took out the sandwiches. She removed the wax paper. She ate one and gave the other to the dog that had stretched his long body out on the bed. It was still daylight when she pulled the curtains together. Her head dropped on the soft pillow and within minutes, she was sound asleep.

DEANNA SAT IN THE YARD at her grandparent's house. Tall grass swayed in the breeze. The light fragrance of mimosa trees filled the sticky hot summer air. The trees' feathery pink puffballs swayed like dancers in the light wind. In the front yard, hundreds of shimmering green June bugs swarmed above the grass as they congregated in the shade of the enormous oak tree. Deanna tied small white flowers together and put the lei around her neck. Then she made another and placed it on her head. "Look grandpa, I'm a princess."

"Deanna why don't we go for a walk?" Charlie held his hand out for her to take it.

"Okay grandpa."

As the sun was going down they walked through the nearby forest. Leaves rustled gently as they walked hand in hand. Charlie showed her plants he used to make salves and elixirs and Deanna talked mostly about the baby rabbit she tried to catch.

They walked until they reached a clearing and Deanna saw the huge rock for the first time. "This was the land of our Cherokee ancestors, this is a sacred place," Charlie said, leading Deanna toward the sacred rock. "Close your eyes, Deanna, listen to the wind, it's telling you somethin'."

"I can't hear anything, Grandpa."

"You will, Wild Honey. Some day you will, just listen."

"Okay, I will listen good," she said as she held his hand. He sat on the stone and Deanna climbed up and sat beside him.

"See those huge mounds of dirt?" Charlie stretched his hand toward the Chota Valley. "Those are the sacred burial grounds of our Cherokee ancestors. They have gone to live with the Creator."

"Who is the Creator, Grandpa?"

"The Creator that I listen to is the God your grandmother tells you about."

"Is that where mommy lives now?"

"Yes, that is where mommy lives," Charlie answered.

"I miss mommy." Deanna still did not understand why her mother went away. She pretended the larger cardboard doll Pearl had given her was her mother, and she was the little girl with the red hair. Her cardboard mommy took her for walks and the little girl picked flowers, then they came home and tried on more pretty clothes.

"I miss her too. But we'll see her again someday." Charlie looked down and touched her cheek with his rough hand.

"How will we see her again, Grandpa?"

"In all of us lives a spirit. God talks to that spirit and if we listen He'll show us the path to find Him and our ancestors that have gone on before us."

"How will I know it's God talkin' to me?"

"God will always tell you the truth and will always show you the right path to find Him. But He also gives us a choice; we don't always follow His chosen path for us."

"What happens if we don't, Grandpa?"

"Then we become lost and wander aimlessly, sometimes makin' the wrong choices and mistakes over and over again."

"If we get lost, can we find the right path again?"

"Yes that's the mercy of God. That's called His grace. All we have to do is ask Him to forgive us and to show us the right path. Now close your eyes and listen and feel the peace and happiness that He puts in your spirit."

As Deanna closed her eyes and placed her tiny hand in his, he felt peace and joy within his spirit. "Thank you, Great Spirit," Charlie said to himself as he sat holding her hand.

"Now do you think I can catch the baby rabbit?"

"Someday you will. Maybe not today, but someday."

The next day James took Deanna to the general store with him. In the small East Tennessee town, entertainment was scarce, so listening to the old men spin their tall tales was as good as it got. Deanna sat on the front porch rocking and drinking Coca-Cola out of a bottle filled with salted peanuts. She listened to the old men's stories while they whittled on pieces of wood and chewed tobacco. When she finished her soda, she put the empty bottle in the wooded crate.

"I'm hungry, daddy." Deanna skipped into the store.

"Okay, I'll make a sandwich when I'm finished stocking the shelves."

ELEANOR SLEPT LATE and when she awoke, she was hungry. She remembered the diner just south of the general store. She quickly dressed and it was one o'clock in the afternoon when she walked into the diner. A tall woman rambled over to her table, stopping to talk to the other customers before finally reaching Eleanor. She set a glass of ice water on the table then took the pencil from behind her ear.

"What can I get fer ye, honey?" she asked with a friendly smile. She took a pad out of the front pocket of her dress and prepared to jot down the order.

"I'll try today's special." Eleanor answered, distracted by the woman's hair. It sat high on her head like a beehive and was bleached blonde. Dark roots were just beginning to show.

"Okay, meat loaf and mashed potatoes comin' right up." She turned around to greet another customer who sat down at a table near Eleanor. "I'll be right with ye, Earl," said the waitress. "Say, how's that new grandbaby?. That makes what now, eight is it?" She returned a few minutes later with a plate and silverware. "Here ye go honey," she said to Eleanor as she sat the plate of mashed potatoes and meat loaf in front of her.

After Eleanor ate, she paid for her meal and left a generous tip for the waitress with the beehive hair. She drove straight to the general store. Her eyes eagerly scanned the store, searching for James and when he appeared wearing a white apron and his arms full of meats wrapped in butcher's paper, a wide smile spread across her face. "Well, who is this young lady?" she asked, as Deanna skipped along beside James

"My name is Deanna, what's yours?"

"Deanna, that's not polite," James said.

"Of course it is," Eleanor said as she looked down at Deanna. "My name is Eleanor."

"Hi, Eleanor, glad to meet you." Deanna put her hand out for Eleanor to shake.

"This is my daughter."

"Your daughter? I didn't realize you were married." Embarrassed, her cheeks redden.

"I'm a widower. My wife died last year."

"I'm so sorry," she said.

"So how was your motel room?" James asked, quickly changing the subject.

"Fine."

"And your companion, how did he like it?"

"He liked it even better; he would not get off the bed to come with me. By the way, I came to buy dog food and to check on buying a newspaper. I'd like to look for an apartment today."

"You want to find an apartment here?" James said, surprised.

"Yes, here. I think White Oak Flats is as good a place as any to settle down."

"If you can wait for about an hour, I can take you to look at one. I know the landlord, she's an elderly lady, and she told me just last week that her last tenant moved out."

"That sounds perfect," Eleanor said smiling up at him.

"Daddy, what about me?" Deanna said, tugging on his apron.

"Why don't you come with us?" Eleanor smiled down at her.

"Can I daddy, please?"

"Sure, if Eleanor doesn't mind." Still standing with his arms full of meat and mesmerized by Eleanor's eyes, he shifted his weight.

"Of course she doesn't mind, she asked me to come with her, silly." Placing her hand on her hip, Deanna looked up at him and shook her head.

The apartment was three rooms and a small bathroom on the second floor of an old house. It had its own outside entrance with a small balcony big enough for a couple of plants and a chair. There was a big back yard with plenty of room for the dog. "This is perfect," she said. The apartment was not as spacious as the one she had shared with her roommates. In fact, it was barely larger than her bedroom at the house in Knoxville.

Her clothes and furniture arrived in a few days. She moved out of the motel and got busy with her new apartment. After a week, and with nothing left for her to do, she found herself at the store almost every day, helping behind the counter and greeting customers. They grew accustomed to her friendly smile and soft voice and were disappointed when she was not there.

ELEANOR SPENT THE WINTER in her comfortable, tiny apartment. She was settling into small-town living and liked it very much. By spring most everyone knew her name and called to her when she drove with the top down on her convertible.

It had been a year since she last spoke to Curtis. He was dating girls his own color now and did not think to call her anymore. The last time she talked to Momma Rose she had mentioned he was seeing a lot of Ray and thought they would be getting married soon.

THE FRIENDSHIP between Eleanor and James had blossomed into a sweet relationship. James had fallen madly in love with her. "I can't give you everything you've been accustom to; all I can give you is my heart," he said one night as he got down on one knee and proposed.

"That's all I need. I'm rich."

"So is that a yes?" He knew she did not love him the way he loved her but he could not imagine living the rest of his life without her.

James and Eleanor were married in June. Deanna was five years old. It was a private ceremony with only James, Eleanor, and Deanna. Eleanor wore a simple white suit and the pearls that belonged to her grandmother and carried a white lace handkerchief, one that Rose had given her.

Deanna wore a dress that she and Eleanor had chosen together. It was light blue with chiffon covering it and had a satin ribbon that tied in the back. She had on a pair of white patent-leather shoes and wore a hat with flowers attached.

After the ceremony, James brought his new bride to the big white house that he had shared with Deanna and her mother Abigale. Eleanor would now call this home and Deanna would have to share her house with Eleanor.

The collie greeted them on the front porch and James swept Eleanor up in his arms and carried her through the open door. He kissed her and Deanna closed her eyes. She ran upstairs and closed her bedroom door behind her. The cardboard dolls were standing on the dresser dressed in party clothes. She was at eye level with them, and had one in each hand, when Pearl knocked on the door.

"Deanna, let's get you changed into your play clothes," she said, taking a pair of pink shorts and a white eyelet blouse out of the dresser drawer.

"I don't want to. I want to stay here," she said, not taking her hands off the dolls.

"Come on little one. You'll have fun."

"No I won't!" Deanna screamed as she ran to her bed, pushing her head into the pillow.

"Deanna, we've talked about this."

"I don't want her here."

"Young lady. Eleanor is your father's wife now, but that does not mean he loves you less or that he stopped loving mommy. Besides, Eleanor loves you. Now come on get dressed and come with me to the party."

In the back yard, there were tables set up with food. And at least fifty of their friends were there to celebrate with them. Blue grass rang through the air. At gatherings music was as much a part of the South as humidity, because of the Scotch-Irish roots.

The celebration continued into the night. Men sat on the front porch, smoked their pipes, and listened as the coon dogs chased raccoons. They told tall tales and occasionally even a true story or two. The women caught up on all the latest gossip and gave Eleanor martial tips.

After the last guest had left, Pearl and Charlie took Deanna to their house. A small group of people had gathered there. Pearl shook her head when she saw the washtub and fence rail. "You are not a part of this are you?" she asked as she looked sternly at her husband.

"No," he said.

"I don't think this is such a good idea. Eleanor is not from around here and I'm afraid she's not used to the old custom of Shivaree," Pearl said as she placed her hand on her hip and shook her finger at them. "Now go on home and leave that young couple alone."

James took his new bride by the hand and led her up the stairs to their bedroom. "My sweet Elli," he said, as he looked into her beautiful green eyes. "You have made me the happiest man in the whole world." Suddenly out of nowhere came loud clanging noises. Eleanor ran to the window.

"James people are out there with pots and pans."

"Oh no, they've come to serenade us," he said in an angry voice.

"What on earth is that?"

"We're being honored, more like teased." He walked to the window and looked down on the group of about ten men and women holding flashlights.

"What are they going to do?"

"The men plan to ride me on a fence rail, and you my darlin' will be put in that washtub and carried around."

"Well that sounds entertaining," she said as she put her shoes on.

"Where are you goin'?"

"I am going to ride in a washtub," she said running down the stairs.

"My sweet Elli, I can see our life together will not have many dull moments." There was not anything he did not love about her. She was as graceful and gentle as a mourning dove. He could listen to her soft drawn-out voice all day; it was like the whispering call the dove makes in the late evening.

"Mother I have some news. I was married yesterday," Eleanor said to Cathleen when she called her the next day. Cathleen was furious. She had better dreams for her only child, and expected her to finish college and marry well.

"You have brought shame to the family name marrying this widower with a child. What are you thinking? And what will my friends think?" she yelled. But Eleanor no longer cared what her mother thought or said. She was safe in her new life, far away from her mother and Warren, and even farther away from her feelings for Curtis.

Chapter 4

FROM EARLY MORNING to late evening, the sun had rained its heat down on the rusted tin roof. An old red and yellow Coca-Cola thermometer hung by the door. It read a scorching ninety-eight degrees. Prince Albert and Red Man had taken refuge underneath the front porch of the small wooded home. Repositioning in the cool dirt, the coon dogs let out a long groan.

The sun was going down, and the cicadas stopped their calling. Dragonflies swarmed around the pond and birds added their voices to the chorus that greets the late evening sunset. Pearl sat on the front porch listening to the sounds of summer. This was her favorite time of day. A breeze suddenly whooshed past her face and through the nearby field. The tall grass whipped like green ocean waves. Over the mountains, gray clouds were forming and a low rumble of thunder rolled through the Tennessee Valley. The ringing of the phone suddenly interrupted the tranquility of the evening.

"Hi mom, it's Rebecca."

"Hello honey, how are you and the boys?'

"That's why I'm callin'. I was wondering if I could send the boys down for a couple of weeks."

"Sure, but is there anything wrong?"

"No, not really, I just need a few weeks of rest."

"I'm sure your dad will be happy to have them around. He has had only us girls to talk to."

"Thanks Mom. I'll put them on the bus Tuesday morning. They should arrive around 10 pm. Is that all right?"

"Sure, your dad can pick them up."

Tuesday morning Pearl rose early to get things ready for her grandsons. She made fresh cookies and baked a cake. She stocked the cabinets with their favorite snacks while Deanna stirred a pitcher of grape Kool-Aid. "Grandma, am I supposed to call Eleanor momma?" she asked, still stirring the purple liquid.

"No, you don't have to if you'd rather not."

"I don't want to."

"What do you want to call her?"

"Eleanor."

"Then I'm sure Eleanor would be okay with that. Deanna you do know she loves you very much and she thinks of you as her own daughter. But she knows you had a mother and she does not want you to feel she is trying to take her place."

That night the bus from Lancaster Ohio arrived, on time, at 10 pm. The boys were tired and went straight to bed. They slept late the next morning. By the time they rolled out of bed, the sun was high in the sky. It was a hot day and the air was thick and humid. They began the first day with pranks; that was their favorite thing. And Deanna became the object of their torment.

"Hey, Deanna, do you want to go to the river with us?" the older boy, Calvin asked. He was twelve, seven years older than Deanna.

"Can I pleaseee, Grandma?" Deanna clasped her hands together and raised them to her chin as she swiveled to side-to-side.

"Yes, if you boys promise to watch out over her and no pranks. Take the cows for fresh water when you go."

"Okay." The younger boy, Troy took Deanna by the hand and they skipped up the worn path to the barn. He was closer to Deanna's age.

"And did you hear what I said? No pranks." Pearl called from the porch.

"Yes ma'am we heard you. No pranks."

The Little Tennessee River was walking distance from the barn and as they walked the cleared path, a skunk scuttled in front of them and into a small hole. "What was that?" Calvin asked.

"Oh that's a pole cat," said Deanna.

"A pole cat. I like cats. Let's catch it!" Exclaimed Troy suddenly interested again.

"Oh no, you can't catch it. It'll spray us!" Troy put his hand in the hole and attempted to grab the skunk. Deanna closed her eyes, preparing for what was about to happen. The skunk ran out of the hole, raised its tail, and sprayed. They all began to cough and choke on the horrific stench. The two cows jerked their heads back and pulled loose from the grip of the older boy. Deanna looked at them with disbelief. "I told you it would spray, dingbat!"

After chasing the cows for a half hour, they took them to the pasture near the barn. Deanna ran ahead of the two boys.

"Grandma, I tried to tell them not to catch it."

"She said it was a pole cat. She didn't tell us it was a skunk," said Calvin.

"City boys. Don't know anything. They are not the brightest bulbs on the Christmas tree are they, Grandma?" Deanna said as she wagged her finger at them.

Pearl filled a tub with tomato juice and water. "I have just wasted six quarts of my best juice. I'll expect all of you to pick enough tomatoes to replace them." They all three took turns sitting in the mixture and then threw their clothes in the tub.

Later that day, after Pearl had gotten the stench off them and out of their clothes, they took the cows back to the river for fresh water. The boys and Deanna played in the water all afternoon before realizing the cows had wandered away.

"Grandpa is going to be mad at you." Deanna said shaking her head.

"He'll be mad at you too."

"No he won't 'cause I'm the youngest," she said to them in an animated voice.

Troy slapped the palm of his hand to his head and rolled his eyes. They spent the next hour looking for the two cows. Finally, they found them in the back pasture and led them back to the barn. "Don't forget to latch the doors or they'll get out."

"Okay miss bossy pants." Calvin said.

"Don't call me that," Deanna snapped.

The sun was going down when Pearled called them for supper. "I'm so hungry my belly feels like my throats' been cut," Deanna said as she ran toward the house. "Grandma they called me bossy pants. I'm not bossy, am I?"

PEARL TOOK THE WATERMELON out of the refrigerator and slivers shaped like crescent moons were lined up on the old metal table that sat on the porch. Each grandchild grabbed a slice and found a spot among the shade of the oak tree. The sweet sticky juice rolled down their chins and collected in the dirt, drawing an audience of ants and flies.

"Shoo fly don't bother me, Shoo fly not bother me or my watermelon," Deanna sang as she swatted at a fly.

The sun was hot. Pearl told the boys to take the cows to the river to water them. "Can we go fishing?"

"Yes, just be careful." Pearl answered.

"We will. Deanna do you want to come with us?" Calvin asked.

"Can I, Grandma?"

"Yes, you can go." Pearl said as she hung laundry on the line to dry.

The river shimmered with crystal-like blue water… A large trout leapt from the water, snagged a fly, and then slid back into the cold river. After the cows drank all they wanted, the boys tied them to a nearby tree. "I can't put the worm on my hook. I don't like worms," Deanna said as she backed away from them.

"Here scaredy cat, I'll do it for you." Calvin took the hook and put the worm on it. Deanna wrinkled her nose and looked away.

They sat on the riverbank for hours; the only thing biting were the mosquitoes. "I want to try one more time before we go back to the house," said Calvin as he stood. "I'm going to cast it way out in the middle this time." He flung the fishing rod back over his shoulder and the hook caught one of the cow's ears. The cow let out a loud bellow.

"Oh no, now look what you've done!" Deanna yelled.

The cow bellowed again, slung her head from side to side, and began to run. The fishing rod flew from the older boy's hand. They stood stunned, with their mouths open, watching the black-and-white spotted cow lope through the pasture. The fishing rod waved from her ear like a flag as the cow ran up a hill and disappeared over the other side.

They gave up the search and walked back to the river, where Deanna was waiting with the other cow. "Grandpas' goin' to be mad."

"We know, Deanna," the two boys said at the same time.

They walked back to the barn and the runaway cow was standing in the doorway, but the fishing rod was nowhere to be found. "Oh no, what are we going to do now?" Troy said.

"Well I guess we'll have to go back and look for it."

"Not me," said Deanna. "I didn't get it stuck in the cow's ear."

"You might start by looking here," Charlie said as he walked out of the stall with the fishing rod.

"We had a little trouble with the fishing rod, Grandpa. I told them you would be mad." Charlie laughed. "Go on down to the house and wash up. Supper is just about ready."

THE NEXT TWO WEEKS Deanna and the boys continued to get in trouble: Falling out of trees, stung by bees, but the worst was accidentally setting the hay field on fire. Luckily for them, it was a cloudy day and a downpour extinguished the fire before the hay was a total loss.

The day before the boys were to return to Ohio, they stood at the top of a hill, each holding an old tire. "Okay, let go and see which tire rolls the fastest," the older boy said. He let his tire go and it picked up speed as it rolled down the hill. The younger boy's tire also bounced down the hill and they both came to a sudden stop, crashing into the side of a house at the same time. A woman, slender as a willow, ran out into the yard.

Deanna's tire bounced up and down picking up speed. It rolled past the woman, barely missing her. The tire crashed against the side of the house and rolled in small circles before it fell onto its side.

"Oh no, she'll throw us in the well!" Deanna screamed as she ran toward home. Pearl was standing on the front porch when the three of them ran through the yard.

"So, I just got a call from Mrs. Millsap. She said tires, exactly three of them, rolled down the hill and crashed into her house. And now she thinks she's having a heart attack." Annoyed, Pearl looked at all three of her grandchildren, moving her eyes from one to the other.

"Bless her, she always says that, Grandma," said Deanna. "And she's probably drunker than a skunk."

"Deanna where did you hear that?" Pearl said, widening her eyes.

"That's what Grandpa says every time she thinks she is havin' a heart attack."

"You're not supposed to repeat everything you hear."

"Then you have to live your life like you're not afraid to sell the family parrot. That's what the preacher said last Sunday," Deanna said with her hand on her hip.

Pearl tried desperately to hold back a laugh. "Now get on over there and apologize to her before I wear all of you out with this hickory stick."

The three of them walked back to Mrs. Millsap's house, taking their time as they walked through the woods. Mrs. Millsap waited on the front porch of her home. A tight bun, about the size of a small hamburger, held her dyed black hair away from her scowling face. Her hands on her hips, she was tapping her black pointed shoe, heel to toe against the porch. She looked at them through round gold-rimmed glasses that set low on her nose. She drew her eyebrows together toward the middle of her forehead.

"Is she a witch?" the younger boy whispered. They pushed Deanna out in front.

"Stop it!" she said looking up at the tall thin woman.

Deanna stared and her mind wandered, as she looked at Mrs. Millsap's long neck stretched up from her shoulders. The woman looked down her pointy nose at Deanna. Her arms were bent and her hands were in a fist resting on her hips, like flapping wings as she strutted to the edge of the porch. The bottom half of her brightly colored dress puffed out. *She looks like a rooster,* Deanna thought.

"Well, do you have somethin' to say or not? Or has the cat got your tongues?" Mrs. Millsap crossed her arms on her mid-section. "Well I'm waitin'. I don't have all day."

"I'm sorry ma'am," Deanna said first.

"Me too," said the younger boy.

"Me too what?" She tapped her foot.

"I'm sorry," he said.

"Well come on, out with it," with squinted eyes she looked at the older boy.

"I'm sorry." Calvin said, looking at the ground.

"Now that's better and I'll not be feelin' my house shake anymore, will I?

"No ma'am," Deanna said.

"Okay be gone with you now," she said raising her hands. All three of them took a few steps back, then turned and began to run. "Stop! Just one more thing."

"OH, NO!, She's going to throw us in the well!" Deanna screamed. The two boys ran past her.

"Miss Guthriiee!" yelled the woman in a high-pitched drawn-out voice.

"Yes ma'am." Deanna stopped and slowly turned around.

"Come here."

"Please don't throw me down the well," Deanna said as she walked to the woman.

"Why on earth would I throw you in the well, Deanna?"

"Because that's where Grandpa says you keep Shine children."

Mrs. Millsap threw her head back and let out a loud cackling laugh. "That's where I keep the shine chillin'."

"What's shine?"

"Ask your Grandpa, he seems to know so much." Deanna's apprehension grew as she watched the woman's slight figure cross the porch. "Here I have three bottles of cola and some stick candy in this paper sack. Since your friends left you behind, you can drink all three of them if you want."

"Thank you, ma'am." Deanna let out a long breath of relieve.

She met Deanna at the bottom of the steps, giving her the paper bag. "You children are as wild as June bugs on strings. Now go on home."

Deanna walked through the woods; nearing home, she sat down on a rotting log and took a stick of peppermint candy out of the box. The boys had been waiting on her, hiding behind a large tree. When they were sure she was not looking, they jumped from behind the tree and growled like bears. She screamed and ran with the strength of desperation through the woods. She stumbled and fell but got up right away. She had to keep running even though she was short of breath. She sensed whatever was chasing her was closing in. The two boys almost caught up with her but she screamed and ran even faster.

"Deanna stop, it's just us," they shouted and laughed.

When she reached the safety of her Grandmother's house, she turned on them. "That's mean. You scared me half to death," she said as she stomped her foot. She bent over, picked up a stick, and threw it at them. They saw the stick coming and ducked behind a tree.

"What do you have there?" they asked, walking toward her.

"Coka-Cola and stick candy."

"Where did you get it?"

"From Mrs. Millsap," she said speaking in a sassy voice.

"Give us some."

"No, she said I didn't have to share 'cause you ran off and left me." She stuck her tongue out at them, and turned and skipped away.

"Come on, we'll be mad if you don't," they teased.

"Well you can get glad in the same pants you got mad in, 'cause I ain't giving you any." They chased her around the yard, finally catching her. "Grandma, help!" she screamed. "Make them stop Grandma."

"Okay that's enough boys, leave her alone," Pearl said as she walked out onto the porch.

"She won't share with us."

"Mrs. Millsap said I didn't have to 'cause you left me." Deanna said and stuck out her tongue to the two boys.

"It's up to you Deanna. You do what you feel's right," Pearl said, drying her hands on her apron.

"Okay, I'll share." Deanna gave them each a bottle of Coke and they filled them with salty peanuts. That afternoon they sat on the porch and told ghost stories until after dark. Deanna came inside the house and climbed on Charlie's lap. "I'm scared, Grandpa."

"Why are you scared, Wild Honey?"

"'cause they've been tellin' me stories about a man that rides a horse but he ain't got a head."

"Oh that's just a story, it's not true. Come on, I'll walk you home."

"Why do you call me Wild Honey, Grandpa?"

"Because your hair is the color of Wild Honey."

"That's silly," Deanna said.

THE ROASTER CROWDED at sunrise and the sun coming through the window caused Deanna to squint her eyes. She jumped from bed and ran down the hall to where her father and Eleanor slept. "Eleanor, Grandpa said I could go to the big town with him when he took the boys to the bus. I need to get ready." She shook Eleanor until she had awakened her, then pulled at her hand until she got out of bed. It was a treat to go to the big town. It had stores with toys and because it was the county seat, there was always people walking around the courthouse, which took up the entire city block.

Eleanor showered and went to Deanna's room where she was waiting. Deanna chose the cloths she wanted to wear. Eleanor brushed Deanna's long hair and placed a bow in it.

"I don't want the bow," Deanna complained. "It looks goofy."

"It does not it's pretty."

"I still don't like it."

Eleanor went down stairs ahead of Deanna to start breakfast. Deanna hurried down the stairs a few minutes later carrying her favorite doll. "Jenny is goin' with me." Deanna said, running through the kitchen.

"You have to eat breakfast," Eleanor yelled as Deanna ran out the back door.

"I don't have time. Grandpas' fixin to leave me."

"Yes you do, they're not leaving for another thirty minutes. So come back in the house and eat."

Deanna sat down at the table and set the doll beside her. She hurriedly ate the bacon and scrambled eggs and gulped down a glass of milk. When the milk was gone, she rubbed her mouth with the back of her hand to wipe away the milk mustache. "It's all gone, may I go now?"

"Yes, you. . . ." But before Eleanor could finish the sentence, Deanna picked up the doll and bolted out the screen door.

"Wait for me Grandpa!" Deanna yelled as she ran through the yard pulling the pink bow from her hair and tossing it aside. Deanna climbed in the back seat of Charlie's car and set the doll beside her, Troy set on the opposite side. Calvin was in the front seat. Charlie laughed as he listened to his three grandchildren chat and remanence about their adventures. The bus stop was twelve miles south of White Oak Flats but a thirty-minute drive on the two-lane highway. They had only been waiting fifteen minutes when the Greyhound bus pulled in behind them. The driver loaded their luggage. Troy and Calvin climbed on the bus and took their seats and as it drove away, the two boys waved to Deanna.

"Them two are thicker than thieves, Grandpa," Deanna said. Charlie laughed and started the old Rambler. He drove around the courthouse square and pulled the car off the street and into a parking space

"Why are we stoppin'?"

"I thought we would stop at the drug store and have lunch."

"Can we have ice cream? Pleaseee…."

"Yes, after we eat." He sat down at the soda counter and picked up a menu. Deanna climbed on the tall stool beside him.

"What can I get for you today?" the woman behind the counter asked.

"We'll have two hamburgers with fries." He laid the menu back down on the counter.

"And ketchup," Deanna said.

"Okay two hamburgers with fries and ketchup comin' right up." After they ate the burgers and fries, Deanna ordered two scoops of chocolate ice cream.

"Are we goin' home now grandpa?"

"We're makin' a stop at Randle Stewart's house first."

"Why?"

"Because one of his mules is lame and he wants me to take a look at it."

"I don't want to stop there. Those kids are meaner than snakes and old Granny Stewart is wacky," Deanna said without conviction.

"Deanna, that's not nice to say about Randle's mother."

"Well, they are and she is."

Charlie turned off the highway onto a dirt road that snaked its way deeper into the rural foothills. He finally stopped in front of a white washed frame house. It sat fifty feet off the road and the gravel driveway was rutted, so the bottom of the car scraped as Charlie slowly made his way to the house. Deanna held onto the door handle as he maneuvered up the driveway. She turned to check on her doll that was still in the back seat. "Take it easy, grandpa, Jenny's scared," said Deanna still holding to the door.

Lavern Stewart waved to them as she worked in the garden; she had on a house dress with tiny blue and pink flowers and wore a large straw hat to protect herself from the scorching sun. Four boys with worn-out jeans and bare feet, played in the front yard and two small girls giggled and laughed as they played silly games. Granny Stewart rocked in the front porch swing.

Charlie stopped the car and the four boys aimed their toy guns and handmade bows and arrows and pretended to shoot at them. The two girls ran to their mother who was walking from the garden. Charlie stepped out of the car and walked to the trunk.

"Hey Mr. Kirkland, it shore is hot ain't it? You're a fer piece from home, what brings ye way up here?" Lavern asked as she removed the straw hat.

"Randle was in the store Saturday and mentioned one of his plow mules was lame."

"Yea he's jest old, I guess."

"Is Randle here?"

"Yep he jest come in. We was jest fixin' to set down fer some dinner. Want ye stay and have some with us?" The two girls stood, one at each leg, peeping from behind their mother.

"Thank you, but we just ate." Charlie opened the trunk of his car and took out a large cardboard box. "Eleanor asked me to give this to you." The box was filled with apples, oranges, candy bars and four pairs of new blue jeans. In a separated box were two dresses for the girls.

Shaking her head, Lavern said, "No Mr. Kirkland I ain't takin' no charity,"

"It won't be charity. Eleanor wanted me to ask if you could pick enough blackberries and make some of that famous jam of yours."

"I expect I can do that."

He took another box out of the trunk; it contained one dozen Mason jars and lids. "Oh I almost forgot. Pearl sent this fabric." Lavern reached into the trunk and gently touched the material. "She said you would not take pay for helping her put up beans this year, and she thought you had mentioned wanting a new dress for the church revival."

"Oh I do, this is so purty." Lavern picked up the bolt of fabric and cradled it in her arms like an infant. "Tell Miz. Pearl thank ye for me." She turned to the boys. "Youins'boys go tell ye daddy Mr. Kirkland's here. And take this box in fer me."

"Good afternoon Mrs. Stewart. Sure is some hot weather we're havin'," Charlie said to the elderly woman sitting in the swing. Mrs. Stewart got up, stiffened her back and was content to stare.

The car was hot, and Deanna opened the door. "Grandpa, it's hotter than the devil's den in here. I want to get out."

"Okay, if you're very quiet you may come with me to the barn."

"Little girl." Mrs Stewart called from the porch. "'Dogs days of summer' is here." She had her eyes fixed on Deanna. "It's a evil time. Dogs go mad and bite ye. Ye stay away from them dogs what foam at the mouth. They'll bite ye and turn ye into one of em. Then ye'll beg for water and scream at the site of it."

Charlie took an old carpetbag out of the trunk of his car. Except for a narrow path, the trail leading to the barn was overgrown with Johnson grass and cocklebur. Deanna walked directly behind Charlie holding her arms in front of her face, not letting the weeds hit her. "Grandpa what did Granny Stewart mean about the dog days of summer?"

"It's just a sayin' Deanna."

Deanna stood in the corner of the stall while Charlie opened white jars of salves and elixirs. He lifted the mule's right front leg, put it down again, and then he began to run his hands up and down the length of the leg. After about thirty minutes of rubbing the mule's front leg with salve, he put all the jars back into the bag. He took Deanna's hand and they walked back to the house.

Randle Stewart was a burly man, the bibbed overalls he wore, stretched tight across his chest. He stood in front of Deanna, his broad shoulders blocking the sun. Her eyes immediately locked on the Mason jars, he held one in each hand. The liquid inside the jars were tinged red and she could not recognize the contents. She backed away as he held the jars out for Charlie to take.

"Here's some meat. I kilt the dear last year. Miz. Pearl can fry it right up fer ye," Randle said as he held out the jars of canned meat.

Charlie set the carpetbag down and politely took the jars. "Thank you Randle that will go right well with some biscuits and gravy." He handed the jars off to Deanna. She turned her nose up and reluctantly took them. "The mule should be as good as new in about a week. Just keep her in the stall for seven days and rub this on her right front leg every day." Charlie gave Randle the jar of salve.

"Much obliged, Mr. Kirkland."

Charlie tipped his hat to Lavern and Mrs. Stewart who had returned to the swing. "Little girl." Mrs. Stewart called to Deanna again. "Ye be careful when it comes 'Dog days of summer' the evil waits fer ye."

"I told you she's wacky." Deanna said as she walked to the car. Looking at the jar of meat Deanna asked. "Are you going to eat this stuff?"

"No, but I didn't want to hurt Randle's feelin's." Charlie said in a low voice.

"Good because that would gag a maggot."

"Maybe the old coon dogs will like it." Charlie said laughing.

"Are they poor, grandpa?" Deanna asked as they drove home.

"Yes, Deanna I suppose they are."

Chapter 5

APRIL 1965, Eleanor had settled into her new life. She helped at the store when she could and became involved in the church community. Pearl taught her to cook and make canned goods. She had passed the cold winter days by quilting with the women of the church. She had tea parties with Deanna, and in the evenings, they sat together and looked down the long driveway waiting for James to come home. When he walked through the door, he would hug his wife and fling Deanna in the air. "How are my two favorite girls today?" he always asked.

Eleanor and Pearl were planting a garden in the field between their two houses. "Eleanor honey, you don't look so well. Sit down in the shade for a while." Pearl brought a glass of water from the house. "How long has it been since you had your last period?" Pearl asked with a big grin on her face.

"I don't know, I've been too busy to keep up with it. Do you think I'm pregnant?" Eleanor looked like she had been knocked off her feet.

"Have you been havin' mornin' sickness?"

"Yes, but I thought that was a virus. It seems all the children at church have had something going on."

"I think you need to see Doctor McKinney tomorrow." Pearl touched her lightly on the shoulder and smiled.

Eleanor saw the doctor the next day. "I'll have the results in the next week or so; in the meantime just go about your regular business. You're healthy and if you are pregnant, I don't expect any problems."

She went about her daily routine at home and at the store but kept her suspicions from James. She wanted to make sure everything was okay before she gave him the news. Two weeks later, Dr. McKinney found her stocking shelves. When she saw him, she took a deep breath.

"Eleanor, you're pregnant. Come by my office later today and I'll get you started on vitamins and give you a book to read." That night after Deanna was in bed and just before she turned out the light, she turned to her husband. "James, I have something to tell you."

ELEANOR DELIVERED a healthy baby boy, who she named David, in January. He had her dark hair and his father's blue eyes. He was a delightful baby and easy to tend too; he cried only when he was letting her know he was ready to eat. Eleanor adored her son and her life seemed perfect.

After feeding her baby she snuggled him in her arms, touched his hair with her lips, and smelled his sweet baby smell. She kissed his chubby rosebud cheeks and the two of them fell into a peaceful sleep.

"Well now isn't this a beautiful picture. Just look at my little girl all grown up with my beautiful grandson." Eleanor quickly opened her eyes and jerked her head around.

"Warren! How did you get in here?"

"The front door was open. You know you should really start keeping it locked." He stared at her exposed breast.

"I don't want you here. Leave now!" Eleanor spat the words at him.

"Oh, now Kitten I made a special trip all the way down here just to see you and to bring a gift for the little boy." She pulled her blouse together and put David in his bassinet. "One of the women in Cathleen's Bridge Club saw the birth announcement in the newspaper. Cathleen is still furious that you were married without telling her and she is too proud to bring the gift herself." He walked to the bassinet and looked down on the baby. "He sure is a fine looking boy." He turned and walked toward Eleanor still holding the present. He set the package on the dresser and moved closer to her.

"James is on his way home," she said in a desperate attempt to get him out of the house.

"No, I just came from the store. I stopped there first. James told me you were here. Oh and by the way he ask me to tell you he and Charlie was making a delivery and would not be home until dark and that Pearl is minding the store while they're gone. So looks like it's just you and me. Just like old times. You remember how nice it was, just you and me snuggling on the couch? You liked that, didn't you? You liked it when I touched you in the special place." He moved closer and picked up a strand of her hair. "I always liked the way your hair smelled." She jerked the hair from his hand.

Eleanor moved toward the bedroom door but he blocked her way. He reached his hand back and turned the lock. It clanged when the latch caught and the unnerving sound made her feel she was twelve years old again. She wanted to scream but she thought of Deanna who was playing just down the hall and she did not want to frighten her.

She backed away until she felt the wall behind her and she could go no farther. His eyes raked her body and then fastened on her face. He leered rather than smiled. His hands ran up her arms then found her breast. "Please don't do this," she pleaded

He then placed both his hands on the wall behind her and leaned in close to her mouth. She turned her head to one side trying to get away from the kiss. Eleanor tried to get her arms up to shove him away, but Warren was to strong and his body too closely pressed against hers. Then he began to paw at her, ripping away her blouse. Her eyes fixed on the gold belt buckle and the initials W.S., she watched in terror as he unbuckles the belt.

"Curtis is not around to help you anymore." He shoved her hard to the bed and before she could move, he was pulling down her pants. Eleanor closed her eyes. She wished this were a bad dream. But the liquor on his breath was much too foul for anything she could have conjured up. He unzipped his pants and forced himself inside of her. All she could do was close her eyes and wait for it to be over. She could feel the cold medal of his belt buckle dig into her stomach as he thrust harder. Then with a sudden jerk, he fell. After a long silent moment, he rose to his feet. Eleanor turned her back to him.

"I wish you were dead," she tried to say, but it came out as a moan.

"Kitten, you're still my special girl and you always will be mine. Don't you ever forget that." He zipped his pants and straightened his shirt tucking it into his trousers. After he fastened his belt, he leaned over Eleanor and touched her cheek. "See that wasn't so bad now was it." He turned and walked to the door, stopping to say, "I'll tell Cathleen you are as beautiful as ever, and the baby looks like his mother."

Eleanor lay shaking all over from humiliation and anger. *Why did I let this happen, I just took it—as if I deserved it.* Eleanor was shamed by her own weakness. *I will never be healed from this sickness I feel. It would have been better if he had killed me.*

Deanna skipped out of her room with one of her drawings in her hand; that was when she saw the stranger leave Eleanor's room. His heavy footsteps clunked when the heels of his shoes hit the hardwood as he walked down the hallway and then down the stairs. She tiptoed to the railing and leaned over to get a better look at the man. When the front door closed, she went back to Eleanor's room and opened the door a crack. "I have a picture for you, Eleanor."

Eleanor did not answer. She lay motionless in bed. The covers were pulled tight around her shoulder and neck. Slow tears seeped from her closed eyes. Deanna walked to the side of the bed and gave her the drawing. She did not look at Deanna, just stared out the window with empty eyes. In the days that followed, she became inaccessible and locked herself in the upstairs bedroom.

Pearl stayed in the guest room and moved David in with her. James moved his things in the small room across the hall. Pearl prepared meals and would leave a tray for Eleanor outside her bedroom door. Everyone pleaded with her to come out of her room but as the days passed, she became more secluded. She became increasingly drawn and pale and no one could understand what had caused her hopelessness. She was in a dark place and no one could reach her.

Two weeks passed. One late afternoon two men came to the house and went upstairs to Eleanor's room. A few minutes later, they came downstairs with her strapped on a stretcher. She was pale. Her thin hand reached weakly for Deanna but she shrank away from Eleanor's tormented face. Eleanor managed a thin smile and then closed her eyes.

Deanna followed behind her father as he walked beside the stretcher. James held Eleanor's hand until the men placed the fragile figure into the back of the ambulance. "Eleanor is sick, but she will be okay," he told Deanna. "She's only going to hospital so she can get better, but she'll be home very soon, I promise." He smiled; it was almost convincing.

IT WAS A HOT SPRING DAY. Deanna sat on the floor staring at the whirling fan and listening to the sound of her voice as it traveled through the blue-gray blur of blades. She was startled when the screen door slammed behind her. When she turned, she saw a tall slender woman and the man she had seen leave Eleanor's room. The women looked angry and the man stood there looking at Deanna.

"Gather the baby's things," Cathleen said in a tone as if she were speaking to the help. She turned to Pearl, saying, "I will be taking Eleanor and the baby to Knoxville where he will be raised properly."

Pearl stood up and put David in his crib. "Eleanor is happy here. This is her home now," Pearl said, looking annoyed. She put on her best smile, leaned over, and kissed

Deanna on the forehead. "Eleanor is comin' home today, little one. I'll be back later to check on all of you."

Deanna was standing near David's crib when she heard her father's car coming up the driveway. Cathleen rose from her chair. Deanna listened to her high heels clack against the hardwood floor as she hurried to the door. She placed her hand on the screen, and gave it a quick push causing it to swing open, slamming against the outside wall before it swung back with a loud clatter.

She marched down the porch steps and walked toward the car. "Hello Cathleen," James said as he took Eleanor's hand and helped her out of the car.

"Mother what are you doing here?" Eleanor looked at Cathleen, then to James.

"I called her when you were admitted to the hospital and again yesterday to let her know you were comin' home today."

"You should not have done that." Eleanor said.

"I thought she needed to know," James said looking puzzled.

"Eleanor get your things. You're going back to Knoxville. I will not allow you nor my grandson to remain in this back-wood hillbilly hell hole any longer," she demanded. Eleanor looked at her, then stepped to the side and walked toward the house.

Deanna was alone with Warren. He looked at her for a long moment before he moved to where she stood. "Hello, Kitten," he said. He touched her hair. *So sweet, little and defenseless, bet you taste sweet, but not now little kitten, you're not ready yet,* he thought as he looked at her. "Do you like chewing gum? I think I have some here in my pocket."

"Leave her alone," Eleanor shouted when she entered the room. "Deanna, go to your room now." Her voice was quick and stern; it startled Deanna. Eleanor had never raised her voice before.

"If you touch her I'll kill you," Eleanor said staring straight into his shark-like eyes.

"Now Kitten, you know I don't mess with little girls. She's still a bit too young for my taste."

"Do not ever come to my home again," Eleanor spewed at him.

Deanna looked at Eleanor; she thought she had done something wrong. She ran up the stairs and to her room then closed the door behind her. She began to cry. She covered her ears to block out the angry words pouring out of Eleanor. And through the open window she could her Cathleen who was still outside with James.

"My daughter should have never married you. She could have married well, a doctor or lawyer or even a United States Senator. It's your fault she had a nervous breakdown, having to live in this God forsaken place." Cathleen's voice screeched with anger. James walked past her and up the steps, when he reached the door he could hear Eleanor screaming at Warren, the angry words spewed from her.

Before he walked inside, Cathleen hurried in the house before him. "Eleanor you're still not well and not thinking clearly. You need to come with Warren and me, we can get you the care you need," Cathleen said as she stood beside Warren.

"Warren I think it's best if you and Cathleen leave now," James said as he stepped between his wife and Cathleen.

Deanna could hear muffled words floating under her door and into her room. Their voices had lowered and she could not make out exactly what they were saying then she heard her grandfather's stern and commanding voice loud and clear. "Warren leave this house immediately and never come back." At last the house was quiet and Deanna heard a car speeding down the driveway.

She was playing with her doll when her father came into her room and sat down on the bed beside her. He brushed her hair away from her face. "Eleanor is lying down. Come out and play with your brother, and I'll make lunch."

Later that evening, Eleanor opened the door to Deanna's room. She picked up the doll from the floor as she crossed the room. Deanna did not stop drawing or look at Eleanor when she touched her shoulder. "Why is Jenny on the floor?" Deanna shrugged. "Hey, you know we have not had a day just for the two of us in a long time. I think we should go to Knoxville tomorrow and shop for some new clothes. How does that sound?" Still drawing, Deanna shrugged again.

"You know, you need new shoes. I think we should get you a shiny white pair."

"With little heels?" Deanna asked.

"Yes, but only small heels."

"Can I have two pairs?" I want red ones, too."

"Why don't we save the red ones for Christmas?"

"Promise."

"I promise." Eleanor paused. "Deanna, about today."

"I'm sorry Eleanor, I didn't mean to make you mad," Deanna said.

"Oh sweetie, I wasn't angry with you. I was angry with Warren. I'm sorry I yelled at you."

"It's okay," Deanna said in a low voice.

"I don't think we should tell anyone what Warren and I were saying to each other. Sometimes when adults get angry with one another they say things they shouldn't."

"Not even daddy?"

"Let's just keep that between us. It will be a secret just between us girls, okay."

"Okay. Did I do somethin' bad?"

"No, you didn't do anything bad."

"Will daddy be mad at me?" Deanna stopped drawing and looked at Eleanor.

"No, daddy will not be mad at you. Now go to sleep we have a busy day tomorrow."

"Good night, Eleanor," Deanna said as she snuggled into the soft sheets.

Eleanor was twelve when Warren came into her room the first time. He sat on the bed and stroked her hair. At first, it was just snuggling then he started touching her and one night he came into her room with his robe on. He locked the door and told her it was time for her to show him how much she loved him. He took her hand and made her touch him. She tried to pull away, but he was too strong. That was the first time he raped her.

She shook the memory from her head and wiped the small tear as it ran down her cheek. "Good night Deanna." She said and turned out the bedroom light.

Down the hall, James waited for her in their room. "Where's David?" she asked in a weary voice.

"He's already asleep. Pearl fed him his bottle and put him down for the night."

"Has she left?"

"Yes, she said she would be back tomorrow mornin' to help out with him."

"That's good, because I promised Deanna I would take her to Knoxville to shop for new clothes tomorrow."

"Are you sure you're strong enough for that? You just got home."

"James, I have done nothing but rest for the past few months. It's time I get my life back to normal."

"Speakin' of normal, that yellin' at Warren didn't sound very normal. What was that all about?" She clenched her hands and her jaw tightened as her spine stiffened.

"Oh that, it was nothing."

"Do you want to talk about the nothing that made you upset?"

"No, I do not". She turned to look into the face of her husband. An unaccustomed emotion entered her heart. "I love you, James Guthrie."

"I love you, too," he said as he put his arm across her chest. She touched his face; love flooded her body and soul.

DEANNA AND ELEANOR walked around Market Square in down town Knoxville. They went into store after store trying on dresses. It was four o'clock in the afternoon and Eleanor had her hands full of shopping bags. "We have one more stop to make before we head home," Eleanor said smiling down at Deanna.

"I'm tired, Eleanor."

"I know, but you'll like this stop. Momma Rose brought me here every Saturday to buy candy."

They walked up to the large glass counter and Deanna looked at all the candy inside. "Hello, Miss Barclay. I haven't seen you here in a while," the middle-aged woman said as she stood behind the counter.

"It has been a long time. I'm Mrs. Guthrie now, and this is my daughter," Eleanor said looking toward Deanna.

"She is lovely."

"I'm not her real daughter, I'm her stepdaughter, but my brother is her real son," Deanna said looking through the glass at the candy counter.

"Oh really, well I think you are a lucky young lady to have such a good stepmother," the woman said.

"Eleanor is lucky to have such a good stepdaughter," Deanna said, still looking at the candy. Eleanor sighed. Deanna had always been an opinionated little thing and always spoke her mind.

"So what can I get you two ladies?"

"Give us a bag of those chocolate-covered peanuts."

"I want two bags," Deanna said.

"All right, two bags."

IN NOVEMBER the air had turned cold and was threatening snow. Charlie was loading the large truck with grocery items, clothing, shoes, and animal feed when Deanna skipped up the wide loading plank. She had on a pair of thick black tights, a pair of rain boots, and her favorite coat – the one with the wooden buttons.

The smell of bananas, apples, orange-slice candy, and moon pies permeated the inside of the truck. Wooden cases of RC cola were stacked in the far back corner. She took off one of her mittens, reached into an opened box, pulled out a moon pie and took an RC cola from one of the cases. She opened the bottle with the opener that was nailed to the inside wall. The lid fell with a clang into a bucket with other lids.

"Grandpa, I'm goin' with you in the rollin' store."

"What about school?"

"It's Thanksgiving vacation, I don't have school today."

"Okay go back inside and tell your daddy you're going with me."

He opened the passenger side door and lifted Deanna into the seat. The truck chugged along the steep mountain road, slowing down at the potholes. Deanna got out at each house, sometimes playing with the children or talking to the women. They stopped along the side of the road by a spring for a late lunch and Charlie made bologna-and-cheese sandwiches. After she finished her sandwich, Deanna ate another moon pie and drank an Orange Crush Soda.

She fell to sleep to the grinding sound of the motor as the truck slowly descended the mountain. Her head was resting on the door window, and she had an empty bottle of soda in her lap. The sun had set and a dusting of snow covered the ground by the time the truck pulled to the back door of the store.

"Wake up, Deanna we're back."

"I'm tired Grandpa, I had a hard day, and I need my sleep," she said, barely opening her eyes.

"Okay, sleepy head, you can sleep while I unload the truck."

Chapter 6

JUNE 1970, James and Eleanor had just celebrated their sixth wedding anniversary. "Elli, Mr. Lawson's on the phone; he says it's important," James called to Eleanor. She took the phone from his hand and smiled lovingly at him as he smacked her bottom.

"Hello, Mr. Lawson."

"Eleanor it's about Cathleen, I'm afraid I have bad news," he said in a quiet but formal voice.

"Mr. Lawson, what is it?" Eleanor asked, puzzled, as she had not spoken to her mother in years.

"Eleanor," he paused. "Cathleen has lung cancer. She's dying and she's asking for you. If you want to see her you should get here today."

"Lung cancer, how long has she known?"

"She was diagnosed about a year ago."

"I can be there in a couple of hours." Eleanor put the phone down and began to cry.

"Elli, what is it?" James asked as he put his arms around her.

"It's mother, she has lung cancer."

"Will she be okay?"

"No, she's dying and is asking for me."

"I should go with you," James said.

"No you stay with the children; I'll call you later." She packed an overnight bag and while James put her things into the car, she called Curtis.

"Curtis, I just received a call from mother's attorney's Mr. Lawson, he said she's dying and he needs me for some family business. As my attorney, I would feel better if you were there as well."

"Of course Eleanor. I'll meet you there in about two hours."

Eleanor drove her car through the rusty gate and up the driveway, toward the big house. The gardens that once were bursting with color were now overgrown with dead weeds. Sparkling water no longer trickled down the tiers of the fountain; instead it lay stagnant, utterly silent. The silence reminded her of too many sobs stifled in a pillow, too many locked doors, and too many glances exchanged without words.

She stopped her car in front of the house and sat a moment before walking to the front door. As she was about to ring the doorbell, Curtis pulled his car behind hers. "Hello, Curtis. How are Ray and the children?" she asked as he walked to the door. The feeling she once had for him was now only one of friendship and respect.

"They're doing well," he said. He forced himself to look away from her as he rang the doorbell.

"Can I help you?" An elderly woman asked.

"Yes. I'm Eleanor, Cathleen's daughter. I'm here to see Mr. Lawson." The woman stepped to the side and waited for them to enter the house. Once they were inside, she closed the heavy door and signaled for them to follow her. Still not speaking, she walked through the foyer to the large living room where Mr. Lawson, was waiting.

"Hello, Mr. Lawson." The heavyset man stood to his feet. "You remember Curtis." She said as she walked to where he stood. "As my attorney, I thought he should be here."

"Yes, hello Curtis," he said as he extended his hand to Curtis. "I was saddened to learn about the passing of Rose." Curtis tipped his head in acknowledgment. "Please have a seat and we can get started." Mr. Lawson waited for Eleanor to be seated, then Curtis. He took a cigar out of his coat pocket, lit it, and sit in a chair across from them. "Eleanor, I'll get right to the point. All of the money is gone."

"Gone, how is that possible?"

"When Cathleen became ill Warren persuaded her to sign all the bank accounts over to him." He drew off the cigar and let the smoke slowly escape from his mouth.

"All of it!" she said, astonished.

"Yes, and I'm afraid there's not money to continue to pay the private-duty nurses; she needs round-the-clock care."

"What did he do with the money?" Eleanor asked.

"After the money was signed over to him, he emptied the accounts. That was six months ago and no one has heard from him since. Warren has a gambling problem and for years Cathleen covered his losses." Mr. Lawson paused. "And there is one more thing you need to know. After you were married, Cathleen put the estate in his name. The house is his."

"I don't care about this house," she said as she looked around. "Curtis, please take the money out of my account and pay for anything she needs. If we're finished I would like to see mother now."

"I moved her downstairs; we set up a make-shift hospital room in the den. It was more convenient for the nurses to have her down here." Mr. Lawson stood up. "I'll be back tomorrow." He took her hand between his and held it for a moment. "I am sorry, Eleanor." She just looked at him and gave a half-hearted smile.

"I'll walk out with you," Curtis said before turning to Eleanor. "Goodbye, Eleanor."

Eleanor walked through the large house. She slowly opened the door where her mother lay. She became ill when she saw her. Cathleen was very thin and her balding head had only a few strands of blonde hair left. Her skin was a pasty grey and her eyes were glazed over. Eleanor stepped lightly, so as not to wake her mother, to the hospital bed where the nurse was taking her vital signs.

"How is she?" Eleanor whispered as tears rolled down her face.

"She's very weak," the nurse replied.

"Warren is that you?" Cathleen asked and turned toward Eleanor.

"No mother, Warren is not here."

"Eleanor," she said in a weak voice almost too quiet to hear.

"Don't try to talk mother, just lie quietly and rest."

Eleanor sat at her bedside until Cathleen fell asleep. A stream of sunlight filtered through the heavy curtains and across the room to the bed. Dust moved in and out of the light like thousands of dancing fairies. She pulled the sheet up around Cathleen's shoulders and looked around the dusty room.

"I'll be in the kitchen if you need me," she said to the nurse before leaving. There was an eerie silence in the old mansion. She moved through the large rooms like a ghost, but never went upstairs. She made a fresh pot of coffee and sat at the breakfast table. She stared into the cup, remembering the last morning she spent in the house. She had left her mother a note, saying she was leaving and would never return.

"Mrs. Guthrie, she's asking for you", the nurse said.

Eleanor rinsed the coffee cup and put it in the drainer. "The coffee is fresh," she said to the nurse before leaving the kitchen. She quietly opened the door leading into the den that was now serving as Cathleen's bedroom, and walked to the bed. The curtains had been opened and Cathleen was looking out the window.

"Mother, you wanted to see me?" Cathleen turned her head and looked at Eleanor. She tried to speak but she was interrupted by a violent cough.

"Mother, don't talk."

"I need to say this Eleanor; I need to tell you I'm sorry for not protecting you from Warren. I always suspected he was abusing you." Cathleen said the words in a voice as if she were talking about the weather. Eleanor stepped back, her green eyes bewildered and hurt.

"You knew, then how could you let him do that to me?"

Cathleen coughed violently again, this time losing her breath. Her thin fingers closed like claws around the oxygen mask and with a desperate attempt she tried to raise the mask to her face. The nurse heard the coughing, rushed into the room, and placed the mask over her nose and mouth. The coughing made her weaker and after that Cathleen fell into a deep sleep. Eleanor stared at her mother for a long time before leaving the bedside. She took a book from the shelf and relocated to the leather-cushioned chair in the corner of the room.

“It’s time for her morphine, Mrs. Guthrie,” the nurse said an hour later when she returned.

“What time is it?” Eleanor asked.

“It’s ten-thirty. Go get some sleep; I’ll sit with her.”

Eleanor made her bed on the couch in the living room and at 6 a.m. the nurse touched her shoulder. “Mrs. Guthrie,” she said softly. “She’s gone; she passed away peacefully five minutes ago.”

Eleanor sat by the bedside until the funeral parlor came to take her body away. Cathleen had made all the arrangement six months earlier and made it clear she did not want a viewing or a service. The next day at the graveside a minister recommended by the funeral parlor said a few words, and read from the Bible. Eleanor placed one red rose on the coffin, then turned and walked away. It was two o’clock in the afternoon when she returned to her home in White Oak Flats.

“It’s good to be home! I hate being away from my family,” she told James that night.

“I should have been with you,” he said, as the couple prepared for bed.

“Perhaps, but I felt someone should stay with the children. We have never been away from them.” She kissed him goodnight, then fell asleep in his arms.

NEARLY A YEAR had passed since Cathleen’s death. Curtis paid all the debts and the nurses out of Eleanor’s trust-fund account. The mansion sat empty; Mr. Lawson had not been able to contact Warren, who had taken the money and disappeared. Until Warren could be notified Cathleen's will remained sealed in Mr. Lawson's files.

It was a lovely Saturday, with no clouds and a slight breeze that had sprung up during the night and chased away the humidity. Eleanor finished laundry and hung it on the line. Deanna's five-year-old brother David was outside with his friends and Deanna was in the kitchen putting the breakfast dishes away when there was a knock at the front door. She opened the door and there was a moment's silence. Then Warren Stone's deep strong voice said. "Look at you, why I would hardly recognize you. Haven't you grown up to be such a pretty girl." Deanna's cheeks reddened and Warren smiled at her. "I'm here to see your step mother is she home?"

"Yes."

"May I come in?"

Deanna pushed opened the screen door and moved to the side to let him enter. "How old are you now?" Warren asked.

"Twelve."

"Ah, youth and innocents it's a rare and beautiful thing. You must have lots of young boys to admire your beauty," said Warren softly. He talked almost in a whisper. He smiled at her innocents and picked up a strand of her long hair. He held the hair to his nostrils for a short moment, then slowly let the locks of hair drop to her shoulder. "Now where is Eleanor I need to speak to her?" He spoke in a kind manner.

"She's in the back yard." He followed Deanna down the hallway, through the kitchen and into the yard.

Eleanor saw a large shadow moving toward her and when she pulled the white sheet back she saw Warren crossing the lawn. Her anger swelled to meet him. "What are you doing here?" She spit the words at him like daggers and ran to Deanna. "Did he touch you?" Deanna shook her head no.

"Eleanor, is that the way you greet your stepfather? I'm still grieving from the loss of Cathleen and to make things worse I'm in a bit of a jam. You see I'm out of money." Eleanor put her hands up to stop him, but he continued to rumble on. "I thought you could lend me some." He scratched and rubbed at his day old stubble of facial hair.

"You are insane if I had all the money in the world, I wouldn't give you a cent," she stared at him, green eyes blazing.

"Eleanor I owe a gambling debt, the man wants his money now, and he is not very patient," Warren whined. "The insurance has not been settled yet and won't be until the Will is read."

"That's your problem, not mine."

"Eleanor, please they're going to hurt me if I don't have the money today."

"I wish they would kill you," she spat.

"Now, Kitten, you don't mean that after all we have meant to each other."

Charlie heard Eleanor's voice become louder. He listened for a few seconds longer, then recognizing Warren's voice guided the horse's foot to the ground. He gave a couple of quick pats to its hind leg and hung the horseshoe on a nail. Before leaving the stall, he picked up the hammer he had been using to shoe the horse and walked the barren path to the house. Without saying a word, he crossed the lawn to where Warren stood and grabbed him by his arm. Charlie was not tall, but exceedingly strong. His fingers were like talons as they dug into Warren's exposed skin.

Charlie kept a firm hold on him. It was not until he reached the car and opened the door he released his grip. He looked up into Warren's defiant eyes but did not back down.

"I told you never to come here again. There will not be another warnin'. Do you understand what I'm sayin' to you, Warren?" Charlie shoved him into the car and closed the door. He stood fearless with his arms folded across his chest, exposing the hammer. Eleanor had confided in him about the rape and he had been the one to convince her to go to the hospital. He promised Eleanor he would never let Warren hurt her again.

Warren did not look at Charlie but kept his eyes straight ahead, as he lit a cigarette. He reached for the bottle of scotch he kept in the glove box, took a long gulp, and after a few minutes, drove away. After he left, Eleanor ran inside the house and threw up. She heaved the vile liquid as if it were Warren she was trying to rid herself of.

"Deanna, come walk with me," Charlie said, still holding the hammer. Without slowing his stride, he placed it in a chair as he passed by. Deanna walked beside her grandfather. They walked through the woods along the path that led to the sacred rock.

"Those mountains over there were once home of the Cherokee. They called the mountains Sha Kon o Hey, place of blue smoke. They lived peacefully, huntin' wild game and fishin' in clear streams. Then the Europeans came and took the land. Our people were forced to leave those mountains and the fertile land that ran along the Little Tennessee River. They were herded like cattle to Oklahoma. The path they walked became known as the Trail of Tears. Many died along the way and others took their lives. Old women mourned for the loss of their home and their loved ones."

He lit his pipe and stretched his hand out over Chota valley. "In just a few years, those sacred burial mounds will be covered by water. This whole river bottom and its fertile land will be gone. This will all be a lake when the Tellico dam project is completed. They have taken our land. But they can't take the Cherokee that flows deep in our veins. I tell you the stories my ancestors told me, so you can tell your grandchildren. Don't ever forget who you are, Wild Honey. You need to know the strength you have inside of you."

Deanna sat on the rock beside him. She looked at Charlie staring out over the valley. He turned to look at her; he raised the pipe to his mouth, inhaled, and then let the smoke seep through his lips. Without speaking, he tipped his head to her and then returned his gaze back to the view of the valley.

Charlie told Deanna stories about her ancestors; he told her how they escaped and hid in the mountains, and of the sacrifice one man made so they could remain in their homeland. He taught her how to listen to animals and how to make the salves and medicines from the bark of trees, roots, and plants.

ONE AFTERNOON IN JULY Eleanor and Deanna were standing at the kitchen sink drying the dinner dishes. "Did you hear the thunder last night?" Eleanor said. "Wasn't it something?" Then she stopped.

"What?" Deanna asked.

Eleanor was staring down at Deanna's white shorts. Deanna saw and felt it at the same time: the dark wet spot of blood. Deanna had started her period.

She was twelve years old and no one talked to her about her body or sexuality; a Southern woman would not speak of the subject of sex but did however, enjoy spending Sunday afternoons, with her husband, behind locked doors.

Deanna's information came from eavesdropping, process of elimination, and filling in the blanks. And from her friend Francine who was two years older. It was Francine that defined French-kissing for her and her best friend Gail, appointing herself their mentor.

She told them what happened the day she woke up with her period. Her mother explained why she had a period, then took her to the Guthrie General Store and got the things she needed. Later that night she told her how babies were made.

"A man and woman start kissin', then he puts his thang in the woman's thang and he spills his seeds inside of her, then a baby starts growin' in her belly," Francine said as she lit one of the cigarettes she had sneaked from her mother's purse. "So if you don't want to have a baby, don't let a man stick his thang in you."

On the weekend, Deanna took David to the river for an afternoon swim. He was looking at the front of her bathing suit in a way that made her blush. “What are those?” he said looking at her bumps. “They look like walnuts.”

“Shut up,” she said. David laughed and jumped in the water, splashing water at her. She jumped in hiding her smile. She only pretended to be angry; actually, she was proud of the bumps growing on her chest. She was no longer a little girl. But she didn’t know if she wanted to play with dolls or think about boys. One minute, it was her dolls and the next a severe crush on the freckle-faced boy who came into the store every Saturday with his dad.

TWO YEARS LATER, Deanna was fourteen, and it was in the middle of a heat wave she tried smoking. It made her gag and light-headed; she turned a pasty color and threw up. That was the last time she tried smoking, she just watched Francine as she blew smoke streams out both her nostrils. One time Francine said “Watch this” and put a lit cigarette in her month and closed it. When she opened it again, the cigarette was sticking out from beneath her tongue, still burning. She said her boyfriend had shown her how to do that.

A mid-July afternoon, Francine and Deanna sat in front of an open window in Deanna’s room. Francine had just lit a fresh Winston when Eleanor entered. The girls turned abruptly and Francine cupped the cigarette in her hands. Smoke was leaking out between her fingers; it became obvious to Eleanor that Francine was smoking a cigarette.

“This whole room smells like smoke,” she snapped as she flapped a dishtowel in the air. Francine rolled her eyes and looked at Deanna.

"Francine, I think it's time you go home; get your things and I'll drive you."

"Oh for crying out loud, Eleanor, just because Francine smokes, it doesn't mean she is goin' to…"

"That's enough out of you young lady, we'll talk about this when I get back."

Eleanor didn't particularly like Francine but she did feel sorry for her. Francine was the oldest of six siblings who lived in a rundown house behind the general store. Her father spent most of his paycheck on whiskey; they never had money to pay for groceries. James kept a running account for them, knowing he would not collect a cent.

David had turned seven the past January and despite Eleanor's best efforts to stop him, James bought him a BB gun. However she did convince him to wait until summer vacation to give it to him. That evening at dinner, Deanna was quiet, still angry with Eleanor for taking Francine home. But David chattered on and on about his new BB gun.

"Would you shut up about that stupid gun." Deanna snapped.

"What's wrong with you, bossy pants?" asked David.

"I'm tired hearin' about it."

"And I am tired hearin' the both of you argue." James responded. Deanna rolled her eyes.

"May I be excused now?" David asked.

"Yes, and don't shoot any birds or animals with that gun. Only cans. Do you hear me David." James said as David ran out the back door.

"Yes sir I hear you." The screen door slammed behind him.

"Deanna you and Gail should stop spending so much time with Francine," Eleanor said after David had left the dinner table. *Here it comes*, Deanna thought. "She's older than the two of you and has more experience and I'm afraid she might be a bad influence."

"You just don't like her," Deanna said in a loud abrupt manner, embarrassed Eleanor had brought up the subject in front of her father.

"You and Gail are good girls. Francine will be pregnant before she finishes high school," James said, not looking up from his dinner plate.

"That's not fair, and that's a horrible thing to say." Deanna knew Francine was having sex but pretended she didn't know what they were talking about.

"Whether it's fair or not, you and Gail can't be goin' to her house. You can't be hangin' out with her anymore," James said.

Deanna threw her napkin on her plate and stormed away. She called Gail, only to find out she had been told the same thing. Deanna was still angry when James knocked on her door. He did not wait for her to answer; he simply opened the door and walked in. Deanna grabbed her pajama top and held it in front of her.

"This is my room. Don't I get any privacy around here?" she hissed.

"First of all you get plenty of privacy and second, you need to lose the attitude, young lady."

"I can have anyone I want for a friend – you and Eleanor can't stop me."

"Yes, I think we can. Remember this is my roof you are livin' under and as long as your feet sit under my table, eatin' my food, you will respect the rules."

"Your rules are old fashioned."

"Maybe, but they're still the rules," he said.

"Just because Eleanor caught her smokin' in my room does not make her evil; she'll not go to hell for smokin'."

"You're right, she won't. Oh by the way, thank you for tellin' me about her smokin'. Eleanor had not mentioned that," he said as he closed the door.

Eleanor was finishing the dinner dishes and humming to herself. James walked quietly behind her and smacked her bottom before throwing the dishtowel over his shoulder. She turned and smiled affectionately at him.

"Did you and Deanna get things worked out?"

"If me losin' my temper and sayin' 'my home, my rules' are workin' things out, then yes we did."

"She'll calm down, her hormones are running wild right now," Eleanor said, handing James a clean dish.

That same summer, Eleanor turned to Deanna and David at supper and asked if they would like to have an in-ground pool in their back yard. David jumped up and hugged her.

"Where are we puttin' it?" Deanna asked. "Do we have to cut down the big oak tree?"

"No, there is enough space."

The next few weeks Deanna woke up to the sound of a backhoe digging in her back yard. And finally, she watched as the new pool filled with water. On Monday morning, she woke up late to the sound of the murmur of the pool filter and David sloshing in the water. From her window, she watched him catch air so that his cheeks bulged out like a chipmunk, jump, and come back to the surface. James did not go to work that day; he stayed home and sunbathed by the pool. By mid-morning, Deanna had her bathing suit on and was lying on a towel by the pool working on her tan.

Deanna started high school in mid-August and she and Gail become members of the future graduating class of 1977. A new girl came to class that year. Her name was Pat and before long, she, Gail and Deanna were inseparable.

Francine did not return to school that fall. The rumor was she had gotten pregnant by an eighteen-year-old boy. He said the baby was not his and it could belong to any number of boys. Francine died that summer; she tried to get rid of the baby by drinking some concoction an old woman had given her. Her family moved to another town after, never paying anything on their grocery bill. James took the credit slips and burned them.

Deanna never mentioned Francine again. She worked hard on her studies and was a straight-A student. Like most teenagers, one minute she was rebellious and selfish and the next, sweet and kind. She was still innocent and had a trusting view of the world and of human nature. She tried very hard to be a good girl, the kind of girl her father wanted her to be.

Chapter 7

MAY 1975 Deanna had turned sixteen and Eleanor promised her a special party. This was the party Deanna had looked forward to for years it was her coming of age party for invited guest.

"Deanna come on we have to be at seamstress for your fitting at eleven o'clock and it'll take a little over an hour to drive to Knoxville" Eleanor called up the stairs.

"Ok comin'." Deanna ran down the stairs and grabbed a strawberry Pop-Tart from the pantry as she hurried through the kitchen and to the car where Eleanor was waiting. As the car hummed along the highway, Deanna talked for a hour about the party. She told Eleanor about the senior boy she had a crush on.

"Do you think he'll be there, and what will I say to him if he is? I'm nervous about it," said Deanna as Eleanor pulled the car to a stop in front of the dress shop.

"Well just be yourself and ask him to dance with you."

"Oh I couldn't do that."

"Why not it's your party, you can ask anyone you want to dance." Eleanor smiled at Deanna.

"But he's the star Quarterback of the football team."

"So and you're the captain of the cheerleading squad."

The dress shop was the same boutique she and Deanna bought the little blue dress she wore at Eleanor and James's wedding. It was the same shop she bought the white shoes, with the little heels, just after Eleanor was released from the hospital and it was where they shopped for all the Easter and Christmas dresses.

Deanna tried on the dress and looked at herself in the mirror. “I love it, don’t you Eleanor?” It was a maxi length dress in apple green with a flutter collar and cut low in the back. Deanna turned around to look at the backside of the dress. “This is perfect. Now, for the right pair of shoes.” Even at sixteen, she looked elegant and striking. Everything about her said she was a woman not a little girl.

Eleanor was talking to the storeowner while Deanna set at the front of the shop looking through a fashion magazine. A man walked into the store, looked around, and removed his sunglasses. That was when Deanna recognized him. It was Warren Stone. His black hair was longer, covering his ears, touching just below his shirt collar. He had long sideburns and a moustache.

With Cathleen’s insurance money Warren had paid off his gambling debts and there was just enough left to allow him to masquerade as one of Knoxville’s elite. And of course he had his share of lonely rich widows to take care of him.

“May I help you sir.” The sales woman walked to where he stood.

“Yes I believe you can. I’m here to pick up three shirts.”

“What’s the name sir?”

“Warren Stone.” The woman walked to the back of the shop. A tall mirror stood in the corner; Warren looked at his reflection and ran his fingers through his thick hair. Then he swiveled suddenly, he was only a few feet from Deanna. He had never seen anyone as beautiful as she was. “Well hello kitten”.

“Hello Mr. Stone.”

"Are you here alone?"

"No Eleanor is with me. She's talkin' to the seamstress."

"You're a little far from home aren't you? Warren asked eyeing her carefully.

"We're pickin' up a dress for by sweet sixteen party."

"Wow you're sixteen now. Happy Birthday." Warren looked as though he was undressing her with his eyes. Deanna smiled and lowered her eyelids.

"Here you are Mr. Stone," the sales woman interrupted him.

"Thank You. Oh and put this on Mrs. Cooper's tab."

"Well see you around kitten."

On the way back to White Oak Flats, Eleanor rambled on about what it was like when she attended her debutante ball. "It was something like 'Gone with the Wind'. Fifty young women all dressed in white satin gowns and long satin gloves being introduced to polite society. But before we were presented we had to complete charm school." The steady droning sound of the car engine lulled Deanna into a light sleep while Eleanor continued to describe the experience.

"What's the point? That sounds borin'," Deanna sighed, as she forced her eyelids open.

"It was very valuable. We were taught to be a lady and the mistress of the house."

"I'm not goin' to be a mistress of the house. I plan to go to law school."

"Then you will need it even more."

"Is there a point to this?"

"Yes." Eleanor looked at Deanna and smiled. "You will be taught skills, like balancing a check book, how to speak properly, how to interview, how to walk, how to dance, what to talk about, who to sit where at dinner parties, how to write letters and thank you notes."

"Now it really sounds borin'." Deanna sighed.

"When we get home I'll get the telephone number of schools in Knoxville. I'm sure we'll find just the right one for you. You'll thank me for it someday." Eleanor reached over and took her hand. Deanna shook her head and looked out the window.

When they arrived home that afternoon Eleanor called the dress shop. "Hello this is Mrs. Guthrie. I was in the shop today with my daughter," said Eleanor into the phone.

"Yes hello Mrs. Guthrie did we forget something?"

"Oh no the dress is perfect. In fact Deanna is upstairs trying it on again. I called hoping, you might be able to recommend a finishing school in Knoxville. I would like for Deanna to attend this summer."

"Yes in fact the mistress is a customer of mine. She's in here often and I have heard nothing but praises from mothers about her school. I have her number if you don't care to wait a minute I can get it for you."

"That would be wonderful."

"Okay here it is Mrs. Guthrie. The name of the school is Miss Vivian's School of Charm. And her name is Vivian Cooper."

"Thank you." Eleanor replied.

On Saturday the back yard was tented and a wooded dance floor was placed under the tent. Caterers were bringing in the food, and a local rock band set up. Later that evening when Deanna walked out on her father's arm the yard was filled with more than fifty guest. Curtis and Ray and their four children were there, college friends of Eleanor and acquaintances of both James and Eleanor. Deanna's Aunt Rebecca, Calvin, and Troy drove from Ohio. The rest were Deanna's school friends and most importantly the senior boy she had invited.

James was teasing her as they walked past the guest and she was laughing with him. And as she was introduced there was an energy that seemed to emanate from her. Eleanor was right behind them and seemed happy to stop and chat with friends. Within a few minutes, Deanna spotted the young man she had invited standing among a group of her friends and she abandon her father and Eleanor to meet them. Within seconds Deanna was laughing and talking and the young man was captivated by her.

There was something mesmerizing about Deanna. She stood out in a crowd, not only for her looks but for her wit and charm. Even the shape of her mouth suggested she was about to say something funny or something you wanted to hear.

When the band started up it broke into a song by the Eagles 'One of This Nights'. Mike, the senior boy asked Deanna to dance. He stayed near her the rest of the evening. They danced, laughed, and sang along with the music. The last song of the night was a slow song. As he held her, Mike kissed Deanna–it was her first kiss.

After the band stopped playing he asked Deanna if she would see a movie with him the following Saturday. She wanted to jump up and down with excitement but she only smiled and agreed. After he turned and walked away she clapped her hands together and ran to Pat and Gail. "He asked me! We're going to the drive-in next Saturday." They all three jumped up and down. "I don't know what I'm going to wear."

After the party and Deanna was in her bedroom getting ready for bed and thinking about her date next Saturday.

"Deanna may I come in?"

"Yes." Eleanor pushed the door open. "Eleanor guess what? Mike asked me on a date."

"Who's Mike?"

"His's the senior boy I invited to the party."

"Oh yes the football player." Eleanor smiled.

"He's so cute."

"Yes he is, but his hair is a little long for my taste."

"Oh Eleanor." Deanna rolled her eyes and flopped on the bed.

"Mrs. Cooper returned my call today. She just had a cancelation for the July class." Eleanor said sitting down on the bed beside Deanna.

"Do I really have to go to finishing school? It'll take up most of my summer. And what if Mike asked me out again."

"It's only for three weeks and it doesn't start until Monday after the Fourth of July. And besides you come home on weekends. Look at the bright side you get away from David for three weeks."

MRS. VIVIAN COOPER was wearing a sleeveless polyester chiffon dress. It was a pastel pink and purple floral print. A neckline of ruffles formed the top and a matching belt tied in a big bow and hung down the side of the dress. Her hair was flicked to resemble small wings at the temples. She spent a large portion of the morning handing out booklets and introducing the other young woman. By late-morning each girl was issued a book by Emily Post.

"Our words expose our sophistications, they tell our listeners of the company we have kept and of our worldly wisdom." Vivian began her prepared lesson. "And proper etiquette is a necessary part of education. It reveals our self-confidence and refinements." She smiled and began again.

At lunch-time Deanna followed the eleven other girls to the back patio for finger sandwiches and iced tea. She found her place at one of the black wrought iron tables and waited for Mrs. Cooper to join them.

After lunch she gave the young women a tour of the mansion. The rooms were large and furnished with antiques. There was a large formal dining room just off a modern kitchen. The industrial kitchen was equipped with double ovens, two stovetops, and two dishwashers and a large walk-in freezer.

"The next three weeks you will learn to plan the menu, shop for food and prepare a meal for a small dinner party as well as host a large party. You will learn where to seat your guest. You will learn to walk, talk, and entertain. You will learn to conduct yourself with all the grace of a Southern Lady." Mrs. Cooper continued as she walked through each room. "You will learn to manage a home, balance a checkbook, and pay house hold bills." They followed her up the stairs. "You will learn how to interview the help and how to be interviewed." She continued down a hallway. "Two girls are assigned to each room and each room has its own bathroom. You will be expected to do your own cleaning and laundry. Lights out at ten and breakfast at eight."

For homework, Mrs. Cooper assigned three chapters from Emily Post and gave each of them a checkbook and a budget for their dinner party. Deanna positioned herself on the bed and began to read. She was still awake when she heard a man's voice and the quiet laughter of Mrs. Cooper. Deanna drifted off to sleep as their voices murmured down stairs together.

By the time the girls gathered around the breakfast table Warren had been gone for hours. He had met Vivian Cooper just after her husband passed away one year ago. He became her devoted companion; it gave him the perfect cover—where else could he be with so many young women.

AN AFTERNOON STORM had taken away the hot gluey weather and a breeze was cooling the night air. Deanna finished her homework and was about to go inside when she saw Warren Stone through the window. He was sitting in the formal dining room. Deanna opened the patio door leading into the den, just off the dining room, trying very hard to go unnoticed. "Miss Guthrie what are you doing down here?"

"I'm sorry Mrs. Cooper I didn't realize it was so late." Warren tilted his head toward the voice.

"Go on upstairs you have ten minutes before lights out."

"Yes ma'am."

Warren was up out of his chair. "Deanna this is a nice surprise." He set his drink down and walked toward her.

"Hello Mr. Stone."

"I didn't realize you two knew each other." Vivian turned to Warren.

"Yes I've practically watched her turn into a young woman. How is Eleanor?"

"She's doing well." Deanna responded. "Please excuse me. Goodnight Mrs. Cooper."

The room was dark when Deanna opened the bedroom door. Her roommate was sleeping. She quietly slipped into her pajamas and brushed her teeth. In the quiet, she heard Vivian's laugh. The street lamp along Kingston Pike came on and she heard Warren's car leave.

The next evening Warren stopped by the house again. It was 9 p.m. and the other girls had gone inside for the evening. Deanna stayed behind to finish her dinner party invitations. Warren stood by the corner of the house and unbeknownst to anyone had been watching her. He waited until she was alone. "Kitten." He said as he stepped from the shadows.

"Mr. Stone you scared me!"

"I'm sorry I didn't mean to."

"Mrs. Cooper is in the house."

"I know, actually I came to see you." Warren moved in closer. "How good are you at keeping secrets?"

"Okay I guess."

"I wanted you to have this." Warren took a gold bracelet out of his shirt pocket. "This belonged to Cathleen. I thought you might like it." He held out the bracelet. "May

I put it on for you?" He reached for her hand and fastened the bracelet around her wrist.

"It's very pretty." Deanna raised her arm and looked closely at the gold locket. It was heart shaped with diamonds. "This is too expensive I can't keep it."

"Cathleen would want you to have it." He patted her hand. "No one needs to know I gave it to you. Eleanor especially, she wouldn't understand. She and I have not been on the best of terms since her mother died."

"Okay."

"See you around kitten." Warren walked back inside the house.

"I'm glad you were able to change your plans next week. I need more adult chaperons for the ball." Vivian said in the cheeriest of voices. "Oh my dear Vivian I always enjoy seeing your young girls transform into young women with such beautiful manners," Warren answered. He took the glass of scotch from her, and smiled before he raised the tumbler to his lips.

Warren started showing up every night, sometimes he talked to Deanna and other times just sat quietly in the den with Mrs. Cooper. Tonight Deanna sat at the kitchen table finishing homework and eating ice cream. "How's Vivian treating you?" Warren asked as he walked into the kitchen.

"Fine."

"May I join you?"

"Yes."

Warren walked to the freezer and took out a carton of vanilla ice cream. He set down at the table, looked over at her, and smiled. "So Miss Guthrie do you have a boyfriend."

"No. Well sort of." The spoon clicked against the dish and the cold ice cream caused her to shiver when she raised it to her mouth.

"So there is a young man you have your eyes on." Warren watched her lips as they closed around the spoon.

"Yes." She smiled.

"So tell me about this young man." He tapped her foot with his and winked at her.

"He's a senior and is on the football team. He came to my birthday party." Her eyes lit up as she talked about him. "He asked me to dance with him."

"So did he steal a kiss?"

"Yes." Deanna blushed.

"I knew it! Who wouldn't want to kiss you." He leaned in closer. "Did you like it?" He was teasing her.

"Yes." She blushed.

"Look at you you're blushing."

"And we've been to the drive-in twice since my party."

"Well if you need any advice about this young man you just let me know." He reached over and took her hand, squeezing it softly. He held it for several seconds. "Has Eleanor told you how I helped her with her boyfriends?"

"No."

He smiled and began the fabricated stories of advice he had given her. They were both laughing when Vivian walked through the door. "Miss Guthrie I think it's time you were in your room."

"Yes ma'am." Warren rolled his eyes and winked at her. She returned the eye roll and they both began to laugh. "Good night Mrs. Cooper.

"If you need any help with that young man of yours let me know."

"I will." They smiled at each other as if there shared a big secret.

THERE WERE TWELVE white dresses hanging in the living room with the name of each girl penned to them. The dresses were long white satin ball gowns. The girls found their name and took the dress off the rolling clothes rack. "Girls quiet please." Vivian gave three rapid claps in succession. "The tailor is here for your final fitting. So let's get started shall we."

It was a tradition the last night of finishing school to attend a ball hosted by Vivian herself. There were fifty invited guest dressed in ball dresses and tuxedo's. James and Eleanor were among the guest along with the other parents of the eleven young women.

The guest were chatting in the elegant reception room. Long tables with lamb chops, green vegetables, and cold shrimp were lined up on the patio and the gardens had been transformed into a tented ballroom complete with a band. A crier announced each girl and their escort as they entered wearing white gowns and satin cloves and the young men from the Military Academy wore dress uniforms.

Warren was wearing a tuxedo like the other men and looked dashing. He was only inches from Eleanor as he held his plate. Looking down at her from his great height, their eyes met. "Warren." Eleanor found she couldn't move at all, she was riveted where she was.

"Hello Kitten, imagine seeing you here. By the way you are still as lovely as ever." She turned quickly and scanned the garden for Deanna. “She’s a beautiful young woman Eleanor. I’ve become rather fond of her.” He said with a smirk. All she could think about was finding Deanna and getting her away from him.

She found Deanna standing at the punch bowl with her escort. “Deanna please come with me.” Deanna looked at Eleanor and saw the serious look on her face. The same look she had the day she came home from the hospital and found Warren in her house.

“What is it Eleanor?”

“Deanna please walk with me.” Deanna followed her inside the house. “You need to get your things we’re leaving.”

“Now?”

“Yes now.”

“But Eleanor the ball doesn’t end until mid-night.”

“Go get your things I said we’re leaving.” Eleanor said in a very stern voice.

“God! Eleanor first you make me come here, now you’re making me leave.”

“Don’t argue with me Deanna, get your things.”

Chapter 8

'THE DOG DAYS OF SUMMER' had settled into the valley and the air between land and sky trembled with heat. The valley held the wet sticky air in like a pressure cooker. It was already eighty degrees and only nine o'clock in the morning. Deanna walked down stairs in her pajamas. "Deanna I'm going to the store to work today and two of David's friends are coming over to swim, so keep an eye on them." Eleanor was finishing the dishes. "There are clothes in the washer to be dried and folded before I get home this evening." Deanna took a glass from the cabinet and poured a glass of orange juice. "And hang your ball dress in your closet it's been laying on your bed for a week."

"Okay." Deanna answered in a half-awake voice. "I have cheerleading practice at four o'clock this afternoon. What am I supposed to do with David and his friends?"

"Drop them off at the store."

"And Mike's picking me up at eight tonight we're meeting Pat and Gail at the Drive-In. 'Jaws' is playing.

Deanna went back upstairs with the glass of orange juice. She sat on the edge of her bed in front of the ironing board ironing her hair trying to get the last of the curls to straighten. Not that it would do any good in the humidity.

"Deanna I'm leaving now. David's outside with his friends," Eleanor called up the stairs.

"Okay Eleanor."

Deanna washed her face in the bathroom sink, changed into her bathing suit, and went down stairs.

"Hello." Deanna saw a blurred outline by the screen door. As she walked closer she could see that is was Warren.

"Hi Warren," she said. "Come in."

"Good you finally called me Warren instead of Mr. Stone. Mr. Stone made me fill like an old man." The screen door slapped shut behind him.

"What are you doing all the way down here?"

"I just missed our little talks." He looked at her young body. "Is Eleanor or your dad home?"

"No they're at the store."

"Are you alone?"

"No my brother and his friends are outback." He walked through the house looking in rooms. She followed him to the kitchen where he was looking out the window.

"Kitten so tell me are you still seeing the young man?"

"Yes we're going to the drive-in tonight."

"Do you need any advice from me?"

"I don't think so."

"Are you sure?""

"No I'm fine." She laughed. "Geese you'd think I was still a little girl. I'm sixteen you know."

"Oh yea, the way you look in that cute little bikini, you're defiantly not a little girl." He moved closer to her. He reached down, touched her bare shoulder, and ran his finger the full length of her arm. "Your skin is as soft as a baby's face."

Deanna blushed; her eyes went to the floor. "Are you still shy? You are. Bet you're ticklish too." She let out a nervous laugh. "Come here let me see if you are." His grip tightened around her wrist. His fingertips dance along her bare stomach.

"Cut it out," she laughed. His hand brushed her breast as he moved to the other side. "Come on, cut it out."

"You ticklish here too?" He was laughing. "What about here?" He leaned down and put his hand on her thigh. "And here?" Then his hand ran up the inside of her leg as he rubbed against her.

"Stop it." But he wouldn't stop. Warren's mood went from playfulness to sinister. "Really stop!" She pulled away from him. "I think you should go. I have to get somethings done for Eleanor before she gets home."

"One minute you liked it and the next you're telling me to stop. You little tease. Better be careful with the signals you put out little girl, someday you'll give someone the wrong impression." He walked out of the house, the screen door slammed behind him. He sat in his car for a long moment before lighting a cigarette. He inhaled deeply then took a bottle of scotch out of the glove box.

Deanna ran up the stairs and into her bedroom. She felt guilty for yelling at him. *May*be *it was just my imagination,* she thought. *I shouldn't have been so mean to him.* She took a shower and set down at her dressing table. That was when she saw him; the insidious evil that awaited. He had crept into her room and was standing behind her. He leaned in and she could smell the stench of cigarettes and liquor on his breath.

"Little Miss Innocence," he whispered.

Deanna saw the evil in Warren's eyes. She jumped up and ran toward the door but he put his strong arms around her middle and held her. She struggled against his strength.

"Let me go!" Deanna screamed. His arms tightened; he was squeezing the breath out of her. She heard her own strangling breath in her ears and the voices of David and his friends outside her window. Their voices faded as her breathing slowed. Her flailing hand fluttered weakly as she made a faint rasping sound. She could taste salt as Warren put his mouth over hers. His tongue flicked in her mouth as though he was trying to win a sword fight.

She could hear her brother laughing again. Suddenly Warren tore at her panties, and then flung her down on the bed. She tried to scream. He raised his thick arm and hit her hard across the face. Her cheek stung from the blow. She looked out the window and listened to laughter as the three boys splashed in the pool. None of this seemed real. She screamed and tried to hit him with her hands but he grabbed her wrist and pressed his knee against her leg, pinning her to the bed.

With his free hand, he ripped her panties off. "Stop. Please stop," she begged as she fought him.

"Listen. It's nicer if you don't fight. Kitten, don't fight, it won't hurt I promise…." He was touching her. His pants were down. She felt her flesh rip; she stopped fighting due to the pain of it.

He glistened with sweat and she could feel his hot breath on her face. "Tell me you like it," he said. "Tell me you like it you little tease!" he repeated.

The voices outside the window faded and all she could hear were the disgusting grunting sounds come from him, they repeated over and over. With every throaty noise came blinding pain. She turned her head away from his face and cried for her mother. The room began to turn dark. When she opened her eyes, he was pulling his pants up.

"We're the same you and me. We're both terrible people, and you liked it, didn't you," he said as he touched her face. Her mind was numb and her insides hurt. He bent down and kissed her on the cheek. She was afraid not to let him. He then turned and walked out the door. She listened as his heavy footsteps grew fainter and she flinched at the slamming of the front door.

She was hurting; she thought he must have split her open. David's voice faded again until she could no longer hear it.................

Her eyes fluttered the voices in the back yard were faraway whispers. She looked at the clock at her beside it was almost four o'clock. She put her hands over the pain and looked at the blood on her white dress that lay crumpled on the bed. Slowly she moved and tried to walk. The room was spinning, but she managed to hold onto the wall until she reached the bathroom.

She collapsed on the bathroom floor, holding the bloody dress to her chest, rocking back and forth, just staring ahead at nothing. She could not even cry. She felt violated and ashamed and dirty, she needed to get the smell of his sex off her. Down stairs the phone was ringing.........ringing.........ringing..........until finally the sound faded away.

"Deanna where are you? Your cheerleading coach called and said you didn't show up for practice. Deanna!" Eleanor yelled up the stairs. There was no answer. "Deanna did you hear me?" Still Deanna did not answer her. "David, where's your sister?"

"I don't know I haven't seen her."

Eleanor went upstairs and saw the trail of bright red drops of blood leading to the bathroom. She opened the door and found Deanna sitting on the bathroom floor, so pale that her skin seemed translucent. She saw the bloody dress and the blood between her legs. She kneeled down beside Deanna. "Deanna are you okay. Did you start your period?" Deanna dropped her head. Eleanor took Deanna's face between her hands and turned it toward her. She gasped when she saw the bruises on her face and wrist. "Deanna, look at me. Who did this to you?" Deanna did not respond. "Deanna who did this?" she asked again.

"Warren," Deanna replied as she fell into Eleanor's arms and began to cry. Eleanor held her and they cried together. She ran a bath and Deanna eased into the hot water. Through the steaming water, she watched her skin redden, streamers of blood sullying the water. Eleanor placed both hands on Deanna's knees, slightly spreading them, letting the water soothe her burning flesh. She then wrapped a towel around Deanna, and led to her down the hall to the bedroom. Deanna's whirling mind produced a flashback. She was three years old, wrapped in a towel, following the two girls from church to her room. She was getting ready for her mother's funeral.

"My dress is ruined," Deanna cried.

"Don't worry about the dress. I'll get you another one." Eleanor helped her into her pajamas and put her to bed. "I'll call Pat and Gail and tell them you are not well."

"What about Mike?" Deanna whimpered.

"I'll call him too."

DR.MCKINNEY tiptoed up the stairs unnoticed and found Eleanor waiting in Deanna's room. She had called him about the rape, but asked him not to say anything to anyone. She wanted to call Curtis first.

He examined Deanna and gave her a shot to help her sleep, and within five minutes, her eyelids became heavy, then closed. He waited until she fell asleep before he turned to Eleanor.

"I can't see that she'll have any permanent physical scars from this, but she will need emotional help. You have to tell James about this, he needs to know," he said, closing his medical bag. "And you need to have that man arrested."

"There is nothing I'd like more than to see him rot in jail," she told him. "But she's only sixteen years old. There's a stigma she'll have to live with for the rest of her life. I don't want Deanna to feel people are staring at her and talking behind her back. She just needs to pretend it never happened."

"You're wrong about this, Eleanor." He picked up his bag and turned to her again. "She's going to need some help with this." He looked at Deanna. "She should sleep the rest of the day and night. But if she wakes up, call me and I'll come back and give her something a little stronger."

"Thank You, Dr. McKinney."

"I've known her since the day she was born. She's a strong girl but this, this is different, Eleanor, and she's going to have to have more than you can give her."

Eleanor withheld their terrible secret from James and chose not to press charges against Warren. That night after James had gone to bed; Eleanor took the dress outside and threw it in the large barrel. She lit a match and watched as the flames burned hotter, consuming both the dress and the secret. Across the lawn, Charlie stood in the shadows. When the flames burned out, he turned and walked away.

THE SOUND of a slamming car door awakened Deanna. There was an urgent knock, and she heard her father open the door. It hurt to move, but she got out of bed and walked to the window. A police car was sitting in the driveway with its emergency light flashing.

"Is Eleanor home? I need to speak to her," the police officer asked.

"Yes she is, come on in Ross," James said. "She slept in this morning, she had a restless night. But I heard her in the shower a while ago, she should be down soon."

"Elli, Ross is here and needs to speak with you," he yelled up the stairs. "Have you had coffee yet?" He asked Ross.

"Yes, but I can always drink another one."

"Then come on in the kitchen." James walked down the hall and the officer followed him. They were standing in the kitchen when Eleanor entered.

"Good morning Ross, how've you been? I haven't seen you at church in a while." Eleanor yawned still sleepy. "Excuse me," she said.

"I'm fine, Ms. Elli." Ross removed his hat. "I need to ask you a few questions."

"Okay," she replied as she poured a cup of coffee. "Please have a seat. Have you had breakfast yet?"

"Yes Ma'am. But thank you anyway." He sat down at the table. "I just got off the phone with a detective from

Knoxville. They found a man lying on the ground outside his car, he had been shot."

"What does that have to do with me?"

"In his glove box they found the car registration. The Mercedes is registered to a Cathleen Stone. Is that your mother?"

"Yes, but she passed away four years ago."

"The detectives thought the man may be your stepfather. He was apparently a victim of robbery. His wallet was missing." Ross took a note pad and pen from his shirt pocket. "When was the last time you saw Warren?"

"Four years ago. It was just after my mother died, he said he owed a debt, gambling I think, and he was asking for money. I refused and that was the last time I saw him." She sat down at the kitchen table. "Oh wait, I did see him about a month ago. He was at a party James and I attended in Knoxville."

"Elli you didn't tell me you saw him there." James looked surprised.

"I just saw him in passing we barely spoke."

"Ms. Elli, they need someone to identify the body."

"I know what he looks like. I can do that." They turned around to see Charlie standing in the hallway. He looked at Eleanor for a brief moment and went with Ross to the car.

After they left, Eleanor went up to Deanna's room. She opened the door and found Deanna standing by the window. "Deanna, Warren's dead. They think it was robbery."

"Why didn't you tell him Warren raped me?"

"Deanna if the police find out he was here yesterday they might think we had something to do with this,"

Eleanor said as Deanna sat in stone-cold silence. "We need to just forget it ever happened."

"All right, Eleanor, I won't tell anyone." *You and I did this together. We are both terrible people.* Deanna heard the words in her head.

THE SUMMER FADED into fall. She tried to pretend she was okay, but she was not the same girl anymore, her spirit had been broken in a violent way and she felt ashamed and humiliated. She was sad most of the time and mostly kept to herself. One day she became ill at school, so ill she spent an hour throwing up in the bathroom. She had never been this sick before. The next day it was the same. Retching every morning and then dragging herself to school. Her grades were beginning to slip.

"What's wrong Deanna? You haven't touched your breakfast," Eleanor said.

"Breakfast is making me sick. And besides, I can't fit into my jeans anymore. I need to lose some weight."

Eleanor sat down at the table and put her head in her hands. She sat there a long moment before she asked Deanna the question she feared the most. "Deanna, when did you have your last period?"

Deanna thought for a moment. "I don't know." It was the middle of October and she had not bled at all, not even spotting. Suddenly without warning, her stomach contracted and her throat filled. She ran to the bathroom, leaned over the toilet and vomited. She was sick again and again until she was weak, and her face was wet with clammy sweat. Then she set helplessly on the bathroom floor. She wiped her mouth with a clean towel, but it did nothing to erase the sour bitter taste inside her month.

ELEANOR had gotten the name of a doctor from Ray, pretending it was for her, and the following week drove Deanna to the appointment. They drove to Knoxville in complete silence and ten minutes after they arrived, a nurse came out and got Deanna. She rose hesitantly and waited for Eleanor to do the same. "Aren't you coming with me?"

"I'll be out here. You'll be fine."

The walls of the examining room were the color of mustard. To the left of the examining table was a trash can with a single white gauze pad stained with blood. Deanna became nauseated just looking at it. The nurse handed her a paper gown. "Get undressed; take your bra and underwear off, the gown opens in front. The doctor will be in, in a few minutes."

She took off her sandals and jeans and pulled the sweatshirt over her head, and put them in a neat pile on the chair. The gown rustled and crinkled as she fumbled with the paper ties. She sat on the table, between the silver stirrups; she reached out and touched one. It was cold.

The doctor was scanning the forms when he came into the room. He stood before her reading. "When was your last period?" he asked. The nurse asked her to lie back as she placed her foot into a cold stirrup and then the other one.

"This is going to be cold," she said to Deanna. The doctor was mumbling something to the nurse. Deanna turned her head and looked at her clothes in a helpless pile. Her heart raced as he began to examine her. When he touched her down there all she could think of was Warren's grunting. The tears leaking from her eyes stained the paper gown. She nodded and shook her head at each question. He paused for a moment while the nurse took blood from her arm. At the door, with his hand on the knob, he turned back to look at Deanna. She seemed like an injured bird frighten and confused. His heart went out to her. He did not encourage abortions often but having this baby under this circumstance could only cause mental stress for her and the baby. "You can get dressed, I'll be back, and then we can discuss your options." He said to Deanna as he lowered his eyes. "Nurse show her mother to my office."

"Yes Doctor."

Eleanor followed the nurse down the hall. The doctor was sitting behind his desk and when she walked into his office he looked up with a sympathetic smile. "Please have a seat Eleanor." He lay the file down and got straight to the point. "Of course we need the blood test to confirm it, but with the exam and my best educated guess I would feel confident to say that she is pregnant." Eleanor began to cry. He got up and walked to the bookcase, turned to look at her and raised his hand to his chin. "There are things that can be done. And there is adoption but under the circumstance I would suggest an abortion."

"I want to be with you when you tell her."

"Yes, of course."

Deanna was quiet on the ride back home; she got out of the car slamming the door with a force created by the last seven days of anger. She did not speak a word, just stormed through the house and went straight upstairs to her room. She sat on her bed surrounded by stuffed animals and dolls. Tears rolled down her cheeks.

"May I come in, Deanna? We need to talk about this." Eleanor shut the door behind her and walked to the bed where Deanna sat holding her doll Jenny, one she had since childhood. "Deanna, you will not be alone, I'll be with you." Deanna simply stared out the window. "Okay, I'll leave you now, but we do need to talk about this." Eleanor touched her shoulder and left.

A week went by before Deanna said anything about the baby. "Eleanor, I've made a decision. I want to keep the baby." Eleanor turned her head quickly toward Deanna.

"Deanna, you're only sixteen. You have the rest of your life ahead of you. Think about what you're going to do about finishing high school and college. And Deanna, people are going to wonder who the father is. What will you tell them?"

"I'll tell them the truth," she snapped. That evening she did not know what to do with herself. She was not hungry. The TV Eleanor and James had given her for her sixteenth birthday sat in the corner of the room, but nothing was on that she wanted to watch. She turned the light out and went to sleep. That night she awoke in a jumble of covers to what she thought was Warren's voice. "*Just a dream,* she thought. She squished her head back into the pillow.

THAT CHRISTMAS was like any other, with one major difference. Deanna and Eleanor shared a dark secret. For Deanna, what was meant to be a happy holiday had a veil of sadness hanging over it. Eleanor and James had bought both their children expensive gifts, but all she could think about was her baby. She sat silently at Christmas dinner, not able to eat a thing.

By February, Eleanor was growing even more concerned about Deanna. She was barely eating and looked tired and pale. "Deanna, we need to talk about this," Eleanor said sternly.. "I've spoken with your Aunt Rebecca and she has agreed for you to stay with her in Ohio until the baby is born."

"You want to get rid of me?"

"No, Deanna. But I think this is for the best. I think we need to make arrangements for an adoption."

"I don't want that. I want to keep the baby," Deanna snapped.

"Deanna, be reasonable. There will come a day when it will ask about its father. Do you want to tell it a monster, a pure devil, raped you? The baby deserves better than that."

She can't wait to get rid of me and my baby – only she wasn't going to, Deanna thought. She made a hot bath as hot as it was the day he had raped her. She eased herself into it. Not that it worked. It never washed him away.

DURING EXAM WEEK, the corridors were a wall of noise. However, Deanna passed among them almost invisibly. Although she was very slim, she was beginning to show. She disguised the pregnancy by wearing sweatshirts. Bellbottom jeans and old sweatshirts seemed to be her uniform these days.

Sometime in the night, Warren's face interrupted her sleep. She gagged, then ran to the bathroom and threw up a pint of hot liquid. She hated him and she wished she had been the one to pull the trigger. She forced herself to breathe slowly and paced quietly, holding the cross her grandmother had given her for her birthday. When she was exhausted, she got back into bed. Outside it was dawn, raining. Her sleep had been stolen. Warren's face was tangled up in her headache. *"You liked it, didn't you?"*

During the day, she looked tired and all she seemed to want to do was sleep. Her best friends, Gail and Pat, could not understand why she did not want a social life. For the next several weeks, her spirits never lifted.

"I'm worried about Deanna. She barely eats, she looks tired and pale, and she cries every time I look at her," James said one night, as he got ready for bed.

"She'll be all right," Eleanor said, dismissing it. "It's been a cold winter and she's working hard in school. If she doesn't improve in a few weeks I'll make her an appointment."

THE DAYS WERE GETTING LONGER and Deanna bought time, day by day. But it was nearing the end of March. Suddenly all of her dreams and fears fused into one big explosion. It was like a bomb had been dropped on her; the whole thing was suddenly more than she could take. She was sixteen years old, pregnant, and scared; she was a child, how could she raise a child? She would barely be able to finish high school, let alone go to college. And if she kept the baby would she see Warren every time she looked at it?. Would she grow to hate it as much as she did him.

She finally decided to talk with Eleanor. "I'm so confused, Eleanor. I don't know what to do anymore." After a long moment of silence, she finally said, "I think the best thing is to give up the baby." She began to cry and leaned on Eleanor's shoulder.

Eleanor handed her a handkerchief. "I think you are doing the right thing," she said. She hugged her and tucked her into her bed that night like a little girl. They shared a smile. Deanna wanted to tell Eleanor she loved her. She opened her month to say it, but nothing came out.

Eleanor's notes to the teachers always started out the same way. "Deanna has been ill with a stomach problem. . . sore throat. . . ," she'd write on days when Deanna felt too depressed to go to school. She never refused to write the excuses, but did not like lying. There were already too many lies.

As the delivery date approached, Eleanor spoke with the school principal; she discussed with him Deanna's emotional state and told him Deanna would be staying with her aunt in Ohio for a few weeks. He agreed to let her take her exams early. James was glad she was going to see a doctor, but he put up a fight at first about her going to Ohio.

"I'll stay with her, James. It's better to take her out of school for a while," Eleanor said one night.

"I guess, but I just don't like the two of you being so far away," James said. After arguing for a week, he finally agreed to the arrangements. Deanna continued to lose body weight and was able to keep her round stomach concealed by wearing the sweatshirts.

Other than Rebecca, no one knew the true reason Deanna was leaving town. Because of her state of mind, it was not hard to convince everyone she needed to see a doctor and rest.

REBECCA WAITED at the Columbus airport for their plan to arrive. When she saw Deanna she took a small gasp. She looked so frail. Her face was pale and her sunken blue eyes surrounded by dark circles. Rebecca met her with a warm hug. She held Deanna tighter and began to cry. "You must be exhausted. Let's get you home. I have a comfortable room ready for you."

Rebecca drove Eleanor and Deanna to her home in Lancaster. When they arrived at the large two-story house it was quiet inside. Calvin her older cousin was away at college and Troy was at an all boy boarding school. Rebecca settled Deanna into a room she had made comfortable for her. Eleanor slept in the next room.

She had been there a month and one night, Deanna suddenly awakened from her sleep. Looking like a child who had been frightened by a bad dream, she stood in her nightgown wet from the waist down. "Eleanor, my water broke." Eleanor touched Deanna's cheek, then quickly dressed and woke Rebecca. They drove to the hospital and there Deanna checked into a private room.

DEANNA'S LABOR was hard. She tried to sleep between the contractions but she tossed fretfully. When she thrashed the covers off, Eleanor tucked them around her again. She stroked her forehead until the distress lines went away. This went on for twelve hours. Deanna took short panting breaths trying to ease her cramping stomach. She had never in her life felt such pain. Then finally, the baby's head began to crown. The nurses rolled her to the delivery room, where the doctor was waiting.

"It's too late to give her a spinal block, the baby is crowning," the nurse said to the doctor as he scrubbed.

"What does that mean?" Deanna looked as frightened as a wild caged animal.

"That means you are going to have this baby natural," the doctor said calmly.

"Oh God, it hurts!" she screamed.

"You need to push, Deanna."

"I can't, it hurts, it hurts."

"You have to push Deanna," he said again. "You can do this."

The pain was worse than anything she had ever felt. With face contorted and eyes shut, she tried to push but she was too tired. She fell back into the arms of the nurse. Her hair was wet from sweat and strands of red curls stuck to her face. She began to cry. The nurse wiped her face with a washcloth and held her hand.

"Push, Deanna," the doctor urged again.

"I can't," she said, crying.

"Yes, you can. That's it, Deanna, push! You're doing fine."

She raised herself upon her elbows and squeezed the nurse's hand and with one final hard push, she heard the baby cry. She fell back into the nurse's arms exhausted. She smiled at Deanna and patted her shoulder. "It's over, you did fine."

"Is the baby okay?".

"Yes," the doctor said as he handed the baby to the nurse. The small bundle cried as she wrapped it in the blanket. Deanna raised and steadied herself on her elbows; she struggled to get a glimpse of her baby.

"What is it?" Deanna asked.

"A little boy."

Eleanor waited for Deanna in the private room. She touched her face as she moved from the stretcher back to her bed. Deanna turned her back and closed her eyes. She told herself she was doing the best thing for him, but she cried herself to sleep anyway. The next morning she woke up and touched her stomach. The life she had felt for nine months was gone.

"Eleanor, I want to see him," Deanna said in a low voice. "I want to tell him that I love him. And I need to say goodbye to my baby." Her arms ached to hold him. She felt empty.

"Are you sure you want to do that?" Eleanor said touching her cheek.

"Yes," Deanna said, still touching her stomach.

"Okay, I'll tell the nurse to bring him to you."

They brought the baby wrapped in a blue and white blanket. Deanna saw his tiny head as the nurse placed him in her arms. She held her baby for what she knew would be the last time. Her heart ached so badly she thought it would explode in her chest. Her heartbroken tears eased her pain a little. She wept openly and loud. The cries came from deep within her soul.

Through tears, she looked into the face of the sleeping baby. "He's beautiful," Deanna whispered. She felt his blond downy hair. She opened the blanket and looked at his tiny feet and hands. When she touched his hand, he wrapped his tiny fingers around hers. "Bye, little baby." She kissed his rosy cheek and caught the tears as they rolled down her face.

THE DOCTOR in Ohio had given Eleanor the name of a psychiatrist in Knoxville. Dr. Wright's office was in one of the tall buildings downtown. "Why don't you get out and I'll find a place to park," Eleanor said.

On the first floor was a coffee shop. Customers emerged, walking past her. Deanna studied her refection in the plate-glass window. Her long ginger hair that she had ironed that morning was her best feature, she thought. Eleanor rounded the corner with a hopeful smile. "This won't be so bad honey," she said, squeezing her hand.

"Oh, easy for you to say, you were not raped and you didn't have to give your baby away," Deanna said, pulling away.

The elevator smelled funny, and though they were the only passengers, it stopped at every floor, opening its doors to no one, while they stood rigidly. As it reached the sixth floor, she turned to Eleanor. "You must really hate me, don't you?"

"I don't hate you," Eleanor said, her hands shaking. "I love you."

"Bullshit," she hissed. "My real mother would have never let anything happen to me and she would not make me do this."

She was the first patient of the day. The upholstered waiting room chairs were old and worn. There was no receptionist. The silhouette of a man passed back and forth behind a frosted window. It stopped, then disappeared. The door open and Dr. Wright walked into the waiting room. He was a short fat man, with gray hair combed to one side, trying to cover the bald spot. He looked over his reading glasses at Deanna.

"You must be Deanna?" he asked. "Come on back." Deanna looked at Eleanor who was pretending to read a magazine.

"Don't say that, my mother was a saint," Deanna hated talking to him. And she hated looking at that ridiculous comb-over and she hated that he always smelled like mouthwash. After four weeks, she refused to go any longer.

"He's a quack and I'll run away if you make me go back," she told Eleanor. The next day, Eleanor told him she was terminating his weekly session at the request of Deanna.

That summer Deanna put on her best smile and pretended everything was just fine. She hid her feelings in the dark corners of her mind. And that was where the demon remained. It stayed quiet, waiting for the right moment to show its ugly head.

Fall came and she acted like any other teenager. There were football games, parties, and dances. By the next summer things seemed to be back to normal. She spent most of the summer hanging out with her friends, Gail and Pat, and finding ways to get into trouble. She only thought about the baby late at night. That was when she thought she heard him cry, and then she would realize it was only the wind or a bird.

The past year had changed Deanna and Eleanor's relationship. Sometimes their Saturday night battles resulted in broken dishes and James just standing looking at both of them in disbelief. Deanna thought Eleanor treated her differently, like a stranger. She spoke only once of the rape. She called it that thing he did to her, and never spoke of Deanna's baby.

By her senior year, college catalogs began arriving in the mail. They were filled with pictures of students and professors sitting together on lawns having pleasant conversations and girls brushing their teeth together at a row of dormitory sinks. She and Pat planned for college and Gail planned her wedding.

Graduation day arrived and she sat in a folding chair waiting to hear her name called. She looked at the large banner hanging above the auditorium. "Class of 1977" was written in big blue letters that sparkled when the light hit them. Finally, her name was called and Deanna walked across the stage. She graduated with honors with the rest of her classmates. That afternoon friends and family celebrated her graduation with cake and ice cream. James and Eleanor surprised her with a car. Later that afternoon, after all the guests had gone, Deanna came down stairs dangling the keys in her hand as if it were a charm on a bracelet.

"Where are you going?' James asked.

"I'm meeting Pat and Gail at the drive-in," she said, casually.

"Don't be late."

"Oh dad, I'm not a kid any longer."

"I know, that's what worries me," he said with a frown.

It was a particular exciting summer for Deanna, as she was going away to college that fall. She had grown tired of small-town living and was ready for a much larger world. She longed for her freedom.

She spent most of the summer with her friends. The three of them hung out by the pool and talked about their future. Gail was getting married in December, Pat was going to the University of Tennessee, and Deanna had been accepted into the University of Georgia.

IN AUGUST, Deanna packed her car and drove to Athens Georgia. The first week of college was hectic. She had books to buy, professors to meet, advisors to work out her schedule, classes to attend, and a dorm full of girls to get acquainted with. It was a big adjustment for her, but it was her first taste of freedom, and she was loving it. She had been there two months when she finally came home for Thanksgiving. She had plenty of stories to tell about the boys she had met and the friends she had made.

"Are you sure you're keeping your studies up?" James asked with a slight look of concern.

"Yes, dad."

On Sunday after Thanksgiving, she was packing to go back to school. Eleanor joined her in her room. "Deanna, is everything okay with you?"

"Yes, Eleanor."

"You just seem so distant and distracted," Eleanor said as she brushed her hair away from her face.

"I'm fine," Deanna said in an unusually cool tone. She turned her head away from Eleanor. She was not fine; she was far from being fine. Late at night when she was alone and closed her eyes she felt Warren again, ramming himself into her—felt that pain, never-ending pain.

"I'll see you at Christmas," Deanna said to David as he loaded her car. Once back at school her friends trickled in the dorm one by one and reported on what they had done over the holiday.

DEANNA SKIDDED THROUGH her first year of college, although she continued to make the Dean's list, began to lose control of her emotions. Her demon was no longer locked in the dark corner of her mind. She became sexually active and went on the pill. That was the only thing that quieted her demon.

In September, Deanna entered her sophomore year of college. She had not been home in eight months and did not talk to her old friends anymore. She was running from her past and the secrets it held. She was not the good girl her father thought she was.

"I can't believe another Thanksgiving has rolled around. Where does the time go," said James as he took the turkey out of the freezer to defrost. "We're getting old Eleanor. I feel it in my bones every day."

"Speak for yourself. I have a lot of good years left." Eleanor smiled at James and winked. Her raven hair had only a few streaks of gray and her skin was smooth free of wrinkles. Her eyes were still bright and the same brilliant green.

"Well then I better go sit down. I'll need all the strength I can muster for later." James was in the den relaxing in his recliner when the ringing of the phone awaken him.

"Hello, dad," Deanna said with a giggle, juggling the phone. "Stop it," she whispered to the boy behind her. He was grinning.

"What, Deanna," James said, trying to hear what she was saying.

"Dad, I'm not coming home for Thanksgiving this year. John invited me, to Vermont for a ski trip," she said, slapping his hand away.

"Sweetheart, we're all expecting you, your grandparents are going to be very disappointed. You haven't been home since last Christmas," James said.

"I know, but I promise I'll come home next month. Have to go now. We have to catch the plane. I'll call you when I get there. Love you. Tell everyone happy Thanksgiving for me."

"Love you too, sweetheart and I expect you to come home for Christmas." James hung up the phone, disappointed Deanna would not be home. He sat in the chair a while longer before he told David and Eleanor she would not be home this Thanksgiving

"Eleanor, I'm worried about her. She hasn't been home in almost a year. Do you think we should drive down to Athens to check on her?"

"James, she's a grown woman and has a mind of her own. She'll tell us if she needs anything. Now come on, let's get to bed. We have a lot of cooking to do tomorrow."

"I guess you're right," James said, as she turned out the lights.

DEANNA'S JUNIOR AND SENIOR YEARS, the demon had quieted and she concentrated on her grades. She saw her family more often and the relationship between her and Eleanor seemed to be better. She went to dinner and movies with her friends. She studied hard for her final exams and in the spring walked across the stage to receive her college diploma with high honors. She graduated cum laude with a bachelor of arts.

She heard clapping from the audience and could not help but smile when she saw David holding up a big sign that read CONGRATULATIONS-CLASS OF 1981.

"So what are your plans now?" James asked.

"Well, I have decided to take a year off and then go the law school. But I want to find a job and work awhile first," Deanna said.

"So does that mean you want to move back home," James said, teasing her.

"Yes if that's all right with you and Eleanor." She looked at Eleanor and saw the pleased look on her face.

"Of course it's okay with me," Eleanor said as she squeezed her hand.

"Hey, do I not have a say in this?" David said in protest.

"No," they all said in unison. The next day James and David loaded her clothing in his truck and headed back to East Tennessee.

Chapter 9

JUNE 1981, Deanna took a job as an emergency-room clerk. The hospital was located at the foot of the Smoky Mountains and about twenty miles northeast of White Oak Flats. Most nights the emergency room had a gunshot or knife wound to make the night interesting. This night was no different. Deanna had alerted the E.R physician and nurses an ambulance was on its way with a car crash victim. Five minutes later the ambulance pulled up to the emergency door. The door slid open and two EMT's hurriedly rolled the stretcher through the waiting room. The patient had been intubated; one of the EMT's gave artificial respirations while a paramedic performed chest compressions.

Everyone worked hectically to save the patient. Nurses scurried in and out of the room, telling Deanna to call lab and x-ray. The paramedic continued to perform CPR. His voice was urgent but calm as he gave the report to the E.R. physician. Deanna went to the door of the exam room and watched as the doctor held paddles to the chest of the patient.

"Got a normal sinus rhythm," the paramedic said as he looked at the heart monitor.

"Deanna call ICU and have them get a bed ready and call respiratory therapy to set up a ventilator," the doctor said to her as he removed his latex gloves.

The paramedic and EMT's gathered their equipment and after the patient was taken to ICU the paramedic turned to Goldie, one of the nurses in the room, and asked. "Who's the new girl at the desk?"

"Her name is Deanna." The nurse patted Lucas on the shoulder. "Don't waste your time. There's a young resident chasing her but she won't give him the time of day," said Goldie.

"Is that Deanna Guthrie?"

"Do you know her?"

"I used to a long time ago." Lucas smiled. "I'm going to marry her."

"Good luck Lucas." Goldie laughed.

Deanna stood at the copier making copies of the patients ID cards. When the last sheet of paper rolled out of the machine, she turned around and that was when she noticed how handsome Lucas McKinney was. He straddled the chair with his chin propped on his hand. He was smiling at her and his dark eyes danced with mischief. She gave him a slight smile and returned to her desk.

"Told you, she's a tough egg to crack," Goldie said with a deep raspy voice. She was a tiny woman with coarse red hair. Her white uniform starched and pressed and the white nursing cap set perfectly in place on her head.

IT HAD BEEN ONE MONTH since Deanna first set eyes on Lucas. And tonight she caught herself staring at him, he was sitting at the desk directly behind her, where he always sat, finishing paper work on the patient he just brought to the E.R. He was very handsome with jet-black hair and magical dark eyes that were warm and inviting. She always said no thanks to whatever he suggested; going out for pizza, seeing a movie, riding through the mountains in his pick-up truck.

"No thanks, Lucas really," she said one night after her shift had ended.

"Any reason in particular you keep saying no to me?"

"I'm just not seeing anyone."

That night Deanna couldn't sleep. She listened to her father's snoring it sounded like a chainsaw. *How does Eleanor sleep with that?* She got up, tiptoed downstairs, and drank a glass of milk. She tiptoed back upstairs and back in bed, she told herself how rewarding it was finally to have a predictable live. To know what you want and to know what shape your life has taken. It was almost convincing.

For the next three nights, she kept a watchful eye out for Lucas: answering the phone, making copies, and listening for his voice on the ambulance radio. Each night as she drove home she made it a point to drive out of her way, just to see if his pick-up truck was at the ambulance station....there was no sign of him.

The weekend before the Fourth of July, Deanna sat at the kitchen table with Eleanor. Outside large droplets of rain hit the stone patio and bounced up again. "How many people are you expecting at the party this year?" Deanna asked Eleanor as they folded red, white, and blue napkins.

"Maybe one hundred. James has two pigs to barbeque this year."

"This party gets larger every year."

"I know, but besides Christmas the Fourth of July is our favorite holiday." Eleanor said beaming with enthusiasm. Food, decorations, and blue-grass music, performed by anyone who brought an instrument, had become a Guthrie family tradition.

Lucas parked his pick-up truck in front of the house. He grabbed the bouquet of wild flowers and ran to the large front porch trying to get to cover before the next crack of thunder. Nervously he rang the doorbell. Eleanor was up out of her chair and answered the door.

"Hello Mrs. Guthrie?" Lucas removed the wet baseball cap from his head.

"Yes."

"My name is Lucas McKinney and I'm here to see Deanna."

"Would you come in?"

"Thank you." He wiped his leather cowboy boots on the welcome mat and stepped inside. Eleanor disappeared down the hallway and a few minutes later Deanna appeared.

"Lucas what are you doing here?" Deanna asked eyeing the bouquet.

"I came to ask if you would see a movie with me tomorrow night." He handed her the bouquet of flowers. This time Deanna did not say no.

"All right," she said.

"I'll pick you up at seven." Lucas smiled broadly. His grin was contagious. Deanna couldn't help but return the smile.

"How about I meet you there?" *At least, that way I can make an excuse to leave if things don't go well,* she thought.

"Okay then I'll see you there." Lucas turned and tried to hide the look of triumph on his face; he had achieved success against difficult odds. He walked back to the truck not noticing the downpour of rain. "Yes," he said as he balled his fist in victory. Deanna went back to the kitchen were Eleanor sat still folding napkins. Deanna had the same smile on her face.

For her date with Lucas she chose a white tee shirt and a pair of jeans. She straightened her curly red locks, which took her an hour to create the smooth hair. She took another thirty minutes to apply her make-up.

"Have fun on your big date." David teased.

"It's not a big date. I'm meeting him at the movie."

"Pardon me. My mistake, I guess you always spend two hours getting ready and straightening your hair." David was fifteen and loved tormenting his older sister. "Deanna's got a boyfriend." He sang as she left the house.

Half way there she looked at herself in the rear view mirror. *Am I driving toward a mistake,"* she thought. *I have just got my life in order. Why complicate it now.* She looked at her hair and liked the way it turned out. *Give it a break Deanna it's only a movie.*

Lucas stopped by the E.R. to drop off paperwork before he met Deanna across town. "Wow look at you out of uniform and all dressed up." Goldie said with a suspicious look. "Where're you going?"

"Can't say. But I'm late; I'm late to a very important date." Lucas sang the words.

"You did it didn't you? You cracked the egg." Goldie winked.

Lucas let Deanna choose the movie. It was a James Bond film "For Your Eyes Only". They sat in the rear of the cinema and ate popcorn like two teenagers. After the movie Lucas convinced Deanna to have dinner with him. It was pizza. "My grandfather lived in White Oak Flats. He was the town's doctor."

"Dr. McKinney was your grandfather?"

"My father and I used to drive down to White Oak flats on weekends to visit him."

"Really."

"You don't remember me do you?" Deanna looked puzzled. "I didn't expect you would. I used to come into the store."

"I'm sorry Lucas I don't." She looked at him embarrassed.

"Don't be embarrassed. I was so shy I was afraid to speak to you."

They finished dinner and at the car she let him kiss her. It was not a passionate kiss just a gentle kiss on the lips.

After their second date they took a walk through a park near the hospital. There was a full moon and it was a cloudless sky. A slight breeze blew away the humidity and the only sound were the sounds of their voices. "I have something to confess." Lucas began with a chuckle. "I had the biggest crush on you. I told granddad I was going to marry you someday."

"Really,"

"Yea, you were the prettiest girl I'd ever seen."

"So why didn't I see you when we got older? Did you stop coming to the store or were you still afraid of me." Deanna laughed.

"No I grew out of my shyness." He winked. "When I was eleven my dad moved us from Knoxville to Montana. He decided he wanted to buy a ranch and raise horses. So I didn't get to White Oak Flats very often after we moved and when I did, I never saw you hanging around the store."

"But apparently you did eventually move back?"

"I did. I began med-school at the University of Tennessee three years ago.

"Is that when you became a paramedic?"

"No I got my license while I was in college in Montana."

"So why did you want to be a paramedic?"

"Dad was a firefighter. I guess it's just in my blood. What about you, what did you do while I was out in Montana taking care of horses and riding ambulances?"

"Oh, nothing as exciting as working on a ranch." Her mind wandered back to the year she was sixteen, but she pushed the thought back to its place in the corner of her mind. "I graduated from the University of Georgia this spring and I'm taking a year off and hoping to be accepted to law school."

He drove her back to White Oaks Flats and when he walked her to the front door, this time when he kissed her good night it was a long passionate kiss. It was gentle; not the kind of kisses Deanna had in the past. It was not full of urgency and desire. It was caring and patient. Nothing about Lucas McKinney was selfish or forceful.

"Lucas, would you come to our Fourth of July party on Friday? It'll be fun and lots of food. And dad always has fireworks after dark."

"What time do you want me there?"

"Four o'clock."

THE TIME THEY SPENT TOGETHER was like a fairy tale. Lucas was the kindest man she had ever met. He made her laugh and they always had a good time together. He was tender and loving. After work he would pick her up and they would go for long rides through the mountains. They spent hours sitting on the tailgate of his truck and talking about the things that mattered to them. They talked about what they wanted to do and places they wanted to see. They spent nights holding hands and kissing.

She had been seeing Lucas six months and up to now had avoided being intimate with him. Her demon was quiet and she did not want to wake it. Deanna flopped down on the bed and cried until her ribs ached. I could have a normal sex life with someone who actually cared about me, she told herself over and over.

"Hey, can I come over for a while?" Deanna asked when he answered the phone.

"Sure, we can watch a movie," Lucas said.

"I'll bring the wine. What goes well with popcorn — white or red?"

"White," he said, laughing.

They sat on his living-room couch drinking wine. He touched her cheek, then began to kiss her. He kept kissing her to the point they could not stop. He asked her if they needed to use protection, and she blushed when she told him she was on birth control. He took her hand and led her to the bedroom. She kept kissing him while she took her clothes off. Nervous, he sat on the bed, and she sat beside him.

"What's wrong?" she asked, touching his face.

"I've never done this before."

"Really! You are one of the most handsome men I know, you could have your choice of any woman."

"I never found anyone I was willing to give that part of me to, until now."

"Are you sure we don't need to stop while we can?"

"Are you crazy? You're the woman of my dreams, the one I've been waiting for."

His mouth kissed her mouth, his tongue touched hers. He guided her down on the bed and began kissing her shoulder, her breasts – not kissing really, but brushing his lips against her skin. He entered her gently, tentatively, waiting. Tears fell from the corners of her eyes, but she was smiling, too. *I deserve this,* she reminded herself. *I'm a good girl. I deserve him.* She'd worked long and hard to feel what he was helping her feel.

His movement quickened, and she caught his rhythm, matched it, over and over. Then he tensed and moaned. Her mind spun, her muscles tightened themselves around him. But their lovemaking brought out all kinds of things that lie buried. She began to see Warren's face instead of his. *You liked it didn't you?,* she heard.

After Lucas fell asleep, she got up and paced in the dark, trying to convince herself as she navigated around furniture that she had turned a corner on her old life. When she got back into bed, she felt the hair on his chest, his breath against her fingertips.

She lay in bed, aching, weeping silently. The voice inside her head grew louder, tormenting her. It kept reminding her of her unworthiness, telling her a good man could not love her. It grew louder and at times drowned out

Lucas's soft snoring. She put her clothes on, kissed his cheek, left him a note, and quietly shut the door.

That night Deanna lay in bed missing her mother again. She was three years old and at her mother's funeral; then sixteen and waiting for her coming of age party, and then she was destroyed by that horrible monster. She cried herself to sleep.

On her day off, she met Lucas at his apartment and when he wanted to make love to her, she asked, "Could you just hold me?"

"Sure, come here." He patted the seat beside him for her to join him on the couch. He put his arm around her and kissed the top of her head. They snuggled that evening, listening to the rain and the storm move over the mountains.

They saw each other almost every day after that and she had managed to push the demon back to the dark corner of her mind. They did make love again; he was gentle and loving. He wrote her love poems and sang her silly songs.

OUTSIDE IT WAS SNOWING, it was coming down in fat chunky flakes. The roads were covered and nearly impassable. Deanna was making a fresh pot of coffee when she saw Lucas coming through the door with boxes of pizza for the E.R. staff. It was going to be a long night. The next shift could not make it in to work; so they all had to stay over and work a double shift.

"Goldie I'm taking my dinner break now," Deanna said as she grabbed two pieces of pepperoni pizza. She looked at Lucas and smiled. "Glad you stopped. I am starving."

"I had to come by to see my girl before I left." Lucas said smiling at her. They walked to the cafeteria. It was empty except for the two them. They talked about the trip he was taking. He was flying to Montana during the Christmas break. His flight was at 6 a.m. the next morning.

"Have you checked with the airlines?"

"Yes, the snow is supposed to stop by mid-night and as of now the flight has not been canceled."

Deanna looked at her watch. "I have to get back to work."

"You still have fifteen minutes and I'm off duty." He took her hand. "Follow me."

She followed him to the front entrance of the hospital. The parking lot was empty of cars and covered in a white layer of fluffy snow that was still coming down as big as goose feathers. The night was moonless and silent. The large lights scattered throughout the parking lot illuminated the snow. Suddenly Etta James was singing "At Last." Deanna looked at Lucas then to the boom box tucked behind the snow covered bushes. He took her hand and they began to dance in the snow under the lights. In his arms and for the first time, she knew what love felt like.

When the song ended there was clapping. Deanna turned her head to see the portico was filled with employees including Goldie who was making whistling catcalls. Deanna raised her hands to her face and leaned into Lucas's chest to hide her blushing cheeks. Lucas squeezed her tighter and laughed. "I can't believe you did this," said Deanna when finally she looked at him.

Unexpectedly a wet sticky snowball whirled toward them hitting Deanna in the back. She turned to see another baseball size clump of snow whizzing at her, she narrowly avoided the direct hit. She picked up a hand full of snow, squeezed it into a ball, and threw it at the two EMT's who were taking another aim at Deanna. In an instance the parking lot was turned into an arena of flying snowballs.

"Okay back to work!" The night shift supervisor shouted from the doorway. "Play time's over we have patients to take care of in case you clowns have forgotten."

Lucas gave Deanna a quick kiss on the cheek. "I'll call you from Montana!" He yelled as he ran to catch up with the EMT's. "I'll miss you. See you in a couple of weeks."

Deanna walked back to the E.R. still thinking of the sweet surprise Lucas had mangaged to pull off. "That boy has it bad for you." Goldie was standing behind her sipping coffee from a white Styrofoam cup. Deanna looked up from the copier and smiled. "Come on take a smoke break with me." They walked outside the emergency room and into the cold. "I should really quit these things." Goldie lit the cigarette. "You'd think I should know better than anyone what they can do to you. But hey, you got to die from something—am I right?"

Chapter 10

IN THE SPRING OF 1982, Lucas received his acceptance letter from the University of Chicago Medical Center– he would be doing his residency there. "I got in." Lucas said to Deanna loudly enough so that the E.R. staff took notice. "We have to do something special to celebrate. And I don't mean sitting on the tailgate of my truck drinking beer and listening to country music."

"Okay you plan it." Deanna looked up from her desk. "I have some news of my own." She held up a letter; the envelope read University of Georgia. "I got in too. I start law school in September."

That Saturday night Lucas and Deanna drove to Knoxville. He had made reservations at Regas. "Lucas this is to expense." Deanna looked at him.

"I said we were going to celebrate."

"Yes but Red Lobster would have been just fine. This is a week's pay to eat here."

"So how often do you get accepted to law school and I get to do my residency in Chicago."

The waiter dressed in black pants, white shirt and tie, and a black vest brought the wine list. Lucas ordered their best wine. "How come you know so much about wine?" Deanna asked.

"It's a hobby. I've always been fascinated by wine making. If I don't make it as a doctor I can always grow my own grapes and sell wine. By the way how do you feel about stomping grapes with your bare feet?" Lucas chuckled.

IT WAS THE FOURTH OF JULY and the Tennessee valley was mired in the 'dog days of summer'. The air was hot and steamy. Without a moment's warning the memories came back so powerfully and unexpectedly it was like she had been hit hard in the stomach. She ran to the bathroom and threw up—the bitter taste in her mouth was as sour as the whiskey on Warren's breath. *You're trapped by your lies. That whole dirty mess of secrets.* She thought as she looked in the mirror. *You haven't been honest with him—not once.*

Later that day Deanna sat on the boat dock with her feet dangling in the cool water. The Tellico Dam Project was completed and the Little Tennessee River was now a lake that backed up to the edge of their back yard. The Great Smoky Mountains seemed to rise out of the water and touch the clouds. Looking from a distance at the tall peaks of the Mountains made Deanna wonder about God. *Was God to far away to hear her?* He felt as distant as the tallest mountain.

"There you are." James said as he stood beside her. "What's bothering you sweetheart."

"Just thinking about Lucas."

"He's in love with you Deanna. I recognize that look. It's the same look I had when I asked Eleanor to marry me."

"Oh dad he's not going to ask me to marry him." *He wouldn't. I won't let him.*

"Come on back to the house Eleanor needs help with the decorations."

That night at the party Lucas stood bchind Deanna. His arms wrapped around her as they watched fireworks burst in red, white, and blue. The lake was as smooth as glass and it shimmered with color as the fireworks erupted.

After the guest left Lucas stayed behind and helped with the cleanup. He had become a big part of her family. He joined them for Thanksgiving dinner, Christmas morning at her house and came to Sunday dinner if he was not working. He watched NASCAR races with David and James on lazy Sunday afternoons even on the Sundays when Deanna worked at the hospital.

Lucas extinguished the fire in the barbeque pits while Deanna and Eleanor gathered the large trash bags of paper plates and cups. It was after mid-night when the clean up was finished.

"Lucas it's so late, instead of driving to Knoxville tonight why don't you stay here. I'll get the guest room set up for you." Eleanor suggested as she put the leftover food in refrigerator.

"And Deanna can sleep in our room," teased James.

"Dad!"

"Come on Lucas I'll show you the guest room." Eleanor rolled her eyes as James.

"And I'll be sitting in the hallway cleaning my old shot gun." James winked at Lucas.

"Dad you're embarrassing me."

"And I'm tying a cowbell around your neck young lady." James said and switched off the kitchen light as he left the room.

"He's kidding Lucas," said Deanna as she walked up the stairs looking back at her father.

"No I'm not."

"Dad don't scare him." She gave James a look. He laughed aloud he always found it amusing to embarrass his daughter.

She tried to convince herself she did deserve him and she did deserve to let him love her as much as she loved him. But late at night she kept hearing Warren, seeing his twisted smile as he told her she was just like him, they were both terrible people.

That summer Deanna began to build a wall and slowly began to distance herself from the feelings she had for Lucas. Shame of her past was stronger than the love she had for him. She began to make excuses as to why she could not see him…she had to work late– had to help at the store–had to get ready for her move to Georgia.

"What's going on Deanna?" Eleanor asked one night as Deanna sat on the front porch steps tracing the outline of her tiny handprints in the concrete.

"They say time is a healer, but I've not done much healing." Deanna looked up and out into the darkness. "I've tried to bury what he did to me but it won't stay buried." She wiped the tears that began to fall down her cheeks. She was silent for a long moment then turned and looked Eleanor in the eyes. "Late at night I think I hear my baby cry and the guilt and shame starts all over again."

Eleanor's eyes filled with tears. She knew all too well the pain Deanna felt. "Deanna." She touched Deanna's cheek. "Love Lucas and let him love you."

THE LAST WEEK IN JULY Lucas flew to Chicago. He rented an apartment near the hospital. It was small, a furnished one bedroom with one bath but would do until he finished his residency. He spent the rest of the week venturing a little farther each day from the apartment. He found a drug store, a market, and a video rental store, not that he would have time to watch movies.

He had one week left before his rotation started and he was missing Deanna terribly. That night he called the airlines and booked a flight back to Knoxville for the next day. He went to sleep thinking about her. During the night he had made a decision—it was the most important decision of his life. The next morning he packed and then walked down the street to the jewelry store where he had been eyeing a diamond ring. The ring cost more than four months' rent. But it was beautiful and she was worth it. He could take extra shifts at the hospital and eat mac and cheese for the next year.

THE FLIGHT TO KNOXVILLE arrived on time. As he waited for his duffle bag to slide down the belt he took the small box out of his pocket and smiled as he looked at the diamond ring.

Lucas smiled when he saw Deanna standing just on the other side of baggage claim. "How was your flight?" Asked Deanna.

"It was fine." He reached for her and pulled her to him then held her for a moment.

"Are you hungry?" she asked as she pulled away.

"No I ate on the plane. If you can call it that."

"So where do you want me to drop you?"

"At my old place. Rents paid up until the end of August and I still have some things to put in storage."

Their footsteps clattered through the nearly empty apartment. Deanna looked at the few remaining pieces of furniture: an overstuffed chair, the bed, and a dresser. Lucas put his duffle bag in the chair, walked into the bedroom and flopped down on the bed. He flopped backward and patted the bed for her to join him.

Deanna smiled and lay beside him. "What's your new apartment like."

"Very small but I won't be in it enough to notice."

"I'm driving down to Georgia next week to begin the search for mine."

He wrapped his arms around her and kissed her forehead. They talked an hour before Lucas stood up. He reached for her hand and helped her off the bed.

"Deanna, I love you," Lucas said and got down on one knee. Deanna watched as he brought a small box from behind his back and opened it. "Will you marry me, Deanna?" She just stood there looking at the diamond ring. Tears began to stream down her face. The silence lasted so long that he began to wonder if he had said it out loud or just thought he had. "Are those tears of joy, or are you sad?" Lucas asked, teasing her.

"Lucas," she began slowly almost a whisper. "I'm a horrible person and if you knew the true me you would think so too," she said, as she looked down at him. "Lucas please get up." She felt ashamed he had kneeled before her–she was not worthy of his respect.

"Deanna, what are you talking about? You're a good person," Lucas said, noticing the panic in her eyes. He raised himself off the floor. "We won't be married right away. You're leaving for law school in the fall and I have two years of residency to finish. We can wait a while."

"Lucas I can't. You'll hate me if I stay. I'm broken and you can't fix me and I don't know how to be anything else." She turned her back to him. "You'll only grow to hate me as much as I hate myself. You don't want this. Don't love me Lucas." She walked out the door without looking at him.

"Deanna I'm begging you not to leave." Things happened so quickly he was unable to think clearly. She had confused him completely. He heard the sound of a car engine and began to run after her. "Deanna wait, don't go."

She drove away crying, her eyes were on the mirror looking back until she could no longer see him. Tears streamed down her face and she started to stop and turn around but she knew she had to let him go, he deserved better. He would make someone a fine husband. He was kind, loving, and honest, all the things that a woman looks for in a man.

Lucas ran until he saw the tail lights disappear into the dark. Tears ran down his cheeks and he felt their sting on his face. He fell on his knees and wept like a baby. Finally, he raised himself up and put the ring back in his pocket. He walked back inside the empty apartment and looked at the bald walls and empty closets. He could never love that deeply again. She was the first person who broke his heart and for the rest of his life she would always be the one who hurt him the most.

At home, Deanna sat with her eyes closed and tears rolling down her cheeks. Leaving him brought back feelings of loss she had tried half her life to forget. It reminded her of the pain she felt when she lost her mother.

"What's wrong, Deanna? Has something happened?" Eleanor asked, panicked. She sat on the bed, handing her a handkerchief.

"Lucas asked me to marry him."

"That's great, Deanna, so why are you crying?"

"Because I said no."

"Why, Deanna?"

"I'm too broken, too flawed. I am a horrible person."

"Deanna, look at me. You are not a horrible person!"

"Stop it, Eleanor. You know what I am. You forced me to keep our dirty little secrets. What would Lucas think of me when he found out about them? I couldn't bear to see the look in his eyes when he discovers he can't stand me any longer."

"Deanna, what Warren did to you was about violence, it was about degrading you. You need to let Lucas love you."

"I will not let him love me!" she wept. "Warren took everything that was good and decent and left the dark side of me. I won't let him love that."

"Deanna, please see another counselor about this," Eleanor pleaded.

Deanna lay on the bed that night to sleep, and to make time pass more quickly. In the stillness, every breath was one more step deeper into the terrible heartache. She pressed the pillow against her head, but even then she could hear the shouts of worthlessness. *If anyone ever found out what you are, what you have done. . .*

Chapter 11

AUGUST 1982, Deanna moved back to Athens to begin law school at the University of Georgia. She found an apartment near campus. And all she had to do now was get through the next three years of law school. The prospect seemed grim and her life felt empty without Lucas. She picked up her phone a hundred times to dial him but each time, she could not find the courage. And Lucas didn't call her or reach out to her. All she wanted to do was hold him until he knew she was sorry for breaking his heart.

At night, her pillow was wet with tears and she woke every morning feeling as though someone had died. There finally came a time that she didn't listen for the phone to ring any longer. The skies of her future darkened; the colors had faded to shades of gray.

She did not make an effort to make friends. She never went on dates and when people asked her why, she said she was too busy. She sat home night after night. Time hung heavily when she was alone and she began to drink too much.

It was three o'clock in the afternoon and Deanna lay asleep on the couch. A knock at the door suddenly awakened her. She stumbled to the door and looked out the peephole. A short stalky woman in a dark suit stood looking at her watch. Deanna removed the chain and opened the door.

"Hi, my name is Linda. Do you mind if I take a minute of your time?"

"Yes, I do mind," she said as she pulled her robe together.

"One of my jobs at the college is to check on our law students from time to time. May I come in?"

The badge pinned to her jacket read Linda Burns, Student Affairs. "Sure." Deanna stepped aside and let her in the apartment. The woman looked at the empty wine bottle sitting on the coffee table.

"How are things going?" she said as she let the leather satchel slide off her shoulder and sat on the couch. "Any reason you have not been coming to any of the student meetings? We have had three already and you haven't been to any of them."

"No not really. With the move and my rigid schedule I'm just feeling a little under the weather."

"So how are you and. . ." she stopped and checked her records; ". . .Professor Brown getting along?"

"Fine."

"He said you skipped class this week."

"Yes, well I told you I've been under the weather."

Linda took a bright red leather calendar out of her satchel and opened it to the next day. "I would like to see you tomorrow at nine," she said as she penciled in Deanna's name. She gave Deanna a card with her name and phone number. "See you in the morning, Ms. Guthrie."

"Pushy bitch," Deanna said after she had left, picking up the bottle of wine and turning it on its end to get the last sip. She opened another bottle and stumbled to the bathroom. She took a sleeping pill and laid on the bed, holding the card and the bottle of pills in her hand. She thought about her mother and father, how they danced together, how happy they were, and how happy she once was. Now there was no life left in her hollow heart. *I could just go ahead and do it, stop the nightmares, stop the pain. End it. I could smash the wine glass and cut my wrist. Or I could hang myself with the curtain cord, or take the rest of the pills, that wouldn't hurt,* she thought. She didn't want to die, but she didn't want to live, either. She had approached some kind of end. But she hadn't reached it.

The wine glass fell from her hand, smashing in pieces on the floor. She was fading, floating. . . She saw herself lying on the bed. Then she saw her mother, dressed in a light blue flowing gown with a ring of wild flowers in her hair. She took Deanna's hand and cradled her in her arms.

THE LIGHT GREW BRIGHTER. "Ms. Guthrie." She heard someone saying her name. She tried to open her eyes but they were so heavy. She felt her eyelid forced open, and a bright light flashed in her eye; then the other eye was opened and the light went to it. She felt a quick jab of pain when the needle broke through her skin, and then cool liquid ran through her vein. The air blowing across her face smelled like plastic. She heard sirens, but she couldn't open her eyes, she was so sleepy.

"Ms. Guthrie, can you hear me?"

This time she could open her eyes enough to see a man standing over her; she reached for the thing on her face and tried to pull it away. He touched her hand and smiled. "There you are," he said. "That's an oxygen mask; you need to leave it on."

"Where am I?" she asked, looking around the room.

"You're in the emergency room."

"Why am I here?"

"The paramedics brought you in, you were unconscious. Do you remember what happened?"

"No." She did not know how long she had lain there unconscious; she closed her eyes and fell asleep again.

She spent the next two weeks in the hospital. She had no recollection of what had happened that night, nor did she remember Linda Burns finding her unconscious the next day. The first two days in the hospital had gaps; she could remember only fragments of their campaign to get her to talk.

"Deanna, do you know why you felt the urge to harm yourself?" Dr. Carter asked. He was a slender man with a short gray beard. His hair was gray and wavy and long in the back. He had very big dark eyes. His appearance and movements were soft, his deep-eyed gaze was direct, and when he spoke, he had a faint accent. Irish, Deanna thought.

"I wanted to die, but this was an accident, I didn't purposely overdose," she answered as she looked out the window.

"So tell me why you wanted to die."

"I don't know," she snapped. "When can I get out of here?"

"This is only the beginning of our real work, Deanna."

By the fifth day, she was ready for his questions. She glared at him defiantly and crossed her arms over her chest. He sat in his usual chair in the corner of the room. He opened her chart, took out his pen, and began to write before he spoke to her.

"Ready to get started today, Deanna?" he finally said looking up at her.

"You're the boss."

He sighed and smiled at her. "What is all this belligerence for? Protection? Okay, let me ask another question. Tell me about your mother and father." He had a way of turning all his statements into fill-in-the-blank questions. "Let's talk about your mother."

"I told you before, this has nothing to do with my mother!"

"You're not angry she left you and that your dad married Eleanor?"

"She's dead, okay; just leave her alone, she was a saint." Deanna did not want him going anywhere near her mother. In her world she was the only thing calm and right.

"A saint?"

"Yes, a saint!"

Tuesday morning was group sessions, Wednesday and Thursday, one-on-one. Early and middle childhood was her easiest phase. Over the next couple of weeks, they talked about her mother. Then they talked about Eleanor.

"Oh my God. I'm getting the two of them confused. I can't separate them. It's as if they are the same person," Deanna sobbed.

"Regardless you told yourself, Eleanor was not your mother, even though you thought of her that way. You had put Abigale so high on a pedestal, Eleanor could never reach it. And when she couldn't, you blamed her. Your mother was not a saint, no one is. She was just a mortal who loved you very much."

Deanna began to sob uncontrollably. Her sobbing and trembling was finally overtaken by profound exhaustion. She felt more tired than she ever had in her life.

"You have made some remarkable strides," Dr. Carter told her at the end of their session.

For the next week, he listened as Deanna wove the network of connection between herself, her mother, and Eleanor. Eventually, she reached the other side and understood her feelings for Eleanor. She came to realize Eleanor had done what she did out of fear and not knowing what to do. They tackled her father next and her feelings for him.

"This is ridiculous! I love my father and he loves me."

"Do you feel guilty because you didn't tell him about the rape and the baby?"

"Of course I did, I mean I do."

"But that's not all, is it Deanna? You wanted him to hold you and tell you the rape was not your fault."

"Yes, I wanted him to still think I was a good girl. I wanted him to tell me I was still his princess."

"But you haven't felt like his princess for a long time, have you Deanna?" Dr. Carter steepled his fingers beneath his chin.

"No."

A MONTH PASSED and she was released from the hospital and eventually went back to school. Linda Burns became her support system, seeing to it that Deanna made her appointments with Dr. Carter and worked with her professors, getting her caught up with the rest of her classmates.

"How do you feel about Eleanor?" Dr. Carter asked. "That's a good place to start."

"Do I have a choice?" Deanna said, smiling at him.

"Don't you always have a choice?" he said, looking through her chart. "You have come to realize you loved your mother – and still do – but she was not the saint you imagined her to be. You have come to the same conclusion about Eleanor – she's not perfect, but she tries to do the best for you. And you have told me you feel like your father will never look at you as a good girl again. Now let's talk about Warren."

"Let's not."

Dr. Carter leaned back in his chair and closed his eyes. "You have come a long way but we still have some critical issues to deal with." He opened his eyes and gazed directly into hers. "Deanna," he said, "you are a healthy young woman, and I imagine that at some point you want to have a healthy sexual relationship. You told me you were sexually active in college with boys you didn't have an emotional attachment to, but when you meet Lucas, with whom you were attracted, and discovered he cared about you, how you felt ashamed. You have to work through that before you can have a normal sex life."

Deanna had been seeing Dr. Carter for a year, once a week. He said she was making a tremendous breakthrough and she did feel as though she were coming to terms with her past. She had obtained a part-time job at a law firm. She clerked for one of the attorneys and spent much of her time at the courthouse. When she could, she would sneak into the courtroom and listen to cases.

"They call him the hanging judge." Deanna heard someone whisper in her ear. She turned to see an angel-faced blue-eyed blonde sitting beside her. "Hi, I'm Sarah. I work in circuit court."

"Nice to meet you Sarah, I'm Deanna. I work for the Stephens Law Firm up the street."

"Haven't I seen you on campus?" Sarah asked.

"Yes. I'm a law student."

"So am I, we should go out sometime."

"I don't get out much, just to class and back and work".

"Well, we need to change that."

SARAH FONTAINE grew up in Savannah Georgia and had been raised by an aunt. Her aunt had recently died, leaving her a beach house there. It was Tuesday before Thanksgiving and school was out for the holiday. She was packing a few things to take home, as she had decided to spend the holiday there and maybe call some friends over for dinner.

"Deanna, this is Sarah. Do you have plans for the holiday?

"No, I'm going to spend my time lounging."

"Well, why don't you come with me to Savannah? You can lounge and look at the ocean at the same time."

"I don't know. You sure I would not intrude on your family?'

"Considering I don't have family to intrude on, no."

Deanna went to Savannah with Sarah for the Thanksgiving holiday. After that she began to spend much of her free time there. She began to think of it as home. She took walks on the beach, and joined friends for dinner at local bars. She loved everything about it and even got used to the hot, humid summers. After graduating from law school, she planned to move there.

THE NEXT TWO YEARS, Deanna was up to her eyeballs in school and work. She went home for Christmas because her father complained he never saw her anymore. And she still was seeing Dr. Carter once a week.

"You said you dreamed about Warren this week, tell me about the dream," Dr. Carter said as he leaned back in his chair.

"It was the same as always, I 'm running trying to get away from him, he catches me but his face is blacked out, he's not talking but I can hear him in my mind. He's telling me I'm a terrible person, that I'm just like him."

"Do you still think you are a terrible person, Deanna?"

"Yes, sometimes."

"Why did you keep your hospital stay from your father and Eleanor?"

"Because daddy would be ashamed of me and Eleanor would feel she had to keep it a secret to protect everyone's feelings."

"Deanna, are you still ashamed of yourself? Look in this mirror, Deanna, who do you see?"

"A big fake. Everything thing about me is fake" Deanna was angry when she left his office. The next week she called to cancel her appointment. But the following week Dr. Carter's nurse called her and rescheduled another one.

"You missed your last appointment Deanna, you were angry with me because I made you look in the mirror," Dr. Carter said, walking to the white insulated coffee pot. "Would you care for a cup coffee?"

"No thank you."

"So why do you think you're a fake?"

"Warren took away every decent thing about me. He took my virginity, my innocence, my trust, and my happiness." Her face was red with anger. "He took my life away from me and everything from that day has been just one big illusion."

Dr. Carter did not respond, but sat very still for a moment before handing her a box of Kleenex. "Deanna, is that why you do not let yourself get romantically involved with anyone? Do you feel you don't deserve them? Do you not deserve to be happy?"

"He told me I was a terrible person, that we were the same, him and me. He said that I liked it when he did that to me."

"When he did what to you?"

"When he raped me," she screamed. "When he raped me!"

"That's right, he raped you. You were the victim, just a young girl. You didn't choose to give your virginity, he took it from you. It had nothing to do with whether you liked it. Warren was a parasite; he could only survive on others people's happiness. He sucked it from the souls of his victims. And each time he did, it made him stronger and made his victims weaker. Are you weak, Deanna?" Dr. Carter moved to the couch and sat beside her. He put his arm around her and hugged her. She cried against his shoulder, sobbing and shaking.

"I'm empty," she said.

The next four months they dove deeper into her feelings about her relationships with other people and her sexual desires. But as hard as she tried, she could not distance herself from the feeling of being a terrible person. However, her job at the law firm and the friendship she shared with Sarah filled some of the emptiness. But she still felt a hole that was created the day her baby was taken from her arms. There were not enough therapy sessions in the world to fill that void.

The following week, Deanna went to her next session with Dr. Carter. She sat on the couch and he sat in the chair across from her. "Why do you still choose to listen to the voice, Deanna?"

"Why do you always begin our sessions with a question, Dr. Carter?

"There's that sarcasm again," he said. "What are you protecting. . . what are you not wanting to talk about? You are a healthy woman with desires, and just because you enjoy sex does not mean you are like Warren. It makes you normal."

"Dr. Carter, I just graduated law school and I think it's time I move on, I'm tired of reliving my past, I'm ready to start my future." She repositioned on the couch. "I'm moving to Savannah next week and starting a new job at a small law office there."

"How's your drinking habit? Is it still under control?"

"Yes, it is, I hardly drink at all and when I do it's because I want to, not because I need to."

"And your sleeping pills?"

"I don't take them often."

"Remember, you don't do sex, drugs or alcohol to be happy. You make your own happiness; you build happiness out of insight and good habits."

"I know."

"If you ever feel you are spinning out of control or that you are slipping back into old habits, call me."

Chapter 12

JUNE 1985, Sarah and Deanna arrived at eight o'clock in the morning to begin their new jobs. The law office was a small house on Lincoln with a brick sidewalk and two steps leading to the front door. It sat off the street, shaded by live oak trees. The old structure had a fresh coat of white paint and the shutters were a glossy black. Red geraniums sat on each side of the door in tall black planters.

The bell hanging on the inside of the door jingled when they pushed it open. A slender woman sat typing at a desk in the middle of the room. Her face was made up with too much rouge and blue eyeshadow and her dyed hair was the color of copper. The pungent smell of coffee and cigar smoke was in the room.

"Hello my name is Deanna and this is Sarah and we're here . . ."

"I know who you are." The woman interrupted Deanna without taking her eyes off the yellow legal pad lying on her desk. She tilted her head back to the office behind her. "And my name is Adeline Cook, but you can call me Mrs. Cook. You will do your own typing, filing, and recording. And I only make coffee for Mr. Hamilton." Her thin fingers struck the keys of the manual typewriter as she spoke.

"Thank you," Deanna said and continued to the small office.

Gerald Hamilton peered over his half-moon glasses and motioned for them to sit in the chairs in front of his cluttered desk. A large fan hanging over his desk pulled streams of cigar smoke up to the ceiling. The small room was shabby and outdated. Stacks of files lay against the wood paneling of one wall and a picture of a bulldog named UGA hung above them. Behind his desk hung his framed diploma from the University of Georgia.

"I see you met Mrs. Cook. Don't worry, her bark is worse than her bite," he said, slapping at a piece of paper as the breeze from the fan whisked it off his desk. He was talking with them and to another person on the telephone, as he often carried on two conversations at once.

His speech was soft, and included a Southern drawl. He had gentle blue-grey eyes and snow-white hair that he wore down to his shoulders. With a mustache and goatee; he bore the resemblance to a Confederate general. Gerald Hamilton was descended from the earliest English settlers and still lived in the family home, with his sister, Blanche Hamilton. Gerald's father began the practice in 1919. When Gerald graduated from law school in 1944, he returned to Savannah to practice with his father.

After he hung up, he looked at Deanna. "Savannah is a peculiar place, Ms. Guthrie. If you are an outsider, you are not easily accepted," he said as he tapped his cigar ash into a large oyster shell. "Rule number one: Savannah takes its parties very seriously. Men here don't rent their tuxedoes, they own them. Do not turn down an invitation. Rule number two: Observe Saint Patrick's Day. Everyone but restaurants and bars close for the day and the drinking starts early in the morning. Rule number three: Always stay in town. Do not shop anywhere else. Rule number four: Get to know all the women at Christ Episcopal Church and become their best friend. Because when a Southern Christian woman turns on you, you better not hope for forgiveness and they won't allow anyone else to forgive you either, especially not their men folks. By the way, services begin at ten o'clock. I am there every Sunday, I will expect you to arrive at nine-forty five, no later. And rule number five: football is a religion not a sport, so don't plan on anyone being in town on game day. Everyone will be making their pilgrimage to Athens to see the Bulldogs play." He stood up and Deanna noticed he wore a light blue seersucker suit and blue bow tie. "Now if you will excuse me, I have a breakfast meeting." He placed his vented straw hat on his head, took his cane, and before walking out the door stopped in front of the picture of the bulldog named UGA and straightened the frame. The two women looked at each other and broke out into laughter.

By the end of July, Deanna had settled into a daily routine. The files were in proper order and she and Sarah did their own filing at the courthouse. Even with the mess, it was still fun to work there.

Deanna loved Savannah. She loved the charm of the city, and the smells of the food and of the salt water as it blew through the streets. Although Sarah had invited her to stay at the beach house, she had rented a place in the heart of the city. It was an old house, converted into apartments. From her second-floor balcony, she could see ships coming in and out of the bay. And from the other side of the apartment the view from the large windows was even more magical. She could see the cobblestone courtyard that was hidden from the view of the street. Thick vegetation grew upward, covering the thick brick walls. And the view gave way to streets lined with live oak trees dripping with Spanish moss. She could see old houses with tall shuttered windows and cornices and beyond the rooftops were church steeples that seemed to reach up and touch the clouds as they drifted by.

From the open window, she could hear water trickle from the fountain that sat in the middle of the courtyard. At night, she could hear street musicians compete with music blaring from the bars and restaurants on River Street. She thought about Lucas only occasionally now, just late at night or if she was reminded of something he had said or done.

She went for a jog every morning and stopped at the same café for coffee and a newspaper. She took long walks through the squares every evening and always walked down Bull Street that took her past the Savannah College of Art and Design known as SCAD. The downtown residents did not respond well to the college. They sometimes lost patience with students and their odd clothes, skateboards, and loud music they played well into the night. But as far as she was concerned, this was the only place to live in Savannah.

DEANNA STEPPED into the courtyard. It had just rained and the air was hot and steamy. It felt like an enclosed tropical terrarium. Once she walked through the old iron gate and out into streets, the breeze offered some relief. She lived six blocks from the office and found it was faster to walk than to drive around all the squares. She walked along the tree-lined streets. Spanish moss swaying in the breeze resembled greenish grey ghosts as it hung from the trees. She stopped at a bakery and picked up a box of fresh pastries for Mrs. Cook. They had come to an understanding; she brought the pastries and Mrs. Cook made the coffee.

The box of sweet smelling pastries was sitting on her desk when Sarah walked through the door. She took one whiff, ran to the bathroom, and threw up. "What's up with you – did you party last night?" Deanna said, teasing her. Sarah only looked at her and made another mad dash to the bathroom. It was ten minutes later when she came out, holding a washcloth to her head.

"I think you're a bit more than hung over, aren't you," Deanna said as she got up and walked to the couch were Sarah sat. Sarah looked at her with sunken eyes.

"Yes, I'm afraid the hangover is going to last another seven months," she said trying to produce a smile. "What am I going to do, Deanna?"

"What we have always done. Survive," Deanna said. "Now for the good juicy stuff. Who is the proud poppa?"

"He's not a proud poppa. In fact, he told me to get an abortion. He has already given me the money for it." Sarah looked at her through sad eyes.

"What are you going to do?"

"I only know I am not going to have an abortion."

"So did you give the money back?"

"Hell, no! I kept it and told him I need more because I was not going to get an abortion in any hole-in-the-wall clinic."

"So how much did he give you?"

"Fifty thousand. His family threw in some hush money," Sarah smiled. "I put the money in a savings account. It'll be a good start for a college fund, don't you think?"

"Hell, yes." And they both laughed.

"So are you going to tell me who the scumbag is?"

"Deanna, you must promise you will never tell anyone. As far as he is concerned I had the abortion and I don't want him to ever know about my baby."

"Okay, okay, get on with it; who is he?"

"His name is Charles Patterson the 3rd," she said with a wink.

"Oh my God! Charles Patterson, of one of the richest and oldest families in Savannah?"

"Yes, that would be him," Sarah said.

"Sarah you little Scarlett!" They laughed and Sarah placed her head on Deanna's shoulder.

"I guess I didn't come from the proper back ground. Heaven forbid someone of my family standing would be permitted into the yacht club."

DEANNA'S FIRST WINTER in Savannah the weather had been unusually mild and the summer heat was unbearable. Even for the locals, it was one of those hot miserable summers. The air conditioner, a small window unit, was rumbling and producing much less than it should, doing very little to cool the old office. The back of Deanna's shirt was wet with perspiration.

She closed her eyes and held a glass to her neck for a long moment. Condensation dripped from the cold glass and provided temporary relief from the sweltering heat. The front door opened and the jingle of the bell startled her. She jerked her head to one side, causing the iced tea to splash out of the glass and onto the front of her white blouse.

"Crap!" she said wiping the blouse with the palm of her hand. "I'm sorry, what can I do for you?"

"My name is Peter Cummings I'm an Attorney with the Dubois Law Firm in Atlanta and I'm looking for a Sarah Fontaine," he said smiling, looking at the way the dampened blouse outlined the lace of her bra.

"Would you please excuse me for one moment?" Minutes later, she returned from the bathroom patting her blouse with a paper towel.

"I'm sorry, you said that you needed to see Ms. Fontaine?"

"Do you know where I can find her?"

"I expect her back at any time. You're welcome to wait if you like," she said, nodding toward the black leather couch.

He was mesmerized by the way her red hair cascaded around her long slender neck and lay against her breast. Like a moth to a flame, he was drawn to her beauty and could not look away even when she raised her eyes and caught his gaze.

"Did you need something else?"

"No, just admiring you," he said, smiling.

Without responding, she continued to read the document that lay in front of her. The air conditioner rattled and spewed and for a long moment, it was the only sound. She smiled to herself, knowing he was still looking at her. Although it did make her feel slightly uncomfortable, she enjoyed the cat-and-mouse game between them. The light musical noise of the jingling bell drew his attention from her and onto the young woman who entered.

“Good Lord, it’s hot enough to fry eggs on the sidewalk,” Sarah said as she walked through the door.

“There’s an Attorney from Atlanta here to see you Sarah,” Deanna said as she pointed toward Peter. He rose from his chair and walked over to meet her.

“What can I do for you?” she asked eyeing him carefully. She was eight and a half months and visibly pregnant. The thought crossed her mind that he might be there to ask questions about her unborn baby.

“My name is Peter Cummings and I need to talk to you regarding your aunt’s estate. My firm represented your aunt in a case some years back. The case has finally been settled and I have a check for you.”

“You didn’t have to bring it all the way down here; you could have just mailed it.” Relieved, she smiled and took the envelope.

“Actually I have a condo on Tybee Island and was driving down for the weekend anyway.”

“Thank you, this is going to help a lot,” she said as she gently touched her swollen stomach.

Peter walked out of the office realizing he did not get the stunning red head’s name. He smiled to himself and continued down the street. He walked along Bay Street and thought about the girl with the long red hair. He found himself attracted to her; he liked that she was feisty and sassy.

DEANNA HAD BEEN ASLEEP for several hours when the sound of her phone ringing awakened her. She looked at the clock on the bedside table; it was 3 a.m. In a stupor she answered the phone “Hello.”

"Deanna, it's time. I need to go to the hospital," Sarah said.

"I'll be right there." Deanna sprang out of bed pulling one a pair of shorts and a tee shirt. She slipped into a pair of flip-flops and frantically moved from room to room searching for the car keys that she eventually found in her purse. After taking a couple of deep breaths and telling herself to calm down, she sped down the two-lane highway toward the beach house.

"Damn it," she said when the flashing lights appeared in her rear-view mirror. She turned on her emergency flashers. "I'll worry about the ticket later," she said to herself. She pulled into the driveway of the beach house and before she could get out of the car, the police officer was out of his car with his gun pointed at her.

"Hands in the air" he yelled.

"Look, I know I was speeding, but my friend is in labor and she's here alone. I'm an attorney at the law office of Gerald Hamilton. The office is on Bay Street, please leave the ticket there."

The front door opened and Sarah walked out of the house and onto the front porch, carrying an overnight bag slung over her shoulder. The light shining from the open door outlined the silhouette of a very pregnant woman. "Deanna, hurry my water just broke," she said as another contraction ripped through her and she doubled over in pain. The officer ran to her side and placed his hand beneath her arm to help her negotiate the two steps leading to the sidewalk.

"We can take my mine." He helped Sarah to the car and Deanna climbed in the back seat with her. The lights flashed as the officer sped down the highway and when it approached taillights, he swerved to the left, passing the slower vehicle. After twenty minutes, the car came to an abrupt stop at the emergency-room entrance.

"Thank you," Deanna said as she helped Sarah out of the car. "You can leave my ticket at the law office."

Sarah was in labor for only two hours. The doctor allowed Deanna to be in the delivery room and she held Sarah's hand while wiping her face with a cool cloth. "Come on, Sarah, you're doing great," she said as Sarah squeezed her hand even harder. Sarah screamed and fell back into Deanna's arms.

"He has a good set of lungs on him," the doctor said.

"He?" Sarah looked at the wet bundle.

"Yes, you have a beautiful baby boy." He gave the infant to Sarah and she smiled down at her new baby.

"I am going to name you Mathew, after your grandfather," she said as she touched his skin.

Two days later, Sarah was up and dressed, anxiously waiting to take her new baby home. She stood watching him while he lay peacefully sleeping. There was a quiet tap on the door. "Come in," she said as she stroked Mathew's blond hair. She turned around expecting to see Deanna, but was surprised to see the handsome young officer who had escorted her to the hospital.

"Hi, I wanted to come by and check on you and the baby. I didn't get a chance to introduce myself." He put out his hand. "My name is Jack Maynard."

"Well hello, Jack Maynard, and I didn't have time to thank you for getting me to the hospital," Sarah said with a smile.

"He's a fine looking boy," Jack said.

"Thank you, I think I'll keep him," she said, still smiling.

"Well, I guess I'll be going. I hope everything works out for you and your son." As he turned to leave, Deanna came through the door.

"Oh, officer I promise I'll pay the speeding ticket."

"Oh, I expect you to," he laughed.

"Well, little momma are you ready to go home?"

DEANNA UNLOCKED the door of the beach house, opened the blinds, and went into the nursery to make sure she had everything ready for the new baby. Sarah was tired and ready for a nap. After she fell asleep, Deanna picked the baby up out of the bassinet; the tiny bundle warmed the front of her. She watched that little gap in his skull collapse and expand, and with each breath, it was almost hypnotic. Tears begin to flow down her cheeks. Her memories rambled through her mind, taking her to all the nights of crying herself to sleep while her arms ached for the little boy she let go.

"Deanna, what is it? Sarah was standing in the doorway.

"Oh, babies just make me all mushy," Deanna said wiping her eyes.

Chapter 13

JULY 1987, Mathew crawled to the desk; he was one-year-old. His big eyes danced as he pulled up to Deanna's lap. "Hey, big guy. What do you want?" she said as she rubbed the top of his head. She brushed his wavy hair with her hand. "You are getting to be such a big boy. You're going to be a hit with all the ladies. All you have to do is bat those big green eyes at them," she said as she put him down. He raised his arms up again. "Okay, I'm a pushover." She reached in her desk drawer. "And if anyone asks, you didn't get it from me." She peeled the foil wrapper off the chocolate; and gave him a small piece he took it from her hand and placed the chocolate in his mouth.

"Hey there's my little man," Sarah said as she entered the office. "Were you good for Ms. Dee?"

"He was a perfect gentleman."

"All right let's get you home. We have to get ready for your birthday party."

"Bye, Mathew I'll see you tonight," Deanna said. She looked at her watch, and had exactly one hour before she met her client at the courthouse. "Mrs. Cook, I have to be in court in an hour and I can't find the file. Do you have it?" She walked over to the stack of files on Deanna's desk and pulled a folder out of the middle of the stack.

"Here."

"I do need to get a better filing system don't I?" She shook her head, remembering the disorganized mess when she and Sarah began working there.

TWO HOURS LATER, the judge returned to the courtroom. "The court rules in favor of the defendant. Case dismissed," he said, as he handed the bailiff the documents. The happy client shook Deanna's hand and walked out of the courtroom. She was gathering her things when she heard a familiar voice behind her.

"That was a great argument." It was Peter Cummings; she had not seen him since the day he gave Sarah the check. His steel blue eyes twinkled as he looked at her.

"So what brings you back to Savannah?" she asked.

"Just a few days at the beach."

"The beach is that way," she said as she pointed in the other direction.

"I know, so I have something to confess. Mrs. Cook told me you were here," he said with a sly smile.

"Oh, really."

"Yes, I convinced her I was perfectly safe and had honorable intentions."

"And she fell for it," Deanna said with a smile.

"No. She said to me, 'Good luck with that one. Honorable intentions will not get you anywhere,' and then she winked. So what do you think she meant by that?" he said with a broad grin.

"I have no idea what she's talking about," she said, flirting with him. "So what can I do for you, Mr. Cummings?"

"Call me Peter, please."

"Okay, Peter Please, what can I do for you?"

"I was hoping to take you to dinner tonight. That is, if you're free."

"Sorry, I'm not free. I have a date with a very handsome young man and I'm afraid not even you, with all your charm, could cause me to miss it."

"I'll not give up and you will give in sooner or later," he said with a grin. He was the kind of man who, if he turned his full attention on you, could be overwhelming. "And again, that was a good job in the courtroom," Peter said smiling at her. "And I'll not give up on that dinner."

"Come on, you can walk me out," she smiled at him. They talked as they waited on the elevator and then strolled through the lobby of the courthouse. She waved to him and watched as he strutted down the street.

A cool breeze blew the smell of the ocean through the streets and Deanna could taste the saltwater in the air. She walked along the antique shops, looking in each window. The shop owners knew her by name and called to her as she walked by. In one of the store windows, she noticed a rocking horse and thought it would be the perfect birthday gift for Mathew. Not giving a thought to how she would get it back to the office, she bought the bulky wooden horse.

She took her high-heels off and replaced them with the flip-flops she had tucked in her leather satchel and walked down the sidewalk. The horse was big and bulky and as she met people, she had to turn sideways to avoid them. Even though there was a breeze, carrying the large toy was awkward and she could feel sweat beginning to run down her back.

"I knew if I waited long enough you would say yes." Deanna turned around to see a gray Mercedes driving beside her. She laughed when she saw Peter Cummings leaning over to the passenger window.

"Are you following me?" she teased.

"I just don't give up if I see something I want. Can I give you a ride, my lady I promise I will be a perfect gentleman."

He smiled and before she could protest, he was out of the car and walking in her direction. He placed the rocking horse in the trunk and opened the passenger door for her. "Where to, milady?" Peter said as he buckled his seat belt.

"Since you're a perfect gentleman you may buy me a tall, cool drink."

Peter drove through the squares and parked his car on Bay Street. They walked down the steep cobblestones leading to River Street and chatted as they walked past the docks and old warehouses. Deanna chose a refurbished old tavern that had stood on the corner of River Street for more two hundred years. It had been spruced and polished and the windows in the tavern still gave a view out onto the street and bay.

They got a seat in the window and watched cargo ships navigate the river. In spite of her effort to remain indifferent, she found herself enjoying Peter's company. He was egotistical, but there was also a caring side to him that he tried to hide with his self-confident attitude.

THREE YEARS LATER under the watchful eye of Gerald Hamilton, Deanna and Sarah became partners at the law firm of Hamilton & Hamilton. Gerald was sixty-four years old and three months away from retiring. Mrs. Cook thought it was time for her to go as well; she had decided to pursue her writing. She said she knew about enough skeletons so that she could live out the rest of her days writing about Savannah's scandals.

They hired a young college girl by the name of Caroline to manage the office. She was a student at the junior college, pursing a degree as a paralegal. Her voice was as soft as velvet and the southern drawl dripping off her tongue left no doubt as to where she was from. Within a few months of hanging the new shingle on the door, they had to hire an assistant to answer the phones and type court documents.

She saw Peter when he was in town, but it did not develop beyond a casual friendship. Deanna did not want anything more. She had dated a few men from Savannah from time to time and she soon learned Savannah's social structure. The men born into the old families had to go to the proper private schools in Savannah, and attend only the right colleges. Then they returned and could only marry a girl from one of the old families with the right background. They had to produce a proper little family. This was the pecking order of the old South's aristocrats.

The day after Thanksgivings, an engraved invitation arrived in the mail. The paper was embossed in gold lettering. It was an invitation to the Annual Winter Ball. The ball is a permanent fixture on Savannah's social calendar and only the cream of Savannah receives an invitation. This was a great accomplishment to be able to make such a prominent place for herself in Savannah's social circle in spite of not being a native. Under his protective custody, Gerald had introduced her to all the right people. But to the aristocrats she would always be an outsider. She would be good enough to attend their parties, but never good enough to marry one of their own.

This year the ball was hosted by a sixth-generation Savannah family. The family was at the very top of society and one of the richest in Savannah. Only a few months earlier the family was able to avoid a dirty family scandal. A grandson discovered after an evening of drinking that the prostitute he had spent the night with was not of the female gender. He had spent the night with a crossdresser. In a fit of rage, he broke the young man's nose, and put him in the hospital overnight. The family wanted this to go away, not because of an assault charge, but because the prostitute was a man.

Deanna negotiated a settlement. The young man agreed to drop the charges and accepted a hefty sum of two-hundred thousand dollars in return for his silence. And now, as far as the family was concerned, the incident never happened. Another one of Savannah's dirty little secrets, that with enough money would remain tucked away in the closet with all the other skeletons.

The last couple of weeks flew by. Deanna was busy trying to get her cases heard before she left for the Christmas holiday. She was planning to go back to Tennessee and spend Christmas with her family. Her brother David and his wife Allison had just had their first child so this was going to be an exciting Christmas for them. She was looking forward to seeing her grandparents as well. Her father constantly complained that she didn't come home often enough, but with her caseload once every six months was all she could spare.

THE TRIAL of the decade was about to begin. Much could be said about it. There was a district attorney who performed brilliantly, but had obnoxious habits of spending too much time with the press. It was very clear that this trial had a purpose. He had political ambitions on a grand scale.

It was nearly nine o'clock on Monday morning when the bailiff called out, "Order in the Court." The courtroom was filled with people wanting to see Deanna take on the district attorney. This was a case that from all accounts should be impossible to win. A young black man from Savannah had been accused of robbing and killing a tourist. The judge brought his gavel down and in a long slurred drawl called the court to order.

"The people will prove that the defendant killed the victim in cold blood," the prosecutor began his long opening argument.

At the end of it, Deanna stood and addressed the jury of seven whites and five blacks. She told them that in the coming days she would prove without a shadow of a doubt that her client had an alibi and that he could not have killed the victim.

Throughout the five days of prosecution testimony, Deanna rose repeatedly to challenge the state witnesses in intense cross-examinations. She was eloquent but vicious. She paused and let the silence in the courtroom emphasize the points she made. "No further questions Your Honor," she said every time she returned to her seat. With the parade of witness finished, the judge called a recess for the weekend.

On Monday morning, the courtroom was filled to capacity. The case had attracted attention well beyond Savannah. Newspapers and television reporters sat in the back of the courtroom. The mood was tense. Deanna looked the jury in the eye, but this time when she spoke, she spoke softly.

She stood before the jury in a packed courtroom and presented her closing argument. She was articulate and compassionate. "This is a young man, uneducated and unsophisticated," she began. She pointed to her client, paused, then turned slowly to the jury again. "This tragic story began with manipulation by the prosecution. Can you imagine how easily this young man, with the mind of a child, could have been coerced into a confession?" It was a splendid performance, and when Deanna finished the courtroom was silent.

The district attorney rose to make his closing statement. "That is all sweet, but what happened was an act of cold-blooded murder, carried out by that MAN sitting there," he said as he pointed his finger at the defendant. His voice was heavy with sarcasm as he continued. Finally, he said, "We rest our case." At that, the judge called a recess and sent the jury to deliberate.

At three o'clock in the afternoon, the courthouse was a scene of turmoil. Spectators had returned to hear the verdict. The bailiff called the court to order, and the jury filed in.

"Madam Forelady, have you reached a verdict?" asked the judge.

"Yes, sir we have. We the jury, find the defendant not guilty."

Gasps sounded throughout the courtroom. The spectators flowed out into the corridor and gathered around Deanna and the young man. They stood in the glare of television lights, while tears of joy flowed down the young man's face. He stood with his arms around his grandmother, expressing his relief. As Deanna spoke to reporters, the stunned district attorney stepped into the elevator. As the elevator door began to close Deanna saw the look of defeat on his face. She felt a rush of excitement and smiled into the cameras.

Cheers rang out when she opened the door to the office. Sarah, Caroline and the staff as well as Gerald Hamilton were waiting on her. "Congratulations, my dear. I have been waiting twenty years for someone to humiliate that pompous ass and you did it, my dear Deanna," Gerald said as he lifted a glass of Champagne to her.

"We all did it – Sarah, Caroline and everyone that worked on this case."

"Nevertheless, the old smug prune lost." He lifted his glass to Deanna. "You have made this office proud."

"Here, Here," they all said as they lifted their glasses.

"Fontaine and Guthrie," Caroline spoke into the phone. "Yes she is. Whom shall I say is calling?" She placed the caller on hold. "Deanna there is a Peter Cummings on the phone for you. Do you want to take his call?"

"Yes, thank you," she said as she stepped into her office. "Peter, good to hear from you."

"I'm surprised you will take my calls now that you are such a celebrity."

"How did you hear?"

"You are all over the news channels. You didn't know. This case has gone nationwide."

"You are kidding me, right."

"No, I'm not. You're famous. You won a case that no one expected you to ever be able to pull off."

"I suppose I just had my fifteen minutes of fame."

"Really, Deanna you saved that kid's life. He was just another poor black kid that no one would miss. A rich tourist killed by a black kid, that makes headlines. The kid was a sacrificial lamb for the DA's run for states attorney; everyone knew that. But what he did not plan on was someone other than a court-appointed attorney taking the case. You did well, Deanna," Peter said with admiration.

TALK ABOUT THE TRIAL, went on for a month. Everywhere she went people stopped to congratulate her or stop by the office to discuss the case. But today she was in a hurry to leave the office early. She had just enough time to stop by the salon to get her hair and nails done before the ball. And she had to stop at the tailor before five to pick up her gown.

The strapless gown fit her like a second skin and showed off her perfect figure. When she moved, the ice-blue satin flowed like water cascading down her tall slender body. She wore a pair of white gloves that hugged her arms past the elbows. Diamond earrings that had belonged to Eleanor dangled from her earlobes. Her red hair was swept up and away from her face. Her skin was soft and a perfect shade of the palest of creamy peach and her eyes were the color of sapphire.

This was the party of the year; it had long been a tradition in old Savannah to parade its aristocrats in view of a crowd. The group of onlookers stood in the streets to get a glimpse of the Savannah royals. The crowd that had gathered in front of the house pointed and whispered as she stepped out of the car.

"Ooooh," she heard from the crowd and, "aaah, she's beautiful," "Who is she?" "That's the woman from the news!" Deanna smiled through her red painted lips. The crowd smiled and waved to her. She glided along the sidewalk, her long slender legs peeping through the slit in her dress teasing the crowd.

Every window of the house was ablaze with candlelight and every room had sparkling chandeliers. Deanna stood outside staring in amazement at the beautiful home where the ball was taking place. This was old Savannah. Ladies in long chiffon gowns walked past her as though she were invisible. They walked with their eyes straight ahead and with a white gloved hand tucked inside the arm of men in black tuxedoes.

At least two hundred guests filled the large room. A pianist played cocktail music and butlers in white jackets circulated with silver trays of shrimp and finger sandwiches. Gerald was working his way around the room, stopping every five seconds to chat with small groups of people, laughing and smiling. He was chatting with a group from the yacht club when he noticed Deanna and waved her over. All chattering stopped and their heads turned to look at Deanna. "There you are, my dear. We were just talking about you," he said as she placed her arm in his.

"All good I hope," she replied as she took a glass of Champagne from a waiter. *Maybe Miss. Vivian's School of Charm is paying off after all.* She thought as she returned her gaze to the men.

"Oh yes, we were just discussing your case, the young black man" said an older gentleman. He was tanned and his snowy hair was perfectly combed. "We were wondering how someone like him could ever afford your hourly rate." The District Attorney was one of the good ole boys who had been raised in Savannah and had attended all the right schools. He wasn't taking the loss very well and neither were his cronies.

"Someone like him couldn't afford my fee. But very few in this town can," she said with a sly grin. "We do a pro bono each year. This was just his lucky year," she replied as she took a sip of Champagne from the crystal goblet.

"Would you excuse us, there is someone I must introduce Deanna to," Gerald tipped his head and smiled at them. She extended her white-gloved hand to rest on Gerald's coat sleeve. Deanna inclined her head in a little bow and smiled at the men. All of their aristocratic pretentions returned in a flash and they returned the smile. "Well done, my dear," he said as he leaned in close. "Simply charming." Gerald whispered and patted her gloved hand. She threw her head back and laughed and the diamond earrings caught the light from the chandelier. The reflecting light cast a sudden aura around her face.

"I told you Savannah was a peculiar place. Look at this circus." Gerald lifted his cane and pointed it around the room. "It is just one giant tent with hundreds of preforming animals." He clicked his cane on the marble floor. "Now where is that partner of yours?"

"She should be here very soon. She called just before I got here to say the baby sitter was running late."

"Ahh… I hear the music starting upstairs in the ballroom," Gerald said.

"This place has a ballroom?"

"Yes, my dear, like I said, one giant circus tent."

"You go on ahead. I'll wait for Sarah and we'll join you later." Gerald walked off in the opposite direction. She smiled to herself. *Of course, there is an elevator.*

She scanned the room, and scrutinized each guest. One distinguished-looking man in his mid to upper thirties stood out. His black wavy hair was gelled and brushed back behind his ears. He was tall and well built, and his green eyes had gold flecks sprinkled around the pupils. Deanna recognized him from the social pages of the Savannah newspaper. Even if she had not seen his picture, she would have known that he was Charles Patterson. Matthew was the spitting image of him; they even shared the same eyes, down to the gold flecks.

Accompanying him was his wife; she was beautiful; a tall, slender, brown-haired woman who was one of the blue bloods with the right background. Just at that moment, Sarah walked through the door. Deanna took a glass of Champagne from the passing waiter and met her at the entrance of the large room.

Before Deanna could warn her, Mr. and Mrs. Patterson walked in Sarah's direction. She looked him in the eye, but they were as impenetrable as ever. He walked past her with an air of sophistication. He had the kind of sophistication that looked down upon the commoners. They were good enough to sleep with, but not good enough to bring to the yacht club.

"The gall of him," Sarah spurted.

"What did you expect he would do?" Deanna gave her the glass of bubbly. "He bought your silence and to him that is that and as far as he is concerned he has never seen you before in his life. You know how it works." Sarah took a sip.

"I should have Corinna cast a spell on him."

Deanna laughed, but then realized she was serious. "Oh come on, you can't believe in that old woman's black magic."

"You can laugh if you want, most people do, but you are overlooking a valuable public service."

"Come on Sarah, don't mess with that stuff."

"I won't because once you start that shit you have to keep it up."

Sarah left soon after. The front porch light was on and Sarah could see the lamp on in the living room and the flicker from the television. She walked in the house very quietly. The baby sitter had fallen asleep on the couch and Mathew was lying with his little head in her lap. Sarah looked at him as he slept peacefully. She sank in the chair beside them. She started to cry, wiping the tears away with the back of her hand.

WHEN THE MOON WAS FULL, like tonight, every squawk of the radio brought excitement and danger. Jack Maynard wanted it and he sought it out. He chose to work the night shift because the hours of darkness were when everything happened. He got an adrenaline rush out of flipping on the blue lights and jamming his finger on the siren button. But tonight he would have to sit in the police car, and wait to catch someone speeding along the two-lane highway. It was his turn to do beach patrol and it was offering no excitement for him; he only spotted cars headed home from a night of fishing, not a night of drinking. He was bored with routine police work. Jack resented this part of his job.

He yawned and checked the clock on the dashboard, it was 6 a.m., time for him to pack it up and head home. The sun was coming up, so he put on his mirrored sunglasses and took one last drive around the Island. He had just turned the bend heading toward the beach when he saw her. He blinked his eyes to clear the orange outline of the rising sun, and when he opened them his breath was suspended by her beauty. Her blonde hair was tied back by a headband. Wispy curls fell around her face. She ran along the edge of the road, her jogging shoes slapping the asphalt steadily. Her big blue eyes looked at him and she smiled as she ran past. He stopped himself from calling out to her as he felt the first ballooning of desire. He watched her run away, knowing it would only be a matter of time before he had her and he would never let her run away from him again.

Dawn came to Savannah and the pale sun burned away the morning mist. It was a cool January morning but the air was invigorating and cleared Sarah's head from the night before. Seeing Charles and his wife at the ball had put her in a dark mood; running always lifted her spirits. She smiled at the officer as she ran past his car. But she did not recognize his face behind the mirrored glasses.

Mathew was up and in front of the television when she returned from her run. "Hey, little man. What are you doing up so early? This is Saturday and we don't have to be anywhere today," she said, sitting down on the couch.

"Good morning mommy."

"What are you watching?"

"Bugs Bunny. I'm hungry."

"You are? How about I make you a bowl of cereal and after I get out of the shower and we get dressed we go for pancakes. Does that sound good?"

"Make pancakes here. I'm hungry now."

"Okay."

They finished eating their pancakes and afterwards Sarah took a shower. When she stepped out of the shower she heard voices. She put her rob on and quickly walked towards the kitchen where the voices were coming from.

"Jack," she said, not frightened but wary.

He stood six-foot two. He was handsome; his red hair and freckled face gave him a boyish quality most people found charming. He was not only charming, but also charismatic and a little unsettling. He poured a cup of coffee and after a pause handed it to her.

"What are you doing in here?" she asked, slowly taking the coffee. She looked over her shoulder to check on Mathew. He was sitting in front of the television finishing his glass of chocolate milk.

"I let him in, mommy."

"Mathew, what have I told you about opening the door by yourself?"

"But mommy, he is a policeman and he drives a police car. He said you rode in the police car the night I was born."

“That’s right, I did.”

Jack interrupted, “I saw you jogging this morning and thought I would just stop in to check on the two of you.”, That was not exactly the motive behind his visit. His broad smile and charm concealed his true agenda.

Chapter 14

MARCH 1991, Deanna stood on her balcony looking down over the floats and marching bands passing through the squares. It was the perfect spot to watch the Saint Patrick's Day parade. Green tinted water bubbled out of the fountains. Crowds lined the streets with cups filled with green beer. The whole town had turned out for Savannah's big affair.

"Caroline, you better hurry or you're going to miss the floats," Deanna yelled through the balcony doors.

"Coming." Caroline hurried to the balcony carrying a pitcher of margaritas and two glasses. "I thought Sarah was bringing Mathew over to watch the parade," she said, handing Deanna a glass.

"That was the plan, then she called this morning to say something had come up."

"Did she say what?"

"No, and I didn't ask."

"Hmm," Caroline said, squinting.

"What do you mean, Hmm? Do you know something I don't?"

"She has been getting to the office late and leaving early and a few days ago, the day-care called looking for her. They said Mathew was not feeling well and they could not reach her by her cell phone."

"That doesn't sound like Sarah."

"I know. I had to pick him up because he was running a temperature. She got back to the office around two o'clock and felt really bad about Mathew but she didn't tell me where she'd been."

"That's strange."

That afternoon Deanna walked to River Street and as she passed a window, she saw Sarah sitting at a table with Jack Maynard. She sat gazing at him, looking awestruck. Deanna definitely had the impression they were more than just friends. They seemed very comfortable with each other as they sat side by side. And it was obvious they were attracted to each other. Deanna felt a shiver run up her spine. There was something cold and dark about him and it was odd that Sarah was being so secretive.

THE CLOCK on Deanna's bedside table read 5:49 a.m. Her head felt like it would explode from the pressure behind her eyes. She swung her legs over the bed and yawned. An hour and half later she was dressed and out the door.

She was standing in the cold-remedy isle reading the back of the packages when she heard someone speak her name. "Deanna Guthrie." She turned to see Charles Patterson standing beside her.

"My name is Charles Patterson," he said as he extended his hand.

"What can I do for you Mr. Patterson?"

"I believe I saw you talking to Sarah Fontaine at the ball this past winter."

"That's right, you did. She and I are law partners; we have an office here in Savannah."

"She and I use to be acquaintances," he said.

"Yes, she did mention that," Deanna a slight grin crossed her face. He looked at her. There was a questioning wrinkle on his forehead.

"I was just wondering how she's doing. I haven't spoken to her in a long time."

"Yes, she did mention that as well and she's doing great. Well, I should be going; I'm due in court in an hour. It was good finally to meet you, Mr. Patterson. Have a nice day." She took a few steps, then turned around as he walked away. "Oh Mr. Patterson there is something I want to ask you." He turned quickly and looked at her. "How are you feeling?"

"Fine. Why do you ask?" he said looking puzzled.

"Oh no particular reason, it was just something Sarah mentioned." *You're lucky you're not covered in boils,* she thought, remembering the curse. She smiled and chuckled as she walked away. "Bastard", she said under her breath.

She went to court and afterward as she stood waiting at the elevator she overheard a couple of county deputies talking about a gruesome murder. It had taken place on the riverfront the night before. The young man was one of the local crossdressers and had apparently propositioned the wrong person. They found him beaten to death; his genitals had been cut off and left by his side. As she passed a newsstand, she got a glance of the young man; his high school picture was on the front page of the newspaper. She cringed when she saw his face. It was the young man whom she had encouraged to take the two hundred thousand dollars to drop the assault charge against the wealthy family.

She sat quiet and pensive in her office that afternoon, staring for a long time at the young face on the front of the newspaper. She was thinking about that young boy and it made her sad. He wasn't mean-spirited; he just liked having a good time.

A FEW WEEKS LATER, on Easter morning, Deanna waited for Sarah and Mathew outside the church. The cathedral bells were ringing when they arrived and Mathew had his ears covered. "They're too loud," he said. Deanna looked at him and smiled. He was dressed in white linen shorts, white shirt with a pink tie and wore a light green linen jacket. Sarah had on a matching linen sleeveless dress and wore a white wide-brimmed hat.

"Well, you two are looking smart, very Easterly," Deanna said.

"Sorry we're late, but someone did not want to wear his tie."

"Well I'm glad that someone did because he looks very handsome."

Gerald Hamilton was seated in a third-row pew. Mathew climbed upon his lap and played with a toy car while services were held. After the service was over a woman with her hair in white curls came over to them.

"Good morning, Deanna dear."

"Miss Emma this is my friend Sarah and her son Mathew."

"What a handsome young man you are," the elderly woman said as she looked at Mathew and then to Sarah's ring finger. Deanna sneaked a knowing glance at Sarah.

"Come with me." Emma led them down the hall. "This is where the children are listening to the Easter story." There were about twenty children seated in a semicircle around a woman with blond hair piled high on her head. She wore a pair of large gold-rimmed glasses. She was holding a children's Bible.

"Jesus loves you," she said.

"Deanna, you know where the Sunday school classes are." Emma took Mathew by his hand and led him to where the other children were sitting.

"Yes, Miss Emma," Deanna said politely. She and Sarah followed the long hallway to a small classroom where there were about dozen other women.

At twelve-thirty, they walked back to children's church where Mathew was standing in the doorway waiting on them. He held up an Easter basket with eggs. "Look mommy, I decorated eggs. I'm supposed to close my eyes then you and Ms. Dee hide the eggs, then I can open my eyes and find them. And look, Miss Emma gave me a chocolate bunny."

"Did you thank Miss Emma?"

"Yes. Do you know Jesus loves me? And he loves you and Ms. Dee too."

"Are you ready to go to poppa Gerald's house for lunch?" Sarah and Deanna walked the couple of blocks to Gerald's house. Mathew chatted constantly about his Easter eggs.

Blanche Hamilton, Gerald's sister, swayed into the dining room, moving gracefully as she took her seat at the dinner table. The table was set with antique blue and white Chinese porcelain. The china had been in the family since the 1800's. It was used only once a year for Easter lunch, then would be packed away until next Easter.

Lunch began with she-crab soup. It was a velvety blend of taste. "Is the soup perfect Gerald?" Blanche asked.

"Yes my dear sister, as always. Blanche bought crabs, going to five different sellers until she accumulated eight." He said to Deanna and Sarah.

"I suppose I seem awfully picky to you," Blanche said after she tasted the soup. "But the soup is just not the same if it is not made with she-crabs. The roe gives it a special flavor, you see. It's a lot harder to find but it's worth the effort, I think."

"The soup is superb," said Deanna.

"I agree, thank you for sharing it with us." Sarah said as she watched Mathew's little face light up in delight as he eats the soup.

"Blanche prepares the soup herself and no one is allowed in the kitchen while she blends her secret ingredients." Gerald said rumbling with amusement. "In Savannah one never asks a Southern woman her politics, religion, or how she makes her she-crab soup."

"Oh now Gerald everyone knows it is made of roe, cream, sherry, thickening, vegetables, and spices." Blanche radiated enthusiasm as she spoke.

"Yes it is the secret spices Blanche will not reveal and how much sherry she puts in the soup." Gerald winked at Deanna. "She always goes in the kitchen with a full bottle but comes out with an empty one. She says she puts it in the soup but she is especially giddy when she comes out."

"Gerald Hamilton! That is not true." Blanches' cheeks reddened.

A pretty light-skinned African American woman in her mid to upper forties cleared the soup dishes. Shortly afterwards, she brought the traditional low country food to the table. The menu consists of shrimp and grits, roasted lamb, sweet potatoes, squash and okra.

"Thank you Serena." Gerald said kindly to the pretty woman.

After lunch, they moved to the living room of the old Victorian home for coffee and dessert. "Gerald would you taste the pound cake and judge if the extract of vanilla bean was strong enough?"

"Yes Blanche the vanilla was fine," Gerald said after he tasted the cake.

"Serena after dessert is served, would you take young master Fontaine to the upstairs guest room? He can enjoy his milk and cookies there, and then put him down for an afternoon nap."

"Yes, Miz Hamilton." Serena gathered Mathew by the hand and began to lead him out.

"Serena, would you stay with him please," Sarah whispered in a voice that only Serena could hear.

They finished dessert and Gerald took a Cuban cigar out of his inside coat pocket. He ran the cigar beneath his nose, taking in the sweet aroma of the tobacco. "Gerald, please retire to the veranda if you are going to light that hideous-smelling thing," Blanche insisted.

"Ladies, would you join me?"

Sarah and Deanna followed him to the veranda that overlooked a pale marble pedestal surround by azaleas. The mansion was one of the oldest in the city and sat in Savannah's most elegant tree-shaded square, back from the street behind an iron fence. Sunlight danced through the large live oak trees onto the pink azaleas that enclosed the lawn.

"The Sheriff's race is going to heat up. That Maynard boy has announced he is entering the race. He's the son of one of Savannah's aristocrats." Gerald flicked the ash of his cigar into a mother-of-pearl ashtray. "Jack is the family's black sheep, one could say. He never had any ambition and he never worked a day in his life. He lived off the family's money until it dried up. If his uncle had not been a county commissioner, he would not have gotten the job in the sheriff's department in the first place." Gerald looked at the end of his cigar. "Their old family home is boarded up and is owned by the bank now. They had to close it down about ten years ago. His poor mother had to sell off the furniture, the paintings, and the silver just to pay the rent. That's the trouble with Blue Bloods, they don't know how to make money, they only know how to spend it."

"Gerald, aren't you a Blue Blood?" Deanna smiled.

"My mother taught me a long time ago the value of a good job. She was the daughter of a cotton grower. She knew how to work."

"How was she ever accepted into the Savannah royals? She didn't come from the right background."

"My father loved her. He threatened to leave Savannah, and never come back. He was the only child and his mother and father did not want to lose him." He took another long draw from the cigar and let it balance between his thumb and forefinger, watching the smoke twirl up to the white fans hanging above his wicker chair. A crystal decanter sat on the table beside him. He picked it up and poured three snifters of brandy, passing one to Sarah then one to Deanna.

"Our money ran out a long time ago. I've paid the bills out of the money from my law practice. Blanche still thinks we're wealthy. Serena helps me with the charade." He smiled affectionately as he said her name. He opened his mouth to speak again, but before he could get the words out, Blanche walked out on the porch and sat beside him.

"It's certainly warm for this time of year," she said, brushing her cotton-white hair away from her face. "Serena," she called out.

"Yes Ma'am," she said meekly as she entered the veranda holding Mathew's hand.

"Would you bring us a pitcher of iced tea?" Blanche moved a straw heart-shaped fan back and forth in front of her face, stirring the air. She did not look at Serena, she only admired the azaleas billowing beneath the oak trees. Deanna saw the loving glances exchanged between Gerald and Serena and realized she was the reason Gerald had never married.

"Mommy, can I hunt Easter eggs now?"

"Yes, but you have to close your eyes while I hide them."

THAT SPRING turned into another hot Savannah summer. The law office was doing very well, keeping Deanna and Sarah busy. They met with a new client nearly every day. However, Deanna's social life was less interesting; she showed no romantic interest in anyone. The whole world seemed to be counting down her remaining child-bearing years. Or at least Gerald was. He had set her up with a wealthy art dealer from New York. The following night he picked her up for dinner, and took her to one of the most popular restaurants in Savannah. The meal was good and the conversation interesting.

"I was thinking I could come in for a drink," he said as they pulled up to her apartment afterward.

"I'm sorry, but I have a very early court case in the morning." She was trying politely to give him the message that he was barking up the wrong tree. She had no intention of going to bed with someone she just met. "Thank you for a lovely dinner," she said politely. She walked around to the courtyard and seconds later she heard him speed away. He was forty-five and extremely handsome; it was clear he was used to having his way with women. Apparently, they never said no to him and he did not like what he heard.

"How was your date last night?" Caroline asked, handing her a cup of coffee.

"Dinner was excellent and the conversation was good, but apparently he was planning on working the meal out in trade."

"And you didn't?" Caroline said, pretending to be shocked.

"Oh be quiet! But come to think of it, perhaps I should have, it's been a long time since someone with his intelligence and money tried to get me in bed," she said with a smile. "What would you have done?"

"Me, I would have paid for dinner just to get him in bed. He's gorgeous," Caroline said showing her the picture of him in the newspaper.

"Yes, he is," Deanna admitted. They both sighed.

THE SUN was going down as Jack Maynard and Sarah walked on the beach. "I've been thinking about something," Jack said casually. "I think we should get married." Sarah stopped and looked at him.

"What brought that up?" she said, surprised. "We hardly know each other."

"I know I love you," he said, putting his arms around her, casting his net of words.

"I don't know. I have Mathew to consider. I'll think about it," she finally said, since he was pressing her.

"What's there to think about?" Jack said, raising his voice.

"I'm tired, can we just go back to the house now?" Sarah walked through the sand ahead of him.

She took a shower and when she came to bed, he turned his back to her like a sulking child. She made a decision that night. She loved him too, and Mathew seemed to like him. She told him yes the next morning over breakfast.

"Great. I knew you would see it my way. I have the next few days off. We can get married then."

"That soon?" she said, sounding surprised. Jack manipulated the people in his life as though they were chess pieces. The next day they were married in front of the justice of the peace in a private ceremony. Sarah called Deanna the next morning and gave her the news.

"Wow!" Deanna said, a panicked tone in her voice. "How did this happen? Do you really know him, Sarah?"

"I know him well enough. I know he loves me and he is good to Mathew," she said defensivcly. "By the way, I'm having a Fourth of July barbeque tonight and I'd like you to join us. I thought I would make it a celebration for Jack and me. Will you come?"

"Yes, of course I'll be there," Deanna replied.

"Great, Caroline and Gerald will be here as well."

Sarah put on shorts and the matching red, white, and blue tee shirts she had bought for herself, Mathew and Jack. Mathew had his on when he met Jack at the door. "Look, Jack, mommy bought us tee shirts. Here's yours," Mathew said, happily handing it to Jack.

"Don't call her that. You sound like a little baby," He set his golf clubs by the door, went to the refrigerator and took out a beer. "Why is all this food in here?"

"We're having a party. Ms. Dee and Caroline and poppa Gerald are coming over for the Fourth of July."

He took a gulp of the beer and set the bottle on the cabinet. "Where's your mother?"

"She's in her room getting ready for the party."

"You should have asked me before you invited all those people over," Jack said to Sarah tossing the tee shirt on their bed.

"I didn't think you would mind. Besides, I wanted it to be a celebration," Sarah said as she brushed his hair back.

"I'm taking a shower." He pulled his golf shirt over his head and tossed it on the bed. While he was in the shower Sarah picked up the clothes he left on the bathroom floor and put them in the hamper. After a long shower he came out of the bathroom wrapped in a towel.

"I thought you would wear this." Sarah handed him the matching shirt.

"I'm not going to wear that stupid thing," he said.

"What's wrong with you? And why are you in such a bad mood?"

"I don't like parties and I don't like any of those people."

"Why? Those people, as you call them, are my friends."

"They don't like me and I don't like them." He let the towel drop to the floor, then pulled Sarah to him. He started kissing her neck and began to unbutton her shorts.

"Jack we don't have time for this, they will be here any minute."

Without speaking to her he put his clothes on and stormed out of the bedroom. Sarah heard the back door slam shut. From the living-room window, she saw him walking down the beach with a beer in his hand. She and Mathew were sitting in a chair eating hamburgers when he returned an hour later. "Jack where have you been our guest would like to toast our wedding."

"Just needed to clear my head." He extended his hand to Gerald and gave a friendly handshake. "Hello Deanna, it's great to see you again," said Jack. He picked Mathew up and began to tickle him. "Did you save me a burger?" He said tossing Mathew in the air and catching him again. He was charming to their guest and stayed close to Sarah the rest of the evening.

The next morning he walked in the kitchen and said nothing to her. He poured himself a cup of coffee and after Mathew left the table, he finally looked up. "You embarrassed me last night in front of your friends," he said with a tone as cold as ice.

"I'm sorry Jack I didn't mean too. What did I say to embarrass you?"

"You questioned me in front of them."

"Jack they're my friends, no one thought anything about that."

"That's right they're your friends not mind." The door slammed behind him as he stormed out. He had slithered into her life quietly and no one noticed when he dug his fangs in and slowly began to poison her mind.

IN NOVEMBER THE SITTING SHERIFF watched in disbelief as the returns came in. Jack's family was still a member of the good ole boys' club that could persuade certain voters. He defeated the sheriff in a landslide. But doubts about him started to circulate as past staff and disgruntled employees passed the word around the county he did not know what he was doing.

Jack was sitting in the dark when Sarah got home that evening. Bottles of beer were scattered around the floor. "Where have you been?" He asked without looking at her.

"Why are you sitting in the dark?" Sarah switched on the light and looked at the empty bottles. "Where's Mathew? And where is Mrs. Williams?"

"I told her to go home and I told him to go to bed."

"At seven o'clock?"

"He was whinny. I didn't want to listen to that stuff. I have enough of that shit at work. Whinny ass employees, who do they think they are questioning me? I won the election fair and square." Jack got up and followed her to the bedroom. "Then I come home to your whinny kid and no dinner."

"Jack I'm sorry you had a bad day. But mind was not easy either. Besides Mrs. Williams made Mathew's dinner tonight, there should have been plenty left for you."

"You didn't answer my question. Where have you been?"

"I left you a message. I told you Deanna and I had to go over a case and we would be working late tonight."

"I saw you at the restaurant today. Who was that man you were with?"

"Oh he's a new client." Sarah answered as she changed into her nightgown.

"He's from Glynn County and lives on St. Simons so why does he need a lawyer from Savannah?"

"Jack you know I can't discus my clients." There was a pause. "Wait, you checked up on him."

"Don't lie to me Sarah. You're screwing him aren't you? That's why he drove up here."

"Jack what are you talking about? I told you he's a client."

"You're lying to me." Jack grabbed both her arms and shook her hard. Then he slapped her with the back of his hand across the face.

"Jack you're hurting me."

"See what you made me do!" he screamed. Finally he shoved her to the floor.

Stunned, Sarah sat quiet, leaning against the bedroom wall. She touched her hand to her burning cheek, then she began to cry. Jack crossed the room and set down beside her. "I'm sorry baby." He reached out to touch her and she cowered as far away from him as she could get

He put his arm around her. "Come here, don't cry. I'm sorry baby, I won't do it again." He pulled her to him. "It's just that I love you so much and I get crazy when I see you with another man." He began kissing her. "Don't be mad at me. I love you baby. I need you." He stood up, took her hand, and led her to the bed. He made love to her and after he fell to sleep Sarah lay crying into the night. Jack was charming but the monster came out behind closed doors.

At the office the next day Deanna set at her desk, her secretary appeared at the door and tapped lightly. "Deanna, your father is on the phone." Deanna looked up. "He sounded serious," she said.

"Hi, Dad." Before she could say anything more James spoke quickly into the phone.

"Deanna, grandma is in the hospital and the doctors said she may not make it through the night." Deanna gasped. "If you want to see her, you need to come home right away," James said.

"I'll leave right now." She looked at her watch; it was 10 a.m. "I should be there by seven tonight."

"Deanna, what's wrong? You look like you've seen a ghost," Caroline said as she walked to where she stood.

"It's my grandmother." Deanna began putting things in her briefcase. "She's in the hospital." She stopped for a few seconds, clearly upset, looking around the office. "Dad said she may not make it through the night. I need to leave now." She shoved files in the leather satchel. "I need to call these clients and postpone the cases."

"I can do that for you." Caroline touched her shoulder. "Are those the files?"

"Yes." Deanna wiped her eyes.

"Leave them. I'll make the calls."

"Has anyone heard from Sarah?"

"Yes she called earlier, she said she was not feeling well and she was going to work from home today."

Deanna rushed to her apartment and packed a small suitcase. She threw in two pair of Jeans, a couple of sweaters, and a pair of sweat paints and sweat shirt. She took a dark suit out of the closet and then reached in the far back behind all the other clothes and found her wool coat.

IT WAS 8 P.M. when she rushed through the double doors of the hospital. She found the elevator and pushed the button for the third floor. When the stainless steel doors slid open and she stepped out into the hallway, she felt she was going to be sick. She ran down the hall and found Rebecca standing outside Pearl's room.

"Hello, Aunt Rebecca."

"Hello, Deanna. It's been a very long time since I've seen you. Look at you, all grown up."

"Yes, fifteen years does that to a person."

"You're pale. . . are you all right?" Rebecca asked.

"I'm just a little sick to my stomach. I haven't eaten anything since lunch. I didn't want to take the time to eat. I just wanted to get here as soon as I could."

"She may not know you Deanna, she's going in and out of consciousness."

"What happened to her, Aunt Rebecca?"

"She has ovarian cancer. She had known about it for a few months but it was too late and too far along for the chemo to work."

"Why didn't someone tell me?"

"She didn't tell anyone. I only found out myself when I got here yesterday."

Deanna stood in the doorway of the room holding the framework for support. She gasped and raised her hand to her month. Pearl's hair was bone white. That was not her grandmother. How could she have just wasted away like that?

Deanna sat in the chair beside the bed. A nurse was in the room giving her medicines through a tube hooked up to her. "Can she hear me?" Deanna asked.

"Sometimes I think she can. She'll open her eyes if I call her name. Go ahead talk to her, she may recognize you."

Deanna looked at Pearl, she was so small and frail. Her thin fingers were gnarly branches, twisting oddly from the stems of her palms, moving slowly across the folds of the sheet. Deanna reached out and took her thin cold hand in hers.

"Grandma it's, Deanna."

Her eyes opened half way, then Deanna heard Pearl's voice, thin and broken. "Deanna. I've been waiting on you." Deanna leaned forward and saw the love in her sunken eyes. She lifted her frail arm and pushed Deanna's hair away from her face. "No need to cry, little one. I'm ready to go be with the Lord. I'm tired." Pearl closed her eyelids and her breathing slowed in sleep. She had slipped into a coma. It seemed impossible that the frail body could summons up the strength to pull air into her lungs and then push it out again.

THE WIND had a bite in it for the sun to be so bright and the sky so blue. Yellow, gold, and red leaves blew across the cemetery, blown by the autumn wind. Deanna looked at the nearby gravestones. Abigale Guthrie, born 1940, died

1962. One tiny stone beside it, the brother Deanna never knew. Pearl was laid to rest beside her daughter.

Deanna stared at the teenaged boy standing with Rebecca's two sons and husband. His red hair glistened in the sun and his eyes were as blue as sapphire. She squinted in the bright sun to get a better look at him. He smiled at her. His wide grin was bright and full of mischief. She had an odd feeling about him, he looked so familiar, and yet she had never seen him before. *Who is he*? she thought, searching his face for answers. He smiled at her again and her heart nearly stopped its beating. *No it couldn't be,* she thought.

Later that day, back at the house, she found him alone in the back yard. "Hi, my name is Deanna. And what's yours?"

"Daniel, but everybody calls me Danny."

"And how old are you Danny?"

"Fifteen."

"I've not met you." Little by little, she extracted the information she wanted.

"I'm Rebecca's son."

"That's strange. I wasn't aware she had another son."

Deanna's eyes flashed dangerously and she put her knuckles into her month to contain her anger. She was shaking all over. She felt betrayed and humiliated. She left Danny and ran inside the house.

"Eleanor!" Deanna hurled the name like a knife. "I have to know. Danny, is he the baby I gave up for adoption?" Eleanor turned quickly, sending a vase tumbling to the floor.

"Deanna please, lower your voice," she said with quiet urgency.

"How dare you. How could you have kept this from me?" she said, her voice growing more intense. Eleanor tried to take her hand, but Deanna jerked away. "Leave me alone!" she shouted.

"I won't, not until you listen to me."

"I don't ever want to listen or talk to you again. I hate you, Eleanor. I hate this place and everything in it. I did everything you told me to do and this is how you betray me? Eleanor, you could have told me where he was!" Her body had long ago recovered from the rape, but she would never be healed from this sickness, she felt. Her teeth bit into her lower lip and her body was trembling. Her heart became as cold as her body.

"Deanna, you need to let me explain," Eleanor pleaded.

"Explain what? Explain that you and Rebecca had this arrangement all along?"

"No, it was not like that," Eleanor said.

Deanna threw her hands in the air and stormed out of the house. She was angry and hurt and never wanted to see Eleanor again. She despised her. The anger she had kept hidden deep in her soul began to manifest itself into complete rage. She hated Warren, she hated Eleanor, and she hated herself.

Charlie sat on the front porch of the small house. He looked out over the majestic Smoky Mountains. The red and gold autumn leaves glowed in the afternoon sun and their brilliant colors reflected on the crystal water of the lake. The crisp fall breeze felt like ice as it blew across his chest. He pulled the old red and black wool blanket around his shoulder and crossed his arms for warmth.

Deanna walked across the lawn. The shadows of the trees were long and twisted and there was a heavy smell of autumn in the air, like apples and wood-burning stoves. "Grandpa," Deanna said as she kneeled beside him. He reached in his shirt pocket, took out his pipe, and filled it with tobacco. "Did you want to see me, Grandpa?"

"Yes, Deanna I did." His tone was expressionless and his eyes were weary; he continued to keep his eyes on the mountains. His hair was no longer coal black; now it was the color of blue smoke. His body that once had the strength of a bear was now feeble and old. He lit the pipe and inhaled. The smoke swirled around his old and wise eyes like an early morning fog rising off deep blue pools of water.

"Grandpa, did you know about Danny?"

"Yes. You cannot change what you lived through in the past. The past is the past, don't carry the things that hurt you the most, you have to let go of them or you will be your own problem, Deanna."

"I can't Grandpa, it hurts too badly, and I'm just not that strong," she said as she laid her head in his lap.

"You have to be strong." He looked at her. "You can always find the strength, you just have to look for it, and you have to want it."

"Grandpa, I'm so confused. I feel there is a tornado spinning around me."

"If you want peace outside yourself, you must first find peace within."

"But how do I do that, Grandpa?"

"Deanna there is no such thing as part Cherokee, being Cherokee is not the color of your skin; it is how you think. Being Cherokee is being spiritual and spiritual seeking is like a treasure hunt. You must go to your sacred place and pray. It will help you find the answers you are looking for so you can move forward without making the same mistakes again."

"But none of this is my fault, Grandpa," she insisted.

"Your present thoughts will determine your future. You choose your own path. You can follow the path of anger and bitterness. Or, you can choose forgiveness and walk the path of peace and joy. To walk this path is a great honor but you have to be a person who prays and you must sacrifice."

"I've sacrificed enough."

"You have to offer your past as a sacrifice." Charlie said. Calling her by his pet name, "Wild Honey," he took his hand from beneath the blanket and touched her hair. "Walking the Cherokee path and thinking right is the greatest gift I can give you. It is not who you are that will hold you back, it is who you think you are not. Keep the faith and be strong."

She rose to her feet. "My faith is shattered." She bent down and kissed him on the cheek. "Goodbye Grandpa."

"Goodbye, my little Wild Honey." Tears ran down his wrinkled face as she walked away. He knew he would not see her in this life again.

"Deanna." She turned to look at him and she saw the deep sorrow in his eyes. "There is an old Cherokee saying. 'When the eagles return, the Cherokee will come home.'"

The following day, Deanna was back in Savannah she sat at her desk catching up on phone calls and penciling in appointments. Sarah walked into her office and slowly sat down on the couch. "I'm sorry but can I call you later this afternoon," Deanna said suddenly to the person on the phone.

Sarah was quiet for a moment, Deanna stood up and walked around her desk. She stared at her and Sarah began to cry. The greenish and purple bruises on her face revealed the effect of Jack's heavy hand. Some tears fell but not a down-pour. As Deanna put her arms around her, she whimpered a little more and eventually calmed down.

"Sarah," she said with disbelief. "Did Jack do this to you?" Sarah moved her head and in a very quiet voice responded.

"Yes he did. But, Deanna, he didn't mean to do it."

"What the hell does that mean, he didn't mean to do it?"

"He's just under a lot of pressure at work and having a ready-made family has been hard on him."

"Sarah, he knew what he was getting when he asked you to marry him. Don't make excuses for the son-of-a-bitch. Bring Mathew to my house; you two can stay with me until he gets help or you decide to kick his ass to the curb. But you have to get away from him."

"He promised me he would never do it again. It's just that I made him mad."

"So that's his excuse, you made him mad."

"Everything will be all right. He loves me. He won't do it again. Please don't mention this to anyone. No one needs to know about this."

"Sarah he has brained-washed you. You know it will happen again." Deanna sat bewildered. *How could Sarah have married a snake like Jack?* she thought. "Sarah, a snake can be beautiful but it's still a snake."

Jack's father was a mean drunk with a volcanic temper. When Jack was growing up, there was not a week that his mother did not have bruises on her arms or face. He often told Jack what happened in the house stayed in the house; it was not anyone else's business….

Jack began to isolate Sarah from all her friends, he did not allow her to go anywhere but to work and back. He knew when she left work and timed her drive home and if she so much as looked at another man he accused her of cheating on him.

A week before Christmas she came to work wearing sunglasses and had bruises on her arms and neck. "Sarah, you can't let him keep doing this to you. You have to leave him." Sarah said nothing. "What did he promise you this time? Did he give you another piece of jewelry to show his love for you?"

"He does loves me, Deanna."

"That's not love. That's control and manipulation."

"Yes, and you know so much about love don't you? I don't see a ring on your finger! You don't know anything about our relationship. You don't know what he can be like. He's sweet and loving and almost like a child. He's always sorry when he loses his temper," Sarah said not looking at her but out the window. "We're going away right after Christmas. He's taking me to London for a week," she said, turning to Deanna.

"He's taking you? That's funny, because it seems to me that it's you making all the money. I don't think he can afford that fancy sports car or spending all his time on the golf course on his county check. Sarah, he's using you and controlling you. Hell, he want even let you go shopping with me. He's isolating you from everyone who cares about you. Can't you see that?" Deanna was raising her voice.

"Just drop it, Deanna."

"I wish I could. You have to get away from him before he kills you. You're my best friend in the whole world. I can't just stand by and watch that."

"Deanna, please don't do anything," Sarah pleaded. She knew that would only make him angrier and he would take out his wrath on her. She also knew everything Deanna had said was true. But she could not leave him, he had a hold on her with complete control; she was his property now. He had verbally abused her so much that she lost all self-esteem and simply did not care any longer. But most of all she knew that fatalities sky rocketed when spouses tried to leave their abusers.

IT WAS THE DAY AFTER CHRISTMAS, just two months after her grandmother was buried, Deanna received word that Charlie had passed away in his sleep. It was as though he had willed himself to die. "No, dad, I am not coming home. There is nothing I can do for Grandpa," she said in an emotionless tone. A few minutes later, she hung up the phone. She got dressed, drove out to Tybee Island and took a long walk on the beach.

There were some people on the beach and some boats on the water in the distance. Overhead, soaring sea gulls, bright white against the cloudless blue sky, cried as they flew around her. The waves crashed thunderously, bringing foam to the shore. The sun was warm but the cold salty sea spray chilled her. She pulled her sweater tighter and looked at the sun-spangled water and the white curls of waves.

Her eyes scanned the water near the shoreline. A gleaming gray shape curved above the water for a moment before disappearing beneath it. Deanna stood and shaded her eyes from the sun. Then immediately in front of her, a dolphin leapt from the water, bowed its back, and dived with a splash.

There were five dolphins in the pod. In front of her one surfaced, cleared his blowhole, and then lazily rocked back down into the water. By then Deanna's dark mood had changed. She smiled and looked out at the dolphins that seemed to be smiling back. "When things are at their worst, Deanna, the only thing left to do is smile," she said aloud.

Chapter 15

EARLIER THAT DAY Sarah did not see the back of his hand coming until it struck a glancing blow on her cheek. Then Jack picked her up and threw her against the wall. Her cheek felt numb and the back of her head hurt. She was numb to any emotions – she was not angry, she did not feel fear, she felt nothing.

Jack paced from one end of the room to the other. He muttered curses, profanity, and vulgarity such as Sarah had never heard from him before. It had never entered her mind that he would turn out to be so violent.

"Just once I would like to come home and not have to listen to that little bastard son of yours." Sarah sat silent as she struggled for words. She felt dizzy. Jack moved toward her and then he began to pace again. "You've spoiled him, he's just a whinny little bastard. He needs to grow up."

"He's just a little boy Jack. Don't ever hit him again." Sarah tried to walk past him but he grabbed her arm again. "Turn me loose Jack." Sarah was defiant. He drew his hand back to hit her again but this time she stared him in the eye and jerked her arm free.

THE SUN had gone down and the beach had emptied of the few people enjoying the sixty-degree temperature. After a leisurely walk back to her car, Deanna drove the five minutes to the beach house to deliver Christmas presents to Sarah and Mathew. She held the shopping bags in one hand and knocked on the door with the other. There was no answer but Sarah's Honda and Jack's Porsche both sat in the driveway. She waited a few seconds, and then rang the doorbell. She had just turned to walk away when she heard the door behind her open. It was Jack.

"What brings you all the way out here?" he asked, disinterested.

"I brought Mathew's Christmas presents."

"Sarah is lying down, she's not feeling well." He stood there staring at her.

"Okay, please give her this one; the rest are Mathew's."

"Sure." He took the bags from her hand and started to close the door. That was when Sarah appeared in her bathrobe.

"Come in Deanna," she said, forcing a smile. Deanna looked at her face. It was red and swollen and her cheek had just a bit of blue tinge. She looked at Jack.

"Jack said you were not feeling well."

"Yes, she has had another one of her headaches. She just took something for it. I thought she was asleep." Jack interjected and answered the question for her.

"Where's Mathew?" Deanna asked turning her eyes back to Sarah.

"He's in his room playing," Jack replied.

"I'll take him these presents. I'm not staying long."

"Wait, I'll get him for you," he said as he stepped in front of her.

"That's okay, I'll go to his room," she said staring at him, not backing down. She squeezed past Jack and walked down the hallway to Mathew's room where he was sitting in front of his TV watching cartoons. She bent over and examined him carefully but saw no signs of abuse. Then she saw the hole in the wall. She looked him straight in the eye.

"Mathew, what happened here?"

"I'm not supposed to talk about it."

"Who told you not to talk about it?"

"Jack said what happens in this house stays in this house." She heard the door creak behind her and she swiveled back to see Jack standing in the doorway.

"Mathew, your mother has dinner ready," Jack said. "The hole in the wall is from Mathew. He threw one of his toys against it. Didn't you, son?"

"Yes, Sir." Mathew glanced toward the floor.

"Jack, I don't believe that. If you lay a hand on him, I promise I'll see that's the last thing you do."

"You need to mind your own business," he said as he grabbed her arm and tightened his grip.

"I'm not Sarah; you don't scare me Jack, and if I were you I would think twice before you lay a hand on me again." He loosened his grip, allowing her to jerk free.

Deanna went back to the living room; Sarah was sitting on the couch with Mathew. She was talking to him but her eyes fixed on Jack as he entered the room. "Do you want another glass of wine?" he asked Sarah.

"No," Sarah said still focusing on his every move.

"Mommy, I mean momma, can I open my presents now? I'm not hungry."

"Sure, sweetheart."

Jack poured a glass of wine. He sat beside Sarah on the couch, across from Mathew. He put his arm around her and smirked at Deanna as if saying, "I know you know, but there is not a damn thing you can do about it." Deanna glared back at him; she despised him for his arrogance. There were days she was angry with Sarah for staying with him, but today was not one of those days. She feared for her and needed to get her away from him, but her hands were tied, Jack was right; at this point there was not a damn thing she could do about it.

"Son, thank Deanna for your presents. I'm sure she needs to be going," Jack said with a twisted smile. Mathew walked over to her and put his arms around her neck.

"Mathew, you call me if you get scared," she whispered to him. "My cell number is on this card. Hide it so Jack can't find it." She put the card in his pocket. He smiled and shook his head in affirmation.

"Okay so I guess I'll see you Monday at work. If you start to feel worse will you call please," Deanna said as she squeezed Sarah's hand.

"I will," Sarah said with a half-smile.

She walked Deanna to the door and Jack followed. He opened the door and as soon as she stepped outside, he closed it behind her with a slam. Deanna got a looming feeling that something terrible was going to happen. But there was nothing she could do about it, not until Sarah decided to leave. She felt a knot in the pit of her stomach as she drove away. She called Sarah the next day, and was relieved when she answered the phone.

"Deanna I can't do this anymore. I'm divorcing Jack. He hit Mathew yesterday."

"Oh my God! Is he okay?" Deanna cringed.

"Yes it happened just before you got here. I made up my mind then."

"Sarah don't be alone when you tell him."

"I'm going to the court house first thing in the morning to get an order of protection. Then we're going to stay with Gerald until Jack gets his things out of my house."

The next morning Sarah waited until Jack left the house before she called Gerald to pick up Mathew.

"Mathew poppa Gerald is coming over to pick you up. We're going to be staying with him and Miss Blanche for a few days." She began to pack his clothes. "Why don't you pack some of your toys but you have to hurry he'll be here in just a few minutes."

"Why are we going Momma?"

She sat on his bed. "Come over here little man." She patted the bed for him to sit beside her. "We can't live with Jack any longer. We're going to stay with poppa Gerald until Jack gets all his things out of the house. After that we'll come back." She kissed the top of his head. "Now hurry poppa Gerald will be here soon." He didn't ask questions, he only began putting toys in his sponge bob back pack. "There's the doorbell. Are you ready to go?"

"Yes I'm ready." He took the stuffed giraffe Deanna gave him for Christmas and ran to the door. Sarah followed him with his backpack full of toys and a small rolling suitcase. Before she opened the door she looked through the peep hole.

"Poppa Gerald I'm staying with you for a few days!" Mathew said as soon as the door was opened.

Gerald rubbed the top of his head. "I've got lots of plans for us. We may even go to the pier to buy she crabs for Blanche."

"Yum, she crab soup."

"Thank you Gerald." Sarah hugged him and her eyes filled with tears. "Mathew you be a good little man for poppa Gerald. I'll see you tonight. And save some she-crab soup for me." She bent down and kissed the top of his head.

"I will mommy." He turned back and waved to her as he walked down the sidewalk hand in hand with Gerald.

"Mathew wait you forgot your raincoat." She ran out into the rain and put the little yellow raincoat on him, then pulled the hood on his head. She bent down and kissed him on the cheek. "I love you Mathew." She stood in the rain and watched them drive away.

Sarah wiped the tears from her eyes and called Deanna but it went to voice mail. "Hi Deanna, it's Sarah. Gerald just picked Mathew up. I'm going to pack and then go to the court house for the order of protection. I should be in the office by eleven. See you then." She hung up the phone and began packing enough clothes to last until the end of the week. She was startled when she heard the front door open. Then she heard Jack's footsteps cross the hardwood floor. She hurriedly closed the suitcase and put it in the floor beside the bed.

"Jack what are you doing back?" Sarah said nervously as he walked in the bedroom.

"I forgot my phone. Why are you still here and where's Mathew?"

"Gerald picked him up. They're going to the pier to buy she crabs." She tried maneuvering the suitcase by pushing it with her foot but it would not go under the bed.

"What are you hiding?" Jack said as he walked around the bed and picked up the suitcase. "Where are you going?"

"Jack." She said as she backed away.

"Are you leaving me?" His face was rigid as he grabbed her by the hair. "You whore. Do you think you can leave me?" He shouted and dragged her across the room then slung her to the bed. As he raised his hand to hit her, she kicked him hard between the legs. He grabbed his groin and fell to the side. "You bitch!"

Sarah jumped off the bed grabbing her car keys and cell phone from the dresser. She ran to the front door but before she could get the door open, he grabbed her long blond hair. "I own you. I'll see you dead before I let you walk out on me." He pushed her into the door and pressed his elbow into her back. She winced in pain. "Who is he?"

"I'm not seeing anyone." She tried to turn her face, but Jack still had his hand to the back of her head pressing her face to the door. He removed his elbow from her back and jerked her around. "Jack please. I'm not cheating on you. Mathew and I won't be your punching bags anymore."

"It's that bitch Deanna. She has turned you against me!"

"She didn't have to. You did that yourself the minute you started hitting me. Get out of my way Jack." She dialed 911 but before there was an answer Jack knocked the phone from her hand. He slapped her across the face then slammed her to the floor. He started kicking her in the head and stomach. She curled up in a ball trying to protect her head and face from the force of the kicks. She felt warm blood run down her head and into her eyes. "Jack please stop," she said in a very low weak voice. "Please don't kill me Jack." She began to cry.

"Shut up whore!" Jack raised his foot, swung it back, and kicked her even harder for crying. She went limp and her crying stopped. The room fell silent….

THE RAIN HAD STOPPED and the day was dry and pleasant. Deanna took her time walking down Bay Street, enjoying the morning sun. She stopped at her favorite café for coffee. After talking to the regulars, she walked to the office. She sat at her desk and tried vainly to organize the stack of paper work. She made some phone calls and her thoughts returned to Sarah and Mathew. She tried to get through to her on her cell phone but it went to voice mail.

"Has anyone heard form Sarah?"

"No, but Jack called about an hour ago. He said she wouldn't be in the office today," her secretary answered.

"Carolina, call my clients and move their appointments. I'm going to check on Sarah."

She arrived at the beach house at twelve-thirty in the afternoon. Jack's Porsche was gone but Sarah's Honda has not been moved since she was there three days before. She rang the doorbell but there was no answer. She ran back to her car for the extra door key.

"Sarah are you here?" Deanna yelled. She heard a low moan coming for Sarah's bedroom. Deanna ran down the hall to where the sound was coming from. "Oh my God! Sarah can you hear me?" Deanna sat down on the bed and Sarah winced and stirred slightly.

"Where is Jack?" Deanna asked.

"I don't know."

"I'm calling for an ambulance."

"Deanna please don't; it will just make it worse," she pleaded.

"You're going to the hospital and I'm calling someone to arrest the son-of-a-bitch."

She called 911 but asked them not to dispatch the call over the radio. Her next call was to the newly elected district attorney. He was young and from Atlanta. He did not have ties to anyone in Savannah and had vowed not to become part of the good ole' boys club.

"Deanna, I am so ashamed I let him do this to me. I'm ashamed I stayed with him," she cried into Deanna's arms.

"It's okay. It's over now."

"No, you don't understand. It will never be over. He'll kill me."

Deanna held Sarah's small body. She had not realized how tiny she was. She looked like a little girl in Deanna's arms. She brushed Sarah's long blonde curls away from her face. It was swollen and purple and blue bruises covered one side. Her right eye was swollen shut. She had taken a severe beating from Jack.

The paramedics lifted Sarah into the back of the ambulance and at the same time the district attorney arrived. "Who did this to you?" he asked looking at her.

"My husband, Jack Maynard," Sarah said through tears. "He will kill me. He promised he would and he said no one would ever find my body."

"Where is he now?"

"I don't know."

From inside the house the District Attorney called the county coroner; he was the only one who could arrest a sitting sheriff in Georgia. Gerald and Caroline arrived shortly after the ambulance drove away. Gerald said he would go to the hospital to stay with Sarah while Caroline stayed at the house with Deanna.

She stepped outside where the DA was talking to the coroner. He was in his mid-sixties and except for the years he was away at college, had lived in Savannah all his life. He knew everyone in the small circle of aristocrats. His son and Jack had grown up together and even attended the same college and were star players on the football team.

They stood on the front porch and as the DA explained the situation, Jack pulled into the driveway in his unmarked police car. He had overheard a 911 dispatcher telling one the deputies about the call from his house. "Hey Sam, what are ya'll doing at my house?"

"They are here because I called them," Deanna cut him off. "Go ahead, hit me too. That makes you feel like the big man doesn't it," she snarled at him.

"I don't know what you're talking about," Jack said with a condescending tone. "What's this all about Sam?" he smirked as he turned to the coroner. Sam looked at him and before he could say anything, a blue and silver Georgia State Patrol car pulled in the driveway and blocked Jack's car. The patrolman stepped out of his car. Standing at least six-foot-five, he put his hat on and adjusted the large brim. When it fit just right, he took his mirrored aviator glasses off and put them in his pocket.

Jack sat down on the steps and before the DA said a word, began to tell his fabricated story. "I didn't lay a hand on her," he said. "She's been going through some mental issues. I didn't want to tell anyone so I've been trying to take care of her myself. We had a fight this morning; she started hitting me. I was just trying to shield myself when she fell, hitting her head on the coffee table. I wanted to call the ambulance but she insisted she would be fine. She was afraid the E.R. doctor would have her committed to the mental ward."

"Tell it to the judge in the morning," the district attorney said. He looked at Sam. "Arrest this man!"

"You can't arrest me. I am the high sheriff in this county." The coroner moved closer to him and took the handcuffs from the highway patrol officer. "Wait a minute Sam, you know me! I wouldn't do this, I love my wife. She means everything to me."

"Jack, you're just like your daddy. He was a mean ole' *sonofabitch* too." Jack's arrogance quickly turned to anxiety. In an instant, Jack turned into a coward.

"Turn around, Jack." Sam placed him in handcuffs, and as the cold metal tightened around his wrists, he began to look like a wild animal that had been captured. "Jack Maynard, you are under arrest. You have the right to remain silent, you have the right to an attorney. . . . . ."

Sam nodded to the patrolman, who had been standing quietly with his hand positioned on the gun hanging from his side. Jack tried to jerk away but the patrolman, who towered over him, only gripped him tighter and picked him up off the sandy grass. His feet dangled in the air a few second before the officer put him down. "Looks like you're going to the Cross Bar Hotel, boy." He placed Jack in the back seat. Jack stared straight ahead as the car pulled away.

"We have to get an order of protection for her this afternoon," Deanna said to the district attorney.

"I'll bring everything to the hospital in the morning for her to sign," he replied as he walked to his car.

Deanna locked up the house and she and Caroline drove to the hospital. Gerald was sitting in a corner chair just staring. Sarah's face was blue and swollen and one eye was covered with a bandage. She was sleeping; the nurse said she had given her a sedative about ten minutes before.

"Have you talked to the doctor?" Deanna asked Gerald as she pulled a chair to the bedside.

"Yes. She has a severe concussion and her cheekbone and eye socket is fractured. She has broken ribs but no internal injuries. However, he says she will be okay in a couple of weeks. He's going to keep her here a few days."

"Will she need surgery?"

"No, he seemed too think it would heal on its own. She was damn lucky, Deanna."

The next day the district attorney brought all the documents over for Sarah to sign. "Where is he?" Sarah asked.

"He's in jail in the next county over."

"But he'll get out. What then?"

"He has to go before the judge first to make bail. That will take a couple of days. And the judge will make sure he understands he can't be within a hundred feet of you."

"That won't stop him. Mathew and I have to go away, at least until after the divorce."

After's Sarah release from the hospital, Deanna took her and Mathew to her apartment. She had filed divorce papers at the courthouse and arranged for Sarah and Mathew to stay in Tennessee until the divorce was final. She had rented a condo in Gatlinburg for the two of them. At least there, her brother David and his wife Allison could keep an eye on them.

Two months after Sarah had relocated to Tennessee, the divorce was final. Jack had laid low; no one had seen or heard from him. "Are you sure you're okay moving back into the beach house this soon after the divorce?"

"Yes, Deanna I have to start my life again sometime. I have the alarm system and Jack knows it would be stupid to contact me before he goes to trial, that would guarantee at least five years of jail time. I don't think even he would risk that," Sarah said, half-convincingly.

"Okay, but I'm telling you now, I don't like it one bit. Come here, little man. Here's my number again, you keep this with you all the time and keep this cell phone. This is like the bat phone. You only use it if you get scared," Deanna said as she looked at Sarah.

"Okay Ms. Dee, I will, but who will answer it? Will it be Batman?" Mathew put the paper in his pocket.

"No it will be Batman's assistant and she will call Batman."

Chapter 16

MARCH 1992 - it was her first week back at work, and Sarah was working her way through the mountain of correspondence and files that had accumulated on her desk in the two months she'd been gone. She had taken half of Deanna's caseload to keep her mind busy and off the upcoming trial. But it was still hard for her to concentrate. And even though she tried hard not to show it, the threat of Jack still loomed in the back of her mind. She called Mrs. Williams, Mathew's baby-sitter several times a day to check on him.

Gerald stopped by the office for a minute, and sat across the desk from her while she finished reading a file. He had no children of his own and loved her like a daughter.

"Are you all right Sarah?"

"Yes, I am. And glad to be back at work. I feel like my old self again."

"Keep me posted," he said, still looking concerned.

"I will, I promise. Now go on. Play some golf or take your boat out. Whatever you retired people do," she said, smiling.

"Sarah, I worry about you and Mathew," Gerald said.

IT WAS THE MIDDLE OF JUNE and Sarah finally received word of the court date. It would be less than a week away. She was anxious to get trial over. Even though she had not heard from Jack, the threat of him still loomed over her head.

"Sarah," Caroline said hesitantly. "A letter came for you."

"Okay just leave it on my desk," she said without looking up.

"It has no return address on it and it has been hand written, not typed," Caroline said. "Sarah, it looks like Jack's handwriting and it has been postmarked from here in Savannah." Sarah took the letter and looked at it closely.

"Oh my God. It is his handwriting," she gasped.

"Do you want me to open it?" Caroline asked, still looking at the letter.

"No, I will," Sarah, said looking terrified. "But will you stay?" Caroline sat in the chair while Sarah opened the letter. She opened it slowly as if she was expecting it to explode.

> *… Sarah, I have never stopped loving you and you can't stop loving me that easily. I think about you all the time. I can't eat and I can't sleep. I miss you so much. I know you still think about me. You can never find another man that makes you feel the way I do. Sarah this is not what you want. It's all those people poisoning your mind. If you go through with this trial, I'll have to go to prison for a long time, is that really what you what? Think about this…*

"I have to get home to check on Mathew. When Deanna gets out of court, will you tell her where I've gone?"

"Did he threaten you?"

"Not exactly. He's just trying to manipulate me."

"Should I call someone to meet you at your house?" Caroline asked.

"No, just tell Deanna to call me later."

Sarah drove to the beach house as fast as she could. She ran into the house calling for Mathew. He was in the kitchen with Mrs. Williams; they were baking cookies–they were startled by Sarah.

"Sarah are you okay?" the middle-aged woman asked.

"Yes, but has anyone called here today? Or have you seen anyone watching the house?"

"No."

"Okay, well I'm home for the rest of the afternoon. You can take the rest of the day off, my treat."

"Thank you, but I can stay if you need me to."

"No, we'll be fine."

"Do you need me tomorrow?"

"Yes. I'll see you at eight in the morning."

"I can let myself out." She got her things and as she closed the door, her cell phone rang, distracting her. She forgot to lock the door.

"Mathew, dinner is ready," Sarah called from the kitchen.

"Be right there, mommy." It was pizza. Even though he was hungry and pizza was his favorite meal, he wanted to stay in his room and play.

"Come on, Mathew, it's getting cold."

He ran down the hallway and skidded across the kitchen floor in his sock feet, holding one of his toy cars. He ran the car across the table and made motor noises with his month. Sarah ruffled his hair, kissed the top of his head, and took the car.

"You may have this back after you eat," she said smiling at him. He wolfed down the piece of pizza and ran back to his room.

Sarah watched him from the doorway. He was the light of her life. She wondered how she could have been so lucky to have had him. He was such a sweet little boy, so caring and kind.

"So Mathew, you'll be having a birthday in a just a few weeks and we haven't talked about your party. Or you haven't told me what you want."

"I don't know. Maybe a super-hero party," he said.

"And what do you want for your birthday?"

"I'll have to think about that."

He was playing with the car when he heard Jack screaming at his mother and she was pleading with him not to hurt them. Mathew tiptoed down the hall and saw Jack circling Sarah, who was sitting on the couch. He was waving a gun as he walked in circles. Suddenly Jack's animal-like pacing stopped and he turned toward Mathew. Mathew ran back to his room, picked up the cell phone, and dialed the number Deanna had given him.

"No, Jack, please don't hurt him he is just a little boy," Sarah pleaded with him. "I'm sorry Jack, I was wrong. I'll do anything you want. Jack, please don't."

Mathew heard the sound of Jack's hand as Sarah took the blow across her on face. He sat frozen on the bed. The door made an eerie squeaking sound as it began to open. Jack stood in the doorway, blocking the light, and his long shadow fell across the room. The gun was clenched in his hand and Mathew could see Sarah lying on the living-room floor.

Suddenly Jack turned toward the noise behind him just as Sarah struck him across the face with a fireplace iron. He fell to the floor and Sarah fell against the wall. “Hide in the closet, Mathew,” she whispered in a weak voice. He ran to the closet and closed the door. He hid between the clothes, holding the phone to his ear.

“My mommy needs help; she’s hurt,” he quietly spoke into the phone.

“Mathew it’s Ms. Dee. What’s wrong with your mother?”

“Jack hurt her,” he whispered.

“Mathew don’t hang up. I am going to call the ambulance and the police. Are you safe?”

“Yes, I’m hiding in the closet.”

“Stay there and do not come out.”

Deanna called 911 then ran to her car. “Mathew are you still there?”

“Yes. But hurry I’m scared. Jack has a gun.”

In the car Deanna kept her foot clamped on the gas pedal, growing more worried every second. “Okay, I don’t want you to talk but I’m on the phone. I’ll talk to you and when I get there, I’ll come and get you. Don’t go out for anyone else. Just stay very quiet.”

“Okay, Ms. Dee.”

“Mathew, was that a gun shot?”

“Yes, I’m scared Ms. Dee,” said a very small voice. For a long moment, there was silence. Then she heard the sound of sirens.

“Mathew, don’t talk. The police are there and I will be there in just a few minutes. You stay where you are I’ll come get you out of the closet.”

Deanna was driving recklessly now, praying Sarah was still alive and Mathew would stay safe. She pulled into the driveway behind the police car. Two deputies jumped out of the car with their guns pointed. Jack sat on the porch with the gun still clutched in his hand.

"Drop the weapon and get on the ground," one of them yelled. Jack slowly put the gun on the ground and dropped to his knees. "Lie down on the ground and put your hands behind your head, now!" One of the deputies kicked the gun away while the other placed Jack in handcuffs.

Deanna ran as fast as she could. "Sarah," she called. "Sarah!" She heard gurgling sounds coming from down the hall. She ran toward Mathew's room. Sarah lay sprawled on the floor with a gunshot wound to her chest. Blood flowed from her chest and pooled on the floor. Her breathing was swallow and labored. Her head lolled back, her month slightly opened, her eyes closed, but with some kind of movement behind her eyelids, as if she were searching for a memory. Deanna knelt beside her friend and touched her face. She sat in the floor and placed Sarah's head in her lap. Sarah opened her eyes and followed Deanna's.

"Where's Mathew?' she asked faintly.

"Safe," Deanna said, her eyes filling with tears.

"Promise me you'll look after him, Deanna."

"You're going to be okay. You're going to be fine."

"You're lying. You never were a good liar. I need you to promise me something. Don't tell Mathew who his father is."

"But Sarah someday he will want to know. He has a right to know."

"But Charles Patterson does not have the right to know Mathew," Sarah struggled to get the words out. "Swear to me, Deanna."

"I promise." Deanna looked into her eyes and saw tears as they seeped from them. Sarah gave a slight smile and closed her eyes.

"Where's that damn ambulance!" Deanna screamed. She tried to will Sarah's chest to rise and fall. She still breathed slightly and her eyelids still fluttered. Deanna cradled her in her arms, rocking her back and forth. Sarah's breathing slowed until there was no breath at all. The sound of the paramedics rushing through the door startled Deanna.

"Sarah, they're here," she whispered. Sarah died quietly; she had slipped away like snow in the springtime on a sunny day. Deanna sank over Sarah's lifeless body and began to sob. "Oh no, no, Sarah, you can't leave me. Please God, don't take her, too."

She had trouble bringing Gerald's face into focus. "Deanna, where's Mathew?" he screamed. She looked into his grief-stricken face. Still trying to focus on him, Deanna remembered Mathew was still in the closet. She pulled herself up off the floor.

"Oh Gerald, how am I going to tell Mathew?"

"Where is he, Deanna?"

"I told him to stay hidden in the closet until I came for him."

She slowly opened the closet door. "Mathew it's Ms. Dee. I'm here with poppa Gerald. You can come out now." He peeped from behind the hanging clothes and saw her blood-covered shirt. He looked at both of them with fear in his eyes.

"Where's mommy?"

Deanna could only think of the words her own father had said to her when she asked him that very same question. She picked Mathew up, carried him to his bed, and sat him on her lap. "Mathew, your mommy has gone to heaven to live with Jesus," she said as tears rolled down her face.

"Mommy will like it there, because the church ladies said God lights it with his love and it's a pretty place." Mathew looked at Gerald, then again at Deanna. "Who's going to take care of me?"

"I will, sweetheart. I promise with all my heart I will always take care of you."

Gerald picked him up and covered his face as he carried him past Sarah's bloody body. He drove them back to Deanna's apartment where Caroline was waiting. She met them at the door and they all sat in shock for a long while. Finally Deanna spoke. "I have to make some calls about funeral arrangements."

After calling the funeral parlor, she looked in on Mathew. He had fallen asleep on the floor behind a chair. She lay beside him and wept aloud. After a half hour, she got up and joined Gerald and Caroline in the living room. "You girls are the daughters I never had and Mathew is like my grandson," Gerald said his heart full of grief.

"Deanna, would you like me to stay here with you and Mathew tonight?" Caroline asked.

"Thank you, Caroline I would like that."

At three in the morning, Deanna was pacing the floor inside the small bedroom. Suddenly tears were rolling from her eyes again and she felt overwhelmed by what had happened, both the reality and the unreality of it. She couldn't deal with any of this, but especially Mathew, who could not stop crying.

"It's all right Mathew. It's all right," she whispered to the poor child, who wanted his mother's arms rather than hers.

"It's all right," she repeated even though she knew it was a lie. She was thinking it is not all right. Dear sweet Sarah who had never hurt anybody had been taken away from Mathew for no reason. She kept hearing her voice, the exact sound of it. *Take care of him Deanna and please never tell him who his father is.*

Caroline was standing in the doorway; she had been watching and listening. "I woke you I'm sorry," Deanna said in a whisper trying not to wake Mathew who had just fallen to sleep.

"I was awake," she said in a calm voice as she walked toward Deanna.

"I don't know how to do this, Caroline. I feel like I am holding his sorrow in my hands."

"All you can do now is open your heart to him and love him just as Sarah would. The two of you will get through this; you will survive." *She let such beautiful pearls of wisdom slip from her mouth without even knowing it.* She walked toward Deanna and put her arms around her. They both teared up again in the cramped bedroom.

THE FUNERAL PROCESSION was three blocks long. It turned down the long parkway lined with people paying their last respects. The limousine drove through the iron gates. Deanna looked out at the graves and thought of how generation after generation was buried there. As they pulled to a stop, a church bell began to ring in the distance. They continued on foot across one of the most beautiful old cemeteries in the world. On both sides, magnificent oaks bordered it and moss-encrusted pedestals and statues were scattered throughout. They walked until they came to a small family plot shaded by a large oak tree. Shadows fell across the four graves that lay inside the curbstone, including the newest one. *Life is a mere shadow on the wall of time, fleeting on a cloudy day,* she thought.

Clouds sailed across the sky. She breathed deeply, tasting the salt in the air. The light breeze lifted her hair that clung to her sweaty neck. "Ashes to ashes, dust to dust…" The minister's voice penetrated the shell of numbness and her mind went back to her mother's funeral. *I'm tired of death, I'm tired of funerals, I'm tired of my life falling away one person at a time.* She was sick of all the sorrow and distress that flourished in her soul like foul weeds. *Why?* she raged silently to God. *Why did You have to take her? Why could it not be me? Sarah was the good one; she was kind and gentle to everyone. I'll never bow my head to You again as long as I live.*

That afternoon Deanna touched the gold cross hanging around her neck. She had worn it every day since her grandmother gave it to for her sixteenth birthday. She took it off, placcd it in a silk bag, and dropped it in her jewelry box.

The days after the funeral seemed to drag by. Deanna felt like she was under water trying hard to swim, to make it back to the surface just to breathe. David and his wife Allison had spent the week cleaning the beach house, making it ready for Deanna and Mathew to move back in. They packed up Sarah's clothes and cleaned the bloodstains off the floor. Allison had done grocery shopping and had the pantry stocked by the time the moving van pulled up to the front door.

A week later Gerald and Caroline dropped by with balloons and gifts. Deanna took the cake out of the oven and decorated it with chocolate icing and candy sprinkles. She stretched a banner across the deck with the words Happy Birthday Mathew written across it. Mathew opened his presents one by one and thanked everyone for them. When she cut the cake, he asked for a second plate. He cut a piece of cake and sat it at an empty place at the table for his mother.

The next day David drove back to Tennessee but Allison stayed to help with Mathew until school started. He played with Allison's son and it seemed to keep his mind off things. Mathew started to school in the fall and Allison and her son went back to Tennessee.

Chapter 17

TWO MONTHS had passed since Sarah's death. In the silence, Deanna stretched and tried to gain the strength to get out of bed. Sleep was becoming a battle; she slept fitfully and was awake for long stretches at a time. Mathew didn't cry as often now, but last night he whimpered for hours before finally falling to sleep beside her. *What am I doing, I'm not a mother, I'm too screwed up to raise a kid. He deserves better than me,* she thought looking at his sweet face.

She made a pot of strong coffee and looked down the beach. The morning light was weak and grey and the tide was coming in. She stared out over the water for a long time, before picking up the phone and dialing Dr. Carter's number.

The next day she drove three hours to Athens to keep her appointment with Dr. Carter. "Thank you for seeing me so quickly Dr. Carter," she began. He rose from his chair and walked around the desk to meet her.

"What's going on, Deanna?" He asked directing her to the couch.

"I can't do this. Furthermore, I'm not sure I want to."

"What happened to make you feel this way?" Dr. Carter said, searching her face.

"I don't know what I'm doing. What do I know about raising a child? What if I screw him up as much as I am?"

"Deanna, every new mother feels the same way. And for the most part they don't know what they're doing, either. It's the child that teaches them how to be a mother."

"This is so overwhelming. I'm tired all the time, I never have time for myself and I feel guilty if I just want to be alone or wish things were back to what they used to be."

"It's scary when you realize for the first time in your life you're responsible for another human being; another person who depends on you for support and guidance. That does tend to make one feel a bit overwhelmed." He took off his reading glasses and leaned toward Deanna. "Ask yourself this, Deanna. Would your life be better or worse without this other person in it?"

After her therapy session with Dr. Carter she waded through the next weeks, going without sleep, not eating and trying to give all she had to a little boy who missed his mother terribly. She sat for a long time at her desk, staring at a piece of paper. Since the funeral, some days her thoughts were just empty cocoons hanging from branches in the gray woods of her mind.

"Ms. Guthrie your two o'clock appointment is here." Deanna looked at her watch not realizing it was that late. "Give me about five minutes." She put on her best smile and again pretended everything was just fine.

"Hi, I'm Deanna." She reached out to shake the hand of the middle-aged woman. The woman smiled timidly at her before extending her hand to return the handshake. "Can I get you anything; coffee, water, a soda?"

"Water would be nice," the woman said. She was about forty-five years old and very attractive. Her blonde hair was cut in a straight bob and she was very well dressed. She wore expensive shoes and carried a very expensive handbag. Deanna thought she recognized her from the social pages of the local newspaper. When she introduced herself, Deanna recognized the family name. She was one of the Savannah royals.

"So what can I do for you?" Deanna said as she gestured for the woman to sit in the chair across from her desk.

"Do you do divorce work?"

"I do."

"I need evidence that can hold up in court," she said, looking a little stronger.

Deanna took a pen from her desk, scribbled something, then asked. "What kind of evidence?"

"Evidence, to prove my husband is cheating on me."

"What makes you think he is?" Deanna looked up at the woman.

"A wife has a way of knowing those things. Are you married, Ms. Guthrie?"

"No."

"Then you wouldn't understand." She took a sip of water. "I'm certain he keeps a mistress."

Deanna leaned back in her chair, steepled her fingers under her chin, and studied the woman's face. "If you decide to file for divorce, considering who he is, it will get very ugly, and it will not be cheap." Deanna leaned forward and crossed her arms on the desk. "And if it goes to trial, it will begin with a motion to counter sue. That can take days or weeks. The first day will be scheduled, and then several weeks later the judge will rule. Sometimes a divorce like this one could take years. Are you willing to go through that, and keep in mind your husband will probably try and drag you through the mud?"

The woman sat across the desk from Deanna. She stared out the window. She sat quietly for a moment before she answered. "I've been no more to him than one of his whores. The only difference is that when it is over I walk away with assets."

"If you're sure you're ready, I'll get a private detective on this right away. When we have enough proof I'll file everything at the court house. In the meantime don't tip him off or he'll turn all his attention to preserving and hiding assets or playing other games and in some cases even destroying assets."

"Thank you, Ms. Guthrie."

"I'll call you as soon as I have something," Deanna said as she walked the woman to the front office.

That afternoon Deanna picked Mathew up at school, she had two crab nets and some cotton string in the truck of her car. Obtaining the crab bait was simple, they just visited the fish-cleaning table at the pier. Mathew chose the fish heads he wanted and placed them in the nets. Seagulls swooped past them as they threw their nets off the end of the pier and into the tidal marshes.

She had her Ray-Bans on and was wearing a pair of cut-off jeans and a tee-shirt that read Pirate's Life For Me. She was a part of the beach community by now. The other anglers knew her and Mathew by name and Mathew chatted constantly with all of them.

They hit the crab jackpot and picked crabs for hours. Mathew took them out of the nets and placed them in a cooler. They scuttled around, reaching out their claws, making scratching noises as they climbed on top of one another trying to reach up the sides to get out. Mathew laughed and hit the side of the cooler. "Stay in there and be quiet you little boogers." He hit the side of the cooler again, but it didn't stop the crabs from making nervous rustling noises.

At sunset, they headed home to make her famous crab cakes. Or, at least Mathew thought they were famous. They sang silly songs that Mathew had learned in school while she sautéed the cakes in a pan of onion butter and bay leaves. She took their plates to the deck and about then a neighbor walked over to share a plate of fresh blue fish. That night, after the neighbor left she and Mathew built a bon fire on the beach and counted stars.

Deanna was adjusting to being responsible for another little human being. She seemed to be less tired, although there were still times she questioned her ability. After her session with Dr. Carter, she had filed a petition to adopt Mathew. At first, he was against the idea because he didn't want to change his last name but Deanna explained it would not change the fact that Sarah was his real mother. She told him he did not have to call her anything but Ms. Dee if he didn't want to.

IT ONLY TOOK the private detective a couple of weeks to dig up enough evidence for her wealthy client. Seems her husband had been a busy man. Not only did he keep a mistress he was also seeing other women as well.

"This is Deanna Guthrie. We have the evidence you needed. Can you come in today to sign the papers?" Deanna heard a long sigh. For a moment, she thought the client had changed her mind.

"Thank God," Deanna heard from the phone.

The next day the woman sat at the conference table across from Deanna and Caroline. Deanna slid the folder to her. She opened it and found pictures of her husband with other women. She began to cry and closed the folder.

"This is not the time to get soft or timid, you can't let your emotions get in the way, nor can you stand on the sidelines just crying, wringing your hands, and whining," Deanna said. Deanna's secretary came in the room with a tray of Diet Coke and three glasses of ice. She sat the tray in the middle of the table and quietly left the room. "After whatever emotional response your husband has to the divorce, he will immediately turn his attention to the assets." Caroline poured each of them a glass of cola. "From that point forward, it is business and he will not care what he has to do or say, for that matter." Deanna took a sip of cola. "His attorney will guide him all the way in being devious, clever, and cunning. We just have to make sure we are all those things and more. So, if you're going to walk away with more that the shirt on your back and a small settlement we have to fight as dirty as they will. Can you handle this?"

"Yes, I believe I can."

"There cannot be, and I repeat, 'I believe I can.' You have to go into this battle expecting to come out a winner," Deanna said to her, as she looked her in the eyes. Caroline began to make notes on the legal pad that lay in front of her.

Deanna met with the client a couple more time before a court date was finally scheduled. "We have a court date. It is in three weeks. We go to court on December the second." Deanna got up from behind her desk and walked to the window. She looked out a few seconds, then turned to the woman. "Your husband has changed law firms. He has retained a firm out of Atlanta to represent him. They are high-dollar and known to represent some of the wealthiest people in the state."

"Can we fight them and win?"

"If I didn't feel certain we could, I would tell you to take the generous offer they have put on the table."

IT WAS 9 A.M. the first day of December, Peter Cummings sat on the opposite side of the courtroom. He was strikingly handsome and looked distinguished and all knowing. He wore a dark suit and a sky-blue tie. His hands were perfectly manicured and every strand of his sandy blond hair was in place. He turned his eyes on Deanna. They were the color of clouds on a cold stormy day. She nodded to him.

"Let the games begin," she said under her breath.

By the end of the second day, the judge made his ruling. Deanna's client stood up, hugged her, and walked out of the courtroom a happily divorced woman. Peter's client, on the other hand, was screaming at him. He shook his head in disbelief and stormed out of the courtroom. Deanna tipped her head to Peter and tried not to look jubilant. He returned the look with a touch of amusement. He put the file in his briefcase and snapped it shut. They exchanged a few casual words before she walked out of the courtroom. Deanna decided not to go back to the office; she decided to go to a local bar instead.

After having two martinis, Deanna heard a familiar voice behind her. "Hello, Counselor."

"Peter. I thought you would be in Atlanta licking your wounds by now," she said with an appraising smile.

"No, not yet. But my ego is bruised just a little."

"Just a little? That ego of yours should be in ICU on life support," she said as she patted the empty bar stool beside her. "Sit down. I'll buy you a drink."

"Bourbon, straight up," he said to the bartender. "I've never had a beautiful woman offer to buy me a drink."

"Is that because you're too busy trying to pick them up?" she said, smiling at him.

"You may be right about that."

They talked for a while and Deanna ordered another round of drinks. She suddenly looked at her watch; it was four o'clock. "I didn't realize it had gotten so late, I need to be home by four-thirty. And by the way, I'm sure your ego will be as big as ever by tomorrow," she said as she patted his arm.

"Would you consider leaving Savannah, Deanna?"

"Why?"

"I could use someone like you on my team."

"I don't think so, my life is here."

"At least think about. You could have a very lucrative career in Atlanta."

"See you around." She smiled and removed her hand from his arm.

Peter smiled and watched her walk away. He finished his drink and drove to his condo on Tybee Island. After taking a shower and putting on a pair of shorts and tee shirt he took a beer out of the refrigerator. The weather was still very warm for this time of year. He walked out onto the deck and watched as people walked up and down the beach taking advantage of the seventy-degree weather.

"Ms. Dee can we build a sandcastle before we eat dinner?" Mathew was waiting with his bucket and shovel when she got home.

"I guess we'll have time to do that before it gets dark." She checked her watch it was four-thirty. "Sure give me time to get out of this suit." Deanna dropped her briefcase on the couch.

"Mathew didn't want me to make dinner. He said he wanted your famous crab cakes." Mrs. Williams said as she gathered her things.

"That's fine. See you tomorrow."

Deanna changed into a white sleeveless dress and as she passed through the living room she picked up a lightweight sweater that lay across a chair. Mathew waited on the deck holding the small red bucket in one hand and a yellow shovel in the other. When Deanna stepped out side he leaped up and off the deck then without waiting on her ran to the water. White waves slapped the shoreline leaving streamers of white frothy foam as they were pulled back into the ocean. Deanna and Mathew walked a few hundred yards at the waters edge before Mathew stopped to build the sandcastle.

Peter took another sip of the cold beer and that was when he spotted her mane of long red hair. Its natural gilded streaks glistened in the sun light as it fell like a warm cloud over her shoulders and down over her bare arms.

"Are you following me counsel?" Peter called to her.

Deanna's blue eyes looked at Peter with that laughing hypnotic intimacy that captivated anyone she had ever known. "I was just about to ask you the same question."

"I live here, or sometimes at least," he said.

"I can't believe we live on the same stretch of beach. We're neighbors."

"I thought you lived in town?" Peter asked.

"I did, but after Sarah died I moved to the Island so Mathew could remain in his own home."

"I didn't know you were his guardian."

"He doesn't have any other family and the father is unknown. I'm all he has in this world."

"Seems to me he is one lucky little guy."

"I wouldn't say that, I'm not the mothering kind. But he's teaching me," she said smiling and looking out over the beach where he was building a sand castle.

"I'm sorry about what happened to Sarah," Peter said and meant it. "How are you doing?"

"It's a strange thing, grief. Some days you think it will kill you. And other times, it's okay. And you can never tell which one you will wake up to."

"I guess there's no remedy, except time," Peter said.

"It's been six months since her murder and it's just as fresh today as it was the day it happened." She looked at Mathew. "I can see his strength and it gives me hope for mine. He's six years old and tries to take care of me. He's just like his mother, caring and trusting to a fault."

"Deanna bring Mathew and come to Atlanta, work with me," Peter said comfortably.

"I may surprise you someday," she said easily. But she didn't seem to care one way or the other.

"What are you doing for dinner?" she asked suddenly.

"I'm drinking it." He raised the bottle of beer.

"Would you like to have dinner with us? I make better crab cakes than anyone on the Island."

"I would like that," he said, grateful for the invitation.

"Great. I'll see you in an hour then."

Deanna took Mathew's little hand in hers and they walked down the beach. "Hey counselor," Peter yelled. She turned around putting the sky blue sweater around her shoulders. "I don't know where you live."

"Fourth house up." She smiled to herself. She found she enjoyed talking to him.

He watched her as she walked up the beach. The white cotton dress she wore made her look like a goddess and the blue sweater made her blue eyes pop. He took another sip of his beer and smiled. She took his breath away. She could be the one that caused him to forget his rules. He turned, went back into the condo, and put on a pair of khakis and long sleeve shirt.

Mathew was surprised when Peter stayed for dinner that night. And he was a little uncomfortable with him. "I have a son about your age; his name is Alex," Peter said, trying to draw him out. Mathew was more interested in talking to Deanna, about his day at school and she listened to his conversation as he chatted on about his sand castle. But he did agree with Peter about the quality of her crab cakes.

"I think we should open a restaurant," Mathew said grandly.

"Maybe we should," Deanna said with a smile for him.

After Mathew fell asleep, she joined Peter on the deck with a bottle of wine. She had two glasses and he finished the rest. By then, he had told her about his mother who had abandoned him at the age of two, and how much he loved his grandmother who raised him.

"She worked long hours cooking and cleaning for the Dubois family. During the summers, there was no place for me to go so I would go to work with her. Sometimes I would sneak into the garage. All day I would sit in their cars and pretend they were mine. I knew at a very young age I wanted what they had." It tugged at Deanna's heart to listen to his childhood stories

"When I finished law school, I was hired by the Dubois Firm. I had interned for them for two years and Bernard Dubois never recognized me. He still does not know I was the son of his housekeeper."

"Peter, I didn't realize you were married or had children."

"That's a complicated story," he said looking at his empty glass. "If you have another bottle of wine and care to listen I'll tell you the sordid details of my marriage."

Deanna walked back into the house and returned shortly with another bottle of wine and wearing a pair of jeans and sweater. The air had turned cool after the sun went down. After she filled the two glasses, she sat down in the chair and propped her bare feet on the deck railing. "I have all night and tomorrow is Saturday." There was a childlike innocence about him, which made him very likeable. She felt drawn to him as a person and as a man.

He smiled looking at her red painted toenails propped on the railing. "I worked hard, won cases and billed more hours than anyone else did. Bernard saw in me the same qualities as he. He did not have a single moral fiber and he soon recognized neither did I. I was just as greedy as he was and would do just about anything for money. So needless to say, when he made the offer I agreed to it."

"What was it, if you don't mind me asking?" Deanna was very curious now.

"He offered me the hand of his daughter in marriage and in exchange he would make me senior partner. So I agreed. Two months later, my name appeared in gold letters on the door, just after Dubois.

Deanna took another sip of wine. "That doesn't sound all that sordid. Women have been marrying for money and position for centuries."

"That's not the end of the story," he said. "Margaret, my wife, does not care what I do as long as it stays discreet and out of Atlanta or as long as I don't embarrass her in front of her friends. I'm her trophy husband; I dress and play the part." Peter did not know why he felt safe enough to open up to her. It was something about this woman. She was different from the others. She almost made him want to be a better person.

Deanna fell silent, thinking about what he had just said. She found the story fascinating, but pathetic at the same time. But she liked him even though he did not have a moral fiber in his body.

"So, what about you counselor? Do you have any dirty little secrets?" he asked.

"It's also complicated. I am screwed up, Peter," she said, staring out into the night.

"You can't be more screwed up than I am."

Suddenly the tragedies of her past overwhelmed her and she burst into tears. Peter took his hand and wiped away the tears that ran down her face. This gesture of tenderness undid her completely and she put her head on her knees and sobbed. He sat quietly beside her, every once in a while rubbing her back.

"I'm sorry," she sobbed. The outburst embarrassed her. She sat up and stared out over the ocean. "I'm usually good at keeping this feelings deep down inside of me. My wounds are well hidden." A faint gust of wind blew her long tangled hair from her face. Peter wanted to take her in his arms and tell her everything would be okay. He looked into her face and he saw not the tough take-no-prisoners female attorney, but a little girl, lost and broken.

The words began pouring out of Deanna like water rushing over a broken dam. "My mother died giving birth to my baby brother when I was three. My father remarried. Then when I was sixteen the stepfather of his wife raped me. Nine months later, I had a baby boy whom I gave up for adoption. And here is the clincher: fifteen years later, at my grandmother's funeral I stumbled onto the fact that my biological mother's sister, my aunt, had adopted him. Since I was five years old, I was expected to keep secrets. No one knew about our dirty little secrets but my step-mother and me, not even my father. I was expected to smile and pretend everything was just fine and never let them see me cry."

"Wow! Okay you win, you may be more screwed up," he teased. He put his arm around her and patted her back. She detached herself from his embrace and wiped her eyes.

"You're an ass," she said, hitting his shoulder.

They sat talking in the moonlight for a while longer. "So what do you do for fun counsel, do you go out with friends, do you date?" Peter took another sip of wine.

"I can't imagine myself dating any more. It's too much work. I have Mathew and my career to keep me busy." She had accepted what she believed her fate to be.

"Don't you want to find someone you can love?"

"No."

"Everyone needs someone to love and have someone love them back."

"I don't."

"You're too young to give up on love. Do you want to live the rest of your life alone?" He was talking to Deanna but wondering if he was actually giving himself the advice.

"I did love a man once, but he deserved better than me. And now I have so much anger inside of me there is no room left in my heart for love."

"That's sad, Deanna," he said, looking at his empty wine glass. "I do the same thing. I get lost in my work and make sure I don't fall in love with the person I'm sleeping with. I don't want demands put on my heart." He laughed at the absurdity of their situation. And so did Deanna.

"We're pathetic," she said as she reached over the table and patted his hand.

Peter looked at his watch. "It's midnight. I better let you get to bed." He reached for her hand and helped her from the chair. "Thanks for the company and dinner, milady. Oh and in case, you don't want to go to bed alone we could have a sleepover," he winked.

"Don't think so," she replied.

"Can't fault a man for trying. Think about my offer."

"Which offer, the job, or the sleepover?"

"Both."

"Good night, Mr. Cummings."

Sleep for Deanna was becoming a battle; she was sometimes awake for long stretches at a time. She habitually read for an hour or so in bed, she had learned in law school that legal publications were wonderful sleeping aids. But lately even that did not work. Her mind raced wildly.

After Peter left she sat long into the night looking out the window. She thought about Lucas. Late at night, in the stillness, she missed him the most. David had told her he had settled down and married a girl and was living in Chicago. She wondered if he ever thought about her. As she thought of him, the torment of her unworthiness grew more intense. She poured herself a glass of brandy. She had discovered that a glass or two would help her sleep. She drank the brandy in one gulp and went to bed.

A sudden storm had stirred up the ocean and waves were crashing against the shore. Thunder rattled the beach and the sound of rain spattered against the windows. Except for the occasional burst of brilliant light caused by lightning, the room was dark.

"Ms. Dee, the thunder woke me up. Mommy always reads to me when I can't sleep." he said, standing by her bedside. She pulled the covers back and patted the spot beside her and he snuggled close. "Better?" she asked as she covered him with the blanket.

"Better, but I still want a story." She sighed and got out of bed, but when she returned with a book, he was sound asleep snuggled with his stuffed giraffe.

SIX MONTHS LATER, and after one year of living quietly in the Chatham County Jail, Jack was facing a trial in

August and the possibility of an execution. He had been forced into bankruptcy and did not have money or assets to hire a lawyer. He was given a court appointed attorney. On August 12th 1993, Jack Maynard was convicted of premeditated murder. Two days later the same jury in the same courtroom returned with a sentencing verdict of death by lethal injection.

He was transported to the state penitentiary in Tattnall County Georgia to begin waiting on his appointment with the needle. On September 1st 1993 he first stepped foot on death row and had to adjust to life behind bars.

Mathew was adjusting well to his new life. The adoption was final six months earlier and the child psychiatrist was amazed at his progress. It had been almost a year since Deanna last spoke to Peter. Then one day, like a bolt out of the blue, she made a decision. And the longer she thought about it, it made even more sense. She decided to accept Peter's offer to work at his firm in Atlanta. She would have to settle the cases she was working on and of course ask for compensation until she built her cliental. And certainly she wanted Caroline to be a part of the arrangement, that is if she were open to the idea of moving to Atlanta.

Deanna went back to work after the Labor Day weekend. She shared her plans and Caroline was surprised by her decision, but also excited about the possibility of moving to Atlanta. "I think it will be good for Mathew," she said kindly. "Will you sell the beach house?"

"No, the house belongs to Mathew when he turns twenty-one he can decide what he wants to do with it. Until then we can use it on weekends."

October had been a busy month and they had decided not to accept any new clients. She waited until the middle of November to call Peter. In December, she met with Bernard Dubois. The Atlanta office of Dubois & Cummings occupied two floors of a building called the Towers that sat on Peachtree Street in downtown Atlanta. Its main lobby was marble and bronze. The partner's offices were on the forty-eighth floor. They were large and richly decorated with oak-paneled walls and Persian rugs.

Deanna was escorted by an attractive young secretary down a quiet hallway, to the corner office of Bernard Dubois. They introduced themselves, shook hands and Bernard leered a bit too long at the young woman until the door was completely closed.

"Welcome Ms. Guthrie," he said, sitting in his burgundy leather swivel chair.

"Thank you."

"I spoke with Peter yesterday, twice in fact. He brought me up to date. You have a very nice record. One that I believe will take you a long way here." Deanna nodded and glanced around the office. Bernard was a neat man with an organized desk. He bore impeccably styled gray hair, and wore a dark Gucci suit and silk tie. One hour later, the meeting was over. "Ms. Guthrie, we will draw up the contract. That is, if you are satisfied with our arrangement."

"There is one more thing." Deanna said. "I would like to bring my own paralegal. She's been with me for a while and I believe my record depends a lot on her."

"Okay," Bernard agreed. "Welcome aboard, Ms. Guthrie." He walked Deanna down the hall to the managing partner's office. "This is Deanna Guthrie," Bernard said. Jim

Baker jumped to his feet, buttoned his jacket, and walked around the large mahogany desk. "Well, I'll leave you with Jim." Bernard shook her hand again and left the room.

Jim Baker was in his early fifties; his words and hands were swift, his desk was not as neat and he looked more like an exhausted accountant. He rubbed his hands together as if he did not know what to do with them and Deanna got the impression he was in a hurry. "Alisha will be your secretary; she's in a pool, but the office manager thinks she will do a good job for you. He walked her to the door and to the elevator and pushed the button for the forty-seventh floor.

When the door opened a young woman with a long brown ponytail stood waiting. "Ms. Guthrie?" she asked. Deanna smiled and stepped off the elevator. The young woman extended her hand. "I'm Alisha, I've been assigned to you." She pushed her glasses back. "Follow me, I'll take you to your office."

Deanna followed her down a hallway filled with young lawyers, paralegals, and busy secretaries. She smiled to herself when she thought about the little office in Savannah. Here the phones rang continuously, copiers and faxes beeped and buzzed; this place was a mad house. "Everything is state of the art," Alisha said as they turned a corner. "Here we are. These are your new offices."

"It's very nice," Deanna said. Alisha's desk set in an open area, with a long conference room behind her. A beautifully polished table set in the middle of the room with chairs on each side. Caroline's office was on one side and Deanna's on the other.

Alisha pushed open the door to Deanna's office and flipped on the switch. It had a nice desk and plenty of bookshelves. She walked around her desk and opened the blinds. "Nice view," she said, looking forty-seven floors below at the people and then out over the high-rises.

"Beautiful, isn't it." It was Peter; Deanna turned and smiled at him. He returned the smile and walked to the window. "I have never gotten used to it." He turned from the view and looked around the room. "How do you like the office?"

"It's more than adequate," she said.

"I brought your keys. Come on, I'll give you the tour, and give you the scoop on parking and security." At the elevator, he turned to Deanna. "Now what about that dinner?"

"You win," she laughed.

DEANNA WAITED UNTIL MAY to move Mathew to Atlanta. She did not want to uproot him in the middle of the school year, so he spent the weekdays with Gerald and she drove to Savannah every Friday night and returned to Atlanta on Sunday. By the end of May, Mathew was settled into his new home in Atlanta. They spent the Memorial Day weekend shopping and decorating his bedroom.

Bernard had been very generous with her incentive and she had negotiated a salary increase for Caroline and moving expenses. Included in Deanna's package was a five-year lease on a three-bedroom high-rise near Lenox Square. The package also included five-year tuition for Mathew at one of Atlanta's top private schools, and a driver to take him to and from school. She hired a retired schoolteacher to stay with him from three p.m. until eight o'clock at night. The schoolteacher helped him with his homework and prepared his meal. And if Deanna had a late meeting she would stay until Deanna got home.

Deanna dedicated her free time to Mathew. It was soccer, movies and just about anything else he wanted to do. He was adjusting and looking well and had made friends very easily at his new school. He'd had a good Christmas this year. They had decorated a tree and placed decorations around the apartment. He got tons of toys and he was thrilled when he learned David, Allison and his new cousin were meeting them in Savannah for New Year.

The week they spent in Savannah was bittersweet. The first day was hard on Mathew; he spent most of the day looking through Sarah's things and old Christmas pictures. By the second day, he was playing on the beach. Gerald came over for dinner and on New Year's Eve they shot off fireworks on the beach. Peter called her promptly at midnight as he said he would. They toasted the New Year over the phone.

"Who was that?" Mathew asked as he wandered into the kitchen.

"It was Mr. Cummings from work."

"It's late for him to call about work." She smiled at him.

She enjoyed the quiet days she spent with her family. She enjoyed the warm sun on her face and tasted the salty air again as she took long walks along the beach. The week went by quickly. Deanna said goodbye to David and Allison and promised she would come visit them this summer. "Have a safe trip," she said as she and Mathew waved to them from the front porch of the beach house.

It was their last night in Savannah and Gerald took Mathew to his house. Deanna called a few of her old friends that she had not seen since she moved to Atlanta and met them on River Street. She had on jeans, a tea shirt and wore flip-flops. Her social life was much less formal than it was in Atlanta. After she left the restaurant, she drove straight back to the beach house.

The house was quiet without Mathew's constant chattering. Deanna felt depressed and she felt the familiar loneliness creep in. Nights were agony for lonely people. She walked slowly across the room, and stood looking out at the ocean for the longest time. She poured a glass of brandy, read a little, put on her nightgown, and went to bed. She had just turned out the lights when her doorbell rang. It was midnight; she couldn't imagine who would be there this time of night. She got out of bed, put her robe on, and answered the door.

"Peter, what are you doing here?"

"I wanted to talk to you," he said quietly.

"Okay, come in."

She stood in the moonlight and her satin nightgown softly touched parts of her body he had only dreamed of touching. Her provocative round breasts were half-exposed, covered only by the soft white satin. Covered yet visible, was a glimmer of white flesh and rosebud nipples.

He stood looking at her and closed the door with a gentle push. In seconds, he was kissing her. And without saying a word he followed her to her bedroom. He undressed her and moments later, they were in bed making love before she knew how she had let this happen. Perhaps it was because they were both such rotten people and they found comfort in each other's arms.

"This is crazy, Peter."

"Maybe, but it is what we both need."

"What, sex?" she said and laughed.

"Well, that too. It was pretty good," he said smiling at her.

"This will never work Peter; you're my boss," she said looking serious.

"So what," he said looking unimpressed. "So you are sleeping with your boss. Do you have rules about that?"

"I do have rules about sleeping with married men. I don't sleep with them."

"You just did." Before she could say anything more, he kissed her again and ran his fingers along her body. And this time she wanted him more – no, she needed him. He was like a drug, a soothing drug. They needed each other and clung to each other until they lay exhausted. She fell to sleep lying next to him.

It was nine o'clock in the morning when she awoke. She felt his body against the curve of her back. She lay there until she felt him stir. She sat up and brushed the hair out of her face. "Now what," she said as she lay back, resting her head on his chest.

"I don't know," he said. Once again, he was overwhelmed by a deep sense of contentment that seemed to make time stand still when he was with her.

Chapter 18

THE YEAR WAS 2002 and their long affair had expanded Deanna's world. Every summer when Mathew was in Tennessee with James and Eleanor she and Peter traveled for two weeks. They went to Paris, Hong Kong, Italy, and Africa. They spent weekends in Savannah. He stayed at his condo, while she and Mathew stayed at the beach house. When Mathew visited Gerald, they spent the whole afternoon in bed.

The feelings Peter and Deanna had for each other over the years were officially nothing more than an affair. Deanna had a cold soul and refused to let anyone into her heart. But she needed him; he had become her addiction. Being with him quieted the demons in her head for a little while. He satisfied their hunger for self-destruction.

Peter put his energies in his work, but when he needed someone's hand to hold, or someone to laugh with, it was Deanna. Peter could talk to her easily, he spoke with her about his own life at times, and occasionally, he spoke of his wife and children. It had been years since he and Margaret had been intimate, physically or emotionally. The only thing she was interested in was showing off what his success had bought them.

Neither ever admitted there was more to it. But Peter noticed that when he could not be with her, how much he missed her. More than he would admit. He tried to pull away from her several times, but each time he was drawn back.

She was a blend of hard and soft, vulnerable and strong, serious and funny. She was responsible, a good mother and a loyal friend. She was capable and brilliant in her field and somewhat of a legend in the courtroom. She was fearless and shrewd and a worthy opponent to the most seasoned attorney.

The years had left Deanna harsh and distant and her chilly demeanor had earned her the title of the Ice Princess. However, at the same time, the people she let into her life knew that beneath the tough exterior was a frightened little girl, for whatever reason, running from her past. And to them, she was kind and thoughtful and often spoiled them with expensive gifts.

She had been at the law firm of Dubois & Cummings nine years and it was just after she made partner she purchased an enormous house on Peachtree Battle Avenue, hired a decorator, and got busy on it. The house was a large two-story brick with wide porches and tall white columns. It had tall ceilings and lovely moldings and hard-wood floors the color of honey. The magnificent old home was the trophy she awarded herself in acknowledgment of her success and victories. Her money and her belongings were a measure of her success and self-worth.

IT WAS A SUNNY FRIDAY AFTERNOON in October just about the last of the hot Atlanta weather. Mathew was seventeen and spending the weekend in Savannah with some school friends and one of their parents and Peter was going to a charity event with Margaret. This was one of those rare weekends that she had planned to curl up with books and fashion magazines. She was actually looking forward to the peace and quiet. It was her house that was usually full of active and very loud teenaged boys and girls.

Outside Deanna's office, the elevator opened. A very attractive woman in her early fifties stepped out and walked into the lobby of Dubois & Cummings. Unlike the forty-seventh floor with all its hustle and bustle and young lawyers, the forty-eighth floor was as quiet as a funeral parlor.

Her designer leopard-print heels tramped across the marble floor and the sound echoed through the office. She wore tight designer jeans, a white silk blouse, and several strands of pearls around her slender neck. In one hand, a tiny dog peered from behind the short light jacket that hung off her shoulders like a cape. In the other, she carried a large designer bag. When she reached the receptionist, her gold bracelets jingled when she removed her sunglasses and placed them on top of her head. The sunglasses disappeared into the mass of long highlighted hair.

Deanna was packing her brief case when Caroline walked into her office looking perturbed. "What has got you fired up?" Deanna asked looking amused.

"Do you remember the princess that thinks we are her royal servants?"

"Which one? We have several of them," Deanna laughed.

"True. But this one really is some sort of princess and she is married to the important English banker."

"Oh, yes – that one."

"Well she's at the front desk and her majesty the queen of bitch is demanding to see you."

"Now Caroline, where's that sweet southern charm of yours?" Deanna winked.

Deanna had represented some of the most prestigious wives and more often than not, she made them the richest women in Atlanta. But she was hard and judgmental and was less inclined to bend or compromise and very straight to the point. Caroline was her exact opposite. Her slow, soft voice and indolent, graceful movements disguised a formidable, strong, and resourceful woman. She ruled with an iron fist in a velvet glove and at times, she had a mouth like a sailor. But the two of them made a good team.

The woman stormed into Deanna's office. She was tall, thin, and in very good shape. She had used the best plastic surgeon in Atlanta for a few nips and tucks but not overly exaggerated, just enough to look rested.

"Did you catch him?" She hadn't hesitated to interrupt Deanna.

"I'm sorry Ms. Guthrie, I told her you were in a meeting," Alisha apologized as she ran in the room after the woman.

"That's all right," Deanna said. She was looking stern and somewhat irritated. "Did we have an appointment this afternoon?" she asked still putting things in her brief case.

"No." The woman replied and handed the Yorkie to Alisha.

"Would you like me to make her an appointment for next week?" Alisha asked. She looked at Deanna, not quite knowing what to do with the dog.

"This should only take a few minutes," Deanna said as she sat down behind her desk. "Have a seat," she said to the woman. Deanna looked at Alisha, who was backing out of the room holding the dog away from her as if she was afraid it would urinate. Deanna held back a laugh.

"Did you catch him?" The woman asked again.

"No, he's being very discreet." Deanna glanced at Caroline who was still standing at the door trying hard not to laugh.

"Do you have any idea how many dinner parties I ran for him? How much nice chit-chat I have made. How many hours I have spent in the spa, so I can look like this. I have been the perfect wife. And he is cheating on me!" she said fumed.

"I'm sure if he is cheating on you our private detective will uncover it," Deanna responded.

"I want your full attention on this. And I want pictures," she demanded. "I expect results and I expect them promptly. If you can't handle that, I will find someone who can." She was working herself into a rage, as Deanna sat quietly. Deanna was silent for a considerable time, giving her the slit-eyed stare, tapping her fingertips gently together under her chin.

"Why don't you do that," Deanna said unemotionally.

"What!" she said, stunned.

Deanna leaned back in her chair and folded her hands behind her head. She signaled for Caroline to bring her the file on the case. "I said, why don't you find someone else to do the work?"

"I'm sorry, I didn't mean to offend you."

"You didn't offend me. I just think it would be better if you found someone else to take the case. We're obviously not the right fit for you." Caroline returned holding a file and a list with the names of other attorneys in town. "I highly recommend any one of these attorneys. I think you will be happy with the one you choose," Deanna said as she handed the speechless woman the list of names.

She looked at the list and after a moment handed it back to Deanna. "Sometimes I'm too abrupt. I want you to handle my divorce."

"Okay then, we will call you, when we have something," Deanna retorted. She rose from her chair, walked around the desk and stood by the door with Caroline.

"I'll walk you to the elevator," Caroline said. The woman put her sunglasses on, as she looked Deanna in the eye. She walked out, teed off at Deanna. Caroline let her walk out the door first and before following her, turned around to look at Deanna who was smiling.

"Checkmate," Deanna said with a shameless grin.

"Your bad," Caroline mouthed, before following the woman. The sound of high heels striking the marble floor told Caroline she was already near the elevator. She had to pick up her pace before finally catching up to her just before the elevator door opened. The woman did not say a word, just stepped inside and pushed the button and as the stainless steel door closed, the dog peeked from behind the jacket and yapped.

Deanna was on the phone with Mathew when Caroline returned. "Call me when you get there," she said before hanging up. She looked up at Caroline. "Maybe we should send her husband a bill. He should be paying us or at the very least thanking us," she said jokingly. Caroline laughed and agreed. Deanna picked up the briefcase and her purse. "See you Monday."

She went back to her large empty house at six that evening. She was exhausted and ready for a quiet weekend. She poured herself a glass of wine, heated up leftovers, and added a salad. She turned on the television and flipped through fashion magazines. Mathew called at nine o'clock to say they were at the beach house. They talked for a few minutes and before they said goodnight she reminded him to visit Gerald. She took a hot bath and went to bed early.

The doorbell startled her when it rang at 1 a.m. It rang endlessly. She got out of bed with no idea who it could be. She looked through the peephole and was surprised it was Peter. He was still in his tuxedo.

"Peter, is something wrong?" she asked as she opened the door.

"I just needed to see you." He looked upset and she could tell he had been drinking. "Is Mathew here?" He asked.

"No, he's in Savannah for the weekend."

"I know it's late but may I come in?"

She stepped to the side. "Are you hungry? I can make you something." They walked through the living room and through the dining room to the kitchen. She offered to make him an omelet, which he accepted. He sat staring at her while she got busy cooking and a half-hour later they were sitting at the table talking.

"How much money did the auction raise?" Deanna asked.

"A couple hundred thousand."

"That's a good start."

"I have to talk to you, Deanna," said Peter, not looking at her.

"What about?"

He looked anguished. He closed his eyes and when he opened them again Deanna was looking straight at him. He felt like a jerk but he had no other choice. He stared at her for a long minute as if searching for the right words. "We have to stop seeing each other." She did not say anything. "We have to stop the affair," he repeated. She looked as though she had been shot, then she stood.

"I have to do it, Deanna. Bernard has found out about our affair and he knows you are not just any women. He is threatening to take everything away."

She walked to the door, wanting to say that she understood. "I'm sorry Deanna, but I have to try to make it work with Margaret. I've worked too hard to lose everything now."

"I hope it works out for you," she said as she opened the door. She felt he had hit her with a wrecking ball.

"I'm sorry Deanna."

"You're sorry? Is that all you have to say?"

"I'll call you tomorrow," he said, sounding depressed.

"Don't call me unless it's business. We have nothing else to discuss."

Deanna lay in the quiet dark room. The voices in her head cut through her like a knife. No decent woman would do the things she had done. She tried to push her thoughts back into the dark corners of her mind where she kept the unbearable. She went downstairs for a drink to help her sleep. She took the decanter of brandy to the living room, filled the elegant crystal glass, and tossed the brandy down her throat.

She sipped her third drink and the brandy sent relaxing warmth through her body. The decanter slowly emptied, as did Deanna's usual control over her mind. Peter had not had to convince her to sleep with him. She came alive when he touched her, when he kissed her. She burned at his touch. Her hands held her aching breast. She abandoned herself to the waves of desire and called out brokenly into the empty silent night. "Peter, I need you." She took a sleeping bill and went to bed.

THE DAYS AFTER PETER left seemed to drag. She had grown accustom to being with him, talking to him, and making love to him. She could keep busy in the daytime, but the darkness closed in on her. The nights were so long and she could not sleep the way she ought to. She had only her thoughts for companions. And she didn't want to think, because she could find no answers to anything. How had she gotten into this mess, she asked herself again and again.

It had taken years for them to part ways and she told herself it was better that way, but she was sad anyway. No one else knew about them, so there was no one to talk to, no one to turn to. It took two months for her to make peace with it.

It was nearly Christmas and in the evenings, she busied herself with shopping. She bought lavish gifts for Mathew, for David, Allison and her two nephews; she enjoyed spoiling them. She gave Caroline and her husband the trip to London they had been talking about for the past five years. Her dad was impossible; she searched high and low before giving up. She finally bought a gift that he and Eleanor both could use.

Deanna and Mathew decorated the impressive old home. They went to a tree farm and bought the biggest tree they could find. They had it delivered and spent all day decorating it.

"Ms. Dee, we should invite everyone down here for Christmas. It's our first Christmas in the house and it looks so Christmassy."

"I don't know, Mathew."

"Come on, I'll call everyone."

"Okay, if that's what you want."

"It is."

The Christmas party she was going to that night was at the home of Bernard Dubois. He had invited several important clients and she was expected to be there. She wasn't in the mood for a party and she had been testy and short-tempered for reasons known only to her. She forced a smile as she walked into Bernard's residence. Other than a couple of people, she knew everyone there. Peter stayed close to Margaret, guiding her with his hand at the small of her back away from Deanna and into the other room. Deanna turned her attention to a man standing beside her. She thought she knew him, then she remembered who he was. Gerald had introduced them at a party once. And much to her surprise he remembered her.

"I was very impressed by you when we met." He spoke in a soft southern drawl. He smiled at her and she noticed he was still a very good-looking man. She had no interest in him, but he was easy to talk to. His name was Samuel Williams; he was a financial advisor who had made a fortune on Wall Street for himself and his clients.

"I didn't realize you were a client."

"I'm not. Bernard is one of my clients."

"I'm very sorry, I just assumed you were since almost everyone here are clients of the firm," she responded, slightly embarrassed.

"That's okay. No offense taken," he said with a pleasant smile.

It was ten o'clock when she quietly got her coat and left. She wandered through her house, lonely, but finally going to bed at 2 a.m. She slept fitfully, thoughts like an unexpected storm interrupted dreams. She felt like she was the only single person on the planet and was tired of explaining why she did not have anyone in her life. She tossed and turned before getting up at four in the morning. Mathew was sound asleep when she walked past his room, she smiled lovingly at him and thought how lucky she was at least to have him in her life.

The next day she shopped for Christmas dinner and was more and more regretting having let Mathew talk her into a family Christmas dinner. She had very little contact with Eleanor over the years. And it felt awkward, to spend Christmas with her, but this is what Mathew wanted. He had always tried to be the peacemaker. He did not know what had caused the rift between them, but he could feel the internal stress of it.

Christmas morning Mathew bounced into her room cradling something in his arms. Deanna stared at him looking stunned and a smile spread crossed her face. He walked over to her bed and sat the Maltese puppy down beside her. "Merry Christmas," he said with a proud smile. The tiny white bundle of fur came to life, bouncing and licking her face.

"Oh good Lord, Mathew I can't believe this. What am I going to do with him?" She said picking up the puppy. She held him for a moment and he licked her face again.

"He's very sweet, almost as sweet as me, and I thought he can keep you company when I go away to college next fall."

"I thought you were going to Emory University and move into our guest house out back," she teased.

"I am but I know you'll still miss me."

"You knuckle head." She gently sat the dog down on the floor and he immediately peed. Deanna smiled and shook her head and Mathew was relieved she didn't seem upset. The little dog ran around the room and sniffed at the furniture.

"Thank you Mathew, this is very thoughtful of you." The puppy was only six weeks old and not yet house broken. She would have to roll up all her expensive rugs. Just as she thought of it, the puppy looked up at Deanna, squatted, and peed again.

"What shall we call you?"

"Beau," Mathew said.

"Why Beau?"

"I don't know. It just sounds good."

"Okay, Beau it is."

The puppy spent the rest of the morning in his crate while she prepare the early dinner. He looked at her miserably and whined. After she put the turkey in the oven and prepared the rest of the food, she took him out of the crate. He ran around the house and peed twice before she could get him outside. She let him stay out for the rest of the afternoon and just as she put him back in the crate, the doorbell rang. "Hi, Dad, Eleanor. You're the first to get here but David, should be here in about thirty minutes."

They opened presents that afternoon, ate dinner, and pretended the elephant was not in the room. Eleanor tried to make conversation, but Deanna changed the subject or ignored her altogether. Finally when Eleanor had all she could take, she followed Deanna to the kitchen.

Deanna glanced around the room when Eleanor walked in to see if anyone was with her. She hated being alone with her. This hatred had only gotten worse over the years. Eleanor had tried many times to make amends but Deanna would have no part of it. She held on to her anger like a priceless piece of jewelry, most of the time keeping it safely tucked away and only taking it out on special occasions or when she wanted to make sure it was still there.

"Deanna, I just wanted to thank you for having us today. It was a wonderful dinner and it meant a lot to James," Eleanor said.

"I only did it for Mathew," Deanna retorted. "I didn't want you in my house."

"Deanna, that's a rotten thing to say," David said as he walked into the kitchen.

"It's okay David." Eleanor said. But then she burst into tears.

"No, it is not mother, I'm tired of Deanna's attitude," he said as he looked at her.

"David, let it go. I'm okay and Deanna is only saying what she feels and this is her house."

"Yes, David this is not your concern. This is between Eleanor and me," Deanna snapped.

"Deanna, you're a spoiled brat and you always have been," David said, raising his voice to her. "I've been in the middle of this for years and frankly I am tired of it. Grow up – you're a forty-three year old woman, for God's sake!. Do you enjoy being the most belligerent one in the room every time our family is together? You just make things harder on yourself by your attitude. Why don't you try being a little less antagonistic?" His words were like shards of glass as he spoke, slicing and wounding Deanna. "Come on, mother," he said as he took Eleanor by the arm.

"You don't know what you're talking about David," Deanna screamed. "I hate your guts, Eleanor, and I am sick and tired of keeping your fucking secrets, oh excuse me, our fucking secrets. He hurt me, Eleanor. And I kept quiet because you asked me too."

"Everyone calm down please," James urged as he walked into the kitchen. "We can hear you two all the way out in the living room. This is Christmas, for God's sake. Deanna can you not forget this feud for one day a year?"

"I think all of you should go now," Deanna said with a stone-cold voice. By now, everyone was standing in the kitchen staring at them. Mathew walked to Eleanor, who had continued crying.

"What happened?" he said, looking at Deanna and putting his arm around Eleanor. "Nonie, are you okay?"

A brief silence fell. "I'll be fine, Mathew," she said as she patted his arm. "Will I see you this summer for the Guthrie Fourth of July party?"

"Yes I'll be there. Wouldn't miss it," he said, hugging her. He walked them to the door. When he returned he found Deanna sitting at the kitchen table with her head in her hands. "I'm sorry Mathew," she said as she looked up at him.

"You don't owe me an apology, but you do owe them one." He turned around and walked out of the room. She heard the garage door open and then close again. The house was suddenly quiet and Deanna was left alone with her thoughts. She began to cry. Her sobbing and trembling was gradually overtaken by profound exhaustion. She felt more tired than she had ever felt in her life. She was sitting in her room with Beau curled up beside her when she heard footsteps in the hall. "Mathew is that you?"

"Yes, I'm going to bed now."

Deanna looked in on him later. She would rather have been stabbed as to have him see that side of her. The day was a blur from emotions running high and the anxiety of the family brawl. She wanted a drink more than she had ever wanted anything. She walked downstairs and took the decanter out of the cabinet. She poured the brandy into the glass and took a reviving swallow and immediately poured another. It was that Christmas day that she began to drink steadily. But it didn't stop the pain of loneliness; she missed Peter more than she had expected. She was alone whether she wanted to be or not and no amount of brandy would make it any different. Deanna was trembling from head to toe, but she made her legs carry her to the staircase and climb the long flight of stairs.

SHE SPENT HER TIME AT HOME wandering from room to room, down the stairs and up again. Her soul was tormenting itself like a frail bird whose wings had been clipped; it was hurling itself against the cruel wires of its cage. She did not notice when winter turned to spring and spring to summer. Or when she needed a drink in the afternoon to steady herself. She looked morbidly depressed and thin – and Caroline noticed it.

"Are you all right," Caroline asked one morning as she poured Deanna a cup of coffee. "I'm hearing more sarcasm than normal, more four-letter words and you are pushing people farther and farther away from you."

"I don't know," Deanna said as she wiped her eyes and blew her nose on her hanky. Then she began to cry harder. Deanna looked at Caroline. She trusted her. She had known her for years and she was her best friend. She had not wanted to share this with anyone but now she needed to.

"Peter and I had a long affair and then last fall it was over just like that. I made a horrible scene at Christmas. I threw Eleanor out of my house, my Dad is ashamed of me, and my brother will not speak to me. And Mathew tries to stay out of my way. I have no friends. You are the only person who likes me and I don't know why you tolerant me."

"Did anyone ever tell you that you had a self-destruction streak?" Caroline asked.

"Often," Deanna said as she stood. She blew her nose again.

"It's not Eleanor you hate. You still hate the man that raped you. He's not here, so you direct all your hatred and anger toward Eleanor. Deanna, you have to let it go. You have to forgive him and then maybe you can forgive yourself. Because if you don't you're going to keep hating and building that stone wall higher. And before long you are going to have everyone who cares about you on the outside and it will be just you and that stone-cold heart of yours."

It was quite a speech. But Deanna knew she meant well. She had known Caroline for a long time. If she believed in what she was saying she pulled no punches, but it always came from the heart. And as much as Deanna believed what she was saying to be true, she wasn't ready to forgive or stop hating.

Caroline hugged her. "You'll be okay and you are better off without Peter. There are other single fish in the sea that would be happy to be with you."

"So says you."

"Come on let's go shopping – that always makes you feel better." Caroline smiled at her friend.

Deanna had come so close to defeating herself. *No more. It was time – long past time. No more brandy.* She flung away that crutch and little by little, she got Peter out of her system. Getting involved with him had been foolish and she was angry and disappointed in herself although she sometimes missed what they shared. But she could look at him now without wanting to tear his clothes off. He was an addiction she was glad was over.

Chapter 19

JULY 2ND 2003 it was Mathew's eighteenth birthday she was feeling better and had gotten her drinking under control. It was a Saturday, and on that sunny day, she took Mathew car shopping. They pulled into the dealership in his old Honda he had bought by mowing lawns one summer. And all the while, he never stopped making wild and crazy suggestions about the kind of car he wanted.

Mathew was trying to talk her into a motorcycle, but that was not going to happen. She did, however, promise to buy him the motorcycle on his twentieth birthday if he finished two years of college. They stopped at the Land Rover dealership, which wasn't far from their house. Mathew eyed a white one.

"I like this one," he said. "Look at all the leg room."

That night she surprised him with a birthday party. She had rented his favorite restaurant, hired a DJ, and had invited fifty of his friends. At the end of the night, she handed him the keys to his new Land Rover. It cost a small fortune but this was his eighteenth birthday. It was easy to spoil him, which she did too often.

The next morning she watched him drive away in his new car. He was going to Tennessee as he did every summer. This was the first year she would be spending the two weeks alone. The first day she lounged by the pool and read. The second day she went shopping. When she got home that afternoon, she laid by the pool for a while, then made herself a salad and gave Beau left-over chicken. She went to bed early and watched a movie.

She could not sleep, finding herself lonelier than she had ever been in her life. She lay in the dark for a while, trying to quieten the voices that were reminding her of her failures and mistakes. She took a sleeping pill, because she did not want to dream. Like ghosts, her dreams must be hidden away. Beau snuggled close to her and nudged her arm. The little dog licked her face and she smiled at him. Then the voice faded away and she fall asleep.

Dawn broke open like a wound that bleeds afresh and her loneliness found her again. On her way to the kitchen, she noticed Beau spinning in circles. She opened the door and he ran to his favorite spot in the back yard and relieved himself. He had been house-broken for a few months and she thought now would be as good a time as any to put the rugs back.

Later that day she moved furniture and unrolled the heavy rugs. By nightfall, she felt the aches and pains of her sore muscles, and began to think about her age. She was forty-four years old and knew from other women there were not a lot of men out there for her. Finding one would be like the proverbial needle in the haystack. *So where are all the fish Caroline was talking about?* Thinking about this made her heart sink even lower.

The next day she visited two museums, went shopping and decided to have dinner downtown. She was having dessert when she saw Samuel Williams with Bernard. They finished their dinner and as they walked past, Samuel noticed her. He said good night to Bernard and walked over to her table.

"Are you eating alone?" he asked.

"Yes."

"Would you mind if I joined you for a cup of coffee?"

"Of course not." With a slight gesture of her hand, she gave him permission to sit down.

"So, do you still have the house in Savannah?" he asked her as he sipped his coffee.

"Yes, but I don't get there as often as I would like."

They talked about Savannah for a while and discovered they had some of the same acquaintances in common. Deanna found she enjoyed his company. He was very charming and amusing, a gentleman of the old school. Although, nothing else about him seemed old. She liked him, in spite of herself. She felt some kind of connection with him, she just wasn't sure what. This was something she had not felt since Peter had left. At the end of the evening, he walked her to her car. She was surprised when he asked her if she would like to have dinner with him the following night.

"That would be nice," Deanna responded.

He suggested a new restaurant in Buckhead and told her he would pick her up at seven o'clock. She thought about him on the way home. He was handsome and about ten years older than she. He was polite and pleasant. His wife had died two years before and he was obviously attached to his children and grandchildren.

The following night, she looked at her watch and realized that Samuel was arriving in thirty minutes and she still had to do her hair and make-up. She rushed around her room and when he arrived, she was ready. Much to her surprise, she had a good time. He was a nice man; interesting, intelligent and good company. The evening was everything a first date should be, easy and peaceful.

She was home shortly after midnight. Beau was curled up on the bed, and he jumped up to greet her when she flipped on the light. She changed into her nightgown, scrubbed her make-up off, brushed her teeth, and went to bed. She turned the light out at twelve-thirty and for the first time in a long time, she did not need a sleeping aid. By 1 a.m. she was sound asleep.

She slept peacefully that night and the next day met Samuel for lunch. He surprised her with an afternoon on his boat. And the day after that they flew to New York on his private jet. They had dinner with some clients, went to the theater with some old friends, then flew back to Atlanta the next day. He was polite, courteous, and thoughtful. He loved to travel and had interesting friends. There were differences and similarities between them that intrigued them both.

They spent days getting to know each other and sharing their views on everything imaginable. Deanna enjoyed their conversations. They spent a great deal of time together; they played tennis, went to museums, to movies, and read books. She did not feel the same chemistry she had when she was with Peter, but she did enjoy Samuel's company.

ONE YEAR LATER, the romance between Deanna and Samuel had progressed nicely. "I'm in love with you," Samuel said softly. "I'm leaving for Hong Kong in a few months. I'll be there for a year and I would like you to come with me."

"Samuel I can't do that. I have Mathew and my career, I can't just leave them."

"Mathew is nineteen years old. He does not need you anymore."

"But I need him."

"I want to marry you, Deanna."

"The two of us married wouldn't work out."

"Why?" He brushed his hand against her cheek.

"Samuel," she said softly. "I can't marry you. I don't love you the way you love me." There were many things she loved about him; his kindness, his intelligence, his since of humor and his tenderness. But she did not love him enough to give up her life for him. Atlanta was where she lived and worked. She couldn't give it up, it would destroy the career she worked so hard to build. She loved her house, she had worked too long and had put too much into it just to walk away. She was not ready to make that choice.

"I hope you come to your senses, because I do love you Deanna." He looked at her, but did not kiss her. Instead, he simply walked away.

After he left, she sat down and thought about everything he had said. Perhaps she should come to her senses. She was not getting any younger. But she didn't love him the way she had loved Lucas or he did not excite her the way Peter had. However, she had grown used to being with him. She would miss their conversations and their friendship.

In the weeks after Samuel left, Deanna kept herself busy and in late July, she and Mathew left for Italy. They rented a car and did all the tourist things. They drove from Rome to Naples, then to Capri. They drove back to Florence and caught up with his artist friends from the Savannah College of Art and Design. And more often than not she spent the rest of the trip alone, but she did not mind. She visited museums, churches, and had wonderful dinners. She did on occasion hang out with Mathew and his friends, they looked at art and sculptures, and she enjoyed having them explain the art from an artist's point of view.

She settled Mathew into the flat before she returned to the states. He would be spending the next two months in Italy before returning to school in September. He and his roommates drove her to the airport. She turned one last time and with a broad grin, he waved and then walked away with his friends.

She took her seat in first glass. Part of her wanted him to return with her, and the other part knew he was a young man stretching his wings. He was simple in what he expected of life and unpretentious. He was serious one minute and whimsical and mischievous the next. He always made his own happiness. He told her happiness was like waiting on a butterfly; you may never catch it, so you just have to find your own wings and fly.

Beau was happy to see her when she picked him up at Caroline's house. He licked her face and did not want to leave her lap. He had spent the last two weeks romping with Caroline's two small girls and seemed anxious to get back to his own home. He ran to her bed as soon as she let him out of his crate. That night Deanna wandered around the house; it seemed very large and quiet. She poured a glass of wine, unpacked and did laundry. At nine o'clock she went to bed. Beau made small circles until finally finding the right spot to curl up beside her. They both fell into a restful sleep.

The next morning she put Beau on his leash and went for a jog. The air was hot and humid. When she returned she took a shower in the guesthouse then walked across the slate patio to the pool. She grabbed a bottle of spring water from the small Refrigerator in the covered outdoor kitchen– after taking the first drink she poured the rest of the cool water into a bowl for beau.

She went for a short swim then took a nap by the pool. "Hello counsel." Deanna was awaked by a familiar voice. She opened her eyes and it took a few seconds for her to focus on the tall figure standing over her.

"Peter! You startled me."

"I rang the doorbell but no one answered, then I heard your watch dog back here," he said, sitting Beau down in the chair beside her.

"Hmmm. I need to teach him to bite undesirables, I suppose."

"Am I one of those 'undesirables'?"

"What do you think?"

"Deanna, I've missed you." Saying it, he leaned down and kissed her; hating herself for it, she responded by kissing him back.

"Peter this does not change anything. I'm not going to do this again." He kissed her again and this time when he stopped she was breathless. "Peter, please don't."

"I'm miserable Deanna, I have been since I left. Can you honestly tell me you don't want this as much as I do?" He untied her bathing suit top and it fell to the ground. "Do you want me to go?"

With every ounce of her, she wanted him to leave. He was arrogant, handsome, charming, debonair, and selfish.

But she was incapable of resisting him and she knew it. She wanted him too much.

"I need you," he said. He unbuttoned his shirt, then his pants fell to the patio floor. She lay watching him undress, and knew she was insane to let this happen again – but also that she was profoundly unable to resist him. Their lovemaking was strong and urgent. She had been starved for his touch.

She was furious with herself for what she had let happen and she was furious with Peter, but not enough to make him leave. They made love again but this time in her bed. She rolled over on her back, looked up at the ceiling, and all she could do was laugh.

"Do you know how insane this is? I can't believe I'm doing this again. You're my drug, Peter. Just when I'm clean and sober I take just one more."

He rolled over on his side and looked at her. "Just think how boring life would be without it." Deanna smiled at him. He was so boyish sometimes, and it was hard to stay angry with him.

Chapter 20

JULY 2ND 2005 Deanna stood looking out through the thick glass doors that gave a view all the way to the courtyard. The garden was perfectly tended and the roses she and Mathew had planted years ago added to the beauty of the old mansion. This was considered one the most beautiful estates in Atlanta.

Antiques she had collected over the years filled the house. Paintings adorned the walls and the six-foot mirror she bought in Italy hung over the fireplace. Expensive rugs spanned the full length of the floors. The crystal chandelier she found in Paris sparkled in the bright July sun. Like Deanna, everything about the house stood out. And like her, all the brokenness was safely hidden behind the stone wall that surrounded the estate.

In the far distance, a dog barked, reminding her of the world outside these walls. She took sip of Irish Breakfast Tea, and then turned from the view of the garden. She looked around the room and admired the workmanship of her newly renovated kitchen. Over a period of five years, Deanna had worked on the house and the kitchen was the final step.

She sat down at the custom-built table and ran her finger along the smooth edge of the wood. The weathered planks were previously a part of her grandparent's home. They had been preserved and sanded to a smooth finish. She closed her eyes and took a long slow breath. Suddenly she heard laughter, as light as wind chimes. The laughter was like a familiar song; then the sweet fragrance of honeysuckle filled her senses. Deanna quickly opened her eyes. Coming from the other room, she heard the chime of the antique clock that had belonged to her mother. She smiled and thought she must have nodded off. She sat there a few minutes longer, listening to the single movement of the hands beat to a rhythm, as it counted the minutes before six o'clock. Soon the soothing sound would be replaced by the noisy disturbance of car horns as people hurried to get to work. She took another sip of the hearty rich tea and enjoyed the last few minutes in her safe haven.

Down the hall, the brisk click of tiny toenails scuttling across the hardwood floors broke the silence. Beau scurried through the house and like a cartoon character, skidded across the slippery floor and crashed head-first into her chair. "Are you okay, little guy?" She gently picked up the six-pound bundle of energy and he began to lick her face. "I guess you are. You have to learn to slow down."

She prepared his favorite breakfast. And while he scarfed down every bite of the roasted chicken, she turned on the TV. "It's time to see what's happening in the real world," she told him. She made another cup of strong tea, hoping the caffeine in the deep red Irish blend would be a good start to her day.

The cheerful weather girl on WLXZ "Atlanta's first to bring your morning news" stood in front of a big screen dotted with numbers. "It's going to be another scorcher out there today, folks. My advice is stay indoors if you can. Temperatures will reach 100 degrees in down town Atlanta and with the heat index; it is going to feel 105. The weather map shows no relief in sight. Yes, the 'dog days of summer 'are upon us and it looks like the hot humid weather will be sticking around for the next few days. If you have plans for the Fourth of the July, you can expect hot muggy conditions through the weekend. Now back to you, Kate and Phil."

Deanna turned off the TV and the words reverberated in her head. *"'Dog days of summer.' 'Ye be careful in 'dog days of summer'. The evil waits fer you.'* She closed her eyes, and hung her head in shame. Her memories, and fears stretched before her like a long highway. She had hoped time would have faded the memories but they were as clear as if they had happened yesterday. She could feel the sticky sweat and the taste of salt and the sickening smell of whiskey on his hot breath. No matter the distance between her and the past, she could not escape the torment. She was still haunted by her ghost. This was a sign her demon was stirring.

She was trying to repress the memories when she heard the sudden burst of water and the cry of someone outside her window. She glanced at the clock, it was 6 a.m.; she was surprised someone would be in her back yard at this hour of the morning. Nevertheless, the distraction rescued her from the persistent memories of her childhood. She brushed back a lock of curly red hair, tied her robe, and walked with bare feet across the polished travertine floor.

The sun beamed through the double doors and she could already feel heat radiating through the glass panes. It was the fifth hot day in a row, certainly breaking a record for this time of year. Deanna looked out onto the porch and a whimsical smile crept across the corners of her mouth when she discovered the cry had come from Mathew. He was standing dripping wet with his face pressed against the thick glass panes. She laughed until her sides hurt at his distorted face peering at her through the etched glass. Holding her cup of tea in one hand, with the other she turned off the alarm and opened the heavy glass doors that led out to the courtyard.

"Good morning Ms. Dee" he said as he bounced into the house.

"Mathew I suppose you forgot the sprinklers came on at six, you knucklehead. What are you doing up so early anyway? I didn't think teenagers got out of bed until noon."

"That's true if I were a teenager, but I turned twenty today," he said with a sly grin.

"Oh, really? I forgot all about your birthday," she teased him, as he walked into the kitchen. With the palm of her hand she flipped him lightly on the back of his head, "Wait, I'll get you a towel – I don't want my new floor wet," she scolded. He pulled the wet tee shirt over his head, which made an even bigger mess.

He tried not to track the floor as he tiptoed through the kitchen. "Great, you have food, I'm starvin'," he said, looking in the refrigerator. He poured a glass of orange juice. With one long gulp, he drank the entire glass. He was finishing the last drop when Deanna returned with the towel.

"The contractor was right; this floor was not a very smart choice for children or pets," she said, sneering as she looked at the wet floor and handing him the towel. "So tell me, what gets you out of bed at this hour?"

Mathew took the towel from her and ruffled his dark wavy hair. "I thought I should get started cleaning the pool before it gets too hot," he said, and then paused.

"So what's up Mathew?" Deanna asked, "I know there's more to this." she smiled and refilled his glass and poured a glass of juice for herself. "You haven't gotten up this early since you were ten years old on Christmas morning."

Leaning against the cabinet a childish smile crossed his face. "Since today's my birthday, I was thinking I could have a few friends over tonight."

She stood looking at him with a rueful grin. She turned her head slightly and squinted, as if she was trying to make a difficult decision. "Depends on how many friends and of course no drinking, you know I can't afford a scandal or a law suit. As long as you agree to those terms and oh yes, there is one more thing, I will be staying in my room."

Mathew groaned as he looked at her with his big puppy dog eyes. He knew she would enforce her rules, and it would be easier just to agree with her, but that was not as much fun. "So what did you say you were going to do tonight? Did you say you were going to the movies?" he asked with a mischievous grin.

"Maybe you should clean out your ears; I think you still have water in them. I said, I would be in my room." She smiled when he let out a rumbling groan.

"Are you kiddin' me? I'm twenty years old and I still have to be chaperoned? Why me?" He put his hands on his chest, pretending to be in pain.

"Stop whining, you're too old to whine," she teased. He was full of playful mischief and his childlike behavior made her forget how old he was sometimes. "If you behave I'll make breakfast and let you eat in my new kitchen."

"Okay, you win," he said, putting his empty glass in the sink. He went outside and began cutting the grass.

Deanna watched him through the French doors. Looking at him, she understood why every girl he smiled at always smiled back. He had that all-American boyish good looks. He had his father's handsome features but he had Sarah's southern charm. He had a quick sense of humor. He was also thoughtful, kind, had an old gentle soul, and could always find good in people. Unlike Deanna, he had not become bitter; he allowed his heart to heal. He once told her that every broken heart deserved to be put back together again, but time had shattered her heart into many angry pieces.

Mathew was the one ray of light she had in her life. He brought joy; he made her laugh with his jokes and told her funny stories. To the rest of the world she was cold and calculating. But he always seemed to bring out the best in her. He had reached beyond her empty soul and filled her brokenness like foam expanding into a crack.

She was gazing out the window, enthralled in her thoughts when Beau started spinning in circles; he was letting her know it was time to go out and his bark would not stop until she allowed him to relieve himself. Walking to the door, she glanced again at the clock as the phone rang.

"Hello?" Deanna said into the phone.

"Deanna it's Dad," his voice sounded strained. "I wanted to catch you before you left for work." She looked worried when she heard his voice. She opened the door and Beau ran to his favorite spot in the back yard.

"Dad what's wrong?"

There was a pause, her father cleared his throat. "Deanna it's Eleanor. She's in the hospital and I thought you should know in case you want to come home." His voice broke.

"Dad, you know how things are between Eleanor and me," she said. "I really don't think me being there will change anything for her."

"Coming home is up to you. She's very sick."

"How serious is it that I should be there?" she said unemotionally.

"I've been with her all night and I think she's getting worse," he said choking on his words. He did not have to say anything more; the sadness in his voice told Deanna her illness was serious.

"Okay, if you really think it's necessary. But first, I need to call the office to see if it is even possible to be away for a few days. If Caroline can rearrange my schedule, I should be there by this afternoon."

"Love you, drive carefully sweetheart." His voice was soft. He did not tell her Eleanor was not breathing on her own and had been placed on life support. She had not regained consciousness since yesterday and the doctor was no longer sure she would again.

Deanna stood quietly in the big house on Peachtree Battle Avenue. She had not spoken to Eleanor since that horrible Christmas dinner. She was torn, because as much as her father needed her, she was not ready to forget the past.

She watched Mathew as he cleaned the pool. With all he had gone through, he still chose the path of forgiveness. He allowed his heart to heal and did not become angry or bitter. And once again, she felt the anger building inside her. A scratch on the back door broke the pained silence. She smiled at her little companion as he sat there, patiently waiting for her to open the door.

She had placed a high value on appearance, possessions, and status. However, looking out over the perfectly manicured lawn, she realized that no achievements are enough to take away the pain that often bubbled up inside her. She wished she could have conquered her demons. Maybe the choices she had made would have been different and just maybe she could look in the mirror and like the person staring back her.

She looked at the clock and suddenly remembered the breakfast she had promised Mathew. She reached far back in the cabinet and behind all the newer expensive pans, she found her grandmother's gnarly old black cast-iron skillet. She peeled off five pieces of bacon and dropped them in the hot skillet. As the bacon began to sizzle, she thought back to when she was a little girl. She often sat on a stool in her grandmother's kitchen watching her prepare breakfast.

Mathew finished his shower. The aromas of the greasy feast filled the house and it only took one breath to know Deanna was knee deep in the breakfast she had promised. Occasionally she would cook one of her southern breakfast. She called it "her heart attack on a plate."

After finishing the meat and taking the biscuits out of the oven, Deanna broke three eggs in a small amount of the bacon grease, cooking them over-easy. When they browned until the edges looked like delicate lace she skillfully placed a spatula under them and flipped them without breaking the yolks. Once she began stirring the sausage gravy, Mathew brought out the jams and poured two more glasses of orange juice.

She was adrift, floating freely in her thoughts and unaware Mathew had been standing near her. She smiled when she noticed him, and then taking a generous portion of the delicious food out of each pan, she placed it onto the dinner-size plates. Mathew took two biscuits, covered them with gravy, and took another for later. The two of them sat down and began spreading butter and jam on the flaky biscuits to their liking. Minutes passed before either one of them spoke.

"Mathew, Grandpa called this morning, he said Eleanor is in the hospital," Deanna said with a calm voice.

"What happened?"

"I'm not sure," she said. "But he thinks I should be there."

"I'm coming with you," Mathew was quick to reply. Eleanor had always treated him as though he were one of her grandchildren and he was crazy about her.

"I think you should stay here until I know more. Besides, you have friends coming over tonight. You can come later, if it's necessary," she said.

"Is Eleanor going to be all right?" he asked quietly.

"I think so, but I'll know more when I get there. She's healthy and strong and in great shape. That can't hurt, right?" Deanna looked at him with cool unemotional eyes. She did not want to tell him, but the sound of her father's voice had told her otherwise.

After breakfast, they cleaned the greasy mess and neatly stacked the pans away. "By the way, I have something for you." Deanna brought out a birthday cake decorated with a red motorcycle and two candles in the shape of the numbers

2 and 0. "I was going to cut this tonight, but since I'll not be here we can eat it early," she said as she lit the candles. "Now don't make me have to call the fire department," she laughed thinking of the birthday when he had started a fire on the deck of the beach house.

The feast was still settling in their stomachs and they were too full to eat another bite but neither of them could resist the delectable chocolate. She cut each of them a small piece and placed one scoop of chocolate ice cream on the plates. As she took her seat, she could remember the very first birthday cake she baked for him. Looking at him now it was hard for her to imagine the young man sitting across the table was that little boy. Although watching him dig into the cake, it felt as though time had stood still and he was the little boy that could melt her cold heart.

"When you finish your cake I want to show you something."

"Okay, just one more bite," he said, putting an extra-large piece of the cake in his mouth.

"Now close your eyes," she took his hand and led him down the hallway to the garage. Do you remember what I promised you on your eighteenth birthday? I said when you completed two years of college I would buy you something." She opened the door and found the light switch and the garage lit up. "Happy birthday," she yelled.

Mathew opened his eyes and his mouth gaped open. Under the bright fluorescent lights, illuminating like a neon sign, was a passion red Kawasaki Ninja crotch rocket. He jumped up and down like a kid, then danced around in a victory dance. He threw his right leg across the motorcycle and grabbed the throttle.

"I have something else for you." She opened the trunk of her car and took out two boxes. Mathew studied the boxes and then laughed at the super-hero wrapping paper. Inside one of the boxes was a red and white helmet with a dark tinted shield and in the other a set of red and white leathers. A small tear collected in the corner of his eye as he thought of the first birthday with her; she had given him an action figure dressed in red and white and a red motorcycle. He covertly wiped the tear as it began to run down his cheek.

He took the boxes and returned minutes later dressed in the leather pants and jacket. "Thank you, and thank you for being my mom."

Her heart melted; it was the first time he had called her mom. "You're welcome, my son," she responded with a smile. As she watched him disappear down the street, she did not think of the son she had lost, she thought only of the son she had.

Mathew pointed the bike east and with no particular place to go he slalomed through traffic until he reached the interstate. He was getting the feel of the bike, and with every mile, getting better at it. He was mastering the clutch and unconsciously leaning into curves and swerving in and out of traffic.

A motorcycle is a strange place to reflect on one's feelings but this birthday was dredging up painful memories for him also. His sleep had been broken by hideous dreams, memories really. He was five years old and hiding in the closet. Jack was yelling at his mother then suddenly he heard her screams and the deafening sound of a gunshot...

For the rest of the morning Deanna prepared for the trip to Tennessee. She put on her favorite pair of old blue jeans, a white tee-shirt and pulled her wet hair back in a ponytail. She applied a little mascara, lip-gloss, and wore only a simple pair of small diamond studs in her ears.

She reached for her watch and stared into the velvet-lined box. The phone call from her father had stirred painful emotions and she was drowning in memories. She stared longer into the jewelry box and a particular piece of jewelry came to mind. It was the small gold cross her grandmother had given her for her sixteenth birthday.

She fumbled through the box until she found it tucked underneath some old letters. She took it out of the silk bag, fastened the gold chain around her neck, then gingerly touched the cross. She had not felt the presence of God in years and did not think she ever would again. She wondered that if she had prayed the right way or did all the right things, would God have heard her.

She reached inside the box again and ran her fingers across the letters; she untied the yellow ribbon that held them all together. Tears began to run down her cheeks and she could hardly see the words written on the aged paper. They were from Lucas; she had saved every love poem he had written to her.

Suddenly the image of him standing with tears streaming down his face flooded her mind. She tried to push it out but no matter how hard she tried, it would not go away. She fell in a miserable heap onto the cold marble. Cries like the sound of a wounded animal escaped her; they came from deep within her soul. All the pain she had ever felt in her life had been hidden there, piled and hoarded in that dark place.

She felt the helplessness of her soul; it was lost and tossed like a ship in a shoreless sea and there was no one to rescue her. She felt alone, more alone than she had ever felt in her life. Deanna's fears—long years if them—crashed in on her like a tidal wave. Beau curled up beside her trembling body and nudged her gently. She looked into the little dog's eyes and he stared at her as if he were looking into her soul. Tears flowed like a river down her cheeks and for the first time in a long time, she bowed her head and prayed. Unsure if God would hear her, she let the words pass through her lips.

"If You're there and will listen please rescue me from this place," she said in desperate hope. She lay there cradling the cross in her hand and slowly drifted away from her place of darkness.

Deanna opened her eyes, and leaned against the toilet. Beau still lay by her side; he nudged her arm, and after he was sure she was no longer in the dark place, he ran to the bed. He jumped up on the comforter and made small circles until he found the perfect spot to lie down.

She looked at her watch; she still had a hundred things left to do. She pulled herself from the floor, splashed water on her swollen eyes, and reapplied her mascara. She took some clothes out of the dresser and put them in the over-sized Louie Vuitton bag. Hanging on the bedroom door was a dark Chanel suit still in the clear plastic cleaner's bag. As an afterthought, she grabbed the plastic bag and threw it on the tote. She had planned to wear the suit in court next week for the Benson case.

"Oh, crap, the Benson divorce trial begins Wednesday," she suddenly remembered. This was a high-profile case; Nicole Benson had asked her to handle the divorce and was not going to be happy with any other arrangements.

She finished packing and then called her office. "Deanna Guthrie's office, Alisha speaking."

"Good morning Alisha, what does my schedule look like today?"

"You have only one appointment this morning – a new client – and nothing tomorrow or Friday. Your first appointment is on Monday."

"Oh, that's right, I'm supposed to start my vacation tomorrow. That completely skipped my mind," she laughed. Peter had canceled; he said he was just too busy this year and she decided not to go to the Caymans alone. She canceled the trip however; she had planned to spend a few days in Savannah. Mathew had decided this year instead of going to Tennessee he would spend the time with her at the beach house. He had finished two years at the Art Institute of Atlanta and was planning to move to Savannah in the fall. He had been accepted into the Savannah College of Art and Design. She smiled when she recalled the time a colleague's daughter had mentioned to her that he was modeling nude in one of their classes. When she had asked him about it, he simply said he was not nude. He had a towel over the important part. She was still smiling when she asked "Is Caroline in yet?"

"Yes, I'll connect you."

"I hate elevator music," she whispered to herself as she waited for Caroline to answer the phone.

Caroline sat at her desk looking over the day's appointments. Taking one last sip of coffee, she answered. "Caroline speaking."

"Good morning Caroline. Dad called this morning. He said Eleanor is seriously ill and he needs me to go back to Tennessee for a few days."

"What happened?" Caroline asked.

"I don't know, he didn't go into details, but he sounded distraught. Can you squeeze my new client into your schedule today?'

"Sure, nothing is going on around here today. In fact if you didn't mind I was going to leave after lunch."

"That's okay by me but, before you leave would you call Nicole Benson, see if you can talk her into moving her trial date to the following week. I don't know what's going on with Eleanor. I may have to stay longer than a couple of days."

"Sure, no problem."

"Thanks. I'll see you next week. Oh, there is one more thing, Mathew is having friends over tonight do you think that hulk of a husband of yours could stop by to check on them. You know, make sure no one is drinking."

"I'm sure Jeff wouldn't mind doing that."

When Deanna hung up, she called Peter. As she waited for him to answer, she found herself growing anxious to talk to him. "Mr. Peter Cummings office." The voice was not his, and she felt disappointed.

There was a pause, "This is Deanna Guthrie, is Mr. Cummings in?"

"Good morning Ms. Guthrie, yes he is, but he is in a meeting with Mr. Dubois. Can I have him call you later?"

"Yes, have him call my cell, he has the number," she said simply.

Peter had just turned fifty and Deanna thought he was more handsome now than he was when she first met him twenty years ago. He was tall, quite good-looking. His slightly graying hair around the temples made him even more distinguished looking. He wore a neatly trimmed mustache-goatee. His eyes were still bright and his smile still just as captivating.

"You and Deanna were seen in public again last night." Bernard walked around the room, then turned suddenly and looked at Peter. "One of Margaret's friends saw the two of you at dinner and said it did not look like business." He walked to Peter's desk and picked up one of his business cards and looked at it a moment before speaking. "You embarrassed my little girl, and she said you were not the least bit apologetic when she confronted you." Bernard raised his eyes from the card and looked at his son-in-law long and hard. "Isn't the cute little thing from the employment agency enough for you?"

He walked over to the wall of glass that looked out over the city. He reached his hands in his pocket and thought deeply for a while. "No one can deny she's beautiful, Peter, but I warned you to stop whatever it is you and Deanna have going on. Son, you only remain in this office because I allow it. Now stop the affair. I can take all this back," he reminded Peter. "We had a deal, live up to it."

Peter sat at his desk and watched as Bernard left the room. He had nothing but contempt for his father-in-law but he had no choice but to do as he said. He had made the deal and sold his soul to the devil a long time ago. Peter had everything: education, wealth, he was a senior partner of a successful law firm, and had a picture-perfect family. The worst part of it was that it all felt scripted.

He eased the desk drawer open and poured a tall glass of bourbon from the bottle he kept hidden. He took a long drink and one hour later opened the door; the place was a quiet. His gaze fell to the five foot seven blonde standing before him.

"I'm sorry, what did you say your name was?" he asked.

"Mandy." She followed him back to his office and looked around the large room. "This is an amazing view," she said standing in front of the wall of glass. "Oh, by the way, Ms. Guthrie left you a message. I told her you were busy." *If I play my cards right,* thought Mandy, *he's going to be busy for a long time....*

"I like the view I have better," he said. Mandy turned to face him. Peter took the paper from her hand, crumbled it, and threw the message in the trash. Her smile was suggestive and inviting. The red dress she wore gave tantalizing glimpses of her nipples. She reached for the zipper of his pants, teasing him until she felt his excitement.

He unzipped her dress and it slipped off her shoulder and slid down her body as smooth as silk. There was no bra, no panties, just her gravity-defying young body. As she lay back on the couch she gazed over his shoulder looking at the door she had left ajar. She was a feline, purring as she toyed with her prey, and Peter had no way of knowing the trap she had set.

On the other side of the offices Caroline sat at the conference table with the door shut; the stunning brunette sat across the table from her. Jewels Patterson was in her mid-fifties and looked incredibly youthful for her age. She and her husband were among the wealthiest couples in Savannah.

"I want the house, the vacation home in Tahoe, half his other assets and alimony. I have been married to that cheating bastard for twenty-five years and he's a fool if he thinks I am going to stand by him again," she said as she dabbed her eyes.

"Does he know you're consulting a lawyer?" Caroline asked as she handed her another tissue.

"No."

"Good, it's wise not to tip him off. We'll get our private detective on it right away. He'll slip up, they always do."

Caroline walked her to the elevator. "Thank you for coming in today, Mrs. Patterson," she said as she touched her arm. "And for being understanding. Ms. Guthrie wanted to be here herself but her circumstance just would not allow it. I expect her back in the office next week and she will call you then."

Jewels blew her nose again. "I was told by friends in Savannah she was not afraid to go up against some of the most powerful families. Is that true?"

"Yes, that is true. Don't worry, she is the best divorce attorney in the state. She never misses on winning an argument."

Caroline walked back to her office and made one last call. She called their private detective. "Hey Cliff, I have a case for you. The client's name is Jewels Patterson and her husband's name is Charles." Caroline laughed. "Yes, that would be him, the one and only, Senator Charles Patterson from Savannah. This one is going to get real interesting."

It was almost eleven o'clock when Caroline closed the door to her office. It was ghostly quiet and her footsteps echoed as she crossed the marble floor. Most all the lawyers were on vacation and the partners had decided to let everyone go home early. She was looking forward to spending a few quiet days at home with her family. She had something very special to celebrate this Fourth of July. Her husband Jeff had just returned from an eighteen-month deployment in Iraq. This was his second tour of duty since the attack on the twin towers in New York City.

"Caroline, I have a message from Mr. Cummings," Alisha handed her the piece of paper. "Do you need anything else before I leave?"

"No. Enjoy your Holliday. See you Monday," Caroline smiled. She read the message and walked down the hall to his large office suite. There was no one at the front desk. And just as Mandy had planned, Caroline approached the partly open door leading to Peter's office. She placed her hand on the door, and with little effort, the door swung opened as her eyes swept the room. Mandy kept an eye on her from the couch as Caroline stood staring at their two naked bodies. Then sensing her, Peter turned his head and her eyes met his. He was at a total loss for words. He had never been in a situation like this and he could not imagine anything much worse.

"What the hell!" Caroline screamed at Peter while he stood there with his privates hanging out. He groaned as he fumbled for his jockey shorts. The two women stared at each other. Caroline was the first to speak. "What are you doing Peter?" She spat the words at him. "How could you do this to her?" She picked the amused girl's dress off the floor and threw it at her. "Get dressed before anyone else sees you," she said loud and clear.

Mandy stood up and pulled the dress over her head. She gave no outward sign that she was embarrassed at all by the situation. "This is none of your business," she said with a twisted smile.

"The hell it's not," Caroline said as she turned on her heel and calmly walked out the door. There was no point in adding fuel to the fire, but she wanted to slap both of them.

"Oh my God, I cannot believe this, Caroline," Peter called, struggling to put his jockey shorts on. Grabbing his pants off the floor, he started to run after her. He would have preferred to poke sticks in both his eyes, than to have Caroline catch him in this compromising act. "Stop, please stop. Let's talk." He was shaking when he caught up with her. "Let's go to your office and talk about this," he said nervously.

She held her hands up in front of him, palms out, and backed away. She looked at him like he was speaking in some strange alien tongue, then turned on him again. "Deanna does not deserve this and you certainly don't deserve her, you son-of-a-bitch." Her eyes danced with anger as they shot daggers at him. Suddenly Caroline moved in his direction and struck him in the chest with the heels of both hands. The blow didn't hurt but the truth of the words did. Peter sat down and put his head in his hands. He was sorry it had come to light in this way but there was little he could do about it now.

He was sure Caroline was going to blow the lid off this. He slumped in the chair, totally humiliated. He hesitated for a long moment, thinking of what he was going to say. "Caroline, life takes funny turns; it has a way of coming back and biting you in the ass." The truth was like a bad taste on his tongue. He knew she had no idea what he was talking about, but the deal he had made with Bernard years ago would always come back to bite him. "Please don't do anything yet," Peter pleaded. "Please wait, and let me tell her."

"To hell with you, Peter." Caroline looked as though she would like to kill him. She had a lot to think about and a lot to decide. She had never understood their relationship and wondered why Deanna would waste her life on a worm like Peter.

Peter still had the panicked look on his face as Caroline walked away. He ran his fingers through his hair as he pondered his next move. This was not going to be without its consequences. He thought about Deanna and wished he had not fallen in love with her; his life would have been much easier.

Chapter 21

DEANNA RUSHED AROUND HER BEDROOM for ten minutes as she tidied up and then looked around one last time. Glancing at her watch, she sighed again, knowing it was time for her to go. She picked up her handbag, the oversized tote, latched Beau in his travel crate and slung the suit over her arm. Then she thought about the condescending voice again that had answered Peter's private line.

The voice was as annoying as nails on a chalkboard. She thought it sounded vaguely familiar and had an odd feeling the person on the phone expected her to know who she was. Then she remembered, she had spoken to her before, the voice belonged to the vivacious girl sent over by the employment agency. It was odd that a temporary employee would be answering Peter's phone and it made her a bit uneasy but she quickly dismissed the thought.

She walked through the house and checked the doors one last time. As she made the last pass and turned on the alarm, she wondered if it was a good idea for her to go. She closed her eyes; she felt anger begin to rise up inside her. As hard as she may try she was not willing to let it go.

She secured Beau in the back seat of her car. The Louie Vuitton tote fit next to him in the seat and she hung the suit in the window. She put her black Hermes bag on the passenger's seat beside her and popped an Aerosmith CD in the player. Deanna could not help but smirk when "Dude Looks Like a Lady" blared through the speakers. She was a product of the seventies and the insane distraction of loud music was welcome anytime.

The clock on the dash displayed eleven thirty; it was later than she had planned to leave and it would take four hours to get to the hospital. However, this should still give her plenty of time to check into the hotel and get Beau settled before meeting her father.

She spent the next couple of hours carefully and calmly dissecting parts of her childhood. The sum of these parts had been the defining influence that had the greatest effect on her adult life. As her black sports car sped along, passing SUVs loaded with kids, luggage, and dogs, she thought of her childhood. She began to unravel the threads that held her memories. Strand by strand the complexities of her life became clearer.

Her mind drifted back and her thoughts were of Eleanor. She thought of the look of panic on Eleanor's face the day she returned from the hospital and found her alone with Warren. Deanna remembered the fear in her eyes and the hatred she had as she spat words at him. She wondered why she had not recognized this before. *Strange, the things you remember, individual images collecting in your mind.*

Deanna was still engrossed in her thoughts when Beau began to bark at the vehicle driving along beside her. She had not noticed the youngsters in the van gawking at her and making inappropriate gestures. She gave a strong and noticeable gesture of her own and sped away, leaving them less assertive. Her car picked up speed and raced down the interstate.

Navigating through traffic had been effortless so far and it was to her advantage that she knew most of the hiding places along this stretch of interstate. *Just ahead in the overgrown thicket will be a patrol car trolling for the next speeder.* She checked the speedometer, decreased her speed and as she had anticipated, there it was, the brown and black sedan.

The vehicle was tucked in the overgrown bushes like an eel hiding in a shadowy cranny. It waited there patiently to snag its next prey. She glided past the concealed patrol car and looked back through her rear-view mirror. She grinned as it disappeared in the distance. "Another one bites the dust," she sang, experiencing the same rush she got when she out witted her opponent in the courtroom.

As she traveled farther, the interstate turned into a rolling parking lot. As far as she could see, cars were lined bumper to bumper and side to side. Deanna checked the time; it was three o'clock. She looked over her shoulder to check on Beau. The little dog was content and secure in his crate, snuggled up to his favorite toys. Just ahead, she saw an exit and at the last second, took advantage of a gap between the cars. Maneuvering through downtown Atlanta had made her more of an offensive than defensive driver. She waved at the driver of a minivan who was flipping her off. "Sorry about that," she said aloud as the sleek M5 series BMW glided off the interstate and down the exit.

The heavy traffic had put her behind schedule. "It's a good thing this stretch of highway is now four lanes and straight, at least I can try to make up for lost time," she said aloud to Beau, as if he understood what she was saying. Deanna felt the power of the BMW as she pressed down on the accelerator. Like a thoroughbred racing for the finish line, the car gained speed and passed everything in its path.

Rolling green pastures speckled with cows and horses lined the highway. Pasture scents flooded in through the open car window. It was not long until the foothills of the Smoky Mountains appeared and she saw a dusky cornflower streak in the distance. She was speeding along, as her mind wandered back to a time of growing up here in this rural community.

She came to stop at one of the two traffic lights and as she waited for the light to turn green, her eyes followed the sidewalk to the last of the four remaining historic landmarks. Most of the little town had succumbed to progress but the Guthrie family store still stood as a memorial. The downstairs that had housed the general store was now called Pizzeria Venti, a popular Italian restaurant. The two-story home of Dr. McKinney, who had practiced medicine for 40 years, remained on one side of the original store. The old post office and drug store sat on the other side. Deanna glanced fondly at the old wooded porch and, for a fleeting moment, visualized sitting on a Coke crate listening to tall tales of old men while cigarettes dangled from their lips.

As she crossed the Little Tennessee River and looked out at what is now the Tellico Lake, she could see the Citico Mountains and in all their grander rising high above them were the majestic Great Smoky Mountains. When she looked at the mountains, it was like wearing blue-tinted sunglasses. Their famous Smoky hue was breath-taking. For the first time in what seemed like a lifetime ago, she felt like she was coming home.

Reminiscing and reveling in the view, she did not see the city police car parked behind a large sign reading

"THANK YOU FOR VISITING AND COME BACK SOON." She looked in the rear-view mirror at the picturesque view and that is when she saw the flashing blue lights. The distance between the flaring lights and her car was closing quickly. It did not take but a few seconds for the black and white Dodge interceptor to overtake the BMW. Slowing down, she pulled her car off to the side of the highway. "Well we're screwed, Beau," she said as she took her driver's license out of her wallet.

She looked at her side-view mirror as the officer walked toward her car. He barely looked older than Mathew. As he approached her, she thought she recognized him but she would not know anyone his age. When he reached her car, she handed him her driver's license and car registration.

"Do you know you were speeding ma'am?" the officer asked.

"How fast was I going?" inquired Deanna.

"You were going seventy in a forty-five. Why are you in such a hurry?" He looked at her license and she saw a slight grin form on the corners of his mouth.

The young officer walked back to his car taking her driver's license with him. Beau was looking at her through his wire crate, "Some help you are, why didn't you warn me?" Deanna sighed as she opened a bottle of antacids. She was still chewing the chalky tablets when the officer returned a few minutes later.

"I'm going to let you off with a warning Ms. Guthrie. But slow it down, the mayor will not be so tolerant if I catch you again," he said handing her the license. "Oh and by the way he said to tell you hi and he's sorry about Ms.

Elli." The young man removed his sunglasses and she saw his eyes. She wondered how she had missed seeing his nametag.

"You're Lucas McKinney's son, aren't you?"

"Yes ma'am I am."

"You look like your father," she hoped he did not interpret her reaction as anything other than surprise.

"How's he doing and how are you?" she asked.

"We're doing okay ma'am. It was very hard on dad after mom died, but he's doing okay now."

"Please tell him I said hello."

"Oh you said hello already, he's the mayor." Lucas McKinney the third laughed.

"He's the mayor of White Oak flats?" Deanna looked confused.

"Yes isn't that a hoot?"

"I thought he had his medical practice. How does he have time to be a mayor?"

"After he was elected mayor he gave up his private practice. He found it was just too much work doing both. He takes his position as mayor very seriously."

"So does he not practice medicine?"

"Yes ma'am he does, he just doesn't have his private practice any longer. When the position of emergency room director became available he closed his office and took the director's position. He's much happier; emergency medicine is what he really wanted to do anyway."

FORTY MINUTES LATER she checked into the hotel near the airport. She had enough time to change her clothes and make sure Beau was settling into his new surroundings.

She swept her hair up and away from her face, the way she often wore it, and then dialed Peter's number. His voice mail answered after four rings. She waited another fifteen minutes and called again. Voice mail again. Everything about this seemed peculiar to her. It was not like him to ignore her calls.

The hospital visitor's lot was overflowing, making it necessary for Deanna to use the emergency entrance. She walked with a hurried pace through the maze of parked cars, feeling heat rising from the payment and burning through her three-inch heeled sandals. The white capris she wore reflected some of the heat but the sun unmercifully beat down on her bare shoulders. She could feel droplets of sweat beading on her neck and running down the small of her back. By the time she reached the large glass doors her silk blouse had begun to stick to her. As the emergency doors slid open, she felt some relief from the sultry heat when a cool blast of air hit her face.

A number of heads turned as she entered the emergency waiting room. She glanced down at the Rolex and gold bracelets and felt out of place. Without saying a word, probing eyes said to her what she already knew. East Tennesseans are people watchers and have a good sense of reading people and they have a saying for someone like Deanna. "You ain't from around here, are you?" A little edgy, she remembered that she had spent the first eighteen years of her life here.

She looked around the waiting area. Things had changed since she worked here. Glass walls divided the clerks from patients and their family members. Ambulances had a private entrance that took patients directly to a room so they no longer had to pass through the main waiting area. She looked behind the glass wall and saw a young paramedic flirting with a nurse. She smiled; the paramedic reminded her of the first time she saw Lucas.

The sound of voices getting off the elevator brought Deanna back from her thoughts and that was when she saw him. Dr. Lucas McKinney standing there, was as handsome as the first day their paths had crossed in this exact spot. Other than his slightly thinning black hair, he had not changed and looked surprisingly young. He was tall, slim, and incredibly handsome in the gray suit he wore.

Two nurses stood beside him waiting for orders. Lucas ran his fingers along his jaw as he talked to them. The muscles in his face tightened as he scanned through the chart, and then wrote orders.

Deanna stood frozen, scarcely breathing. Should she speak or turn and run in the other direction? Just as she decided to run for it, Lucas looked up from the chart he was reading. The lines in his face softened. As their eyes met, her breath caught and instantaneously she felt her stomach doing somersaults.

His world turned upside down. There stood the first girl to break his heart and he had not loved that deeply since. His heart started racing. He thought he was over her until she smiled at him. She looked beautiful and delicate and the pale green blouse looked incredible with her red hair. He stood staring at her with ecstasy just as he had twenty-four years ago. There was a moment of awkwardness and then he spoke. “It’s good to see you, Deanna.”

“It’s good to see you too,” she said looking into his eyes.

"So tell me Ms. big fancy lawyer are you chasing ambulances or just happen to be passing through the emergency room?" he joked.

"That would be contingent under certain conditions. Are you still riding on them?"

Lucas chuckled. "No, I'm not riding ambulances anymore; I'm too old for that," he said, still looking into her eyes. "I've been to see James and although he's trying to be strong he's not holding up so well. I know what it feels like, to be in his shoes," he said with empathy. "I don't know what I would have done without Luke. He'll be grateful that you came home; he's going to need both you and David to help him through this."

"I'll stay as long as he needs me," Deanna said.

"If you need me later, here's my phone number." He wrote his personal cell number on the back of his business card and as he gave it to her, his hand brushed hers.

"Thank you," she said softly.

He held back for an instant then without a word put his arms around her. He pulled away from her finally. "It's good to see you," he said again. He watched her walk away and was amazed at how good she looked. She looked better today than she did all those years ago when he had first laid eyes on her. He thought she could not be more beautiful than she was back then, but the years had only made her more stunning.

When Deanna reached the elevator, she turned and looked back at him. "By the way I forgot to thank you for forgiving me my speeding ticket, Mr. Mayor." She smiled at him and then stepped into the elevator. Turning around, she gazed into his dark eyes and could not release herself from his penetrating stare.

Lucas was captivated; he tried to look away but stood frozen, not able to take his eyes off her. He peered into her eyes until she disappeared behind the stainless steel doors. He stood with his heart still racing, terrified of what he was feeling. He had not thought about Deanna in years but, after all this time, seeing her rekindled love in his heart.

It was six-o'clock when the elevator doors opened and she stepped into the hallway. She felt the knot in her stomach begin to tighten; the last time she walked these halls she had said good-by to her grandmother. That was twenty years ago and she still missed her tremendously. She had made the world wonderful and as long as she was there, she could make everything all right. How Deanna wished her grandmother was still here; she would hold her close, and all her troubles would go away. No, she did not want her grandmother to be here. She was glad her grandmother did not know the awful person she had become.

She navigated the long hallways and after making several wrong turns, eventually found the intensive-care waiting room. There was an elderly man, wearing a red volunteer's vest, sitting at the desk. He looked up from his newspaper when she entered the room.

"Can I help ye?" the man said.

"My name is Deanna Guthrie and I'm looking for my father, James Guthrie. Do you happen to know where he is?"

"Yer brother has been lookin' for ye. He asked me to tell ye he's gone back to ICU to see yer mother. But only two can go back at a time. I'll call back there and let'em know ye is here," he said with a friendly East Tennessee smile.

"Thank you," she replied.

"The coffee is makein'. I jest put on a fresh pot, help ye self to it," he said with a thick Appalachian brogue.

Deanna smiled at him. His accent was charming. She remembered her on Scotch-Irish dialect and laughed to herself thinking about the weeks she spent in finishing school and of a very frazzled Mrs. Vivian Cooper. *Miss Guthrie it is pronounced morning, not mornin' and you are going to the store, not fixin' to go the store....*Now all of sudden it made her melancholy to think this old language has nearly disappeared.

She took a white Styrofoam cup from the stack by the coffee pot and poured a cup of the black coffee, then found a chair in the far corner away from the other visitors. She did not dare to smile or even look at them; that would be an open invitation to engage in conversation. Appalachians are talkers and striking up a conversation comes very easy for them.

In one corner of the room, there was an elderly man sitting alone, he looked like his whole world was being taken from him. She was drinking her coffee and still absorbed in her thoughts, when David sat down beside her. His cold hand caused hers to recoil when he touched hers.

"Hi, Deanna, I'm glad you came," he said, looking worried.

"Hi, David how are you doing and how's Dad?" she asked.

"I'm okay, just tired. But I'm concerned about Dad; he hasn't slept since yesterday."

"What happened, David? Dad hasn't told me anything about Eleanor." He hesitated for a long moment.

"She's in critical condition, she's unconscious and on life support." Deanna was stunned. Her father had not indicated Eleanor's condition was that serious.

"Is she going to be okay?"

"It's too soon to tell," David said honestly. "She had a heart attack," he continued. "And no one knows how long she was down before Lucas arrived. They're doing an EEG on her now to check her brain activity." By the time he finished explaining it to her, Eleanor's condition seemed very grim.

"A heart attack, but she was always so healthy. She made sure Dad ate right and they exercised regularly," she said, as though it would change the outcome. "How could this happen?" Deanna fell silent.

"The doctor said it was hereditary."

"Where is Dad now?" she finally asked.

"He's with Mom."

James was sitting at his wife's bedside clinging to her hand as two nurses worked to change the IV and check the monitors. It had been more than twenty-four hours since Eleanor fell unconscious and the doctors has given him little hope for her recovery. They knew by the EKG that her heart had been badly damaged. She was running a high fever and her heart was beating irregularly, and now her kidneys were beginning to fail. Her vital signs were poor and she was wavering between life and death.

"Can we get you anything, Mr. Guthrie."

"No, I'm fine." All he could think about was his wife lying there, fighting for her life.

"Poor man, he's not left her bedside since she arrived in ICU," one of the nurses said.

Deanna was still staring at the wall and David had not said another word. Thirty minutes passed before she turned to him. "David, I'm sorry the way I treated you and Eleanor that Christmas. I don't have any excuses for the way I behaved." She had not spoken to either of them since and David did not respond to her statement.

"Lucas was with Dad the whole time. He even rode in the ambulance with Mom to the hospital. He's a good man," he said, changing the subject.

"Yes, he is," Deanna said, remembering he had given her his cell number. She stepped away and took the card from her purse. Hesitating a moment, she dialed the number. "Hello, Lucas, it's me, Deanna."

"Hi, Deanna, is everything okay?"

What she really wanted to say was that she was sorry for the way she had let it end between them. And that she had picked up the phone a hundred times and tried to dial his number, but at the last moment, lost her nerve. "No change here, I just wanted to thank you for what you did yesterday and for checking on Dad today. That was very kind of you." She just kept it all inside.

"Deanna," he whispered.

"Yes, Lucas."

"I think you should take James back to the hotel tonight. He needs to rest. I don't want two patients. The nurses will call you if there is any change in Eleanor's condition. I'm stopping at city hall for a little while but shouldn't be there more than an hour, and then I'll be home the rest of the evening. I'll check on her throughout the night. By the way I left an order in the pharmacy for James, it will help him sleep." She had just turned his world upside down: He realized time or distance had not weakened his love for her….

"Okay, thank you Lucas," Deanna did not want to hang up, she needed to hear his voice.

"Goodbye, Deanna."

"Lucas," she whispered. There was silence on the other end of the phone.

Chapter 22

THAT AFTERNOON the council meeting ended early. It was a welcome break for Lucas, after such an emotional day. As he was leaving, he saw young Luke in the parking lot. They talked for a little while before he drove home.

EIGHT YEARS EARLIER, when Luke was only thirteen, his mother was diagnosed with breast cancer. It was a battle she lost after two years. When Luke turned eighteen he left for college and Lucas found himself alone in a big house with nothing but time on his hands. He threw himself into his work and spent most of his time with his patients. He tried dating again, but that had not worked out for him, he was not interested in learning the new etiquette of dating.

He felt like a fish out of water. As months passed the yearning to come back to East Tennessee became stronger. He sold the home Luke had grown up in and moved back to East Tennessee. He started a new practice and the first patients were James and Eleanor Guthrie– he quickly became a part of the Guthrie family again. When James offered to sell him twenty acres of his farm, he took the offer, and built an impressive log home in White Oak Flats and began raising horses.

His grandfather had been the town's doctor and mayor until he died some twenty years before, and like his grandfather it did not take Lucas long to become a part of the small community. It was after his son Luke began working for the city that he ran for public office. It began as a dare but he found himself drawn to politics and it suited him well.

LUCAS DROVE HOME from the council meeting that afternoon deep in thought. He was glad Luke had not mentioned Deanna. He had to sort out the feelings that had ambushed him. He sat on the couch staring out at the mountains and found it difficult to think about anything but her. Trying to get her out of his mind was like trying to forget someone he never met. After an hour he changed into an old pair of blue jeans and a tee shirt and headed to the barn.

He saddled one of the horses and rode along the barbed wire, looking for openings in the fence. The sun was beginning to set and the cicadas emitted their sober drone. Their high-pitched raspy call rang through the valley like a circular saw tearing through two-by-fours.

The sun had set by the time he rode back into the barn. This was his favorite time of the day. The relief from the heat paired nicely with the growing silence as the cicadas quit their calling. In the distance, a pair of mockingbirds sang to each other. Their song was like the last smile at sunset. The gentle snorting noise the horse made added to the peacefulness.

He cleaned the stalls and fed the horses, and then took a beer out of the antique Coke machine. He sat down on a bale of hay. Beneath his mellowness was intense heartbreak. As much as he tried, he was not going to be able to save Eleanor; there had been too much damage.

Losing patients was hard to endure but losing someone close to him was even more difficult. He felt helpless; the same way he felt when Lisa had cancer. He took a long gulp of the cold beer and then dialed his phone. He knew the doctor on call would inform him of any change in Eleanor's condition, but he wanted to check on her for himself.

"ICU this is Ms. Gentry," the voice on the phone said.

"This is Lucas McKinney. I'm calling about Eleanor Guthrie. Is there any change in her?"

"No, Dr. McKinney I am afraid not," the nurse said.

"Are the results of the EEG back yet?" Lucas asked, although he was pretty sure what the results would be.

"Yes, sir they are. The neurologist is here now. Would you like to speak with him?" After waiting for several minutes, he heard the neurologist on the other end.

"Hey, Lucas, Yes I have the results and as we feared there is no brain activity," he spoke in a quiet rush of words as if trying to finish quickly.

"Does the family know yet?" Lucas asked.

"Only the son and daughter-in-law, her daughter, and Mr. Guthrie had already left for the night. The son thought it would be best to let his father sleep and tell him tomorrow. I'll go over the results and they can make a decision after that," he said. "I wish it were better news Lucas."

"Thank you," Lucas said and hung up. He sat in the stillness a few moments longer. The only sound in the barn was the hum of the Coke machine and the gentle sound of the horses as they munched on hay. Lucas drank the last of his beer and strolled back to the house.

"Hey, there you are. We grilled steaks. I left you one inside, and there are potatoes in the microwave," Luke said, not taking his eyes off the big screen.

"Thanks, but I think I'll get cleaned up first," Lucas answered. He grabbed a towel and used the outdoor shower. This was a house of bachelors and neither of them were modest about showering outdoors.

The warm water felt good as it ran down his tired body. He looked up at the stars and his thoughts returned to Deanna. He thought about the first time they made love. There was no one in the world like her and even his wife had not made him feel that much of a man.

As he stepped out of the shower, it was obvious he felt like a man again. He quickly stepped back inside and turned on the water. When the cold spray hit him, he let out a scream. The high-pitched cry sounded like a siren wailing and it continued until the cold water discouraged his arousal.

"What was all the screaming about?" Luke asked, when his father joined them.

"Oh that, I forgot to turn the hot water on," he answered with a smile as the image of himself dancing under the cold water flashed through his mind.

For a better part of an hour, he enjoyed the company of Luke's friends. It was about ten-thirty when Lucas said goodnight to his son and the others. As he got ready for bed, he found himself feeling lonely and thinking of Deanna again. He picked up the suit coat he had worn earlier and he could still smell her perfume. He inhaled slowly. He swore that, come what may, he would never let her out of his life again. He loved her from the first moment their paths crossed and now he had been given a second chance. As he lay in his empty bed, he drifted off to sleep thinking of her

BEAU LICKING HER FACE awakened Deanna. She checked her watch; it was 5:30 a.m. Her father was still asleep in the other room. David had convinced him to return with her to the hotel and the sedative Lucas had prescribed was working. She quietly put on her running clothes, put Beau on his leash and went out in the cool morning. It was a beautiful morning. A slight breeze that had started during the night had chased away the humidity.

Along the Appalachian horizon, the emerging sun illuminated the distance hills. As it slowly rose above the mountains, dazzling layers of red, orange, and yellow drifted across the sky. Blankets of mist dispersed around the mountaintops. Wispy smoke-like fog, shades of blue, violet, and deep indigo, hovered over the peaks and valleys of the ancient Appalachian Mountains. It was six-thirty when she returned to her suite. She checked on her father and quietly closed the bedroom door, took a shower, then called David. "Good morning, how are you?"

"We're okay, we sent the boys home last night and Allison stayed with me," David replied, sounding exhausted.

"Dad's still sleeping. I'm not going to wake him, I'm hoping he'll sleep for a few more hours. I'll let you know when we'll be there," Deanna said.

"The neurologist came in last night, he gave us the results of the EEG and it was not good news. Dad is going to have to make a difficult decision in the next couple of days." David choked on his words.

"You mean Eleanor does not have brain activity?"

"No, the only thing keeping her alive is the ventilator," he replied.

"I had no idea," Deanna said with sorrow. She had not expected that. She sat in the stillness as she listened to the restful breathing of her father. After a while, she forced herself to move; she stood up and walked to the window. There were so many questions, to which she did not have the answers. A lot had happened in the past twenty-four hours; it was a lot to absorb.

She could not bear the thought of telling James about Eleanor. Thinking about it, she decided to leave the responsibility to her brother. She needed to talk to Caroline about her new client, but suddenly that did not seem important to her. The words Lucas said repeated in her mind. *"Your dad is going to need you and David to help him though this."*

She evaluated her choice of clothing. The knee-length shorts, white tee shirt, and sandals seem to be appropriate. She looked pretty and young, and as always, very fit. James joined her for breakfast. He had showered, shaved and had put on the clean shirt David had brought him. At seventy-three, he was still a handsome man and was in great shape for his age. He was extremely strong and active, physically and mentally.

"You look lovely today sweetheart," her father said as he kissed her fore head. "Did you get any sleep on that couch?"

"I slept fine," she answered with a warm smile. "How about you?"

"Like a rock. I don't know if I fell asleep or passed out, but I'm fit as a fiddle today." He looked in good spirits as he sat down at the table. "I see you ordered enough food to feed every guest in the hotel. I can't eat all of this," he teased her.

"I didn't know how long it had been since you last ate or what you would feel like eating so I ordered a little bit of everything," she said with a grin.

"Coffee and toast would have been just fine, but I suppose I can't let all this food go to waste," he said as he filled his plate with pancakes and eggs and bacon and added some fruit. Much to Deanna's surprise, he ate a huge amount of what she had ordered. "It's a good thing Eleanor doesn't allow me to eat like this often, I would be as big as a bear," he complained.

"I don't think I twisted your arm," she added, but he looked serious as he glanced back at her. There was little else said during breakfast and by the time they left the hotel they were both in somber moods.

When they arrived at the hospital, James looked at her with the most serious eyes Deanna had ever seen. His silence was a blood-curdling scream of anguish. She held his hand, "We can't do anything about what has happened, but I'm here for you Dad, and I'll stay for as long as you need me," she said, as she squeezed his hand.

He placed his free hand on hers. "Deanna, I know there was a lot that happened between you and Eleanor." He paused. "She told me about Danny." Deanna looked at him in shock. "There was a lot she kept to herself, and I could tell it was too painful for her to talk about, but it was eating her up inside. After we left your house that Christmas she was so upset I finally got it out of her what happened. She told me about Warren and that he had raped you." Deanna turned her head and stared straight ahead. "Eleanor had to come to terms with a lot of things, but the one thing she could not come to terms with was that she asked you to keep the secrets. Deanna, there is a lot you never knew about Eleanor."

"I know she betrayed me, dad. There were nights I thought I could hear my baby cry, then I would remember that I had given him up for adoption. Eleanor knew how I suffered with that guilt and she never told me where he was." Her words were burning hot and crispy.

"Deanna, that was the terms your Aunt Rebecca demanded. She agreed to adopt Danny but didn't want him or you to ever know who he was."

"Did she ever tell him he was adopted?"

"Yes, he always knew he had been adopted. He was happy, Deanna; your aunt and uncle did a good job raising him, and he grew to be a fine man. Eleanor made sure he was well provided for. She set up a trust fund for him and she paid for his education. He's a cardiologist and lives in Ohio with his new bride."

"Did you keep in touch with him?"

"Yes, we saw him from time to time." James looked out the window and after a brief pause turned to Deanna again. "Deanna," he said hesitantly, "last year just before your Aunt Rebecca died, she told him everything. He knows who his biological mother is."

Finally Deanna was able to look at him. "Does he know about Warren?" She dropped her head and her tears were a river running down her cheeks.

"Yes."

When they got out of the car, it was ten thirty. There was not a word spoken between them as they walked the hallways of the hospital. The full impact of what was about to occur was beginning to hit Deanna. And she was growing more anxious about telling her father about the prognosis. Maybe, with any luck at all, the EEG had been wrong and when he saw Eleanor again, she would be out of the coma. It was all she could hope, for her father's sake.

When they reached the ICU waiting room Deanna could see David talking to a group of people. They all stopped and looked at the two of them as they entered. Deanna did not know anyone but the strangers seemed to recognize her. She was glad her choice of clothing was more casual, she felt more at ease with herself as she prepared to meet them.

She smiled and gave a nod as she joined her brother in the center of the crowded room. Deanna did not find it at all odd that so many people were waiting to offer support to her father. This was the way of the South. Southerners think of each other as family even though they are not actually related.

"You must be Deanna," one of the women said as she held out her hand and introduced herself. "I'm Betty," she said with a warm smile. "My husband and I have attended church with James and Eleanor for many years and I know we're not kin, but she's like my own sister. Eleanor spoke of you often, she was proud of you," Betty said as she held Deanna's hand.

Deanna's eyes squinted in obvious confusion the moment she heard this, and Betty noticed it. "I'm sorry," Betty continued, "I'm going on and on about things and I know you want to see Eleanor before visiting hour is over." She patted Deanna's hand.

Deanna did not find herself without words often, but she was speechless by what Betty said to her. She sat down across from David; she looked puzzled, someone had slapped her hard across the face. She had never thought of Eleanor being proud of anything she did. It was one thing for her father to know how Eleanor might have felt but for her stepmother to tell other people was baffling to her.

"Deanna, are you alright?" Allison asked. Her face was ghostly pale and Allison thought she might pass out. "Would you like me to get you something to drink?"

"No, thank you," Deanna said softly. "I was just thinking how little I know about Eleanor," she said, looking preoccupied. Allison touched her hand in response.

A young man dressed in casual clothes and wearing a white lab coat over them entered the waiting room. He spoke to the volunteer sitting at the front desk. He turned around and scanned the room, and when he saw David, he walked in his direction. She could see his name on the lab coat; it was the neurologist, and she was surprised at how young he looked. He was talking to David when James returned from ICU.

She could tell by the look on her father's face that there had been no change in Eleanor's condition. He walked slowly across the room and found an empty chair away from Deanna and the others. He began to sob. It had been two days since Eleanor's heart attack, and he finally allowed himself to release his emotions. He had remained hopeful until now, but seeing her this morning James knew his wife's situation had become less hopeful. Her condition had gotten the best of her; she was deep in the coma. At this stage, he could only grieve.

Everyone allowed James his privacy and the doctor told David he would let him have a few minutes before they met. Fifteen minutes passed before James could utter a word. He took a white handkerchief out of his shirt pocket and began to unfold the perfectly pressed cloth. He wiped his eyes. "Eleanor always made sure I had a clean ironed handkerchief. She would say to me, grown men do cry." James cleared his throat and refolded the wadded handkerchief he had in his hand.

He was sitting in the same chair when the neurologist returned and broke into David's conversation. James looked at the young doctor in pained silence and felt helpless as a baby. "Where are they going?" he asked Deanna in a low voice. Then as she touched his hand, he understood. The doctor was waiting for them in the hallway. He led them into a private lounge.

"Mr. Guthrie, the EEG shows no brain activity," the doctor said with compassion.

"What does that mean?" James asked, trembling from head to toe.

"I'm sorry Mr. Guthrie, she will never wake up from the coma." He did not pull any punches. "It's impossible to tell how long she'll survive like this. It could be days or even weeks, but her vital signs are growing weaker and her kidneys are shutting down." He paused to give his words time to sink in. "Mr. Guthrie, we need you to make a decision. We can put her on dialysis if you wish, but she's too compromised; it will only prolong her life, not save it." He paused again and looked at all of them. "Alternatively, we can take her off the ventilator and let the natural progression take place," he said, placing his hand on James's shoulder.

There was a long silence. The neurologist confirmed what they already knew, more or less, and James thought prolonging her life would attack the dignity of his wife. She would not want to lie in bed like a living corpse. He looked at the neurologist and cleared his throat. "Eleanor would not want this. I can't put her on dialysis," James said finally. Again, his eyes swelled with a sea of tears.

"I'm sorry, Mr. Guthrie," the doctor paused. "Given the grave nature of things and if this were my wife I would make the same decision."

They stepped out of the room. "We can disconnect the ventilator when you're ready. Take as long as you need to say goodbye to your wife. You can let me know tomorrow and we'll set up the time. In the meantime I have arranged for a cot to be brought to her room."

James nodded, thanked the doctor, and walked down the long hallway to ICU. When he reached her door, he wished as he did every time that he would find a change on the other side.

With all that had happened over the past twenty-four hours, Deanna had forgotten to call Caroline. She suddenly remembered she needed to ask her about a new court date for the Benson case. Then she thought of Mathew; he would need to know about Eleanor. She took a sip of coffee to still herself before making the calls.

She called Caroline first; the phone rang several times before there was an answer. Deanna closed her eyes when she heard the recording; she had forgotten the next day was the Fourth of July. That was one of her father's and Eleanor's favorite holidays.

Before she dialed Mathew's number, her phone rang. "Deanna, it's Caroline," she said sounding concerned. "I'm afraid there is something I need to tell you. I'm sorry, this is very awkward." She paused. There was no easy way of saying what had to be said.

"Caroline what on earth is it? Has something happened at work?"

Caroline did not answer her right away; she chose her words carefully. It was questionable she would keep her job after this, but it would be almost worth it for Deanna's sake. After a pause, she lost her nerve. "It can wait. How are things there?"

"Things are not going well. Eleanor is on a ventilator, the neurologist told us she will never come out of the coma and Dad has decided to take her off life support. I'll not be in the office Tuesday. Did you speak to Nicole about postponing her case?"

"Yes, and at first it was futile to try to change her mind– she has the flexibility of a steel rod. I suggested someone else go to trial with her, but after a lengthy conversation she finally agreed to postpone it. The clerk will call on Monday to give us a new trial date."

"Thank you. You're the best. Now what did you need to tell me?" Deanna asked.

"It's not important. Is there anything I can do for you?" Caroline sounded calm but she was anything but. As she thought about it, she decided she would say nothing more; Deanna had enough on her mind. All it would do at this point would add more heartache. Caroline said goodbye and hung up the phone. *Peter Cummings is a son-of-a-bitch, rotten to the core and he needs a steel rod up his ass,* she thought, and then laughed as that image danced in her head.

Deanna walked down the corridor to the end of the hall and stared out the window for a long time. She was still staring into space when she received a text. She was relieved to see it was from Peter. Deanna could only assume he was returning her message from yesterday. Then, as she opened the text, for a moment her hair stood up on the back of her neck.

A half-hour later, she was standing there heartbroken when David walked up. And when Deanna turned with red swollen eyes, he could see she had been crying. He had no idea she had received a text and it would have never occurred to him he had walked up on a defining moment. "It's visiting hour and dad wants you to come to ICU," David said firmly.

"Okay, I'll be right there." She took a hanky out of her purse. She had acquired the habit from Eleanor of always carrying a handkerchief. It was one of the tender memories of her. She blew her nose and hurried down the hallway. David stood at the double doors waiting for her to catch up. Without saying a word, he pushed the door open that led to ICU.

Bright fluorescent lights illuminated the halls and Deanna could see that it was very busy but orderly as nurses attended to their patients. All the rooms were occupied; some of the patients were awake, but most were sleeping, or sedated, or maybe comatose. There were many sounds coming from the rooms; beeping monitors, coughing, moaning….

Deanna could hear the beeping of the heart monitor and the ventilator as it cycled, pushing air into Eleanor's lungs. She slowly opened the door; she stood in the doorway for a few seconds and taking a deep breath, entered the cramped room. Her eyes immediately focused on the crisp white sheets. The lamp above the bed provided little light but the sheets illuminated in the dimness and revealed the gentle motion of Eleanor's chest as it methodically rose and fell.

She had two days to prepare herself for this, but nothing prepared her for the way she would feel. Just seeing Eleanor made her ill; it was though Eleanor was no longer there; she was just an empty shell. She no longer had a china-doll face. Her face was swollen almost unrecognizably. She had been intubated for the ventilator and her mouth taped up. Tubes and wires were hanging from her like tangled spaghetti.

Two nurses stood by her bed. One was checking the monitors and the other was repositioning the endotracheal tube. Deanna said nothing and did not approach the bed. She stood there for what must have been five minutes.

"The doctor just left. She has a fever. He was considering giving her something to lower her temperature, but he said there was no need, that this was just the natural progression." James was speaking to no one in particular, but to everyone. He sat motionlessly in the small chair in the corner of the room while Allison stood by his side.

Deanna jumped, she had not seen them in the shadow; her eyes had been focused on Eleanor.

"Is Mathew coming?" James asked without looking up.

"I haven't called him yet, but I will as soon as I get back to the waiting room," Deanna said, still not taking her eyes off Eleanor.

"Don't wait much longer, I want all three of the boys here tomorrow," James was quick to reply.

"Okay, Dad, I'll do that right now." She was enormously relieved to be able to leave the intensive care unit. She did not stop at the waiting room; she stepped in the elevator and went to the first floor. She took a huge breath of fresh air as soon as she reached the outdoors.

She was leaning against a post when she saw an elderly man sitting alone. She recognized him; she had seen him yesterday sitting alone in the waiting room. Deanna had the impression he was in the same agonizing waiting game they were. He looked very tired, and she felt sad for him. She sat on the bench next to him.

"I'm Deanna," she said while taking a bottle of water out of her purse. "I noticed you had a little something on your shirt and it's too nice to let it stain." She handed him the water and a clean handkerchief.

The old man smiled at her and took the bottle of water. "Thank you, my wife is on me all the time for staining my clothes," he remarked. His hand shook as he poured the water on the handkerchief.

"Here let me do that for you, I raised a son, I have to do this after every meal, and he's only twenty-years-old," she joked. "I saw you in the waiting room yesterday, are things going okay?"

"My wife is in ICU, she had a stroke three days ago. She's being moved to a private room today. And after that I'm told she will be going to a nursing home," he said as he took a pack of cigarettes out of his shirt pocket. "Louise, that's my wife's name, tells me these cigs are going to kill me. If I live another nine months I'll turn ninety in April. I think that's long enough to live, don't you?" He tapped the side of the half-empty pack against his hand until a cigarette appeared. He placed it between his lips, pulled it out of the pack then offered one to Deanna. She shook her head. "You don't smoke?" he asked.

"No. I tried them once a long time ago. But they didn't agree with me." She smiled remembering the summer she had tried smoking. She turned green and threw up and Francine had laughed at her.

"Better you never started," he said as his trembling hands lit the cigarette. He exhaled slowly, making smoke rings. "Are you from here?" he asked.

"Yes, born and raised." She smiled as she said it. She went back inside, found a chair near the waterfall, and listened to the sound of the water as it trickled down the slate stone. She closed her eyes and felt the cool mist gently whisk past her face. Deanna knew she had to be stronger than this. Her grandfather taught her that deep within she could always find strength; she just had to search for it and more than that, she had to want it and accept it.

Before calling the airlines to make the flight arrangements for Mathew, she sat thinking about her grandfather and the last words he spoke to her. *"The past is the past. You can't carry around the things that hurt you the most, you have to let go of it, or you will be your own problem, Deanna."*

The next flight out of Atlanta was at seven o'clock in the evening, arriving in Knoxville at seven forty five. She dialed Mathew's number and as she waited for him to pick up, she suddenly felt extraordinarily burdened by telling Mathew about Eleanor.

He answered the phone with a yawn. When he recognized it was Deanna's voice on the phone, he started to become alert. He had been up since 4 a.m. to finish his lawn work before the heat became unbearable. "He's asleep," Mathew kidded. "Can you call back later, oh, say about seven o'clock this evening?" he said, rolling over on his back. When he heard her voice again, he sat up in bed. "What is it?" He had no idea what he was about to hear, but Deanna's voice sounded strained.

"I'm afraid I have some bad news about Eleanor," she began.

"How serious is it? When?" With her explanation, Mathew could feel a lump in his throat as he quickly jotted down the flight number.

Deanna had arranged for a car; he had two hours to get dressed and packed before it arrived to take him to the airport. He opened his closet and took a bag off the shelf. He threw shorts, tee shirts, jeans and a dark suit in the large tote. He did not take time to eat; all he could think about was his grandfather and Eleanor.

Shortly after she spoke to Mathew, Deanna walked back to ICU. When she stepped inside the room, she found her father in the same small chair. He had placed the chair near Eleanor's bedside and was holding her swollen hand.

She looked like a lifeless doll, so still there in her hospital bed. Her spirit seemed to have already returned to its maker. It was hard for James to understand that the woman he had been married to for forty-two years looked like a stranger to him now.

"Did you call Mathew?"

"Yes dad, he'll be here tonight," she answered, walking around the bed.

"Tomorrow is the Fourth of July. I want all the boys here one more time."

Deanna pulled a chair beside her father and sat quietly listening to the sound of the ventilator. After a while, James began to cry. "I've decided to take her off life support tomorrow." All he wanted to do was tell his wife one last time how much he loved her.

"I should have paid more attention. A month ago, when she started having trouble sleeping and was exhausted all the time, I should have known something was not right. It was not like her to be so tired. She just thought it was the heat."

"Dad, how could you know this was going to happen," Deanna said, trying to comfort him.

"Eleanor was a stubborn woman; she would not slow down. The day she had the heart attack, she had asked me to go the drug store to get antacids. And she promised she would go to the doctor after the party. While I was gone she had gotten sick and vomited before she passed out. By the time I got home it was too late, she was lying on the floor. I called Lucas and he was there right away. But he couldn't save her, Deanna. He tried but it was too late. This is my fault; I should have made her go to the doctor, but

Eleanor had never had any trouble with her heart before. I just didn't know."

"Dad, this is not your fault. I know you feel like it now, but no one blames you," Deanna said as she put her arm around him.

David and Allison joined them later. They all sat in silence for the next hour. A sharp hunger pang hit and Deanna realized she had not eaten in hours. It was almost four o'clock. She was suddenly weak, tired, and hungry. "Dad, I think I'll go back to the hotel, Beau has been locked up in the room for hours and I'm sure he needs to go out." She got up and put her hand on his shoulder. "I'll wait on Mathew's plane to arrive and we'll be back later. Do you want me to get you something to eat before I go?"

"I'll make sure he goes to the cafeteria in a little while," Allison said.

"Dad, you eat something, okay?" Deanna bent down and kissed the top of his head. She touched David's arm. "I'll be back in a few hours."

She had a lot to think about; starting with the text she received from Peter. At first, she thought the message had been for her to meet him at the airport at six. She assumed he was flying to Knoxville, but after reading further, she realized Peter had sent her the text by mistake. She read the words again as if the more she read them they would somehow change.

Since the moment they met, he had been her drug. There was something about Peter that intoxicated her. He had expanded her world beyond anything she could have imagined. It had been a dance not easy for her to learn and had frightened her profoundly at times.

Chapter 23

THURSDAY JULY 3RD, It was almost four o'clock in the afternoon. The whole forty-eighth floor of the Towers was enveloped in otherworldly quietness. Peter sat silent and motionless behind the large mahogany desk. His father-in-law's terms sliced through him like a steel blade and he felt his heart had been carved right out of his chest.

He stared expressionlessly into the bottom of his empty glass and expressed an aura of quiet desperation. For the better part of an hour, he tried to drown his feelings. But as hard as he tried, he could not deaden the feelings he had for Deanna.

Their involvement with one another had been unpredictable. He had wanted her from the first time he saw her. She had looked like a goddess that day as she walked across the shoreline wearing a sheer summer dress. An emotional friendship had happened sudden and with vivacity. She had touched him deeply. She was everything he thought a woman should be. She was intelligent and funny and had been an unexpected gift, suddenly appearing in his life.

He refilled his glass, rose from his chair, and crossed the room, a little unsteadily, to the matching black-leather couches that sat directly in front of the twenty-foot wall of glass. He sat down, all the while, sipping his bourbon as he stared out from the art décor designed building. In front of him stretched Atlanta, with its high-rises that cast their dusky shadows from Mid-Town to the gold dome of the state capitol building. Peter had never gotten used to that panoramic view.

Hanging on the wall were photographs of his wife and three children. The black and white pictures conveyed the seriousness of royal portraits. As he stood to leave, he raised his empty glass to the painting of Bernard. Peter stared at the painting, looking at the self-satisfied impassive face, and he despised him. He continued to stand quietly and raised the glass to the view Bernard so gladly dangled in front of Peter like a priceless family heirloom. He seethed with loathing for his father-in-law and everyone else. Even himself.

"And to you, my Queen," he said as he turned away from the portrait of his wife hanging on the lustrous mahogany-covered wall. He sat the glass down on the corner of the desk and picked up the half-empty bottle of bourbon. As he turned to leave, he caught a glimpse of a crumbled note he had thrown in the trash. He retrieved the paper and read the muddled writing. Once again, he felt the cold steel blade slice through his soul; he had made it his pact and now he had to live with it.

He turned out the light and idly walked through the large offices that occupied the entire 48th floor. As he walked passed the last office, he saw a young boy standing in the doorway. He looked to be about six years old.

"I'm sorry sir. I had to bring my grandson with me today. I had no one to keep him. He won't touch anything; he's a good boy. Miss Caroline said the office would be closed today and everyone would be gone, she said I could come early so I can get my cleaning done and I can get back to the hospital," the woman said as she motioned for the boy to come back inside.

"It's all right," he said as he ruffled the boy's hair. "Who's in the hospital?"

"My husband, he has lung cancer, I told him those cigarettes was going to kill him someday," she said as she shook her head.

Peter smiled down at the toothless grin smiling back at him. The boy held a toy sports car toward him, proudly displaying it to Peter. "So you like cars. So do I," he said, taking the plastic toy. "This is a beauty. Work hard and mind your grandmother and one day you can buy a nice shiny one, but remember it's not the most important thing you will have." He gave the toy back to the boy and then took five twenty-dollar bills out of his wallet and handed it to the woman. "Take a cab today and you and the boy have a nice dinner tonight." Then he handed her another twenty, "and maybe you'll have time to buy him something special."

"Thank you sir, and tonight when I pray for my husband, I'll ask God to remember you."

"I'm afraid you'll be wasting your time. I've already sold my soul to the devil."

"Oh no sir, time spent in pray is never wasted," she said in a soft drawl. "Bless you sir," and with that, the women turned and continued her cleaning.

As he waited for the elevator, he thought about his grandmother. He once asked her why she did this for a family that did not appreciate the sacrifices she made for them. "It pays the bills, my boy," she replied.

The elevator opened in the underground parking garage. Side by side and bumper to bumper, expensive cars filled the spaces: Porsches, Ferraris, Lamborghinis. A canary-yellow Ferrari squealed through the multi-level garage and came to a stop on a dime in front of Peter.

"With this heat I figured you would want the top on and the air conditioner running," the smiling young garage attendant said as he bounced out of the car and held open the door. "Big plans for the Fourth sir?"

"Yes, mind numbing plans, my boy."

"Have a good one, now sir," the energetic young man said as he waited for Peter to get in the car.

"Thank you Billy, I'll give it my best shot," he said handing him a five-dollar bill. He sat the bourbon in the seat beside him and eased out of the parking garage. He turned left on Peachtree and in moments navigated the crowded streets of Atlanta. He passed the Ritz-Carlton, then swung left on Ellis. The fine leather seat pushed against Peter's back as he floored the accelerator and sailed onto I-75, disappearing into the sea of traffic.

Behind the mirrored lenses of his aviator glasses, his stormy blue eyes were even colder now. His mind was blank as he drove south from the city. That was now his one true talent, the ability to focus on nothing.

The traffic heading out of the city had slowed to a crawl. One hour later, after a hot frustrating ride, Peter pulled the car into the secured lot. The yellow Ferrari screeched to a stop, sending the bottle of bourbon to the floor. Peter closed his eyes. He opened them again and quickly picked up the bourbon. He felt the cool glass on his lips and took a long burning gulp. He let the empty bottle drop to the floor; the liquor was taking its toll. Peter felt dizzy. His thoughts were cloudy. Images of Deanna suddenly flickered in his mind like an old movie.

Her eyes, her face, her body. He tried not to think about her but his mind kept picking at it like a festering sore. He gripped the steering wheel. His jaw was set. His face rigid. Then the rage drained out of him as quickly as it had flared up. Using iron control, he withheld all his emotions. He got out of the car and turned to the attendant, his face once again calm. "Call a cab, I need to get to the airport."

Peter sat in the back seat of the cab, once again his mind blank. "Which airline, sir?" The driver watched Peter through the rear-view mirror. "Sir," he said again. "Which airline?"

"Delta." Peter checked his watch; it was almost five o'clock. He paid the driver and walked through the glass doors, where he bought two tickets. He left one at the ticket counter for his traveling companion and took the other, then was herded through security with the rest of the crowd.

THE HIRED CAR, one arranged by Deanna to take Mathew to the airport, had arrived promptly at four o'clock. Traffic heading out of the city was frenetic and made the drive to the airport tedious. Mathew tried to relax in the back seat. Finally, at ten minutes past five o'clock, the car stopped at the passenger drop-off and Mathew stepped onto the sidewalk. He checked his watch, looking like he was in a hurry, which he was. He checked the flight times; his flight to Knoxville was on time. The ticket

Deanna had purchased was waiting on him at the ticket counter. He checked his bag and hurried through security.

He checked in at gate 28 and hunkered down for the forty-five minute wait. That was when he saw Peter Cummings. He looked relaxed, tanned, and toned. He was wearing khaki pants and a blue silk golf shirt and he wore the pair of very expensive Prada Driver shoes Deanna had given him for his birthday. He had an aura of power and success about him; even dressed in summer casual suave, it was hard to ignore. Everything about him had subtle elegance to it that drew the right people to him.

He considered ignoring Peter but after thinking about it, decided to do the polite thing and say hello. He walked halfheartedly the short distance to the lounge. And as Peter opened a newspaper, Mathew noticed his perfectly manicured hands and that he wore the Breitling watch Deanna had also given him.

Before he reached the table, he spotted her, a busty blonde girl in her mid-twenties. She was dressed in short cut-offs, a low-cut peasant blouse, and wore a pair of five-inch wedged heeled sandals. She had a large colorful beach bag and a small overnight bag slung across her shoulder.

Mathew recognized her, her name was Mandy; they had met a couple of months earlier at Peter's fiftieth birthday party. She had too much to drink that night and Mathew had volunteered to drive her home but Peter said she could sleep it off in his office.

The men at the other table suddenly fell silent as she paraded past in a display of long tanned legs. Her mass of blonde hair tumbled around her doll-like face. She laughed boldly, looked them over with a long sensual gaze and then ordered a beer and a shot of tequila from a passing waiter. Peter looked up from behind his newspaper and his steel blue eyes narrowed as he peered over his reading glasses. His lips curved in a half smile and she made eye contact with him as he folded the paper.

"Are you looking for company tonight?" she said with a brown eyed-wink. Her voice was low but sultry. Almost like Marilyn Monroe.

She moved toward him and reached into the large bag, took out a folder, and slid it across the table. Peter ran his finger along the edge and toyed with the corner before opening it, he then flicked through the contents.

He closed the folder and put it in the tote bag sitting beside him. Then he laughed harshly. His next reaction took Mathew by complete surprise. With a slight twist of his head, Peter had a view of the men at the other table. Their eyes glued to the girl; they sipped their drinks and watched. He raised his glass to the men, and with one gulp, he finished the bourbon.

"You are a bad girl; I may have to punish you later," he said, taking off his glasses. She was still grinning when she stood behind him at the table. She playfully pressed her breasts against his back and whispered something through lips that were painted cherry red. As she nuzzled his ear, he rolled his eyes back and moaned then pulled her around and placed his mouth on hers. As they kissed, all Mathew could see was the back of her blonde head, and Peter's hand running up between her bare legs.

Mathew stood there immobile; he wanted to look away and get out of there, but before he could actually move, the kiss was over. Sitting down at the table, and glancing over

Peter's shoulder, Mandy raised the glass of tequila to her lips. She threw her head back and with one swallow, the shot was gone. Then in slow circular movements, she suggestively ran her long nail along the top of the bottle of beer. There was an awkward pause. Despite his best efforts not to, Mathew was gawking at her. By the time he could release his stare and walk away, Mathew was pretty sure she saw him before he headed back to gate 28.

It was six forty-five when he boarded the plane and found his seat by the window. He could not get the image of the two of them out of his head. *Was Peter Cummings a complete idiot? Or even a member of the same species as respectable men?* Mathew thought.

He felt the plane gradually move away from the passenger boarding bridge. Soon it was inline on the tarmac; he would be in Knoxville in forty-five minutes. He closed his eyes as the plane began to taxi down the runway, picking up speed, and with a sudden thrust, the plane was in the air. Mathew had suspected the affair between Deanna and Peter, but she was always discreet, careful not to expose him to their relationship. After thinking about what he had just witnessed he decided, without delay, he would reveal to Deanna what Peter really was.

AT THE HOTEL, Deanna had just return from her walk with Beau. She took a shower then lay silently thinking about Peter and Lucas. She thought about how starkly different the two men were. Peter was fueled by power and Lucas by passion. It was remarkable to think how Lucas had come back into her life by sheer happenstance. There had been no communication between them in years but she could not deny the strong feelings she still had for him.

She dozed, and then got up at seven o'clock. Beau lay contentedly on the bed beside her, and her father's clothes that he had worn the day before lay cleaned and pressed. From her hotel room she could hear planes as they made their approach and departures. Mathew's plane would be arriving in forty-five minutes; she called the front desk and arranged for the shuttle to pick him up.

Her hair was still damp; she ran her fingers through it and fluffed it with her hands, that was all it needed. She wore a simple pair of navy linen slacks, a pullover lavender tunic and matching cardigan. She fastened a string of pearls around her neck and wore matching pearl and diamond earrings. Tilting her head from side to side, as she looked at her reflection, she ran her finger along the smooth black pearls. Her time in New York quietly drifted through her mind. Dismissing those thoughts, Deanna slid on her sandals, and went to the hotel restaurant.

The waiter had just brought the food when she spotted Mathew. He looked like a typical college student coming home for the summer with all his clothes squeezed into the duffle bag. She grinned when she saw he wore his favorite old tee shirt and cargo shorts and wore a pair of flip-flops. Seeing her, Mathew smiled and joined her at the table. He placed his bags in an empty chair beside Deanna. Sitting down he rubbed his hands together in anticipation of eating the double-bacon cheeseburger and home fries.

"I thought you might be hungry," she said with a smile. "How was your flight?" she asked as the waiter placed the linen napkin in her lap.

"Can I get you anything else ma'am?" the waiter asked as he refilled her water glass.

She smiled graciously at the young man, "No we're fine, maybe dessert later for the eating machine over there," Deanna joked, as she nodded toward Mathew.

"The flight was fine," he said taking a bite of the burger. "I saw Mr. Cummings in the airport."

"Oh, really," Deanna replied trying to sound surprised as she raised her fork to take a bite of salad.

"Someone met him there," Mathew continued after swallowing his food and taking a drink of his soda.

"Did you know who she was?" she asked, playing with her salad and trying not to sound too curious.

"What makes you think it was a female?" he said with a grin. "And yes I did know her; she was the blonde with the big boobs at Peter's birthday party."

"Mathew! That's a horrible thing to say about a young lady," she scolded as she took a sip of water.

"Okay, the girl that had too much to drink and Mr. Cummings let her sleep it off in his office. One, she's no lady and two, I don't think that was all she got off in his office that night," he said with a sneer.

"Her. The girl from the employment agency," Deanna said as she choked on her water. *She could not find her way out of a paper bag,* she thought. The puzzle was now coming together, Peter cancelling the trip with her, the girl answering his office phone, and Caroline's strange phone call. Peter had been sleeping with her.

"Did they see you?"

"No," Mathew replied. "Or at least Mr. Cummings didn't. But I think she did. I think her little show in the airport lounge was for my benefit," he continued.

"Little show?" Deanna said, putting her glass down.

"You don't want to know, Mom," he said shrugging his shoulders and shaking his upper body. He swallowed the last bite of his burger and burped. "I think I ruined my appetite, no dessert for me," he said raising the napkin to his mouth and shuddering again.

Deanna laughed at his gesture and motioned for their waiter. As she signed the check, she told Mathew to leave his suit out and she would get it pressed tomorrow. "Oh, get your grandfather's clothes they are laying on the bed," she yelled at him as he ran to catch the elevator.

She gave the valet her parking ticket. Deanna's brow creased in thought and she mumbled under her breath. "Little show. What do you suppose she's up to?" Deanna thought the girl was as flakey as a snowfall, but perhaps she did not give her enough credit. Mandy could be cleverer than she thought.

"Ms. Guthrie." She turned quickly to the speaker. It was the valet, handing her the keys.

"I'm driving," Mathew said, running to the car.

Deanna looked at the young man, shook her head, and then gave him his tip. He opened the passenger's door and she slid in the seat beside Mathew. As she was fastening her seat belt, he sped down the street. "Slow down, I can't get pulled over again, I don't think I can get you out of the ticket here," she said, looking not worried but amused.

"Pulled over again," Mathew said with a cackle.

"Never mind, just drive."

Mathew walked into the ICU waiting room just behind Deanna, and her two nephews, aged fourteen and sixteen immediately came to greet them. The room was empty except for a few of her father's friends. Betty was talking to Allison about preparing some meals for the family. Deanna joined her sister-in-law in the conversation while Mathew told his cousins about the awesome birthday present Deanna had given him.

"Thank you, Betty for being so kind and thoughtful," Deanna half whispered as Betty put her arms around her to say good night.

"Eleanor would have done the same thing for me. I could not count the meals she prepared for families and the visits to hospitals. She was a wonderful person and friend," Betty said as she cupped Deanna's hand in hers. "It was about twenty-eight years ago, just around the time you left for college, that I met Eleanor. My husband and I had just moved here and didn't know anyone when we got the news my mother had passed away. There were so many things to do before the funeral, and in the midst of all the turmoil, the phone rang. It was Eleanor; she said she had heard about my mother and asked if there was anything she could do for us. It was dinnertime when we came home from the funeral and food was the last thing on my mind. My boys were starving and I had just started to make something when the doorbell rang. There stood Eleanor and James with their arms full of dishes of food. She had made dinner for all of us. I was so amazed by her generosity and kindness. We've been close friends ever since," she continued. "You know she loves Mathew. When I saw them together it was like looking at two peas in a pod, they were always cracking jokes and he kept her laughing," Betty said as she looked over at him.

Betty said goodbye to Deanna and Allison and seeing her leave, Mathew excused himself and followed her to the hallway. She held him tightly for a few minutes before disappearing into the elevator. Mathew was still standing outside the waiting room and staring down the long corridor when James appeared from behind the double doors. He walked down the hall and embraced his grandson.

James sat down with all three of his grandchildren and they sat quietly for a few minutes. Then he began to explain to the boys about Eleanor's condition. They listened intensely as he told them of the decision he had made. They had a long list of questions for him and after he explained to the best of his ability, they sat silent for a while.

James stood up and walked out of the waiting room and they all followed. All three of his grandsons walked side by side down the long hallway and Deanna, David, and Allison followed behind. They waited outside Eleanor's room until the nurse finished taking her vital signs. When she had finished she turned and smiled at them compassionately and touched James on the arm as she left.

James entered first, then Mathew right behind him. Mathew was standing on one side of his grandfather and the two boys on the other. James put his arms around his grandsons and they all stood there in silence for what seemed like an eternity. Mathew was the first to move; he bent over the bed and touched Eleanor's hand. "I'm here Nonie." Mathew said before he kissed her forehead. James smiled; Mathew had started the nickname his first summer with them and it stuck.

It was later that evening when Deanna walked back to the waiting room. She stared out the window gazing at the glow of the streets as the sun went down behind the tallest building. She hated herself as much as a forty-six year old woman could. For the next few minutes she stood motionless, it was unthinkable, and easy to believe the pain she had caused her father and Eleanor. Only God knows how deep the wounds went.

Thirty minutes later to the second, she still stood frozen staring out at the sky. The clouds emanated a red glow like burning coals heaped on a hearth. Off in the distance she could see flashes of lighting as the sky lit up like fireworks.

"Yep, we'll going to get a heat storm tonight," the rusty voice said.

Deanna swirled around; lost in her own thoughts she had not heard the woman enter the room. The woman wore a red vest that swallowed her tiny frame and her hair was silver – the color of brushed aluminum.

"Do I know you?" asked Deanna. "It seems we've met before," she said, studying the woman's face.

"Yes you do know me," she replied. "I worked as an emergency room nurse. I caught you and Lucas McKinney in the supply closet one night," she said with a raspy laugh. In that coarse laugh, you could hear every cigarette she'd ever smoked.

"Oh my goodness, you're Goldie!" she said, forgetting the anguish she had felt just a few short minutes earlier. "I couldn't look at you for a month after that without turning red in the face."

"That little deed is still good for donuts and my special cup of coffee," Goldie said holding up her cup. "Lucas brings my hush treat by every time I work," she said taking a bite of the sugar-covered donut. "You just missed him; he brought my weekly bribe."

"Your bribe?" Deanna asked.

"Yeah, he still becomes embarrassed when I mention the closet," Goldie said, laughing. "You know that boy moped around after you left. He was wasting away and still pining over you when he met Lisa. It was a shame about her cancer."

"Yes, I knew about her illness and was saddened by her death," Deanna said.

"We all thought he would just dry up when she passed, but it was the opposite, he seemed to blossom. When he moved back here, he just fit right in as medical director. He's a fine man and only has one vice that I can see; he has a tendency to work too much."

"Oh, I know he is also the mayor of my home town," Deanna said with a smile.

"It's a pity you didn't see him," Goldie said as she raised her cup of strong coffee.

MATHEW AND DEANNA left the hospital at midnight and headed back to the hotel. Sleep came in brief naps, interrupted by long periods of staring at the ceiling. She rolled from side to side trying to make herself comfortable. At one point, she got up and stared through the darkness.

Sunlight was an hour away and she had slept less than three hours. She made the coffee strong, and sipped it on the bed while she watched the morning news. There was no movement in Mathew's part of the suite. After she showered and dressed, she moved around the suite very quietly.

She sat at the table sipping coffee and reading the paper until Mathew woke up. She ordered breakfast and was finishing her toast when he stumbled to the table in his pajama bottoms and tee shirt. His voice was scratchy and his eyes were puffy and red. He played with his food, nibbling on toast and pushing the eggs around on his plate

Deanna cuddled her coffee cup in her hands and they sat without talking. She was still holding the cup when her phone rang. She looked at the caller ID, and then across the table at Mathew. It was Peter; she excused herself and went to her side of the suite. She stood looking at Peter's name on the screen. She knew she had to say something but there was a long empty pause.

"Hello, Deanna."

"What? I can't hear you," she said finally, she immediately knew he was not alone, he was whispering into the phone and she could hardly hear him.

"I'm sorry I missed your phone call, I just found your message. What did you need?" he asked calmly. His cool demeanor was better than any hand of poker he had ever played in his life.

"I only called to let you know I'll not be in the office next week but Caroline has rearranged my schedule. We'll talk when I get back." Deanna hesitated for a fraction of a second. She had to fight herself not to scream at him through the phone. Instead she pretended she was not at all concerned he had not returned her call. "There is one more thing, though," she said with an unruffled voice. "I want you to understand something, I think it's indelicate of you to call me while she's in your bed." She bit her tongue to keep from unleashing her anger on him.

It was her tone that conveyed to Peter the betrayal she felt, even when her words did not. Before he could say anything else, she was gone. Peter held his hung-over head in his hands. The sun was like ice picks in his eyes. He had a splitting headache since 4 a.m., when he stumbled into bed. From twenty feet away he could see Mandy lying passed out naked on the couch. He closed his eyes and let the darkest of dark thoughts creep though his mind. Never having to open his eyes again would be better than the loathing he felt now.

His eyes popped open again and he reached for the bottle of bourbon lying on the bed beside him. "Damn it!" he yelled, throwing the empty bottle against the wall. The alcohol coursing through his veins no longer dulled the pain. Instead, it greased the wheels of rage. Shards and splinters of jagged glass scattered across the floor as he fell hopeless back into bed, holding his head with both hands.

"My God, what are you doing!" Mandy screamed. "My head is pounding. Oh I get it," she said playfully, her blonde hair brushing across her bare breast as she rose from the couch. "We're out of liquor," she said, climbing into bed with him. She ran her finger from his exposed naval down to the sheet that barely covered him.

Peter lit a cigarette, and then took his time to speak. "Put your clothes on, we need more bourbon," he said. Ironically, being intimate or even friendly with Mandy was more than he could stomach. He drew on his cigarette.

Then he watched the bright end of it cool and become ash. He threw it in the ashtray, and gave it an angry twist.

"Whoa, that stung," Mandy said, her tone sharpening to an edge. "You cannot have it both ways," she said reaching for a cigarette and sliding it in her mouth. She picked up the lighter and played with it a few seconds before lighting the cigarette. She tilted her head to the side as she lit up and took a deep puff. She smirked as she glanced at the small video camera she had hidden the night before. "So this is the game you want to play. Well, you will be nicer to me later," she said while propping up on the pillows.

With a jaunty toss of her head, Mandy laughed while covering her naked body with the sheets. Peter lifted his head and shot her a look with cold blue eyes. "Do me a favor, Mandy. Shut up and wipe that arrogate smile off your face," he said as he walked the short distance to the bathroom. Mandy's last line echoed in his head. It was something about the way she said it that made Peter think she had something up her sleeve. And sure enough, Mandy did.

The bathroom door slammed behind him with a violent jolt and his head throbbed even harder. Through blood-shot eyes, he came face to face with his own reflection. The unshaven face of a man he no longer recognized was staring back at him. Peter stood there, trying to justify what he was doing.

He took two aspirin from the bottle and swallowed them. His mouth was dry from the night of heavy drinking and his head pounded with every heartbeat. His eyes were full of all the things he had not said to Deanna. He had never told her he loved her, he had never indicated anything to her other than admiration.

Gouging her out of his heart no matter how painful it was to either of them was something he had to do. He hated himself for hurting her, but this was the way it had to be, at least that was what he was telling himself. It was harder than he had imagined it would be to let her go. But he was not willing to give up his wealth or position of considerable stature in the Georgia legal community. He did not care how he held on to them, or for that matter who paid the price. Somewhere along the way, he had completely forgotten about what is right and wrong.

Suddenly his face grew as pale as the white towels that were draped across the shower. This one was going to come with a steep price. He drew in a deep breath and closed his eyes. He was hoping that when he opened them this would have been all a bad dream. But no, it wasn't, this was real. Deanna was gone.

Deanna held the phone in her hand. The enormity and suddenness of Peter's betrayal shocked her. There was something very cold and calculating about his behavior that she could not understand, because he had never betrayed her with another woman. Peter was like the seasons; he left and returned but was never far away from her. It was all a part of the patchwork of their relationship.

The bitter tears stung as they ran down her face; they were like acid rain falling on fragile petals. She sat down on the bed and put her hands across her middle. Her heart ached, not just because of the loss of Peter but also because of the lonely ache of wasted years. With all she had done to protect her heart, she realized that even the coldest of hearts can suffer deep wounds.

She sat there a few more minutes before she stood to her feet; she blew her nose and wiped her eyes. As always, Deanna pulled herself together and even now, she maintained an air of unflustered composure. She had a way of pretending everything is just fine when in reality it was just the opposite. Besides, she had far more things to be concerned about. Today, her father and Mathew will need her to be strong. She packed her bag and gathered her things; five minutes later, she sat down at the table with Mathew. Her face was blotched red from crying.

"The call sounded serious," he said. "Was that about Eleanor?"

"No," she replied. "It was about work."

"Didn't sound like work to me."

"I'm going to take Beau for a walk. Get your things packed, I'll be back soon and we'll leave for the hospital." Deanna did not want to discuss the conversation.

Outside, Deanna felt the heaviness in the air. Above the mountains, half-black and heavy clouds were forming and long rumbles of thunder rolled through the valley. Thick liquid heat hung over her head like a wet sponge. Deanna lifted her chin to the gust of wind and walked the few steps to the door.

Chapter 24

JULY 4TH, it was four o'clock in the afternoon when Deanna pulled into the hospital's parking lot. The weather had turned rainy, not brief showers but rain that lasted for hours. She slowed her car, keeping an eye on the people that scurried to take cover from the fast-approaching storm. Suddenly flashes of forked lightening tore through the thickened clouds. Then cracks like a cannon ball tumbling down a marble staircase caused Deanna to jump in her seat. Her jaw tightened. She felt like a nervous cat about to lose one of its nine lives. Mathew sat silently, unmoved by the explosion; his expression was despondent. Deanna had not seen that look since the dark days after his mother's death.

"Mathew," she said quietly. He dragged the back of his hand across his eyes.

"I'm going to miss her." The sadness in his voice was heartbreaking. Deanna felt her eyes spilling tears as she tried to soothe him.

After a few moments, he looked at Deanna. "There's something I need to ask you, mom." She looked at him, puzzled for a moment.

"Sure, what is it?"

"I need to know about Jack."

A momentary look of surprise showed on her face and she felt a sinking feeling in her stomach. "Are you going to tell me what this is all about?" she asked.

"I've been having the dream again. There are questions I need answered."

"Okay, do you want to talk about it now?"

"Yes."

A brief silence fell. "Jack hurt me." The voice was almost a whisper.

"I know he did and I am so sorry. I wish I had done more to protect you and your mother," she said.

"After he hit my mother he came in my room. He hit me and told me that I was a no-good little bastard. Where is he now?" A degree of coldness she had not heard before crept into his voice.

"He can't ever hurt you," said Deanna. Tears starting again in her eyes. She hated Jack for what he had taken from Mathew. Now, she hated him even more.

"Mom I need to know," his voice was a whisper, almost a chant. "I want to see him. I have something I need to say to him." His face was as impassive as a stone statue.

"He's in the state prison on death row." The words slowly trickled from her mouth.

Deanna looked at Mathew's determined face. He murmured a wordless affirmation and looked out the window. The silence in the car was thick and unbroken. Minutes passed, then a loud deep rumble of thunder erupted as the air was suddenly heated by lightening. Mathew only stared out the window, unaffected by the noise.

"When is the date of his execution?"

"Next month," the words tasted bitter in her mouth.

Mathew continued to stare out the window with an expression she could not read. Somewhere in there was the boy he used to be. Somewhere in there was the man he had become. His expression softened and a slight smile crossed his face. She returned the smile as she looked into his face.

He had the face of his father but the heart and soul of his mother.

"I can't remember what her voice sounded like. I can see her in my mind but I can't hear her voice. Tell me about her."

"Sarah and I met in college. She was my best friend but she was more like my sister," she began. "She was this blonde-haired, blue-eyed southern belle with the face of an angel. When we walked into a room together, all eyes would go directly to her. She was funny, charming, and intelligent. She could hold the attention of everyone in the room. I, on the other hand, may as well not have been there; no one ever noticed me when I was with her," Deanna said with an expression of amusement. "She was a good lawyer, she loved her work and was full of passion. But, you were her pride and joy. She was totally in love from the first moment she laid eyes on you."

"Why did she marry Jack?" he asked pointedly. Mathew's voice grew hard again. Jack had abused him, abused his mother, and robbed him of his mother's love. He wanted to hate him. He told himself he was glad he was going to die. However, Mathew did not hate him, nor did it give him peace knowing that Jack was going to die for murdering his mother. He had channeled his hatred years ago in other directions.

"Jack was charismatic and it was almost as if he had cast a spell over her." *But most of all he was a manipulator. He knew Sarah was vulnerable and he took advantage of that.* But she did not articulate the thought. "They seemed to be happy, at first. Then he started drinking too much."

"Why did she stay with him?"

"That was a question I asked her every time she came to work with a black eye. She always made excuses for him," she said with a degree of frost creeping into her voice.

"Then I don't understand how she could stay with a man that hit her. How could she be that weak?"

"Sarah was not weak. She was a victim of domestic violence and had become trapped in a cycle of abuse. She was afraid of Jack and she felt ashamed that she stayed with him. Jack was a violent, damaged, abusive man. He was a bully. He would hit her in a fit of rage or because she said or did something he didn't like and other times it was just for the sheer control. Then he would beg her not to leave him and he always promised he would never do it again. He could be so charming at times and he made her feel like she was his princess, then the cycle would start again. This was all a part of his control."

"I still don't understand why she stayed in that abuse."

"I don't know either, Mathew. She wanted to leave but he had done something to her mind. That's the thing with battered women; it's difficult for them to move out of the shadow of their abuser. But when he hit you she had the strength to leave."

"I didn't protect her," Mathew said, clearly distraught.

"Hey, you were only five years old. It was not your job to protect anyone. I'm sorry, Mathew. I should have protected you both." Deanna took a breath and continued. "She did divorce him and he was charged with assault."

"Then what happened?"

"Jack came to your house and that was when you called me. I called the police and then drove as fast as I could to your house, but it was too late I found your mother lying on the floor."

Deanna had not thought about this in a long time. She felt a chill dance through her. She could recall it so clearly in her mind. The house, Jack sitting on the front porch with the gun clutched in his hand. Sarah lying on the living room floor and the smell of warm blood. She remembered the promise to his mother she had made as she lay dying in her arms.

Mathew wiped his eyes again, fresh tears running down his face. He squeezed his eyes shut. He looked Deanna in the eye. "Who is my father?"

She looked down at the floor and shook her head. She hesitated for a moment, remembering the secret she had promised to keep. She closed her eyes. When she opened them again, he was looking straight at her. Mathew stared at her for a moment. She had never done anything so difficult in her life as to honor the promise she had made.

"We should go; this storm is getting worse."

The storm was in full fury with no signs of letting up. She looked out into the dark sheet of water. "We're going to have to run through this downpour," she moaned. Deanna hunched her shoulders to lift the collar of her rain jacket higher on her neck. The wind blew streams of water under her umbrella and down her back.

By the time they reached the portico, Mathew's dark mood had passed. He was laughing so hard he could hardly catch his breath. "You should see yourself, you look ridiculous," he said as his grabbed his side. The gusts of wind in the rainstorm had turned her umbrella inside out.

"Okay, wise guy. Knock it off." Hair dripping, feet wet and pants sticking to her, she shot him a look. She was trying hard not to laugh.

A crack of thunder shook the window. Mathew leaped like a racehorse leaving the starting gate. He did not stop until he was inside the hospital. Deanna was right behind him. "Now who looks ridiculous," she said, breaking into laughter. Mathew was more soaked than she was. "I guess I'm going to need another umbrella, this one seems to be broken."

"I'll buy you another one for Christmas," Mathew said, pretending he was sad.

Deanna struck him lightly on his leg with the broken umbrella. "But what am I going to do in the meantime," she frowned.

"Here this fixes it," he said straightening the broken wires.

"Nowhere on earth is there a more thoughtful son than you are," she said rolling her eyes and shaking her head.

"I know, right," he said with a playful grin.

Once again visitors filled the waiting room. By now, Deanna had come to recognize most of their faces and found it comforting to know how many friends were there to offer moral support, if nothing else. She and Mathew stopped in for a brief moment to show their appreciation. Then she took Mathew's hand and continued down the long corridor leading to the ICU.

Deanna paused at the doorway, and before she could continue through the door, a sudden realization filled her with anguish. Her heart began to ache for Mathew and her family. Her heart ached for the lost years. She wished she could tell Eleanor how sorry she was for all the pain she had caused. Suddenly, tears choked her throat; all the calm and false bravado was gone, and she was a mess. She could not stop crying, sobbing openly.

"Mom, are you all right?"

Deanna took a deep breath but her voice continued to shake and her tears to flow. She could not answer him, she felt as though she were going to vomit. She was usually calm and in control but now she was falling apart. Looking worried, Mathew clutched her hand in his. He watched her face, but asked no further questions. He was on the verge of tears himself. Without saying a word, he led her through the doors and into the ICU.

The door to Eleanor's room was closed and from outside they could hear the ventilator and the heart monitor beep each time her heart beat. They could hear the gentle whimper of her father. Mathew quietly pushed open the door. James was sitting beside the bed, crying for his wife. Deanna had always thought of her father as strong but seeing him now without Eleanor, he was collapsing. David and Allison stood holding hands, ready to burst into tears. The boys were standing beside them. Deanna and Mathew quietly walked to the corner of the room, unnoticed by her father.

Just before five o'clock a young women entered the room with a stack of papers. She stood silent for a moment before interrupting. "Mr. Guthrie," she said in soft gentle voice. "I'm the social worker. I know you want to spend this time with your wife and I will not be long."

James looked up and the anguish in his eyes was heart-breaking. He was a broken man. Only two days earlier, he had been a lively man planning a Fourth of July celebration with his beloved Eleanor. And now, suddenly in a matter of days, he was an agonized old man.

"I have release forms that have to be signed before we can take your wife off life support."

Hearing that, James dissolved into sobs, he was in no condition to do anything but sit in the chair. She was wonderful with him and David. She was deeply sympathetic, compassionate, and patient. It was an hour later when the release forms were finally signed.

"The neurologist and Dr. McKinney will be here at eight o'clock and after she is taken off life support she can be released to the funeral parlor," the young woman said with kindness.

None of them had thought about that yet. They had been dazed by what had happened and too worried about James. "If you like, I can call the funeral parlor and tell them someone from the family will call them later to discuss arrangements," she said while holding James's hand. "I'll be here until ten o'clock and this is my number if any of you need anything or have any other questions please call me. I reserved the chapel and it's ready now. It sometimes helps to spend some time away from all of this before the doctor arrives. Then afterward you can use it for as long as you need." She was saddened for them. She knew how much they had been through and could only imagine how hard it was.

"Thank you," Deanna said, following her into the hallway. She told her the funeral parlor to call and thanked her again. As soon as she walked away, Deanna went back into the room where her father clung to David. He put his arm around James and they walked out to the waiting room.

"I think we all should get a bite to eat," Allison said as she stood near Deanna. "It has been hours since any of us have eaten and we need to get James to eat something," she suggested sensibly.

"That's a good idea. I'll stay here in case the social worker needs to discuss anything else and I can handle any legal forms."

Deanna was left alone in the room. She walked to the window and stared out at the storm. Clouds half-black and heavy churned violently. Suddenly a sharp crack of thunder shook the window. She cringed and jumped back. She stared at the machines and tubes attached to the empty shell. That was all that was left of her stepmother. Deanna reached out and took the swollen hand in hers. She put her head near Eleanor's shoulder and wept aloud like a child. Tears ran down her face as she listened to the sounds in the room. The clock continued to count down. She laid down on the cot, closed her eyes, and fell into a deep sleep.

*****

Chapter 25

JULY 4TH 7:55 P.M. Deanna slowly awakened from a sleep so profound her dreams had been muddled fragments of memories and fears. Again, she heard the sounds of the ventilator and the clock counted down the minutes. She looked into the face of Eleanor and watched the gentle rise and fall of her chest as the ventilator continued to breathe for her. She turned her head to see Lucas sitting beside her. He lovingly swept a lock of hair from her face; he looked her straight in the eye, silently reassuring her. They sat silent, just the two of them, waiting.

The rain had stopped and the sun broke through the dark clouds. Long rays of light made their appearance through steam, causing a ghostly glow outside. For an instant, Deanna felt a calming presence. She glanced at the clock hanging above the bed; it was 7:58 p.m.. James entered the room, followed by David, then Allison and the three boys. The neurologist had phoned to say he was on his way.

She touched Eleanor's fingers and gave up her place to James, who stood looking at his wife, with tears streaming down his cheeks. He could hardly speak. James gently touched her hand and kissed her fingers. "Goodbye, my beautiful Elli girl."

A nurse and a respiratory therapist stood by the bedside. The nurse monitored Eleanor's vital signs. James tried not to get in their way, and the therapist showed him where to stand. At eight o'clock the neurologist walked in. He spoke briefly to James then gave the therapist a nod, signaling it was time. With one flick of switch, the room plunged into stillness. The gentle rise and fall of Eleanor's chest stopped. An unnatural calm descended over the room. Her blood pressure began to drop. The rhythmic beep of the heart monitor began to slow. Then finally, one continuous alarm sounded and a straight line ran across the screen. The doctor's quiet manner told them it was finished. He walked to where James was standing and gently placed his hand on his shoulder.

"If you would step out for one minute, they will get the machines off her and then you can come back in and stay as long as you want." When he turned to leave, Deanna saw a small tear roll down his cheek. Lucas put his arm around James, led him from the room and they all followed. No one spoke. After a few minutes, the nurse and therapist stepped out of the room. The nurse stopped long enough to tell them they could go back inside.

The machines were moved to a corner. The room was eerily quiet and her lifeless body lay on the bed covered by the white sheets. The wires and tubes were gone and the breathing tube had been removed. Seeing her without all the tubes did not make it easier. They all hugged for a long moment and choked on sobs again. "Let's get you home, dad. Mathew will drive you. I'll stay for a while longer and call the funeral parlor from here. I want to make sure they're on the way," Deanna said sadly.

"Okay." James shook his head and followed Mathew to the car like a submissive child. The full impact of it all had hit him hard.

It was ten o'clock when she stepped out of the elevator and looked across the lobby. She saw Lucas standing just beyond the glass doors. The doors slid open and Deanna stepped out into the muggy air. "How was James when he left?" Lucas asked.

"He was a mess. I don't know what's going to happen to him. I'm wondering if he will manage without Eleanor. I never realized until now, he was totally dependent on her."

"You can't judge by these past few days," Lucas said. "He's in a state of shock. He will learn to manage. I did." At that moment lighting flashed through the sky and a low rumble of thunder rolled through the valley. "Come on, let's get you home before the storm hits again."

"I have my car here."

"No, actually you don't." Deanna looked puzzled. "My son, Luke, drove James's car home and James and Mathew drove yours."

"I have to go back to the hotel to get Mathew's and my bags, and my dog is still there."

"Oh, by the way there is someone who wants to see you," Lucas pointed to the back seat of the extended cab.

"How did you get him?" Deanna asked with a suspicious look, when she saw Beau snuggled up in his crate.

"Mathew gave me his key." Lucas smiled at her. "You're all checked out and your bags are in the back seat."

"Thank you." She smiled at him. "I need to reimburse you for the room."

"No you don't."

"No, really you don't need to do that."

"Don't be silly." He smiled at her and walked to the passenger side of the truck. "I'm trying to show that we mountain men can be just as cavalier as your city men, so don't mess it up for me," he laughed as he opened the truck door.

Deanna smiled and walked to where he stood. "I remember." She touched his arm. He placed his hand at her elbow to assist her into the truck. "Is this truck big enough for you?" she teased.

"You know what they say about men and their toys," he replied, looking proud of himself.

The light from the dashboard cast a pale glow on Deanna's face. She laid her head back and looked at him. The way he gripped the stirring wheel with one hand and rested the other on his upper thigh – he had a sex appeal and did not even know it. It was an image that excited an old memory.

When they arrived at the house, it looked silent. Not a light showed through the blinds. Lucas carried Beau and the bags to the front door and said good night. She was exhausted when she walked through the front door. The house was so still, and then the sound of laughter shattered the silence. She heard the three boys upstairs, they were laughing about something they had seen on TV.

"How's Dad?" she asked. Allison was sitting at the kitchen table with David.

"He's doing okay. I gave him a sedative and he's sleeping for now at least," Allison said with an exhausted yawn.

"You two should go home and rest. It's going to be a busy day tomorrow." Deanna had called the funeral home and started the arrangements. She told them they had to go there in the morning and pick out a casket. And they had to set a day and time for the funeral.

Deanna walked through the house; the shadowed corners of the rooms were strange to her now. It felt like a hundred years since she was here last. The old clock standing in the entry way struck eleven o'clock. Deanna stared at the familiar old piece, this house had not been the most comfortable part of her life, but it was a major part. There had been good memories, bad memories, peaks and valleys and peaceful times.

Her legs felt as heavy as lead as she carried her bags up the stairs. Mathew and her nephews were watching television in the guest bedroom. "Mathew, your bags are at the bottom of the stairs. Good night, boys." She looked in on James; he was in a restful sleep. She pulled the door shut and walked down the hall to the little back bedroom.

She sat down on the bed and looked around for a long quiet moment. It looked the same; nothing had been changed since she left home. The house filled with an immeasurable silence, as Deanna sat long into the night. Her mind drifted aimlessly, never staying on one thing very long. Her thoughts were being carried along by the events of the past few days. Then finally, sleep came and she fell into a restful sleep.

She woke up early the next morning to the smell of coffee as it drifted into her room. She picked up her bag and walked down the hall to the bathroom. The door to her father's room was open and when she looked in, his bed had been made. Today was going to be nightmarish; she wondered how he would handle the stress of making the arrangements. She showered, dressed and put on her makeup and then checked on the boys. They were sound asleep. Her two nephews were in the bed and Mathew lay splayed out on the floor. She closed the door and went downstairs.

Lucas was sitting at the kitchen table with James while Beau scurried around the kitchen. Lucas had gotten there early and had scrambled eggs, bacon, and toast waiting at the table. He told James he had to eat to stay strong, and much to Deanna's surprise, he was eating and not crying for the first time in twenty-four hours. She poured herself a cup of black coffee and joined them. Beau playfully jumped in her lap, almost spilling the cup of coffee.

"Whoa, little guy, settle down," she said, as he tried to lick her face.

"Allison called about an hour ago, she'll be here at nine," Lucas said as he looked at her.

She glanced at her watch; it was almost nine. "Dad, you need to get dressed. We need to leave soon." James just sat, staring out the window. "I think you and Allison should go. You can make the arrangements. Just keep it simple. Eleanor would disapprove, if it were too showy." He turned his head toward Deanna. He did not look well; his face looked gray. "I think I'll go back upstairs and lie down for a while." He was relieved to let Deanna and Allison make the decisions.

They went to the funeral parlor and were back in a few hours. They had done all the unpleasant things, chosen a casket, the flowers, set the day and time for the viewing, and planned the funeral. They had decided the viewing would be on Monday after the holiday weekend, with the funeral on Tuesday. They had taken a suit– it was the color of lilacs. Allison said it was Eleanor's favorite. The funeral director had requested they bring several pictures of Eleanor to place around the room and one of her and James together.

Lucas was playing with Beau when they walked through the door. This time Beau did not run to her, he was enjoying the game with Lucas. He had fed Beau and let him out several times. Deanna looked around the kitchen; it was full of containers filled with food. Friends had been coming by all morning with arms full of casseroles and trays of cold cuts.

She followed Lucas outside. "Thank you," she said.

"I'm going to the hospital for a few hours, but I'll be back.

"Would you have dinner with us later? David and Allison are coming over," she said as he got into his truck.

"Sure, that would be nice."

That night they all had dinner together at the house. Allison and Deanna warmed the casseroles and made a large salad. Lucas brought a bottle of very good wine from his collection. James never looked up, he ate but didn't talk, was apparently tired and depressed. After dinner, he left the room with a grief-stricken face. They all sat and talked late into the night. Mathew and his cousins listened to their crazy childhood stories and memories that surfaced at times like these.

After everyone left, Deanna turned out the lights and went upstairs. She quietly opened the door to James's room. He was crying again. She wondered if she should give him another sedative or not. She went to her room and changed into her pajamas and when she checked on him again, he was asleep. On her way back to her room, she heard the TV in Mathew's room.

"May I come in?"

"Sure." Mathew was watching something, and she picked up the remote and lay next to him on the bed.

"How are you doing?" She asked.

"I'm good." They talked until he fell asleep. She turned off the TV, turned out the light, and went back to her room. Sleep came easy that night.

Clouds had crept back in, and Deanna woke up to the rumble of thunder in the distance and a spattering of rain on the window. Mathew and her father were still asleep. She showered and went downstairs and let Beau out. She had already called Caroline and was taking the next week off, but she had to go back without fail on the following Monday. She could not see how she could stay even one day longer. The Benson case was set to go to trial on Wednesday 16th. Caroline was sending the files by messenger, so she could begin preparing for court. She had also sent a lovely bouquet of yellow roses and a thoughtful note to Mathew.

Deanna spent the rest of the morning receiving containers of macaroni and cheese, fried chicken and potato salad. Lucas stopped by to visit James, but he was still asleep from the sedative Deanna had given him the night before. He checked on him but said he did not want to disturb his rest. Lucas and Deanna sat on the front porch drinking sweet tea while a soft rain fell on the roof.

"This was not the way I had planned to spend my vacation," she said in a washed-out voice.

"I know, Deanna. I'm sorry."

It was one o'clock in the afternoon when James joined them. He had gotten a lot of mileage out of the sedative. The sun had found its way through the clouds and a rainbow hung in the sky. They all three sat in the stillness for a few minutes longer appreciating its beauty, the colors were so bright and vivid.

"Good morning," Mathew said, still groggy after having just awakened.

"Good morning to you as well," Deanna said as she pointed toward the clock. He rubbed his eyes and poured a class of juice from the container. James said very little; the past few days had been very hard on him and he looked like he had aged a decade. He finished his meal and afterwards went back upstairs to lie down again.

Traditionally, funerals in the south were social occasions, with lots of visiting and eating. Dozens of friends stopped by the house that afternoon. The house was chockfull of visitors, so much so that they overflowed onto the front porch. The number of visitors began to overwhelm Deanna; she could not listen to one more conversation or participate in one more story about her childhood. She had to get away from their clamoring voices, she couldn't breathe, she was going to hyperventilate. She felt like she needed a drink to calm herself down.

She slipped through the crowd and found her favorite place in the backyard. Lying beneath the old oak tree, she watched white puffy clouds drift lazily in the sky. She took long, slow breaths pulling the air in and letting the stress out; with every cleansing breath, the need for a drink subsided.

A quiet breeze whispered through her hair. She closed her eyes; she could smell the sweet smell of honeysuckle vines and the old-fashion pale pink roses that grew untamed in the back yard. She thought back to a time when living was easy and her life was fun, not yet touched by all the misery and distress she had experienced. She remembered riding in her grandfather's old farm truck. The old truck reeked of metal, sweat, and hay, and would creak and shake as they ran over potholes on the dirt road. Cows hunkered down in the shade and would gaze lazily, as they slowly rolled by.

Lucas stood for the longest time watching her. When she sensed he was there, she smiled at him. "Hey, mind if I join you?" he asked.

"I was just thinking about when I was a little girl growing up here on this farm." She sat up, looked at him and with a quiet laugh, she began. "The year my cousins visited I must have been five years old. We got into so much trouble that summer. And I had a mouth on me; they called me miss bossy pants." She laughed aloud. "I would get so mad. I would stomp my foot and wag my finger at them."

"I hear from good sources you're still somewhat bossy," Lucas said as he looked at her and grinned.

"Oh really, who would tell you such a thing?" She played with a strand of her hair and smiled at him. She stared into his eyes for a long moment; then she lay back onto the ground and placed her hands beneath her head and watched the clouds drifting by. "I remember riding in the bed of grandpa's truck and looking up to see large clouds of cotton float through the blue sky. Dust from the dirt road would billow in the air. The truck would stop under the trees, the tailgate would slap down with a clang, and out would jump bare-foot kids, running to the river bank for a late afternoon swim. I was so happy back then."

"Are you not happy now Deanna?"

"No, Lucas, I'm not." Deanna stood slowly and walked toward the patio, stopping to let Lucas catch up to her. Lucas stood a few feet away. "I'm sorry," she whispered. She stared at the ground and wiped her eyes, then turned to face him. "I'm not asking you to forgive me. I just wanted you to know I am sorry I hurt you." She breathed deeply for a moment and wiped her eyes again. Lucas took her hand but before he could respond she turned slowly and walked into the house.

The guests had left and James had gone to bed early. David, Allison, and the boys were watching the NASCAR race on TV. Mathew was in the kitchen making a sandwich and invited Lucas to stay and watch the race with them. Deanna made sandwiches and joined them in the den.

They talked and teased each other and for a moment, life seemed normal. From the day she arrived they all had meals together, and she felt as if she were back in the bosom of her family. Even in the midst of sadness, this seemed to be where she felt the happiest. Here with her family, her job in Atlanta seemed unimportant. Yet that was where she lived and worked. It was her life.

The next day friends and relatives continued to drop by with food. The visitation at the funeral home was that night. Hundreds of Eleanor's friends were there, including childhood friends of Deanna and David, and people neither of them knew. They spent two hours shaking hands. They were all drained; David and Allison went straight home after the visitation. Deanna was too tired to talk or think and after she made sure her father was asleep, she went to bed. They still had Eleanor's funeral to get through the next day.

THE FUNERAL SERVICE was simple. Only immediate family and Lucas attended. The pastor kept it short and very sweet. After he said his final words, James got in the limousine without speaking to anyone and sat next to Deanna. He stared out the window on the way to the cemetery. David and Allison were in the car with them, Lucas was with Mathew and Deanna's nephews in the second limousine.

James stood alone next to the grave for a long time, and everyone left him alone. The man that was there to cover the grave sat patiently and waited. Deanna pulled a handful of weeds from her grandmother's grave and ran her fingers over the name. She thought back to when she was a small child and all the days she spent with her. She was a fine Christian woman, sweet and kind. Deanna thought back to summer days playing in the river, climbing trees, fishing, and rummaging through the old barn. But her fondest memories were about grape Kool-Aid that Pearl would prepare for her after a long day of play. Grape was Deanna's favorite flavor and it was fun knowing that when she came in dirty, wet, sweaty, and tired there would be a full glass waiting for her.

She chuckled thinking about that thin slip of a girl, like a new moon; barefooted, ragged, with neglected hair and Eleanor trying to brush her long tresses each night before she put her in the tub to soak away the dust and dirt.

Deanna turned her thoughts back to Eleanor and her father, watching him as he stood motionless beside Eleanor's grave.

He was thin and colorless, and his pale stricken face was as empty as his staring unseeing eyes. Eleanor was his soul mate. He could not bring himself to believe she was gone. "How could this happen?" he said as tears rolled down his cheeks. He cried her name. It was a cry of a soul filled with loneliness and fear. He stumbled toward the grave.

"Dad!" Deanna screamed. Stunned, they all stood there watching him. Deanna began to run, her high heels slipping in the grass. She grabbed him and his arms dropped to his side. He moaned softly, then his body crumpled in Deanna's arms. Just as she was losing her grip on him, David and Lucas caught his limp body and lifted it upright.

"Come on, Daddy, let's go home," Deanna said brushing away tears of her own. The burial was the last act of a painful ritual that had seemed endless.

One hundred people had come to their house to remember Eleanor, and women from her church had served lunch for them. This was the last step in the Southern tradition. It was five o'clock in the afternoon when the last guest left. Betty was in the kitchen putting away the leftover food.

"I have never been so tired in my life," Deanna said as she grabbed the roll of tin foil. "I haven't had a chance to ask how you're doing, Betty."

"The reality of it has not sunk in yet. It's as though she has gone away for a weekend and will return at any time. I can't believe I'll never see her again," Betty said. She was crying, having just realized how much she was going to miss her friend. "I can't believe she was buried today. It is all so unreal," she said. As they cleared away the dishes, she told Deanna stories about the two of them. "She taught me a valuable lesson – to treat everyone with kindness, generosity, and compassion."

"You learned your lesson well."

It was seven o'clock when Betty left, and Deanna was exhausted. She found Lucas chatting quietly with her father. He had come by to check on all of them. It was such a strange time. Eleanor's passing had left such a huge hole in all their lives and the community. She realized that Eleanor was more than just a wife and mother. She was loved and admired by so many.

Chapter 26

THE NEXT MORNING Deanna woke before dawn. She lay quiet in the dark room, still tired from the day before. James slept down the hall; the longer he could sleep, the better. She wrapped herself in the silk robe she had brought with her and crept quietly down the dark hallway and down the stairs. She sat quietly at the table; the kitchen illuminated only by the light above the stove. It was warm and friendly in the dark room and the smell of coffee brewing was dark and sweet. She stepped out on the porch with a cup of the freshly brewed coffee and raised it to her lips, savoring the aroma as she took a sip.

The first rays of dawn touched the mountains. They strained through the trees, and were soon turning yellow and then orange. There were no clouds, nothing but dawn's brilliant colors against the dark sky. It rose higher and the rays of sunshine looked like a thousand glittering diamonds sparkling on the crystal blue water of a lake.

The morning air was fresh and cool; dew covered the freshly mown grass. She breathed the sweet smell of summer and looked across the front yard. Honeysuckle vines grew up and over the white fence, hummingbirds sucking the sweet nectar out of the yellow blossoms.

Dense swags of wisteria climbed the white columns of the front porch. This is where she had spent her childhood and the handprint on the front porch steps was hers. She had forgotten how peaceful it was here. There were so many memories, but until now she had only remembered the depraved ones. Her heart grew tender with sweet childhood memories and the love of her kindred.

She heard a vehicle coming up the driveway, and saw his truck when it came into view. It was Lucas. When he got out of his truck, he carried a toolbox. "Is James awake yet?" he asked as he stepped onto the porch.

"No."

"I don't have to be at the hospital until later this afternoon. I thought I would distract James by keeping him busy fixing things around the house."

That sat and talked for a while, but neither of them mentioned the conversation between from yesterday. Eventually James joined them. His whole body seemed to droop when he came and sat next to them. It was hard for him to believe Eleanor was gone. It was exactly one week ago that they sat on this very same front porch planning the Fourth of July party. His adjustment was going to be hard. He was not used to taking care of himself; he had relied on Eleanor for more than half his life and he was going to be lost without her.

Eventually, the three of them went inside and Lucas cooked breakfast while Deanna went upstairs and showered. After she dressed, she found Mathew and James sitting at the kitchen table chatting with Lucas.

"What are we talking about?" Deanna said as she walked into the kitchen.

"Grandpa and every widow in the neighborhood knocking on his door bringing him food," teased Mathew.

"Yeah, your're going to be a hot commodity," Lucas warned.

"I'm not interested," James said miserably.

"But they'll be interested in you," Deanna said with a wink. Except for James, they all laughed.

"So Mathew what are you up to today?," said James, changing the subject.

"Do you mind if the boys and I take the boat out today? I promised to go water skiing with them."

"Sure, the key is in the drawer," James nodded, realizing how lonely he was going to be when they left.

James and Lucas got busy with the fix it projects and Deanna cleared the dishes and straightened the house. She went upstairs to make the beds and as she walked around her father's and Eleanor's bedroom she was shocked. She gasped because it hurt, seeing all the familiar pieces. Every little thing she had ever given Eleanor was proudly displayed in a glass cabinet. One by one, she picked up the items she remembered so well. On one shelf, she found a photo album, entirely filled with pictures and newspaper articles about her.

Eleanor had saved articles from Deanna's high school; pictures of her at her sixteenth birthday party, pictures of her and the other cheerleaders at football games; the year she was homecoming queen; all the Valentine and Christmas dances. There was an article about her graduating from law school and another when she made partner at the law firm. There were clippings and pictures of her important cases and awards.

When she heard James and Lucas talking downstairs, their voices brought her back from her thoughts. She returned the album back to its place on the shelf.

Lucas was putting the tools in the metal box when she walked down the stairs. "Some week," she said.

"Yes, it has been. But I think everyone is going to be okay."

"Drive safely," she said as Lucas got in his truck.

At least a dozen people stopped by to check on them, once again bringing baskets of food. There was a wide assortment of snacks and cooked meals. Deanna looked at all the food and sighed. A smile spread across her face as she remembered what Eleanor would have said: "Think of all the starving children in India. I bet they would like to have some of this to eat." Deanna put the prepared meals in the freezer for James.

James searched the cabinets as he walked through the kitchen. He looked tired and frail and had lost several pounds. "What are you looking for, Dad?" Deanna asked, looking puzzled.

"My car keys. I know this is where they are supposed to be."

"I saw them upstairs on your dresser. Sit here and have a glass of tea. I'll get them for you." She was back in a couple of minutes with the keys. "Where are you going?"

"To the cemetery," he replied.

"Let me drive you," Deanna said as she reached for her purse.

"I can drive myself. I'm not helpless," he snapped. But he was; the adjustment was going to be hard. He had been married for more than forty years and now he was alone. He did not even cook.

"I'm sorry. You're right," she said and kissed his cheek.

Deanna went out to the pool and went for a swim. She swam laps with powerful strokes up and down the length of the pool. She was in great physical shape but was tired when she finished. Beau jumped in and looked like a drowned rat when he came out. It made Deanna smile to watch him. She lay in the sun and dozed.

Later that evening she heated up one of the casseroles friends had brought by. James didn't eat, and had skipped lunch, too. "Dad, you have to eat something," she scolded.

"I'm just not hungry."

After dinner, Mathew took James on the lake. He was trying to get his grandfather out of his black mood, but had only a small success. James had always liked the water but without Eleanor by his side, he was just not interested

They took the boat out on the water. James was depressed but he enjoyed being with Mathew. He joked around and by time they returned and walked back to the house, James was laughing, admitting they had a good time.

They found Deanna sitting at the pool with her old high-school friends. Gail was a Realtor now and on her third marriage and Pat was a former Miss Tennessee who had just moved back to East Tennessee with her husband.

"Do you remember Friday nights after the football games how we would circle the drive-in looking for boys," Gail said, laughing at the memory.

"Yes, that was the seventies form of speed dating." Deanna joined in the loud laughter.

"Oh, Deanna do you remember when we raided James's homemade wine? And when he found out about it he had a fit," Pat recalled.

"Yes, he grounded me for a month."

"You should have been grounded longer, that was my best wine," James said. They all laughed and he and Mathew went inside.

"I have an idea." Deanna looked as though she had a plan; in the old days that look would have meant doing something forbidden by their parents. "Tomorrow, I have to go over a case file but let's go to P.J.'s Friday night." They all agreed to meet there at nine o'clock on Friday.

THURSDAY no one stopped to visit; that gave Deanna the chance to read the file on the Benson case and prepare for the trial. That evening she again warmed food left by their friends after the funeral. After they eat and as she cleared the table, Deanna noticed James had eaten everything on his plate. "I'm glad your grandfather is eating again," she said to Mathew as he strolled through the kitchen.

"Do we have popcorn?" he asked as he stood staring at the shelf in the pantry

"I think I saw some on the top shelf."

"Grandpa and I are going to watched a horror movie on TV tonight."

"Sounds like fun; can I join you?"

"Sure."

A loud thunderstorm rolled through the valley and raindrops slammed hard against the windows. Deanna joined James and Mathew in the den; they had a big bowl of popcorn sitting between them.

After the storm passed and the rain stopped, James eased to his feet and stretched. "Think I'll let Beau out." he said.

"Okay, but hurry back, it's getting to the good part," Mathew said.

"Deanna, you have a visitor," James called from the front porch.

Deanna looked at Mathew and he just shrugged. She slipped her flip-flops on and walked to the door. She smiled when she saw Lucas propped against his truck. He had his arms folded across his chest and legs crossed. He was wearing faded blue jeans and a cotton plaid shirt with the sleeves turned up. His black hair hung slightly below the Stetson hat. He was country through and through, right down to his boots and Deanna thought she had never seen anyone look better. Suddenly Beau stuck his head out of the open truck window.

"Are you trying to steal my dog?" Deanna said as she stepped out onto the porch.

"Well, you kids have fun," James said.

"Is this a conspiracy?" she asked as she turned and watched James go inside the house.

"Hey, I paid good money to get everyone to cooperate," Lucas said.

"So where are we going?" she asked.

"Is it okay if we go to my house? We can sit by the pool."

"That's perfect," Deanna smiled.

He reached in through the truck window and brought out a bouquet of wild flowers, and then kissed her cheek as he gave them to her. She smiled at him and got into the truck. They drove up the driveway to his house and suddenly being alone with him made her nervous.

He opened the hand-carved wooden door and found the light switch. In all its splendor the cathedral ceiling and exposed timbers lit up with a welcoming ambiance. Deanna's eyes took in the sophistication of the room. The grandness came in part from the long tall windows that show cased the lake and the mountains in their full glory. The stone fireplace rose from the floor, passing the second-floor balcony, and disappeared into the pine ceiling. The house seemed as if it had been lifted from a lodge from somewhere in Montana.

Lucas removed his hat and hung in on the rack beside the door. His boots striking the hardwood floor echoed in the large open space. Deanna watched him as he sauntered across the room and continued to do so as he reached in the tall cabinet for a vase. He had an irresistible male grace about him.

"Are you checking me out?" he asked, looking amused.

"I was admiring you," she confessed. Feeling embarrassed, her cheeks reddened as she looked away from him. A warm smile spread across her face. "You are one fine-looking man, Lucas McKinney."

"You are either crazy or blind," he said with a chuckle. He handed her the vase and as she placed the flowers in the water, she smiled at him. Inadvertently, he had set her anxiety to rest.

Lucas opened the glass doors and stepped outside. The deck ran the full length of the side of the house and no matter what direction you looked, you could not see another man-made structure. Deanna sat Beau down and walked to the rail. The sweet aroma of honeysuckle and wild roses perfumed the air as she inhaled the pleasing fragrance.

"Every time I step out here, I can't believe how blessed I've been," he said.

"It is a peaceful place," she replied.

The rain had left the evening unusually cool for this time of year. She moved closer to Lucas and tucked her arm in his. She loved the way the air smelled after it rained. She loved the earthiness of it and the way it left everything fresh and clean. The experience evoked these mountains and one of her favorite memories of growing up in this place.

A full moon had replaced the storm clouds; it shined down on the mountains and cast a golden reflection over the calm water of the lake. Like winged stars, fireflies flashed and danced, pale in the bright moonlight. Her mind drifted back to her childhood. She remembered catching fireflies and experiencing the simple joy of watching their light flick on-and-off, on-and-off. She remembered the sweet peace of falling asleep watching the soft glow inside the Mason jar.

Suddenly, without warning, the charming memory was replaced by the image of Warren and the sickening smell of whiskey on his saturated breath. It was a haunting memory that refused to die, even in Lucas's calm presence. Deanna stood, peering out into the darkness. The night-blackened lake seemed to be a wide abyss, like looking into deep murky waters that ran nowhere. She shuddered and shook her head as if to clear it of the dark thoughts dancing inside it. She shut her eyes, trying to block out the memory.

"Are you cold?" Lucas asked softly. And as he looked down at her, he saw only sorrow in her eyes. And he had no idea why.

"What? I'm sorry, for a second there, I was somewhere far away," she said looking up at the canopy of glittering stars. Beau's angry bark interrupted the silence of a falling star as it streaked across the sky. A chubby raccoon stood on his hind legs staring up at them. Releasing Lucas's arm, Deanna walked across the wooden deck to get her fearless companion. She laughed as she picked him up. "Yeah I bet you could whip him with one paw tied behind your back. Come on big fellow, let's get you inside."

Lucas stood at the door; he laughed and patted the little dog's head. "I feel much safer with you here," he said with a chuckle. Then placing his hand at the small of Deanna's back, he directed her inside. She sat down on the overstuffed sofa and Lucas vanished to the covered patio in the back of the house.. After a few minutes, he returned carrying two glasses and a bottle of his best white wine.

"Thank you, this is nice," Deanna smiled as she leaned back on the leather sofa and looked at him. By now, she was totally at ease, and felt like a bird that had escaped from a cage. But most of all she was surprised at how familiar this felt.

"Good," he said sitting down. They sat side by side; he had an arm around her. They talked endlessly for hours, just relaxing and enjoying each other's company. He chatted about his work in the ER and about his accomplishments as mayor. They talked about their boys. For now, at least, she felt as if time had stood still and that she had all the time in the world.

"Why did you never marry?" he eventually asked.

"Oh, I don't know. Too busy, I suppose. Or too scared." Little by little, Lucas chipped away at the barrier surrounding her.

He stood and helped Deanna to her feet. Taking her hand, he led her to the kitchen, stopping at the large granite-topped island, where he picked up a tray of cheese and fruit. As she stepped out onto the patio, she was impressed by the elegance of it all. Candles were lit in large hurricane vases and orange flames danced in the stone fire pit. It was all so beautiful; she was touched by his thoughtfulness. He had taken the time to make everything perfect.

"Do you believe in second chances, Deanna?" He turned and looked her in the eye.

"Not really. I never gave it much thought," she said. "I don't feel I deserve one. I've been a dreadful person to most everyone I know. Do you believe in second chances, Lucas McKinney?"

"Yes I do, and I dare to hope for them," he said, pulling her close to him.

He held her so tight Deanna could feel his heart beating, but he did not kiss her. For an instant, she was disappointed. When he finally released her, she looked at him; his eyes were deep and wise and sad. There was something warm and tender in the way he looked at her. He touched her hair and gently stroked her face. Deanna smiled at him nervously, her flawless skin flushed, and her long red hair gleamed as it hung past her shoulders.

Lucas turned quickly, wiping a tear that had begun to run down his face. He did not want Deanna to see his emotions; he feared she would do what she did best and run away from him again. He had so much to say to her but knew this was not the right time. There were still unspoken words hanging thick in the air.

"I think you got me drunk," he said trying to de-escalate the emotions that had nearly unhinged him.

"Are you afraid we may behave scandalously?" she said, laughing at the thought and taking another sip of wine.

"That's appalling. Not only do you want me drunk, you want to take advantage of me as well," he said, winking at her.

"That would be a lot harder than getting you drunk," she said with a giggle. She felt light-headed. "So how long did it take you to get over me?" she asked, feeling tipsy.

"Oh, about thirty minutes."

"Is that all?" she laughed.

He held her hand and led her to a table and then ambled over to a stack of wood, picked up a log and threw it in the fire. Deanna enjoyed watching him and this time when he caught her sneaking a look, she did not turn away. He smiled at her and when he took his seat, she lifted his hand to her lips and then kissed it.

"You are a remarkable man," she said, her eyes full of tenderness. He took her hands in his. She had long, slender fingers and beautiful graceful hands. There was such softness to her, such gentleness, and so much femininity. He leaned in and kissed her and then looked into her eyes. They were the kind a man could lose himself in.

"I hope you don't mind," he said, taking delight in seeing the surprise in her eyes, "but I took the liberty; shall we dance?"

She recognized the song coming from the overhead speakers. It was an old love song "At Last", with Etta James. That was their song, she was surprised Lucas had remembered. Without saying a word, he led her to the middle of the floor and held her close. They were in perfect rhythm with each other as they glided around the stone floor. With a strong arm around her, they moved from song to song. She moved closer to him. He said nothing, closing his eyes as he held her. It was all so familiar to him.

Deanna was enjoying his warmth as she nestled close to him. Tonight she felt happier and more at peace than she had in years. There was no awkwardness, nothing strange or uncomfortable. At that exact moment, the perfect moment in time, she began to think perhaps God would give her a second chance.

They were still out on the floor wrapped in each other arms when the music stopped. For a moment, neither of them moved. "The music has stopped," Lucas said regretfully as he released her from his embrace. He watched her eyes as she smiled at him. Her delicate eyebrows formed a perfect arch over her blue eyes. "I don't think you are a dreadful person at all. I think you are much harder on yourself than you should be," he said as he kissed the top of her head.

They walked to the table and he poured them another glass of wine. She only sipped at hers and nibbled at some cheese. Suddenly she was afraid he would see the ugliness she kept hidden behind her smile. As their eyes met over the glasses, it was Deanna who lowered her eyes under the intensity of his gaze.

Lucas saw the change come over her and worried he had pushed her too far. "Are you all right?" he said gently, remembering all too well the look in her eyes. He was crossing barriers and knew that if he ventured too far, it could be a dangerous thing. At that moment, all he wanted to do was take her in his arms and tell her he was in love with her, but that would only complicate things.

"I'm fine," she replied. "I had such a good time tonight. You're very good to me," she said solemnly. As different as their lives had been, they were still like magnets drawn to one another by a force they could not control. His pull was strong and she had not dared to touch him again. She was sure they would be treading in deep waters if she did.

"So did I," he said, taking her hand he helped her to her feet. "But I don't know how, you are such a horrible person and a complete bore." She laughed softly, and he kissed her hand. "Come on, let's get you home."

Sleeping in the chair beside her, Beau stretched out on his side. He began to make high-pitched whining sounds while his petite legs moved in quick short strides. "He must be chasing that raccoon," Deanna laughed as she reached down and stroked his white silky fur.

He stretched again and opened his eyes. Looking around, he jumped off the chair and ran to a grassy area at the edge of the yard. Bullfrogs exchanged coarse croaks and jumped into the pond. An evening fog was rising off the lake and it had turned the view of the back yard into a soft-focus stage set with red roses blooming beneath the large elm trees. The outdoor lights glowed in the background. A coyote yelped to her young and the fearless little dog ran back to the porch. He stood near Deanna and watched as Lucas smothered the flames with water.

Red embers sizzled and popped as the water hit the hot coals and circles of blue smoke whirled and danced. Looking into the smoke, she saw the face of her grandfather. His haunting blue eyes stared back at her as the smoke whirled and danced. She felt his spirit and heard his voice again, "Your path is what you choose it to be, Deanna."

She picked up the tray of cheese and empty bottle of wine and walked barefooted into the house, carrying her shoes. Deanna yawned as they walked to the truck. "Thank you again for bringing me to your home."

She seemed subdued; her voice was almost a whisper and for an instant, she sounded very young. Under the clothes and makeup and the woman she presented to the world, she was still the sad little girl hiding behind the smile. There was something pure and innocent about her, but few people had seen those qualities. And at that moment, all Lucas wanted to do was to take her in his arms and protect her from what had caused her so much pain. He wished that he could spend the night with her and hold her until she fell asleep. But he knew this was out of the question; he would not do anything she might regret.

He drove her home and walked her to the door. "How about breakfast tomorrow? I make a mean omelet," he offered, still standing close to her.

"That would be nice," she whispered in a tired voice.

"Good night. See you tomorrow morning," Lucas said as he kissed the top of her head.

"It's a little late, young lady," James said from his room. It reminded her of her youth – nothing had changed, except she was now forty-six years old. He was sitting in bed reading when she looked in on him.

"Hey Dad, can't sleep?" she said, sitting down on the bed. She let her flip-flops drop to the floor and curled in bed beside him.

"How was your evening?" he smiled. "Don't think I don't see what's happening with you two. He's a good man, don't let him get away again."

"Oh Dad, don't be match making. I can't see myself settling down any time soon."

"You just haven't found the right guy yet. Open your eyes – there is one standing right in front of you. He may not wait forever."

"I'll worry about that when the time comes," she said.

"You could have a good life here, Deanna. Life is short and goes by so fast. When you find love, hold on to it, don't let it slip away. Be with the one who makes you happy, the one who makes you laugh, and cherish every moment. Love that person and let him love you."

James put his arm around his little girl. "Princess, what that man did to you was not your fault. You deserve to be happy. Lucas wants to love you, so open your heart and let him." Deanna began to cry and laid her head on her father's shoulder. He held her until her crying stopped.

Deanna walked down the hall and looked in on Mathew, who was sound asleep. Beau jumped up on her bed and made small circles until he found the perfect spot. Deanna turned the light out. The night was quiet except for the chirp of crickets and the hoot of an owl now and again.

In that moment, she realized that what she felt when she was with Lucas, as much as desire, was an extraordinary sense of happiness and peace. She pulled the fresh sheets over her. Her head felt light, her whole body relaxed, and she plunged at once into a deep refreshing sleep.

Chapter 27

THE FIRST HINT OF SUNSHINE angled through the blinds. She woke and stretched; she had slept extremely well. She shaded her eyes from the sun. Her legs lay tangled in the crisp sheets while her upraised tee shirt exposed her mid-section. She felt a soft breeze tickle her bare skin as the overhead fan revolved in slow lazy circles. She reposed peacefully, her eyes fixed on the slow moving blades. Iridescent colors danced across the ceiling as the sun reflected off the pool below her window.

The seductive smell of fresh coffee revived Deanna. She brushed the tumbleweed of red hair away from her face. She unraveled her long legs from the sheets and stepped onto the cool hardwood. Scanning the room for Beau, she suddenly heard his high-pitched bark coming from outside.

The tiny ball of white fur was running wildly around the pool. Lucas chased a raccoon from one side of the pool to the other. He had the cutest grin on his face as he tried to capture the rowdy animal in a net. Then in one final swoop, he snared the creature, carried him to the outer perimeter of the yard, and released him. Deanna turned away from the window and slipped her shirt off, showered, and combed her hair and twenty minutes later, stepped out onto the patio.

"Good morning, Sleeping Beauty," Lucas said with a warm smile. Then handing her a cup of coffee he kissed her cheek and pulled a chair out for her.. "Did you sleep well?"

"Yes, as soon as my head hit the pillow I was out like a light. This mountain air is intoxicating! Oh wait, or was it all the wine you forced me to drink last night?" she said sipping the hot coffee.

"I forced you to drink? I thought it was the other way around," Lucas said, teasing her.

"Where is everyone?" Deanna said, glancing at her watch.

"Mathew and James were up at sunrise. They stopped by my house to get another fishing rod," Lucas said, sitting in the chair across from her. "They said to tell you they would not be back until late this afternoon."

Deanna took another sip of coffee. "Oh, okay. Why are you here so early?"

"I promised you breakfast?" he said, savoring every precious moment with her. He wondered if this morning would be the beginning or the end for them.

"Breakfast sounds good; what about that omelet you promised?" Beau jumped up in her lap and lay down. "By the way did you let him out this morning?"

"Yes, when I walked in the house I heard him upstairs whining and scratching on your bedroom door. I knocked, but you didn't answer, so I opened the door and the poor little guy was spinning in circles. Wow, I have missed those beautiful long legs."

"So I suppose you saw?" Deanna felt her face flush.

Lucas found it amusing that she would be embarrassed. He leaned back in his chair; a knowing smile on his face. He did not wait for her to respond; instead, he stood up, shaking his head and asking a question that surprised even him. "So when do I get to see more of them?" Her wit and charm had brought out the playfulness in him and he thought never in a million years he would he have asked her that this morning. No sooner than he said it, he regretted his boldness.

"Hmm. . . I have to admit, that does have a certain appeal to it," Deanna said, smiling from behind her coffee cup.

Lucas laughed; her response was even more surprising than his question. As he strolled into the kitchen to make the omelet, Deanna leaned back in her chair, her eyes finding their way to ceiling fan. Slowly she exhaled. Flirting with him had an arousing excitement about it. But she knew it was a dangerous slippery slope.

"I can't believe I'm doing this," she muttered to herself as she took another sip of coffee.

Lucas returned with a tray of food. They had orange juice and toast, and a delicious omelet made with fresh eggs with bright yellow yolks. He had added grated cheese, mushrooms, and fresh spinach. And to top it off he lightly drizzled his perfectly creamy homemade Hollandaise sauce over the omelet.

They shared the pot of coffee as they enjoyed each other's company; Deanna felt sheer joy watching him. His chiseled face looked beautiful to her as he sat there just drinking coffee. And then his eyes moved toward hers and he smiled across the table..

"You're spoiling me," she said

"Don't you think you deserve it?"

They had shared a wonderful evening together; to Lucas, it was like finding the missing pieces of himself. There was a void in him he never realized until he saw her again. It was not that he had been unhappy before, it was that other things had occupied the empty space.

As she put her coffee cup down, she was grinning at him. "What are you smiling at?" he asked with a look of amusement. "You're in a good mood this morning," he said as he reached for her hand. Her mood was contagious, suddenly they both burst into laughter.

"So when are you going back to Atlanta?"

"Tomorrow, I have a high-profile case on Wednesday, so I need to get back in the office on Monday."

They cleared the table and put the dishes in the dishwasher. After that, they sat next to each other on the deep cushioned couch. Her bare feet were on the coffee table and they peered over her toes and watched TV.

"What kind of work do you do?" Lucas asked.

"Divorce cases mostly. I seem to be very good at reducing husbands to rubble." Deanna leaned forward and took her tea glass from the table. She sipped and thought a moment. "I think I take my hatred out on them."

"What kind of hatred?"

"Oh Lucas, there is so much I didn't tell you." Deanna did not move for a long time. Her eyes were wet, but she said nothing. She wiped them with the back of her hand, drying her hand on her jeans.

And then her eyes moved toward his and she smiled. Her eyes were so deep and gentle; she was like a young doe sniffing the air and liking what she sensed. Deanna's lips parted, she knew her eyes had to be telling him how much she longed for him to kiss her.

Lucas looked at her and without hesitation, put his lips to hers and kissed her. It was a long, slow kiss, filled with all the sadness and loneliness they had both felt for so long. There had been no one else since his wife died, he hadn't desired anyone. He welcomed Deanna tenderly into his open heart.

When they stopped kissing, she was breathless, and so was he. They felt the joy of being together and realized they were starving for one another. The years of longing had finally caught up with them and they could not get enough of each other. Deanna could not fight her overwhelming desire for him, nor could Lucas fend off his desire for her. They both needed to catch their breath before they went further, or they risked drowning in each other.

All she wanted was to kiss him and hold him. She wanted to feel his skin touching hers and she wanted to nuzzle him. She couldn't get enough of his kisses; he wanted her more than ever before and they knew they could not restrain themselves.

"I know we should stop," she whispered between his kisses, but she did not want to. She had protected herself for all these years and now she was ready to open her heart. All she wanted was for him to make love to her, and to give him the deepest part of her. Deanna was ready to abandon herself.

"Deanna listen to me, we do not have to do this. Do you want to stop?" he asked, pulling away from her. He was trying to keep control of the moment. She hesitated, then looked at him long and hard. There was a brief moment of silence and she closed her eyes.

"I want you Lucas. . ." she whispered. It was totally out of her control now.

With a single movement, he swept her up in his arms and carried her up the stairs to her room. She looked into his eyes as she unbuttoned his shirt. She pulled his shirt away; he was solid muscle, chiseled to perfection and tanned. She ran her hands along his sculptured muscles. She began kissing every inch of his exposed chest, feeling his sleek skin against her lips. She felt a tingle of pleasure and was swept away by desire. After a few seconds of complete silence, she took the deepest of deep breaths and exhaled.

Lucas laid his head back and closed his eyes and all he could focus on was how amazing she felt. She pressed her body against his, sweeping her hair against his skin. She could feel his arousal and his desire for her. She stared deep into his eyes while biting her lower lip; finally, she pulled her tee shirt over her head. Within seconds, his hands found her breasts; as he caressed them tenderly, he leaned down to kiss them. She moaned as he took off her bra; the feel of their flesh on each other was spellbinding. He kissed her, then stripped the rest of her clothes away, taking in every inch of her perfect body.

As he tore off his boots her desire for him flared into passion. He dropped his shirt on the floor, then his jeans. A moment later, he placed her on the bed. Looking into her eyes he gently let himself down on top of her. He was kissing her everywhere, savoring the sound and the feel of her as she moaned beneath him. She was kissing him like he had never been kissed in his life. As he entered her he was kind and gentle as he'd been that first summer. She pushed back all her anger and hurt and distrust and within seconds she gave herself completely to him. They were both overcome with passion they held nothing back.

They made love for a long time, with all the passion of two people swallowed up in pleasure. Lucas felt he was going to disappear inside her as he cradled her in his arms. Feeling him there caused her to soar to new heights and when they both reached the summit, she felt her soul soar with his.

Still cradling her, and supporting himself with his elbows, Deanna could feel his heart pounding. His sighs were soft and suddenly he released all that had been pent up inside of him for so long. When it was over, they lay exhausted and absolutely still, not moving a muscle.

It was Lucas who moved first. After taking a couple of deep breaths he gently moved off her. He rolled over on his side and looked at her more tenderly than he had ever looked at any woman. "I love you, Deanna," he whispered into her hair.

She smiled at him. He had awakened a part of her that she had kept numb for so many years. She had never in her life been as happy. What he had allowed her to give him would be the glue that would mend the shattered pieces of her heart back together. As she lay in his arms, he kissed her with tenderness and knew he needed to comfort her, to soothe the wounds in her soul, just as he had needed to drink from the peaceful fountain she offered.

"There's a lot I need to tell you, a lot of secrets and lies," she said in a faraway, little-girl voice. She began to tell him of the secrets she and Eleanor shared; the words came from deep inside of her. He kissed the tear that had escaped and began to trickle down her cheek. She was pale and her haunting eyes welled with yet more tears.

"I love you, Deanna," he said, caressing her with his voice. And he meant it more than he had ever loved in his life. "I don't understand the reasons why God took Lisa. But I do know that God brought you back into my life."

She started crying again, so he held her tighter. Suddenly the shame she had felt for most of her life was gone and all she wanted to do was kiss him, and hold him, and feel him on top of her again. Within minutes, as they kissed and his hands wandered, they found each other again. What she felt was an unspoken bond they had for each other from the first time they made love – a bond that had remained unbroken through the years.

They spent the rest of the day in bed; he rubbed her back until she fell asleep. Deanna was snuggled in his arms when voices drifted up the stairs and into her room. She looked at the clock; it was four o'clock in the afternoon. "Oh shit, they're back!" Deanna jumped out of bed and scrambled for her clothes. "This is your fault," she said as she threw his pants at him. Lucas laughed and got out of bed.

"Hi Dad, you're home. How was the fishing, catch anything?" she said as she walked through the kitchen.

"Where's Lucas? I saw his truck outside."

"He's around. He stopped by, before his shift at the hospital."

"Mom," Mathew said as he took a pitcher of sweet tea out of the refrigerator. "Your shirt is inside out."

Deanna felt her cheeks redden. "So are we going to have fish for dinner or what?"

She heard Lucas's voice on the front porch; he was talking to James. She could still fill the heat in her cheeks as she walked outside. "Lucas, I'm meeting some old high school friends tonight. It would be nice if you could be there." She smiled. "We're meeting at P.J.'s at nine o'clock."

"I'll meet you there about ten." Lucas got into his truck. Good Bye James I'll get by tomorrow to check on you."

"See ya' Lucas." James turned to go inside. "Deanna come up stairs to my room when Allison gets here. I have something that Eleanor wanted the two of you to have." He turned and walked into the house.

"Okay dad."

Thirty minutes later Deanna and Allison walked into the bedroom. "Oh my goodness. Dad where did all this come from?" Deanna stared at the exquisite pieces of jewelry displayed on the bed.

"These belonged to Eleanor's mother and her mother before that."

"These are heirloom pieces. They're beautiful. I can't believe I've never seen these before."

"Some of these pieces are almost a hundred years old." James sat on the bed beside the jewelry. "When Cathleen's will was read she had left all the jewelry to Eleanor. She put them in a safety deposit box and never looked at them again."

"Dad there must be thousands of dollars here." Deanna said touching one of the diamond bracelets.

"This was a part of Eleanor's life she never talked about. Eleanor was a very wealthy woman when I married her." A tear dripped off his face and fell on one of the pieces. “I think the fair thing to do is let each of you take turns and choose.

“You go first Allison. You were more of a daughter to her and treated her kinder that I ever did.” said Deanna regretfully.

Chapter 28

IT WAS NINE O'CLOCK when she parked her BMW near the docks. It was beginning to get dark and a full moon hung over the Appalachian Mountains. The band was starting up; she could hear the electric guitars and drum and the deep velvet voice of the singer. The words of his country song blared through the open door. People sauntered in and out of P.J.'s and the men eyed Deanna as she strolled through the gravel parking lot. She had the sinuous grace of a dancer and the tall lithe body of a runway model. Her tight jeans hugged her hips perfectly as they swayed to the beat of the music.

Her eyes burned as she walked through the crowd and smoke. The only light came from the neon beer signs and flickering candles on the tables. She scanned the dimly light room, searching for Pat and Gail. When her eyes adjusted, she spotted them and their husbands sitting at a table near the dance floor. They had already had a round of beer.

"Hi, Deanna glad you could finally make it," they teased.

"What? I can't hear you," Deanna said, cupping her hand to her ear.

The smell of beer and barbeque hung in the air. She motioned to a server who took her order for a plate of ribs. The others were on the dance floor while she sat checking her phone. The band played, beer flowed, and so did the pick-up lines.

"Good evening, pretty lady." A tall handsome young man sat down at her table. "Can I buy you another beer?" he said with a smile that could light up the entire state of Tennessee.

"No thank you," she said as she smiled at him.. *He couldn't be more than twenty-five,* she thought.

It was about ten o'clock when Lucas arrived. He searched each table and smiled when he saw her. Her red lips caught his eye as she laughed at the young man's jokes. The light from the candle caused her face to shine with a golden glow and the dangling diamond earrings she wore sparkled as they danced in and out of her red hair.

The band was playing a slow song when he reached her table. "Sorry man, she's with me," Lucas said.

The young man placed his fingertips on the brim of his base cap and tipped his head. "Pleasure to meet you ma'am," he said in a slow southern drawl and sauntered over to another table.

"I got here just in time. Any later I would have to resuscitate the poor boy."

"Oh, and why's that," Deanna smiled.

"You were about to give the young gentleman a heart attack. Folks around here ain't used to you big city Atlanta girls."

"Well I do declare sir." Deanna said in a Southern Georgia accent.

"May I have this dance?" He felt like a kid again as he reached out for her and took her in his arms. He pulled her close and placed his hand to the side of her face as he kissed her tenderly.

Deanna snuggled in his arms. As he held her, she closed her eyes and the crowd disappeared. It felt like they were the only two people on the dance floor as she moved with his body. In his arms the world was a magical place. Her world in Atlanta seemed a million miles away and it was hard for her to compare the two.

"Last call for alcohol!" It was mid-night and Deanna was still lost in the sweetness of his arms when the bartender called to the crowd. "Y'all can keep drinking, but you can't drink here."

"It's only twelve o'clock. Why don't you ask your friends to meet us at my house?" Lucas suggested. "I'm sure you ladies still have a lot of catching up to do."

They all agreed, and at twelve thirty in the morning they pulled into his driveway. Lucas built a fire in the pit and Deanna chose a bottle of wine from his collection. They sat on the patio where they laughed, caught up on old friends, and talked about their lives until three in the morning.

Deanna sat by the fire, beside Lucas and rested her head on his shoulder. She was receiving enormous comfort from her old friends. This was where she seemed to be happy. There was a sweetness to these mountains, a kind of magical serenity that made old friendships as solid as family and family as comforting as old friends. She did not want the night to end; she wanted the warmth of it to last forever. But that was not possible; her life was in Atlanta.

THE SUN WAS BRIGHT through the window when Deanna stumbled out of her bed the next morning. Her sleep had been uneasy. She had to stay in the shower a little longer than usual to clear her head. She finished packing and carried her bags downstairs as the smell of freshly brewed coffee led her to the kitchen. She met Mathew as he headed for the door. He said he would be back in a couple of hours. She poured a cup of hot coffee and made toast, then found James sitting outside on the porch.

"Good morning, Dad. Have you had breakfast yet?"

"Yes, I made myself some toast."

"Dad I hate to leave you, but I have that case next week," she said as she sat down in the swing beside him.

"I'll be fine."

She hoped he would. He had put the dishes in the dishwasher with food on them yesterday, and she had to teach him how to do his laundry. They sat in the peacefulness of the morning, drinking coffee and talking about Eleanor. Deanna reminisced about the good times they shared. The bad things were a distant memory now.

Down the driveway a car turned the bend and followed the white fence to the house. The black Cadillac came to a stop in front of them and when the door opened, a tall thin man stepped out, wearing a pair of dress pants and a white shirt turned up at the sleeves.

"Good morning, James," he said as he stood at the bottom step.

"Come on up and have a seat, Curtis," James said. "What brings you down here?"

"I have something for Deanna," he replied.

"Can I get you a cup of coffee?" Deanna asked.

"Coffee would be nice." Curtis looked distraught. He was sitting near James when she returned with a tray with coffee, a pitcher of cream, and sugar. James left them alone; Deanna handed Curtis a cup and took a seat beside him.

"Eleanor left this in my custody. She had given me instructions to make sure you got it when she was gone." Curtis handed her a fat envelope. She recognized the handwriting on the front. The writing was starkly black on the creamed-colored paper. She touched it gently before she opened the stiff envelope. She looked anxiously at the words. Her eyes moved quickly over the smooth handwriting. As she read it in the bright morning sun, the letters squirmed like a snake in front of her eyes.

> *...Deanna, I have done terrible things, and I have asked you to keep horrible secrets. Secrets that no child should ever have to keep. I know this letter is too little too late. And there aren't words that would ever be enough to take away the pain you have suffered...*

Deanna read page after page. She felt like crying, each page was darker than the last. She stopped reading and let the pages fall to her lap. She did not know how long she had stared at the jumble of pages before she picked them up, found her place, and read to the end.

She stared at the letter, at first too shocked to hurt. She could not even cry, all her tears had been spent in the emotional storm of the past week. The blood drained from her face and she felt a moment of dreadful hopelessness. "Curtis, why did she not tell me any of this?" She lifted her eyes to him.

"Eleanor wanted to spare you the pain of knowing everything. She thought if you didn't know about her abuse, somehow it would be easier for you to forget yours. She thought because you were young you could put it behind you. And she wanted to protect you from all the gossip and whispers she had endured as a young girl. But she regretted every day of her life that she had asked you to keep that secret from James."

"So why did she not report my rape and have him arrested?"

"Eleanor called me that day. She told me what Warren had done and needed my advice. Deanna, you have to realize that was a different time. You would have been questioned by the police and would have been put on the witness stand. His attorney would have made it appear you were to blame or that you were lying about the rape. And unfortunately, a jury usually ruled for the defendant, leaving the victim shamed in the community. So I advised her against it. She didn't want to but I convinced her to wait until she heard from me. But I already knew what I was going to do."

Deanna stared at him; at first, she could not comprehend what he was telling her. "I couldn't let him do this to another woman." She listened closer to make sense of it. "Sometimes a person just does not deserve to live. It's as simple as that." She took a short gasping breath when she finally realized what he saying.

"Curtis, did you kill Warren?" she asked, not really wanting the answer. Curtis looked down at the ground. He squared his shoulders and then lifted his eyes to meet hers.

"I was fifteen the first time he raped her. I told him I would kill him if he touched her again. It wasn't until he raped you that I found out he had raped Eleanor when David was only six-weeks-old."

"Oh my God, that was why she had to go away. Did Dad know what had happened to her?"

"No. She didn't want him to suffer with that knowledge."

"Why didn't she tell the police that Warren had raped me?"

"When the police showed up at her door asking questions, she thought Charlie had shot Warren. She had confided in him that day and later that night she saw him get into his car carrying something in his hand and he did not come home until very late in the night. She didn't tell the police the next day, because she thought she was protecting Charlie."

"Curtis you still did not answer my question. Did you kill Warren?" she asked him again.

"Yes. And if I had it to do all over again, I would do the same thing and now I'm ready to accept the consequences."

"Did Eleanor know it was you?"

"No, no one knows but you and I."

"Give me a dollar," Deanna said. She stood up and walked toward him.

He reached in his pants pocket and took a dollar bill out of the gold money clip. "She gave me this gold clip the day I graduated from law school. She said she didn't think I would get rich being a lawyer because I wouldn't make money doing pro bono work. She gave me one of those contagious laughs and said at least I would have some gold in my pocket even if I didn't have money."

Deanna saw a tiny tear in his eye. "She was my one regret. I loved Eleanor, I loved her since I was ten years old and she loved me, too. But we could not be together, not a black man and a white woman." Deanna touched his hand and he smiled at her. "I married Ray and she married your father. We were both lucky – they loved us knowing how we felt about each other and they were willing to accept it. Ray gave me four beautiful children and Eleanor, she fell madly in love with your father."

Deanna took the dollar from his hand. "Now we have attorney-client privilege," she said.

Finally, she held the letter in her hand and with slow deliberate movements, she picked up a box of matches. Striking the match made a sound like thunder. They watched the flames consume the letter. When she could no longer hold the burning pages, she let them fall. They slowly drifted and by the time the charred paper came to rest on the floor, the flames had quietly devoured the ugly secrets. "Secrets . . . we shall keep our secrets," she said.

"Deanna, there was a paid up life-insurance policy on Warren. Cathleen was the sole owner of the policy and since Eleanor was her next of kin, the life insurance came to her. It has grown to be a small fortune. Eleanor wanted you to have all of it. She said it would never be enough to pay for what Warren had done to you or to make up for the mistakes she had made." Curtis smiled warmly at her. "Her family trust will be divided between James, you and David, and she has set up trust funds for the three boys. Deanna, you're now a very wealthy woman. And the old mansion in Knoxville belongs to you now. After Warren died for some reason Eleanor never sold it. She said you would know what to do with it."

After Curtis left, she followed the path to her grandfather's sacred stone. When she reached the place where Charlie had shown her the ways of her ancestors, she sat down on the huge rock. She looked down the long graceful curve of the Chota valley, and the sweep of the shoreline. Her eyes followed the water until she saw the place where it covered the sacred buried ground of the Cherokee.

Deanna recalled a time in her life before the purity of a child had become stricken with shame. The stain of it had marred her existence for years as she wandered blindly, looking for the peace and love she felt as a child. She stared ahead, facing her demons: her mother's death, the savage rape, giving up her baby, Sarah's senseless murder, and the sad ending of Eleanor's life....

She began to question her so-called successful life. She had chased selfish things; prizes that shine no more than discarded gum wrappers. She closed her eyes; recalling every footstep of her life and every bad choice she had ever made. She listened to the words of her grandfather.

> *"Sometimes you have to go within to remember who you are. Close your eyes, Deanna, listen to the wind, it is telling you something. In all of us, life is a spirit. God talks to that spirit and if we listen, He will show us the path to find Him and our ancestors that have gone on before us. God will always tell you the truth and will always show you the right*

path to find Him. But He also gives us a choice; we don't always follow his chosen path."

"What happens if we don't, Grandpa?"

"Then we become lost and wander aimlessly, sometimes making the wrong choices and mistakes over and over again."

"If we get lost, can we find the right path again?"

"Yes, that is the mercy of God. That is His grace. All we have to do is ask Him to forgive us and to show us the right path. Now close your eyes and listen. Feel the peace and happiness that he puts in your spirit."

Still sitting on the sacred stone, she bowed her head and prayed. "Lord, God, please help me make peace with my past. I have tried to do this on my own, but my demon only attacked harder. I looked for peace in alcohol, sex, money, and success. I tried to fix my brokenness but I only made the same mistakes over again and I hated You for my failures. I am lost and broken. I'm asking for Your mercy. I give to You my past, and my brokenness. Help me to forgive myself so that I might forgive others. Please help me to find the path You have chosen for me."

Sitting there cross-legged, Deanna felt the awakening of her spirit and suddenly surrounded by immeasurable silence. She opened her eyes and saw two eagles, circling overhead. Then their loud screeches echoed through the

Chota Valley. They flew in spirals, ending where they had begun and repeating this path over and over until coming to rest in a tree by the water's edge. The majestic birds sat perfectly still for a long moment before taking their final flight. They circled once again gliding in the updraft of the breeze

Deanna knew God had given her a second chance and that the Cherokee had come home.

Chapter 29

THAT AFTERNOON Deanna and Mathew drove back to Atlanta. On the way Mathew chatted endlessly. He would be moving back to Savannah in a month to begin his studies at SCAD in the fall. As she listened to him talk about his plans, she knew what she needed to do. She was at peace with her past. And her future.

The next day she sat in the stillness of the house on the quiet reflective Sunday afternoon. She spent a lot of time just sitting, stroking Beau while he lay sleeping in her lap. She had a sense of peace and by Sunday night, she was sure that her decision was the right path for her. There were no voices haunting her and the decision had been an easy one. As she picked up the pen and began to write on the cream-colored paper, she smiled contently remembering the expensive monogramed stationery was a gift from Eleanor. She ran her finger across the raised letters of her name and began writing her resignation letter. The letter was simple and to the point. She folded the paper, put it in the matching envelope, and wrote Bernard's name across the front.

Later that night she called Curtis, asking him to start filing the paper work for a foundation for abused and battered women. The foundation would be called The Eleanor Foundation for Abused Women. She also wanted him to begin work on the old mansion. The house that had held so many horrible secrets of Eleanor's childhood would now be a safe haven for battered women and would be called Sarah's House.

The money from the insurance policy had grown over the past thirty years. There was over five million dollars in an account. It would be used to restore the old home for women with young children and teen-aged girls. More rooms would be added to the guesthouse, to provide a safe place for women with teen-aged boys. The foundation would teach these women skills, help them find jobs, and to relocate if necessary. Their children would be homeschooled while they were there. The house would be a place where they can feel safe and can recover.

There was a lot to do. A full-time counselor would need to be on staff for the women and children. Security guards would have to be there twenty-four hours a day to keep them safe. They would need someone to home-school the children and to help with job skills and job placement. She and Curtis could handle the legal work and fund raising. But she would need someone to manage all this. She immediately thought of Caroline.

Monday morning July 14, she made an appointment to meet with Bernard. She also made one to meet with Peter; she owed him at least that much. It was mid-morning and Deanna was sitting at her desk going through her messages when she came across Jewel Patterson's name. She read the notes Caroline had written on the paper. She leaned back in her chair and a wide grin spread across her face. *This is going to be an easy one,* she thought. "Sarah, this one is for you," she said aloud.

She was still going through messages when Caroline came through the door with a cup of coffee and Deanna's favorite pastry. "How are you doing?" she said as she sat the coffee and pastry on her desk.

"Okay."

"I hope that's true, and I hope you still feel that way after I tell you what I wanted to a week ago when I spoke to you on the phone," she said as she sat down.

Deanna looked at her dear friend. "I know about Peter and Mandy. Mathew ran into them in the airport."

"Really? And you're okay?"

"A lot happened over the past week. Things that will change my life forever." Deanna leaned in closer to her desk and propped her arms on it. "I need to talk to you. I want you to hear it from me." Caroline looked worried as Deanna began to tell her about her decision to resign. "Being back in East Tennessee gave me a sense of normalcy that I wasn't sure I was ever going to get back in my life. When I first got there all my defenses were up – and then I connected with old friends and family. I realized I could have a normal life there. Funny, how things have a way of turning around. The things I got away from are the things drawing me back."

"Deanna, are you sure this is what you want?"

"Yes, I have never been more sure of anything in my life." She told her of her plans for the foundation and Sarah's House. "And that's why I have a question for you. How would you feel about moving to East Tennessee? I need a director I can trust and I trust you more than anyone in the whole world."

"Wow," Caroline said.

"I know it's sudden, a lot to be thrown at you, but would you please think about it?"

"When are you leaving?"

"As soon as I can get my cases wrapped up."

Caroline shook her head in amazement; she had never seen Deanna this happy or excited about anything. And her whole face lit up when she talked about Lucas.

"Well, all righty then, I guess I need to talk to Jeff and the girls to see how they feel about living in the hills," she teased.

"You do know they wear shoes and even have indoor plumbing. And bust my britches, they even have cable TV!" Deanna teased in her Appalachian accent. Caroline became serious again. Deanna could tell something else was troubling her.

Caroline looked out the window and took a few seconds before she began. "Peter has been missing since last Monday. He was here for a while Monday morning after the weekend of the Fourth of July but no one has seen or heard from him since. And his phone goes straight to voice mail."

"What about Mandy, is she here?"

"No, and we have discovered Mandy is not her real name, she has several aliases. And she was never from the employment agency." Caroline paused. "She is some hooker Bernard hired." Deanna dropped her head in disbelief and closed her eyes. Thoughts began to run through her mind: Bernard was behind Peter's actions. She could not get her head wrapped around the fact that Bernard would go to this length. "Deanna," Caroline spoke quietly. She raised her head and her eyes met Caroline's. "Cliff has uncovered the fact that she has prostitution charges in three states."

"Is there a chance she is with Peter now?"

"We have her on surveillance camera in Peter's car using his ATM card. That was on Monday afternoon."

"I know where he might be. He has a condo in Savannah, he told me no one knew about it. Can you get Cliff on the phone? We need to make a road trip. And could Jeff go with us? We might need some muscle."

The drive from Atlanta to Savannah took four hours. The sun was beginning to set as they crossed the bridge to the Island. They were quiet, fearing they might find the worst. But none of them expressed the possibility he may not be alive. The memory of rushing across the bridge and finding Sarah lying on the floor with a gunshot wound was weighing heavy on Deanna. She tried to push the memory of that day out of her mind as she wiped the tears that had begun to run down her cheek. She had to keep praying Peter was alive. He had to be.

The last mile was the longest. Deanna prayed harder. "Turn here. This is the condo," she said to Cliff. He turned his SUV into the parking lot. He made a slow pass and her heart sank when Peter's car was not there. He turned the SUV around and out of the corner of her eye, Deanna got a quick glimpse of yellow tucked between two large SUVs. "There it is," she said, pointing to the canary-yellow Ferrari. Cliff quickly stopped the car and they all got out at once. Deanna's heart was racing as she ran to the front door, Jeff right behind her. Cliff knocked on the door several times but there was no answer.

"How are we going to get in?" Jeff asked as he looked at Deanna. She ran back to the SUV and returned seconds later with the key in her hand. She handed it to Cliff and he unlocked the door. She suspected by now they knew her relationship with Peter was more than professional.

"Peter, it's Cliff, are you here?" No answer, just music coming from the bedroom. As they approached, they could hear the shower. Cliff called Peter's name again.

Jeff turned to Deanna. "Maybe you should stay out here," he said as he touched her shoulder. The shower stopped and the two men hurried to the bedroom.

Peter was lying in bed unshaven and barely conscious. He had lost weight and was severely dehydrated. Cliff quickly scanned the room and found white powder and some needles. He checked Peter for needle marks and found them up and down his arms. Jeff called 911 and gave them the address and his name.

Deanna rushed into the room and ran to the bed. "Is he alive?" She saw he wore the watch she had given him for his birthday, then her eyes fixed on the needle tracks.

"Yes," Jeff said. Her knees became weak and she sat on the bed. She gently touched Peter's cheek and he opened his eyes slightly.

"Where's Mandy?" She looked around the room. Cliff pointed to the closed door, saying, "Someone's in the bathroom."

Jeff walked to the door and stood beside it waiting for her to come out. The door opened, he grabbed her arm and pulled her out. At first she had a look of shock on her face, then she just smiled at the three of them. "Sit down," Jeff said as he slung her in the chair.

"Well you found us," she said with a smirk.

"The police are on their way," Cliff said.

"What for? We're two consenting adults," she said smiling.

"Let's start with your outstanding warrants, PHYLISS OR MANDY or whatever the hell you are calling yourself today!" Deanna stood up and walked across the room. "Then add kidnapping, forgery, and the use of illegal drugs, and I personally know Peter does not do drugs and I don't think he shot himself up," Deanna said.

"There was no kidnapping or forgery and two adults can do what they want in their own home," Phyllis countered.

Deanna opened the file and took out the picture of her in Peter's car using his ATM card. "Give me your phone." Phyllis pointed to the bedside table. Deanna scanned through it and found pictures of Peter and Phyllis in bed together. "Let's add extortion to the charges," Deanna said.

"That proves nothing; everybody takes pictures," she said smiling.

Cliff was searching the room when he discovered the recording device she had hidden. He put on latex gloves and looked at the video. Even he was shocked at what he saw. "Deanna," he said. "I need to speak to you in private." She looked at Phyllis, who was smiling. Deanna shot her a look, then joined Cliff in the next room. "The police are going to be here any second now and we need to make some kind of deal with her. I don't think Peter will want this public and it sure will be if any of this goes to court."

"Is it that bad, Cliff?" He shook his head in confirmation. Deanna locked her hands behind her head and walked to the window. She stared out over the ocean for a brief second. She turned to look at Cliff when she heard the sound of the sirens. "Okay."

"Here's the deal, Phyllis. Kidnapping, extortion and forgery will get you twenty-five to life. We are willing not to mention any of this when the police get here. But if any of what is on that video or the pictures ends up going public, I will personally see to it that you rot in prison. Oh and by the way, the statute of limitations does not run out on felonies like kidnapping, extortion, and forgery. Do I make myself clear?" Phyllis listened to her with a wooden face, then shook her head in agreement.

"I didn't understand you. What did you say?"

"I said yes," Phyllis said.

"Don't you cross me on this; you can't begin to know what I am capable of." Deanna turned to walk away. She stopped, turned back around, and made a fist, and punched Phyllis hard in the nose. "That's for Peter. He's too polite to strike a woman." The blow knocked Phyllis off her feet and back down in the chair. She touched her hand to her face; looking at the blood on her fingertips she leaped from the chair. Cliff placed his hand on her forcing her back down. "Sit down," he said, "before you trip and hurt yourself again." She gave him a sullen glance and wiped the blood from her face with the back of her hand.

Deanna did not stay with Peter at the hospital that night; she stayed at the beach house instead. Cliff called Bernard to give him the details. He told him of the deal they had made with Phyllis, and considering Bernard had hired her to seduce Peter, he agreed with the decision.

Jeff drove Peter's car with Deanna back to Atlanta. Caroline called Deanna in the car as they were driving. It was 8 a.m. in the morning. "Good morning. How are you?

"A little tense, among other things." said Deanna.

"That's understandable. Deanna I thought I should warn you before you get here. Mr. Dubois called a meeting this morning with the senior partners. The official word for Peter's disappearance is that he just decided to go on a walk-a-bout to meditate. And he's coming back with new energy and ideas."

"Tell me you are kidding me. Who's going to believe that crap?"

"Honest that's what he said, I just read the memo."

"He should have said he is coming off a bender. Everyone would have believed that."

Cliff stayed at the condo to clean up and get rid of the drugs and stayed there until the Peter was released from the hospital. Three days later, they were back in Atlanta.

Friday morning, Deanna sat across the desk from Peter. He was clean-shaven and looking like his handsome self again. As far as anyone in the office knew, he had been away on vacation. Deanna was somber as she addressed him.

"Deanna, I'm so sorry; I never meant for you to find out the way you did."

"That's not why I'm here. I don't need an apology from you."

"Then I will just thank you for rescuing me. I hear you have a mean right hook." He winked.

"Yes, I should have used it on you as well," she said. "Peter, I wanted to tell you before I spoke to Bernard. I owe it to you that you hear it from me first." She repositioned herself in the chair. "I'm resigning effective immediately."

"Deanna, don't you think that's a little extreme?"

"It's not for the reason you might think, Peter. You and I have been through this song and dance before and it never made me want to leave. I love my job and I love Atlanta. And Peter, I never admitted it, but in my own way I loved you." She had tears in her eyes as she said it.

"Why not just take a year's leave of absence? You can take care of your father and then come back."

"This is not where I belong anymore. Going home made me realize that. I'm selling the house and moving back to Tennessee."

"Are you sure? This is a lot for you to give up." He looked shocked and had tears in his eyes.

"Yes, I'm sure."

"I loved you too, Deanna."

She dabbed her eyes with her handkerchief and slid a folder to him. "Cliff found this in your condo when he was cleaning up. I thought you might want it back."

It was the folder Phyllis had given him at the airport. He opened it and a broad grin crossed his face. Deanna smiled and walked out of the office, there were no words left between them.

Peter looked at the pictures of Bernard and Phyllis's nude bodies in bed together. He smiled to himself, then put the folder away in his desk drawer and took out the bottle of bourbon he kept hidden there. He sat at his desk and stared at the view through the twenty-foot wall of glass.

The meeting with Bernard was less emotional. He was angry at first and told her she was throwing her career away. She thanked him for the opportunity he had given her and left his office. The deed was done. Now all that was left for her to do was put the house on the market.

She was on the phone with the Realtor when Caroline appeared in front of her. "Charles Patterson is here with his attorney; they are in the conference room," she said after Deanna hung up the phone.

Deanna looked up and smiled. "Ask Mr. Patterson to come to my office without his attorney. He may want to hear me out before we start the mediation."

Caroline showed Charles to Deanna's office and after he sat down, she offered him a cup of coffee. Her long slow southern draw was dripping in sweetness and southern charm. She gave him the coffee and politely smiled at him before leaving.

Charles sat quietly across from Deanna. He wore a black suit, white shirt and purple silk tie. His wavy black hair was combed and behind his ears. He drank his coffee and made himself comfortable.

"So we meet again, Mr. Patterson." She would not meet his eye but instead she continued to shuffle papers on her desk.

"Meet again?"

"Yes, Sarah Fontaine was my law partner in Savannah." She still wasn't looking at him. She picked up a document and scanned the pages.

"Looks like you've done well for yourself," he said casually. He creased his trouser leg, making sure to adjust his pants at the knees so the crease would not bag. "I'm eager to hear what you have to say," he said finally.

"So," she said laying down the document and picking up another one. "First of all, your sex life is your own business and it's nothing personal to me." She laid the document down. "But it is your wife's business. And that brings us to the point," she said not tipping her hand yet.

"You don't have anything on me or we would not be here talking about a settlement." He smiled and took another sip of coffee.

"Charles, may I call you Charles?" Deanna fixed him with ice-cold eyes. "Let me throw some light on this. You want to be re-elected, don't you Senator, and maybe even considered for President someday. A dirty little scandal may hamper those plans."

"What, a divorce? That's nothing," he said in his arrogant tone.

"This is a picture of a check for fifty-thousand dollars you wrote to a certain young girl twenty years ago." She turned her phone facing him, so he could Sarah's picture.

"So, she had a crisis in her life and needed money. I was just helping her out."

"What about this one?" She flipped to another photo. "This is a signed affidavit from Sarah Fontaine stating that she was pregnant with your child and that the money was for an abortion you demanded she get. Look at the witness's signatures. You will find one of them is mine and the other is Gerald Hamilton's, dated November 27th 1986. Gerald and Sarah took the secret to their graves, but I'm still here." Charles stared at the floor. "A good conservative like yourself running his campaign on a pro-life position wouldn't want this to hit the media now, would he?" Charles shifted his weight in the chair, anger flashing from his eyes. "I'm certain if your divorce went before a judge, involving a man with your political standing, there would most certainly be TV cameras in the room. And the whole mess would play out on every TV channel in the country."

He stared at her for a long silent moment. "How much is this going to cost me?" She slid the documents across the desk. He looked through the papers, took a pen from inside his coat pocket, and signed the document. "Are we done, Ms. Guthrie?"

"Yes, we are Mr. Patterson." She dealt with him like a cleaver deals with meat.

August 5, Deanna was packing things in her office, when Caroline walked in smiling from ear to ear. "What are you smiling at? Are you glad to finally get me out of your hair?"

"I wish. But that's going to be impossible, if I'm living in Knoxville."

"You're not joking with me are you? Are you saying you're coming with me?"

"Yes, I gave the old coot my resignation today," she said with a big grin. "Now about my sign on package," she laughed.

Chapter 30

AUGUST 10TH 2005 thirteen years after Sarah's murder, Jack Maynard was lead down a hallway. In a bright room with only a single gurney, a tall man stood beside a rolling tray. A stethoscope hung loosely around his neck. Jack walked into the room and looked at Mathew who stood on the other side of a large window.

Jack was placed on the gurney and his hands and feet strapped to the bed. He was asked if he wanted a final pray. "Yes," he said. "I atone for the sins I have committed."

After the prayer the fatal chemicals were injected. His eyes fluttered then they opened. They fluttered once more and Jack Maynard died. He was pronounced dead at 6:05 a.m. His mother and father had long ago passed away, sparing his mother the agony of knowing her only son had died by lethal injection. And unbeknownst to Deanna, Mathew had made his peace with Jack and prayed for his soul.

AUGUST 17TH it was on Saturday morning, Deanna wandered the rooms of the big house one last time. She was flooded with memories of all the birthday parties, a witness to years of family history, with scuffmarks and wall dings to prove it. As she moved from room to room, she saw physical evidence of the scratches the door suffered when Beau was a puppy. The nick in the baseboard was from Mathew when he dropped his weights. Every room told a story.

She found herself crying, not for the loss of the house she had in the past, but for the hope she had for the future. She walked out of the house for the last time. She took her aviator sunglasses out of the glove compartment of her BMW and put them on. With a quick glance in the rear-view mirror and at peace with the image smiling back, she drove away from the house on Battle Field Avenue, and into her new life.

The sun was going down when she turned off the road. She drove up the driveway and stopped her car in front of Lucas's house. She walked through the door and stood in the kitchen of the big log home, watching through the window as Lucas made his final round in the hay field. She made two glasses of sweet iced tea and stepped out onto the covered patio. When he stopped the tractor, she walked barefoot through the smooth grass of the back yard.

He jumped off the tractor, removed his favorite old baseball cap, and knocked the dust off his jeans. Deanna watched him as he raised his old tee shirt to wipe the sweat off his face.

"Lucas."

He looked toward the sound of her voice. "You came back." He seemed surprised.

"I came home."

She walked slowly toward him, her face beaming. He met her half-way. "Lucas," she said. "I love you. I've always loved you." He reached his arms around her and pulled her close. She leaned on him there for a few moments. "Lucas, I don't want to live my life without you." He leaned over and kissed her, and she responded, removing any lingering doubts about her feelings for him.

"Do you believe in second chances, Lucas McKinney?"

"Yes I do, Deanna Guthrie."

"Then ask me again to marry you."

He picked her up and carried her inside. "I have something that belongs to you." He let her down slowly and then led her by the hand upstairs to his bedroom. He walked over to a jewelry box and took something out. "Let's put this back where it belongs." Deanna eyes filled with tears when she realized it was the same engagement ring from all those years ago.

Before she completely lost it, Lucas kissed her again, then got down on one knee and proposed. "Deanna Guthrie, will you be my wife and promise to love me forever and ever?"

"Yes. I will love you to the end of my life."

APRIL 5TH 2006 on a beautiful sunny spring day, Deanna and Lucas were married in a simple outdoor ceremony. Caroline was her matron of honor and her two daughters were flower girls. She wore a strapless lace dress and carried a bouquet of wildflowers. Her mass of red curls were loose and held up and away from her face by two antique diamond studded combs and she wore a diamond bracelets, all from Eleanor's collection.

David and young Luke stood by Lucas and watched as Deanna promenaded the aisle on the arms of Mathew and James. Lucas thought he had never seen her look as beautiful as she did that day. He took her hand and lightly kissed it. She knew he would never let her fall. She gave him an endearing smile that told him she would never leave. She kissed the tear that was on his cheek and they said their wedding vows.

The reception was in the back yard of the big white house she had grown up in; friends and family where there to celebrate with them. Goldie told the embarrassing story of the supply closet; it made Deanna's cheeks turn red. Mathew and Luke told stories of their childhood memories, Pat and Gail told of the many things they did in high school including the day they and ten others from their senior class piled in the back of Charlie's old pickup truck, skipped school and spent the day on the river. They thought they had gotten away with it until they started home and the old truck broke down.

Hundreds of white lights were strung from trees, and the flickering of candles on each table created a soft glow on the cobblestone patio. The band began to play "At Last" and the magic of the mountains surrounded Deanna with perfect peace. At that moment, she knew she had found her way back and this is where she would always belong. Old friendships had been renewed and family bonds had been woven stronger.

"Dance with me," she said as she took Lucas by the hand. He took her in his arms and they moved as one as they danced to their song. In his arms, she found what she had longed for; someone she could love and to let him love her back and someone to accept her brokenness. That night after the cake had been cut and the guest were gone Lucas took her back to their home and carried her over the threshold of the log house. She made love to him for the first time as his wife and his tenderness was as sweet as morning dew on a rose. His gentle touch was like a warm blanket; his hands were always caressing her, as though he was making sure she was still there. Her eyes were as blue as heaven when he gazed into them. He kissed her again and the kiss was deeper. They could feel each other's body quiver and she sensed, as did he, that the fiber of their beings had blended and become one. She was his and he was woven into her. That night as she fell asleep in his arms, she knew she would never feel the ache of loneliness again.

They honeymooned in France. The first week in Paris, much of their time was spent in bed. For the next two weeks, they toured the French countryside. It was everything a honeymoon should be. It was fun, spontaneous, and full of passion.

When they returned to White Oak Flats. Deanna moved into the log home with Lucas, and he did not mind when she decorated the house the way she wanted. She hung the chandelier from Paris in their bedroom and the tall antique mirror from Italy over the fireplace. The expensive rugs covered the hardwood floors. She placed the table made from the old weathered wood in the kitchen. Most all his furniture had been moved to Sarah's House, making room for hers.

IN LATE JULY, Deanna drove Mathew's Land Rover to Savannah and he followed behind on the motorcycle. He was returning to the Savannah College of Art and Design and they spent the next few days getting the things he needed to begin classes in September. She took him shopping for new furniture so he could redecorate the beach house to his taste.

Deanna spent a few quiet days just walking the beach before Lucas drove down on Saturday. That night they took Mathew out to eat at the Boar's Head Grill and Tavern on River Street. It was his favorite restaurant in Savannah. They began the meal with she-crab soup. "It's not as good as Miss Blanche made." Mathew said to Lucas. "But it's the next best. By the way mom, did I ever tell you that Miss Blanche gave me her recipe for she-crab soup."

"What! Are you kidding me? She gave up her secret." Deanna eyes widened. "So tell me Mathew what are her secret spices."

"Can't tell you. Now they're my secret spices." Mathew laughed.

When they finished the soup Mathew suggested to Lucas he try the shrimp and grits. And they all agreed it was the best they had ever tasted. Then they topped it off with desert and coffee. Mathew had a generous portion of Jack Daniel chocolate pecan pie and Deanna and Lucas both had crème Brulee'.

The next morning Lucas put Deanna's bags in the car. She held on to Mathew and cried. "I promised myself I was not going to do this," she said wiping her tears with a handkerchief.

"Mom, I'm not leaving the country. I'm only eight hours away."

"You promise you'll come home for Thanksgiving and Christmas and for the Guthrie Fourth of July Party."

"Yes, Mom, I promise."

He walked her to the car and hugged her again before she got inside. He gave Lucas a quick hug. "Take care of her, Lucas."

"I will, I promise."

Mathew watched them drive away and as he turned to go inside, he raised his tee-shirt to his face and wiped the tears that had begun to run down his cheeks. He poured a glass of freshly squeezed orange juice and walked outside to the deck. In the early-morning light, he saw a dolphin leap out of the water.

He was watching waves splash against the shore when he felt a cold nudge of his hand. A stray dog had wandered over and set at his feet and was looking up at him with big black eyes. Mathew patted the scruffy dog's head. The dog wagged its tale and its pointed ears perked up. "Okay, come on, I'll make one of my big southern breakfasts." The content looking dog leaned his head to one side then to the other.

Mathew turned to go inside the beach house; the white and brown dog jumped up, ran on ahead, and curled up on the rug in front of the kitchen sink.

His round black eyes followed Mathew's every move as he placed eight pieces of bacon into the hot skillet. When the bacon was a nice crispy brown he put the skillet to the side and broke four eggs into a bowl and added a little milk. "You know my mom used to make this for me; she called it a heart attack on a plate." The dog jumped to his feet and licked his lips. "Welcome home," Mathew said to the dog as he sat a plate of scrambled eggs and bacon down in front of him. "I think I'll call you Duke."

BY THE END of September, Sarah's House was open. Deanna was busy with fundraising events and awareness. Caroline and Jeff had settled into their new home in

Knoxville and their daughters were happy at their new school. Jeff worked with surrounding sheriff departments and local police to assure the house was a safe haven for battered women and their children.

The old mansion in Knoxville that had once held so many of Eleanor's family secrets was now a place for a new beginning. Out of the ashes sprang new hope for women who had suffered years of abuse from men who claimed to have loved them. In Sarah's House, they moved out of the shadow of their abusers. They could move freely, think for themselves, and make plans for their future. They could rest their heads on their pillow at night and fall to sleep knowing they would wake the next day to see their children.

OCTOBER 28TH the crisp air smelled of pine needles and fallen leaves. Deanna walked along the path until she reached a small pool with a waterfall making a joyful noise. She sat on a stone bench next to the pool and thought about her life – how it all seemed so unreal. She gave herself permission to accept the feelings about her abuse and to accept that those feelings would always be with her. She was not entirely healed and probably never would be. *That does not make me a bad person or a weak person; it just makes me a survivor,* she thought.

"Deanna."

She turned her head toward the voice. She gasped when she saw the young man standing in front of her. She looked at his red hair, then his face, his nose, and his blue eyes. "Danny!" Her voice sounded as though it was pushing through a thick cloud. *I'm dreaming,* she thought.

There was a sudden gust of wind, and he was engulfed by rustling and flickering shadows as high spirals of leaves fluttered about him like a swarm of butterflies. Then he answered in a low voice. “Yes, I’m Danny.”

Deanna took her hands from her face and stood up. She took slow, hesitant steps toward him. He opened his arms for a quick embrace, and at the same time, they began to cry. There was another long silence, during which time she continued looking at him. She could feel her heart pounding. Fresh hope and anticipation returned, even though tears were still streaming down her cheeks.

She heard her own voice, quiet and desperate.

“Danny, where do I begin?”

THE END

Made in the USA
Columbia, SC
06 November 2020

24074848R00281